"Admit it. You want me just as bad as I want you..."

Gabby's eyes darted to the side. "I'm sure you could have your pick of ladies in town."

"I'd pick you."

Her gaze flicked to Ethan's and held. "Well that's good, because I have another rule for us. No kissing or sleeping with anyone else while we're doing this. It might be just pretend, but I won't be made a fool of either."

"I would never make a fool of you, Gabby." He gazed into the honeyed depths of her eyes.

"And this... attraction, it won't be a problem for you?"

Oh, it was a problem all right. "I can control myself if you can."

Her cheeks flushed a warm pink. "It won't be a problem for me."

"Well then, I guess we have a deal."

Acclaim for the Love to the Rescue Series

EVER AFTER

"Lacey's Love to the Rescue contemporary series keeps getting better and better...Olivia's foster dogs, her fluffy kitten, and Pete's dog provide delightful diversions while the humans build their own forever home."

—*Publishers Weekly* (starred review)

"4 1/2 Stars! Lacey's latest is filled with huge doses of humor and passion...[Her] modern storytelling style, with its crisp dialogue and amusing banter, will keep readers engaged until the very end."

—*RT Book Reviews*

FOR KEEPS

"4 Stars! With one super-hot cowboy, one spitfire of a woman, and several lovable dogs, Lacey draws readers into a tender story that will make your heart melt. An engaging plot and colorful, genuine characters make the author's latest a sweet, enjoyable read."

—*RT Book Reviews*

"Your heart will be captured many times by the genuine scenarios and the happily-ever-after for all, both human and canine."

—HeroesandHeartbreakers.com

"Lovable men and lovable dogs make this series a winner!"

—Jill Shalvis, *New York Times* bestselling author

UNLEASHED

"Dog lovers rejoice! The stars of Lacey's cute series opener, set in Dogwood, N.C., have four legs instead of two, and their happy ending is guaranteed."

—*Publishers Weekly*

"Delightful...a great story...You'll fall in love!"
—MyBookAddictionReviews.com

"Both the man and the dog will rescue your heart. Don't miss it!"

—Jill Shalvis, *New York Times* bestselling author

"Endearing! Rachel Lacey is a sure-fire star."
—Lori Wilde, *New York Times* bestselling author

RUN TO YOU

RACHEL LACEY

FOREVER

NEW YORK BOSTON

Copyright © 2016 by Rachel Bates
Excerpt from *Crazy for You* copyright © 2016 by Rachel Bates

Cover design by Elizabeth Turner
Cover images © Blend Images/Gettyimages
Cover copyright © 2016 by Hachette Book Group, Inc.

Forever
Hachette Book Group
1290 Avenue of the Americas
New York, NY 10104
forever-romance.com
twitter.com/foreverromance

First Edition: August 2016

Forever is an imprint of Grand Central Publishing.
The Forever name and logo are trademarks of Hachette Book Group, Inc.

The publisher is not responsible for websites (or their content) that are not owned by
the publisher.

The Hachette Speakers Bureau provides a wide range of authors for speaking events.
To find out more, go to www.hachettespeakersbureau.com or call (866) 376-6591.

ISBN: 978-1-4555-3754-9 (mass market), 978-1-4555-3753-2 (ebook)

Printed in the United States of America

OPM

10 9 8 7 6 5 4 3 2 1

For my Grandma Mae, who was every bit as feisty and awesome as Dixie.

Acknowledgments

First and foremost, thank you to my amazing family for always being supportive of this career that sometimes turns me into a bit of a zombie and often involves long, crazy hours. You've made it possible for me to realize my dreams, and I'm so grateful!

Huge thanks to my editor, Alex Logan. I am so lucky to have you in my corner. My books are so much better for having your input—and this is particularly true of *Run to You*! Also thank you to Madeleine Colavita, Elizabeth Turner, and everyone else at Grand Central Publishing who helped bring this book to the shelves.

To Sarah Younger, my awesome agent—thank you for everything you do. You always have my back, and I really can't imagine doing any of this without you. I'm so happy to be a part of Team Sarah and NYLA.

A huge shout-out goes to my friend and critique partner, Annie Rains. I'd be lost without our random daily e-mails! Thank you so much for your friendship and your endless support on everything book-related. Who knew what we were starting when I sat in front of you at that Cherry Adair workshop back in 2011? Now we're both published authors, and we even share our awesome agent. I can't wait to see what's next!

Thank you to my sister, Juliana, for being awesome (as always!). I think I've used you as an expert in every book I've written so far—this time you were my "bad boy advisor." Obviously, you are a woman of many talents, and thank you so much for sharing them with me!

Many thanks to my #girlswritenight crew, Annie Rains, Tif Marcelo, April Hunt, and Sidney Halston, for your late-night writing motivation and plotting sessions. Without you, Off-the-Grid Adventures might not exist!

Thank you to Marie Johnson for being my EMT resource and answering my many questions for medical accuracy.

A huge thank-you to all the friends—both in "real life" and in the writing industry—who've helped, supported, and cheered me on along the way. Writing books can be a lonely job, but I've been so lucky to have you guys by my side. Love you all!

And last, but definitely not least, I'd like to send out big, warm hugs and thanks to all of my readers. It is just the most amazing thing to know that people are reading my books, and I am so grateful for each and every one of you.

RUN TO YOU

CHAPTER ONE

*E*than Hunter braced his feet against the edge of the wooden platform, glanced down at the ground some forty feet below, and pushed off. With a yank from the harness, he was flying. The wind whistling in his ears, combined with the scream of the hand trolley over steel cable, silenced his thoughts for the first time all morning.

He let out a whoop, an adrenaline-fueled war cry, as he soared between trees and over a small ravine. The zip-line carried him about eight hundred feet, ending on a wooden platform similar to the one he'd kicked off from minutes earlier.

Here he unclipped from the line, unfastened his harness, and took off his helmet to check the Go-Pro camera he'd attached. He thumbed through its menu, searching for the video he'd just recorded. It wasn't there.

He swore under his breath. Somehow he hadn't recorded a single moment of his trip down the zip-line. And he had to get this video sent off tonight to the college student he'd hired to design the website. He'd have to hike back and take the whole course again. His empty stomach grumbled in protest.

Ignoring it, Ethan climbed down the ladder and headed for the trail that would take him back to the top. This was the end of the line, the fifth and last leg of the series of zip-lines he'd built, taking him from the main building deep into the forest behind. For now, the zip-lines were his, a place for him and his buddies to get their thrills without putting any-one's lives at risk.

But soon, when Off-the-Grid Adventures opened, this would be the start of a business venture that could set him, as well as his friends Mark Dalton and Ryan Blake, on the way to fulfilling a dream. A way to put their dare-deviling ways to good use, cementing themselves as upstanding citizens and making some money while they were at it.

And as of last night, bringing this dream to fruition had taken on a new urgency. His grandmother's words haunted him like an unwelcome ghost, flitting in and out of his vision and making his chest feel too tight.

"An aneurysm," she'd told him over supper. "I saw it my-self on the scan. Because of the location, it's inoperable. The doctor said it could stay like that indefinitely, but he thinks chances are high that it will rupture sometime in the next few weeks or months."

Weeks. Months.

Dixie Hunter was the strongest woman he knew. She'd endured more in her lifetime than anyone ought to, had raised him since he was twelve with a firm hand and a smile on her face, and at seventy years old, she still walked a mile into town each morning to have breakfast at The Sunny Side

Up Café because, as she said, she had two perfectly good legs and needed the exercise.

And now he was to believe that a bulging blood vessel in her brain was going to take her life sometime in the next few months?

She'd taken his hand across the table, tears shimmering in her eyes. "I need to see you settled before I go, Ethan. I need to know you've got something or someone to keep you out of trouble when I'm not here to nudge you back into line."

A hawk called overhead, drawing his gaze toward the blue sky peeking through the swaying treetops above. Settled for him would never include a family, but this place would keep him out of trouble. He just needed to make sure Off-the-Grid Adventures opened in time for Gram to see it.

He picked his way across the stream, taking a shortcut back to the start of the course. One more ride on the zip-line, and this time the damned camera had better work. He absolutely could not afford a delay.

Up ahead, a woman sat on a large, flat rock by the stream, her back to him, arms crossed over her knees. Ethan stopped in his tracks. He owned this property, but it bordered the public forest so it wasn't unheard of to find a hiker wandering through his neck of the woods.

What was unusual was that he didn't recognize her. The population of Haven, North Carolina, numbered somewhere in the vicinity of seven hundred, and he could say with some confidence that he was acquainted with all the female residents in his age range.

The woman before him had light brown hair hanging almost to her waist in long, loose waves. She wore a white tank top that hugged her slender frame, accentuating the curves at her waist, and a billowy blue skirt that swirled around her ankles. Intriguing. Different. And without seeing her face, he knew he had never seen her before.

"Hi there," he called out.

She scrambled off her perch with a startled squeak, almost pitching face-first into the creek. With one hand on the rock for balance, she turned to face him.

And *hot damn*, she was gorgeous. Her eyes were a shade darker than her hair, as wide as they were wary. She looked a little out of place here in the woods dressed like that—he didn't know any local women who went hiking in a skirt—but most interesting were the black leather boots peeking out from under its folds. Not girly dress-up boots. These looked more like combat boots, and for some reason, paired with the blue skirt they were smokin' hot.

"Sorry." He held his hands out in front of him. "Didn't mean to startle you."

"I—well—oh!" She swatted at something near her face. "Ouch!"

He stepped closer. "Something sting you?"

"Yes, it's okay. I'm not allergic. Ack!" She let out a little shriek, ducking and swatting around her head.

Ethan lunged forward, spotting several yellow jackets buzzing around her head. "You must have disturbed a nest." He put a hand on her arm and tugged her away from the rock where she'd been sitting.

With another shriek, she jumped, landing flush against him, her face pressed into his shirt. Just as quickly, she pushed past him, leaving behind the faint scent of honeysuckle and the warm impression of her body on his.

Something he'd like to explore…later. He glanced back and spotted the nest she'd accidentally trampled, now easily visible thanks to the swarm of angry wasps flying in and out. "We've got to get away from that nest."

He nudged her ahead of him, swatting at yellow jackets. One of the little fuckers stung his arm, and it hurt like a son of a bitch. He smashed it beneath his palm. "You doing okay?" he asked the woman ahead of him. His arm was on fire from one sting, and she'd received several.

"There's one in my hair. Oh God—" She clawed at her head.

"Let me." He disentangled her fingers then combed through her hair until he found a yellow jacket busily stinging her scalp. He squashed it. "Got it."

He inhaled the scent of honeysuckle from her hair, then winced at the angry welt already forming on her scalp.

"My skirt—" She grabbed it in her fists, shaking madly.

They'd gone up her skirt? *Oh hell.* Ethan wasn't touching this one with a ten-foot pole. "Ah—"

She stomped and twirled until thankfully a yellow jacket escaped from the folds of her skirt. Ethan ground it into the dirt before it could strike again.

"Please tell me that was the last one." Her hands flitted anxiously by her face, which had flushed a dark pink. Two red welts had risen on her left cheek, and another was visible on her forehead.

Damn. "I don't see any more. You said you're not allergic, right?"

"Yes. I mean, no, I'm not." She dabbed at one of the welts on her cheek and winced.

"Either you really pissed them off or they like the smell of your shampoo. Let's keep going to put a little more distance between us and their nest." He led her along the path by the stream, walking briskly.

"I came from that way." She pointed in the direction of one of the town's hiking trails.

"I figured, but you wandered onto my property, so I'll drive you back to wherever you're parked."

"Your property?" She pulled back. "I'm sorry. I—"

He shook his head. "Don't even worry about it. I think we lost the yellow jackets. Let me have another look at you."

She stopped short, her pretty face now alarmingly red and splotchy. "Thank you for your help, but I should really go back the way I came."

"No way I'm letting you out of my sight right now. Hang on. I have an ice pack." He reached into the pack he wore slung over his right shoulder. "I'm Ethan Hunter, by the way."

"Gabrielle Winters—Gabby. An ice pack does sound great. You're awfully well prepared." She blew out a breath and waved her hands in front of her cheeks.

"I like living on the edge, but I always keep a basic first aid kit on hand. Then I can at least patch myself up...well, most of the time." He winked at her.

Her lips curved in the faintest of smiles.

Ethan found her 100 percent captivating, even in her current wasp-stung condition. He cracked the ice pack to activate it, then handed it to her.

She pressed it against her forehead with a sigh of relief.

"You got a lot of stings. Sure you're okay?"

She grimaced. The hand holding the cold pack, he noticed, was shaking. "Actually—" And then she stepped backward, tripped, and landed with a splash in the stream.

* * *

Gabby let out a startled squeak as she landed flat on her butt in the stream. But then...oh, the cold water felt so good. Her skin was on fire, like a million stingers were never-endingly piercing every inch of her body. She lay back in the stream, splashing more water over herself.

"You okay?" Ethan leaned over her, offering a hand to pull her up.

She shook her head. The cold water felt too good. Her skin might burst into flames if she got out now. She pressed a cold, wet hand to her forehead and squeezed her eyes shut. Why did she hurt all the way to her toes when she'd only been stung on her face? Somewhere in the back of her pain-wracked brain, she was aware she was making a total fool of herself in front of Ethan Hunter.

Of course, if she had to get stung by yellow jackets after wandering onto some guy's private property and then fall on her butt in a stream, of course said man would have to look like he belonged on the cover of *GQ* magazine.

With his tousled blond hair and tanned, muscular arms, Ethan Hunter looked more like a movie star than a Boy Scout. He might be the hottest guy she'd ever met. And *oh God...*

She moaned, watching as his cold pack floated away. Her heart was racing, and her skin...her skin felt like it was being devoured by ants.

"Gabby, you're scaring me."

"I'm okay," she answered, this time letting him pull her to her feet. The pain increased tenfold as she left the cold caress of the water. She was torn between the desire to claw at herself until she bled or cover her eyes and scream.

Speaking of eyes, Ethan's had darkened considerably. Following his gaze, she looked down to see her breasts outlined beneath her now soaking-wet white tank top, her nipples visible through the thin shell of her bra. Her skirt was also plastered to her skin, probably highlighting her panties in similar fashion. Crossing her arms over her chest, she turned away.

What a nightmare. She needed to send him on his way, pronto. This little encounter was headed from bad to worse, and if she didn't get into a cold shower in the next ten minutes, she might spontaneously combust.

He pulled out a cell phone and held it to his ear. "Hi, Max. I'm so glad I caught you. Got a minute?" He paused. "Great. I'm with a hiker who got stung by yellow jackets, at least half a dozen stings, and most them are on her face and scalp. She says she's not allergic, but—"

"I'm not," she repeated, "but my skin is on fire."

Ethan repeated this to whoever he was talking to, then looked at her. "Are you having any difficulty breathing? Any itching or swelling in your throat?"

She shook her head. "Just my skin. And my heart is really racing."

He spoke into the phone again. Gabby knelt by the stream and scooped a fresh handful of water to splash over her face. Who cared what kind of impression she made on Ethan at this point?

"Hey." He came up behind her. "My friend Maxine is an ER nurse. She says you're probably just reacting to the amount of venom in your system, but we should get you checked out to be safe. I'll drive you to the clinic. I wish I had some Benadryl to give you in the meantime."

"Oh." She stood, backing away. "I guess it's probably a good idea to get checked out, but I can drive myself."

He gave her a look that said *hell no*. "I have a change of clothes in my Jeep. I doubt the shorts would do anything for you, but I can at least offer you a dry T-shirt."

"That's really not necessary. I'll drive myself straight to the doctor, I promise." She yanked at a chunk of her hair, desperate to relieve the burning, crawling sensation on her scalp. She had to get away from Ethan. He was too charming, too smooth...too *everything* she no longer trusted. She'd come to Haven to take care of herself for a change, and that's exactly what she intended to do.

He shook his head. "You can call someone to meet us at the road if you want, but there's no way I'm leaving you out here by yourself."

She shivered, biting her bottom lip to keep from screaming in pain and frustration. There was no one for her to call, and the longer they stood here talking, the more likely she was to strip naked right in front of him and jump back in the stream to sooth her wasp-bitten skin.

Ethan's blue eyes narrowed, and he shoved his hands into the pockets of his cargo shorts. "You're not from around here, right? I'm a strange guy you met in the woods. How can I put your mind at ease?"

She shook her head "Forget it."

He cocked his head with a smile that might have made her swoon if she wasn't so miserable. "I could get my grandmother on the phone for you. She'll vouch for me, and she knows everyone in town."

"It's okay, really. I trust you." She shouldn't, but she did—enough to let him drive her to the clinic anyway. And maybe he was right. Maybe she shouldn't be alone right now in case it turned out she was allergic after all. "Thank you for caring."

He shrugged. "Of course. I imagine you'd do the same for me if I'd been the one who stepped in a wasps' nest."

This was true. With a resigned sigh, she clenched her fists

against the urge to claw at her flaming skin and started walking beside him, presumably in the direction of his car. Her misery was compounded by the wet clothes that clung to her with each step.

Ugh.

"You new in town or just visiting?" Ethan asked.

"Both." She wiped a strand of wet hair from her face, grimacing when her fingers brushed against one of the wasp stings. "I've been here since April."

Two months, spent mostly holed up inside the little cabin she'd rented or wandering the woods behind it. A habit she'd modify now to make sure she stayed far the hell away from Ethan Hunter's property. She couldn't wait to forget today ever happened.

"But you're not staying?" he asked.

She shrugged. "I'm not sure how long I'll be here."

"You have family in town?"

She shook her head. After she'd left Brad, she'd stayed with her parents for a while, but it hadn't taken her long to realize she'd merely left one suffocating situation for another. So she'd packed up her SUV and hit the road, leaving her hometown of Charlotte behind. A quiet mountain town called Haven sounded perfect. And it had been, more or less. She'd needed a place to curl up and lick her wounds before she was ready to go back out and face the world, and she'd found it.

"Been to the spa yet?" Ethan asked.

She shook her head again, rubbing her hands up and down her arms, which only seemed to intensify the burning sensation in her skin.

"Definitely check it out. You've heard of the natural hot springs here, right?"

"Yes." Not only did they sound fantastic, but they were

rumored to have medicinal properties that calmed the soul. And hers could certainly use calming.

"How're you holding up?"

She paused and pressed a hand against her heart. It raced like a runaway train, making her light-headed. "You ask a lot of questions."

"You seem kind of quiet, and I need to keep you talking to make sure you're okay." He gave her an easy smile, but his eyes were sharp, watchful.

"I could use a cold shower and some Benadryl, but I'll be okay." She bit her lip. "In fact, I'd really rather go straight home."

"No way. I'd never forgive myself if I sent you home and you went into anaphylactic shock or something. There's a clinic on Weaver Street that'll get you right in. I've been there more times than I care to admit. The nurse practitioner who works there is an old friend of my grandmother's. You'll be in good hands."

They came out into a large grass yard behind a little white house. A red Jeep Wrangler was parked in the driveway. She'd seen this house before, driven by it many times. In fact, the cabin she was renting was just up the street. "You live here?"

"Nah. I used to, but I bought a condo downtown last year. My friends and I are turning this place into an extreme outdoor sporting facility—Off-the-Grid Adventures."

"Extreme outdoor sports?"

"Yeah. Zip-lining, rock climbing, that kind of thing." His eyes gleamed with pride.

"Wow, that sounds, um...exciting."

His lips quirked. "You look horrified."

"Sorry. I guess I'm not adventurous."

He looked like he was about to say something, but then

he shook his head. "I'll drive you to the clinic and then take you home. Where are you parked? I can get someone to drop your car off at your place later."

"I walked."

"Really? Where do you live?"

"Just up the road actually."

His brows lifted. "Oh, you must be renting the Merry-weather place."

"Yes."

He opened the back of the Jeep and pulled out a light blue T-shirt that said, I'D RATHER BE GETTING HIGH, with a graphic showing someone hang gliding. "Sorry. This is all I've got."

"It's okay. I'd rather be getting high than stung by wasps." She laughed in spite of herself. "Thanks for the shirt."

"My pleasure." His gaze flicked briefly to her breasts, still outlined in embarrassing detail beneath her wet tank top.

Her cheeks burned even hotter as she turned her back and pulled the shirt over her head.

* * *

Lord have mercy. Ethan scrubbed a hand over his eyes and tried to wipe the dirty thoughts from his mind. Gabby Winters was turning him on big time, even red and blotchy from the wasp attack, still slightly bedraggled from her tumble into the stream, and wearing his ridiculously oversized T-shirt.

Nurse Meyers had examined her, dosed her with Benadryl, and given her a tube of anti-itch cream to take home. Her symptoms seemed to be a reaction to the amount of yellow jacket venom in her system, not an allergy.

Gabby settled on the front seat of the Jeep, looking slightly more relaxed, probably thanks to the Benadryl. She leaned back and closed her eyes.

"I'll be right back." He left her in the Jeep and walked into the pharmacy next door. He grabbed a couple of jumbo-sized candy bars, a bottle of water, and a package of Benadryl tablets. After paying for his purchases, he snagged one of the candy bars for himself and walked out to the Jeep. He handed the bag to her. "For later."

She peered inside, her eyes widening. "Thanks, but you didn't have to—"

He waved her off. "The least I could do. Now let's get you home."

Neither of them spoke on the short drive to her house. It was a classic-looking mountain cabin, with wood-paneled walls and a real wood-burning fireplace. He knew because he'd done some work on the deck a while back. The Merry-weathers had moved to nearby Boone a few years ago and now rented the place out to vacationers.

In the driveway, Gabby climbed out of the Jeep and gave him a small smile. "Thanks again for all your help today."

"Any time. See you around." He watched until she was safely inside, then turned back toward the center of town and his condo. He ripped open the wrapper on the candy bar and took a big bite. His stomach had been growling since before he'd found Gabby in the woods. It was too late now to go back and make a video of the zip-line. He'd have to shoot it tomorrow morning and hope it didn't delay production on the new website for Off-the-Grid Adventures.

He chewed through the candy bar in the time it took to drive home, but it didn't come close to filling him. The left-over pizza in his fridge ought to do the trick. The roar of a Harley behind him on Main Street could mean only one thing: His good buddy Ryan Blake had arrived in town. A grin worked its way across Ethan's face. Tonight was looking up after all.

He swung into the space behind his building and watched as Ryan parked beside him. Shit was getting real now. Ryan was here, and Mark planned to arrive by the end of next week. They'd requested to have the property on Mountain Breeze Road rezoned from residential to commercial to allow Off-the-Grid Adventures to operate there, and it was taking longer than expected, but with any luck, they'd be accepting customers by the end of the month.

He stepped out of the Jeep. "Well, look what the cat dragged in."

Ryan grinned at him from behind mirrored shades. "Good to be home."

Ethan pulled him in for a hug and a clap on the back. "Good to see you, man. You check out your new digs yet?"

Ryan nodded. "Got here this afternoon. The place looks nice."

The old brick building in front of them had once housed the town's newspaper offices. It had sat empty for over a decade, but last year, Garrett Waltham, a local businessman, had bought it, renovated it, and converted it into three spacious condos. Ethan, Mark, and Ryan bought them, ready to turn this old building into their newfangled bachelor pad.

Ethan's stomach growled again. "You want to head over to Rowdy's for a beer and some wings?"

"Definitely."

They walked down the block to Main Street. Rowdy's

was just around the corner, ambitiously named for this laid-back town, but occasionally, if enough alcohol was consumed, it lived up to its name.

Ethan and Ryan took a table near the front where they could see the game on the TV behind the bar.

"Hi, Ethan," their waitress, a pretty blonde named Tina, said as she approached their table.

"Hey, Tina."

She adjusted the neckline of her top, giving him a better view of her cleavage, then turned to his friend, her eyes widening. "Ryan Blake?"

"Yo." Ryan gave her a friendly look, his gaze sliding from her face to her breasts.

Dog. Ethan shook his head with a grin.

"I'm Tina Hawthorne. I was in class with your brother."

Ryan's eyes narrowed. "Excuse me?"

"Bro, she means Mark," Ethan said.

"Right. Good to see you, Tina." Ryan's posture relaxed. He and Mark had been foster brothers for a few years in high school after they'd both been taken in by Howard MacDonald in Silver Springs, the next town over from Haven.

After being bounced around the foster care system, Old Man MacDonald had been a welcome respite, a stable home where they were treated fairly and with respect. Ethan had gotten even luckier. After only a year in the system, Dixie had shown up and taken him in. Luckiest day in his damn life.

Tina had her hand on Ryan's biceps, admiring his tats. He showed her an eagle he'd had inked on his right arm, and next thing Ethan knew, she had lifted her shirt to show Ryan a little blue bird tattooed on her hip.

It was cute. So was she. Ethan sometimes flirted with

Tina when he came here, which was often. She'd never shown him her tattoo. But tonight he didn't care because his thoughts were still occupied with Gabby, her honeysuckle-scented hair and those gorgeous caramel eyes. There was an air of mystery around her that intrigued him.

He wanted to see her again. Soon.

He and Ryan ordered a pitcher of beer and a platter of wings from Tina, then settled back to watch some baseball.

"You heard from Mark?" Ryan asked.

Ethan shook his head. "He said he'll be in next week, so he'll be here."

His phone pinged with a text message. He swiped it from his back pocket and grinned.

What's this I hear about you escorting our lovely friend Gabby Winters to the clinic?

It was from Gram, the tech-savviest seventy-year-old he'd ever known.

She stomped on a yellow jacket nest. She's pretty sore, but she'll be okay, he wrote back. How do you know her?

Silly question. Gram knew everyone in town.

We met at the garden store. She's a sweetheart.

Entirely too sweet for the likes of him, and they both knew it.

"Who are you texting?" Ryan asked. "You better not be planning to ditch me for a chick on my first night back in town."

Ethan held his phone up so that Ryan could see the screen.

His friend chuckled. "Tell Gram I said hi."

He did, and Gram replied that she'd like to have them all over for dinner soon. Ethan's gut twisted uncomfortably. He'd scheduled her to see a specialist in Charlotte on Monday for a second opinion. This guy was supposed to be the best. Surely he could find a way to save her life.

Because Ethan had no fucking clue what he would do without her.

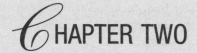

CHAPTER TWO

*G*abby opened her eyes to one hell of a hangover. Only she hadn't been drinking. This was more of a post-wasp hangover. A dull pain pulsed between her eyes, and her whole body ached. With a groan, she rolled out of bed and padded into the bathroom.

The good news was that, other than the red welts on her face, she looked normal, or as normal as she ever looked first thing in the morning. Yesterday's red-splotched, flames-from-hell skin was gone. Just the memory of it made her cringe.

She rubbed some anti-itch cream on her face, freshened up, and wandered into the kitchen for a much-needed cup of coffee. She started the Keurig and tapped her fingers restlessly against the counter until her mug had filled with piping hot caramel vanilla roast—her morning addiction.

She brought the coffee with her into the living room.

The view from this room had sealed the deal the first time she'd seen the place. It was a far cry from the condo in downtown Charlotte she'd shared with Brad. Here her only neighbors were chickadees and cardinals and the occasional deer. Beyond the back deck, the yard dropped off in sweeping views of the Great Smoky Mountains.

It was breathtaking.

She sipped gratefully from her coffee, listening to the birds chirp outside the window as the caffeine slowly permeated her system. She'd made such a fool of herself yesterday in front of Ethan Hunter. He was handsome and charming in an effortless way, the kind of guy who probably had ladies lined up around the block waiting for the chance to date him. Once upon a time, she might have joined that line, but not now.

Now she just wanted to put yesterday behind her and move on. She'd come here to do things on her own, after all. But the utter silence in the house was a bit unnerving. She'd been toying with the idea of stopping by the animal shelter after work today. Maybe she'd adopt a cat or a little dog, something to keep her company without any of the emotional baggage that came with a member of the human race.

She finished her coffee and took a long, hot shower. Then she blew her hair dry and put on makeup, hiding the red welts on her face as well as she could. She could have just stayed in her pajamas since she worked from home, but for some reason, she'd always felt compelled to get dressed and make herself presentable anyway.

She came back through the kitchen for a granola bar, then headed for the spare bedroom, which currently served as her office. She booted up the computer, already mentally running through today's checklist. There was a bug in the interface she hadn't been able to find yesterday. That meant it was her top priority today.

A knock at the door interrupted her thoughts. A knock? In the two months she'd lived in Haven, no one had come to her house, not even a door-to-door salesman. She'd tried and largely succeeded at staying off the radar, even in such a small town.

The knock came again, harder and louder this time. A man's knock.

With a frown, she started toward the front door. A niggle of fear twisted in her stomach. It couldn't be Brad. Only her parents knew she was here in Haven.

Gabby pressed her eye to the peephole. Ethan Hunter stood on the other side. She blew out a breath, ignoring the little thrill that ran through her at the sight of him. What in the world was he doing here?

She flipped the deadbolt and opened the door. "Ethan?"

"Hi." Today he wore a gray T-shirt that said, ATTITUDE & ALTITUDE, and depicted a man rock climbing. Ethan's wavy blond hair looked as if he'd just run his fingers through it, while his lips curved in what appeared to be his trademark flirtatious smile. "I came to see how you were feeling, but you look as if nothing out of the ordinary happened yesterday."

"Thanks, I think." She ran her hands over her cotton skirt. "I'm feeling much better today."

"Glad to hear it. I brought these for you." He held out a bouquet of flowers, and *oh*...they were gorgeous. A mixture of daisies, lilies, and all kinds of flowers whose names she didn't know, but they were all bright and colorful. She couldn't keep the huge smile off her face.

"Thank you." She took them from him and pressed her nose into their depths, inhaling their sweet scent. So lovely.

One of her very favorite things in the world, yet so wrong coming from this man she barely knew. "You didn't have to do this."

"I know." He gave her another heart-stopping smile. "But I've never known a woman who didn't like getting flowers."

"Would you, um, would you like to come in?" Because it was awkward that they were still standing in her doorway, but to have him inside her house felt dangerous...in a thrilling kind of way. No doubt about it, she was attracted to him. A lot.

"Sure." He followed her into the living room, moving with the easygoing confidence of a man who probably never felt out of place anywhere. That kind of swagger ought to turn her off, but seemed to be having the opposite effect.

He walked to the window, taking in the view of the mountains beyond. "So what do you do for a living? I can't believe I haven't bumped into you around town before."

"Oh, I work from home. I'm a software developer." She fiddled with the flowers in her hands, then turned toward the kitchen to look for a vase.

"So you write computer code?"

She nodded. "For video games."

"Really? I've never known anyone who designs games. Do you get to play them, too?"

"I do, after they're finished. That's the best part, really." She felt herself smiling as she rummaged through cabinets. "Sorry. This place came furnished, and I have no idea where a vase might be."

To her surprise, Ethan joined her in the kitchen, helping her search. "So you're a gamer?"

Gabby bit her lip. "Yes." A lot of men disliked women

stepping into what they perceived as their territory. Brad had continually gotten bent out of shape that she could beat him at almost any game.

Ethan pulled open another cabinet. "That's cool. I don't play much myself, but my buddy Mark—he's big time into it. He likes that adventure series, *King of the Desert*."

Her fingers closed over a slender blue vase, which she nearly dropped in surprise. "Oh, I helped design that one."

"No shit?" Ethan took the vase and the flowers from her. "Okay, I'm seriously impressed."

"Really?"

"Are you kidding? That's awesome." He filled the vase with water and put the flowers inside. "You are totally badass."

"Oh. Well, thanks." The tight confines of the kitchen had them standing way too close. His cheeks were coated in several days of scruff, making him look even sexier. She was staring at his lips, imagining them on hers, and goodness, her hormones were out of control. "Um, would you like some water? Or coffee?"

"A glass of water would be great." The glint in his blue eyes told her he knew exactly what she was thinking. His gaze flicked to her mouth.

Gabby resisted the urge to lick her lips. "And you, what do you do for a living?"

"I do a lot of odd jobs around town. I helped build your deck." He nodded in the direction of the back window. "But my friends and I are opening Off-the-Grid Adventures later this month, so that's my main focus right now."

She ducked her head. "Right. You told me that yesterday."

"No worries. You were rather preoccupied." Another charming smile. He should patent those, because they were pretty intoxicating. "I'm also the swim coach at Pearcy County High. We're off now for the summer, although I offer private lessons year round to my students."

"Oh. So you swim?" *Duh.* God, she was doomed to say stupid things in front of this man.

"Yeah. I swim." There was humor in his smile now, and she had the annoying feeling she was missing something, but the thought of Ethan in swim trunks had short-circuited her brain.

"That's great." She turned away and rummaged in the cabinets again, this time for a glass. Then she reached into the fridge for the pitcher of filtered water and filled it for him.

"Thank you." He took a long drink, still standing way too close. "If all our permits come through, we hope to open by the end of the month. The zip-line course is complete. You should stop by. I'd love to take you out on it."

"Oh." She took a step back. "Thank you, but I'd rather keep my feet on the ground."

"Not a fan of heights?"

Or of risk-taking in general. "No."

He grinned, a cocky grin that should have sent her running, but didn't. "How long are you in town?"

"Through the end of the summer." She'd have to go home to Charlotte sooner or later, but for now, hiding out in Haven seemed as good a plan as any.

"I'll get you in a harness by then."

She frowned. "Don't be so sure about that."

"Oh, I'll get you up there. It's a great way to conquer your fear."

* * *

Gabby crossed her arms over her chest, chin up. "I never said I was afraid."

Ethan felt an uncomfortable tug in his stomach. He'd just been teasing, but now she *did* look frightened, and he felt like an ass. "No, you didn't. Well, we've got lots of other things on the docket. Rock climbing, hiking, an outdoor survival skills class taught by my buddy Mark that should be really kick-ass." Although he didn't like thinking about Gabby out in the woods with Mark, nor did he like the idea of them playing *King of the Desert* together.

The truth was, Ethan liked her, so much that he was toying with the idea of asking her out. By all appearances, she was the type of girl he shied away from: the type of girl who would eventually want something more than he was able to give. But if she was only in town temporarily, a casual relationship might be just what she needed right now, too.

She eyed him cautiously. "Well, the survival skills training does sound interesting."

Damn him for mentioning it. "I think it's going to be great. Mark is former special ops so he definitely knows his stuff. Good skills for anyone to have."

"You never know when they'll come in handy." She glanced at the clock above the sink.

"I should let you get to work."

"I suppose so. Thanks again for stopping by, and for the flowers. That was really sweet of you."

Sweet. Now there was something he didn't get called every day. "You're welcome."

She followed him to the front door.

He turned toward her, allowing his fingers to brush against hers. "So I'll see you around then."

She nodded. "See you around."

He walked out to the Jeep, already thinking of excuses to see her again.

Ryan was waiting when he pulled in the driveway at Off-the-Grid Adventures.

"You ready to see this place or what?" Ethan asked.

"Ready." Ryan took off his helmet and swung off the bike. "I get to help test the zip-line course, right?"

"Damn straight." Ethan fell into step beside his friend as they walked down the path behind the house. "And how 'bout some rock climbing afterward?"

"Last one to the top's buying lunch." Ryan gave him a smug smile.

"I know better than to take that bet." Ethan stopped in his tracks. The ground below the zip-line platform was littered with beer cans, cigarettes, and other trash. One of his brand-new harnesses lay tangled in the mess. "What the fuck?"

"You have a party without me?" Ryan said.

Ethan raced up the steps to the platform. Gear was strewn about, mixed with yet more beer cans. Worse, the hand trolley wasn't clipped to the safety line. "Someone's been up here."

"Ya think?" Ryan stepped onto the platform behind him, surveying the mess.

"The zip-line's been used." Ethan strode to the edge of the platform and looked toward the other end of the line. The trolley hung halfway between platforms, an empty harness dangling from it. "Someone was out here last night."

"Or a bunch of someones." Ryan kicked a beer can. "Drunk someones."

"Teenagers." It had to be. Getting drunk and riding a zip-line in the middle of the night without proper training—

or any training—was stupid and dangerous and exactly the kind of reckless thing he would have done when he was a teen.

He went back down the stairs, headed for the second platform. Ryan fell into step beside him. "We'll need to start locking up the gear and maybe post some NO TRESPASSING signs, too," Ryan said.

"Yeah." Something Ethan should have done already. It was nothing but dumb luck that whoever had been here last night hadn't gotten hurt out on the course. He and Ryan came up to the second platform, finding more beer cans. The ground below the platform was all scuffed up. Several deep gouges had been carved into the earth.

Something darkened the dirt at one edge, and there were droplets on the nearby leaves. It almost looked like—

"Blood," Ryan said, his voice gone deadly serious.

A trail of blood drops led from the platform into the woods. Cursing a blue streak, Ethan took off at a jog with Ryan at his side. They followed the blood all the way to the road. Muddy tire tracks marred the grassy edge of the pavement where a car had been parked.

Ethan yanked his cell phone out of his pocket and dialed the Pearcy County Sheriff's Office.

* * *

Gabby spent the morning deeply imbedded in computer code, weeding through line after line to find the piece that was making her action sequence buggy. "Aha!" She clapped her hands when she finally spotted the problem—someone had inserted the wrong reference type into one of her parameters.

She fixed it, then stood and walked into the kitchen to

refill her water glass and contemplate lunch. She had just opened the refrigerator when she heard a knock at the front door.

Again? No visitors for two months and now two in one day? This wasn't Ethan. The knock was quieter, less insistent. Slowly, she walked to the door and pressed her eye to the peephole.

An older woman stood on the other side. She wore sunglasses, her silver hair styled in a short, spiky 'do. She looked vaguely familiar, but Gabby couldn't quite place her. She pasted on a friendly smile as she turned the lock and swung open the door.

"Hi," the woman said. "I'm not sure if you remember me. I'm Dixie Hunter. We met at the garden store last month."

"That's right. Nice to see you again, Dixie." Gabby stepped back and invited the other woman into her house. Both she and Dixie had been selecting flowers for their yards, and Dixie had struck up a conversation. Gabby had left with a mixed selection for the hanging baskets on her front porch. It was probably silly buying flowers for her rental house, but seeing the pretty blooms outside each morning made this place feel more like home.

"Your flower baskets look great," Dixie said as she followed Gabby into the living room. Despite her age, she exuded a kind of energy and vitality that left Gabby feeling a bit wilted in her presence.

"Thank you. Is there something I can help you with?" she asked, because she still had no idea why this relative stranger was here in her living room.

"Well, I heard what happened yesterday, and I came to make sure you were okay. It must have been terribly frightening with the wasps attacking you like that." Dixie shuddered.

"It was pretty bad." Gabby fought a shudder of her own. "But I'm feeling much better today. How did you hear?" Small towns, man. They boggled her mind.

"A friend of mine saw you at the clinic, and she said my grandson was with you, so I got the scoop from him." Dixie's eyes twinkled mischievously.

Gabby pressed a hand to her mouth. "You're Ethan's grandmother?"

"I sure am. I brought sandwiches from the deli on the chance you haven't eaten lunch yet." She held up a white paper bag in her right hand.

"I haven't, and wow, thank you. That was very nice of you." Gabby motioned toward the little table in the breakfast nook. "Would you like some iced tea?"

"Love some. Thank you."

Gabby poured two glasses and sat with Dixie at the table.

"I brought two Havenly Ham specials," Dixie said. "It's got ham, Swiss, lettuce, mustard, and pickles."

"This is delicious," Gabby said after she'd taken a bite. She'd mainly eaten at home since she'd arrived in Haven, believing—perhaps mistakenly—that she was keeping herself off the local radar. Apparently she'd been missing out on some seriously good sandwiches.

"Best sandwich in town. Do you like to read? We local ladies have a book club that meets the second Thursday of every month. You should come, get to know people."

Gabby chewed and swallowed another bite of her Havenly Ham sandwich. "I do like to read. I'll definitely keep that in mind."

"I'm hosting this month. We're reading *The Girl on the Train*, but it's very casual. Come even if you don't get a chance to read it."

"I'll check my calendar and let you know."

"Those flowers are lovely." Dixie nodded toward the bouquet Ethan had brought over that morning. "Who are they from?" The twinkle in her eye made it clear she had already guessed.

"Ethan brought them. He came by to make sure I was okay, too. I'm afraid I made quite a spectacle of myself yesterday."

"Nonsense. I'm just glad he was there to help. Did he get a chance to show you the new facility he's building? It's going to be quite the new local hot spot, I imagine."

Gabby shook her head. And she had no intention of seeing it either. "Ethan and I—we're not—"

"You don't need to explain a thing." Dixie glanced again at the flowers on the countertop. "My grandson has a bit of a reputation, I'm afraid, but don't let it frighten you off. The girls, they still see him as somewhat of a local celebrity. You're different. I can see that."

"A local celebrity?" That nagging feeling was back...

Dixie grinned broadly. "Well, he brought home two Olympic gold medals and one silver from Beijing in 2008. Men's fifty-meter freestyle, men's one-hundred-meter breaststroke, and the men's freestyle relay."

Yeah. I swim, Ethan had said with humor in his smile.

Gabby's sandwich slipped from her fingers. No wonder his name sounded familiar. An Olympic champion. *Holy shit.* Yeah, she remembered him now. He'd been the hottie all the girls—herself included—were swooning over that summer. "I hadn't made the connection."

"No reason for you to. He's a good boy, my Ethan. I'll get going now because I'm sure you need to get back to work. So I'll see you next week at book club?"

Gabby stood. "I'll think about it."

"I'll leave you my number." Dixie pulled a piece of paper

from her purse and wrote her number on it. "Great seeing you today, Gabby."

"Thank you so much for stopping by, and for bringing lunch. I owe you one." She walked with Dixie to the front door.

"No you don't. But I'd be happy to lunch with you again anytime. Just give me a ring." With a wave, she was gone.

Gabby stared after her from the front window, watching as she got into her SUV and drove away. What a cool lady. Despite dropping by unannounced—something Gabby would have normally said she didn't appreciate—she liked Dixie a lot. Maybe she'd go to her book club. Maybe it was time to get out of the house and meet some people in town.

She ran her hands up and down her arms. She'd gotten awfully comfortable living like a hermit, but this wasn't her usual style. With a sigh, she walked back to the kitchen, pausing to press her nose into the flowers Ethan had brought her. Nice. The flowers, the man, and his grand-mother.

But she wasn't here to make connections. She was just here to heal.

Still, the house seemed to echo with emptiness after having had visitors. The afternoon dragged on as she worked out the final bugs in her code and put it through a series of tests.

The house was definitely too quiet. And she knew the perfect way to fix it. After she'd shut down her computer for the day, she headed straight for the car. There was just an hour left before the Pearcy County Animal Shelter closed for the day.

She tapped the address into her phone, and the automated voice of her GPS app guided her through downtown Haven and out onto the winding mountain roads beyond. God, she lived so far out in the middle of nowhere! Such a far cry from the hustle and bustle of Charlotte.

After ten minutes on a winding road leading down the mountain, she came to a lonely traffic light, then a handful of stores, and finally the animal shelter. It was a nondescript white building with several fenced dog pens jutting from its sides.

She walked inside, greeted by a boy with short-cropped black hair who didn't look a day over eighteen.

"Can I help you?" he asked.

She nodded, her stomach tingling with either excitement or dread, she wasn't quite sure which. "I'd like to adopt a pet."

The kid behind the desk perked up. "Great! Dog or cat?"

"A dog, I think. A small one. Maybe someone who's been here awhile."

"Oh, we have plenty of those." He stood and extended a hand. "I'm Logan."

She shook it. "Gabby."

"Nice to meet you, Gabby." He led her down a hall behind the reception desk and into a bright room lined with dog runs on either side, fronted with something similar to a chain-link fence. Behind each one, a homeless dog waited.

A large dog that more closely resembled a bear barked at her, lunging forward against the gate. She took an involuntary step back. "Definitely smaller. Maybe even a cat."

Logan showed her a beagle named Lucy, a terrier mix named Tootsie, and a Pomeranian named Leo (probably because he looked like a baby lion). In the next kennel stood a tiny brown dog with enormous ears. He took one look at her and ran to cower in the back corner of his kennel.

"This is Sir Lancelot. He's a Chihuahua mix. He's been here almost six months."

Gabby stared at the little dog. "Sir Lancelot, you do not look like anyone's knight in shining armor."

"He might not be a fighter, but he'd make a great companion," Logan said.

And right now, that sounded exactly like her idea of a knight in shining armor.

CHAPTER THREE

*E*than's fingers gripped the steering wheel so tightly they were starting to go numb.

"Honey, calm down. It's going to be okay," Dixie said from the passenger seat. She reached out and touched his arm. "Thank you for insisting I get a second opinion and for coming with me. But we both knew it most likely wasn't going to be good news."

It was not going to be okay. His grandmother, his only real family, was dying. And it was not fucking okay. "There has to be something they can do, Gram. We'll get another opinion. We'll find someone who'll operate."

She made a tsking sound. "Well, I'd rather not have my brain cut open anyhow. But Dr. Haskell is one of the best in the country, and if he says my aneurysm is inoperable, I believe him."

Ethan had brought her to see a specialist today hoping for a miracle. Instead, this morning's MRI showed that the aneurysm had grown since her first scan. It was so large now that Dr. Haskell felt certain Gram didn't have much time left. It was rare that they'd even found it before it burst, but she'd started having terrible headaches and gone to have them checked out. Now they were stuck in some kind of hellish limbo waiting for her to die.

Ethan slammed his fist against the steering wheel. "There has to be a doctor out there who can do something."

"Nonsense. Honestly, I feel blessed to have found out about it ahead of time. Now I can live these next weeks knowing they're my last and make sure I don't put off anything I've been meaning to do. I'm an old lady now, Ethan. It's my time."

"You are not that old," he said through gritted teeth. Seventy was not old enough to die. Not his Gram.

"Maybe not, but I've lived a full life."

"You lost your only child when she was twenty-nine years old, and then you gave up your dreams and your freedom to raise me. You deserve better than this, Gram." He glanced over and saw the grim set of her mouth. He rarely mentioned his mother. Losing her had been bad enough for him, but surely it had been even worse for his grandmother.

"Raising you was an honor, Ethan. I wouldn't have traded it for anything. Life is too short for regrets. We make the best out of the cards we're dealt, and that's all we can do."

"And sometimes that's not good enough."

"No, it's not, but it's out of our hands. I can think of a lot worse ways to go. I feel great, except for the headaches now and then, and that shouldn't change. If I'm lucky, I'll pass in my sleep and never feel a thing. Stop strangling the steering wheel."

If he could have, he'd have ripped the damn thing right out of the Jeep and smashed something with it. He couldn't lose Gram. Couldn't speak over the painful clog in his throat.

"You'll get through this." Her voice had gone soft.

He turned off Highway 321, beginning their ascent into the Pisgah National Forest. The Smoky Mountains smudged the horizon ahead of them, dark and hazy like the emotions flooding his brain.

"I made a bucket list," she said, her voice stronger again now. "There are only a few things on it. I want to try out your new zip-line course."

He shook his head with a bitter laugh. "You got it."

"I'm so happy Mark and Ryan are coming back to town. It'll be great to see the three of you guys working together."

They fell silent for a few minutes. He couldn't wrap his brain around the things he'd heard from Dr. Haskell that morning. He and Gram had so much to talk about when they got home. So many decisions needed to be made, decisions he did not want to think about.

"I invited Gabby to book club," Gram said.

"What?"

"I really like her. Those flowers you gave her were lovely. You're a catch." She winked at him.

Did Gram think he and Gabby were a thing? He was considering asking her out, but they were far from an item. Before he could answer, his cell phone rang. He reached for it and saw Ryan's name on the screen. "Hey," he answered.

"Yo, I just got a call from Deputy Ziegler. They finally tracked down our bleeder."

"Yeah?" Ethan straightened in his seat.

"Kid was treated at the ER for a broken leg and a scalp laceration. Said he fell out of a tree," Ryan said.

"A fu—" He glanced at Gram. "A friggin' tall tree. He's lucky that's all he broke."

"Tell me about it. Anyway, he eventually admitted he was

out at our place with four of his friends, drinking and joy-riding on the zip-line."

Shit. What a nightmare.

"And I didn't call you earlier," Ryan continued, "because you were with Gram at her appointment, but I got a call this morning from someone on the Haven Town Council. She said they have some concerns about Off-the-Grid."

"What the hell?"

"I'm guessing they heard about what happened on our property the other night. She's going to stop by around two to discuss it with us. What time will you be here?"

"I could be there by two if I drive straight to the office."

"All right then. Just wanted to give you a heads-up."

"Thanks." Ethan disconnected with a frown.

"Everything okay?" Gram asked.

He told her what they'd just learned. "And now someone from the Town Council is coming over to discuss their concerns with us."

His grandmother scoffed. "That must be Lorraine. She always has had a stick up her ass."

He rubbed a hand over his mouth to cover a smile. He knew Lorraine Hanaford, and Gram was right on the money. "You mind if we stop by the office first so I can take care of this? Shouldn't take long, then I'll drive you home."

"Take all the time you need."

Forty-five minutes later, he pulled into the driveway. A blue sedan followed him in and parked beside his Jeep. He stood and watched as a short brunette got out of the sedan, her hair teased and sprayed like she had stepped right out of the eighties. She extended a hand. "Ethan, it's good to see you again."

He took it and shook. "You, too, Lorraine."

Lorraine looked anything but pleased to see him, which

was nothing new. She'd never been a fan of his. Might've had something to do with the time he'd gotten into a fistfight with her son Devon back in high school.

"I spoke with your business partner, Ryan, this morning," she said.

"That's right."

Dixie came around the Jeep with an overly cheerful smile. "Lorraine, how are you?"

Lorraine's eyebrows rose. "I'm well, thank you. And you?"

His grandmother's smile faltered, and Ethan felt like someone had just socked him in the solar plexus. "No complaints."

"Let's step inside," Ethan said. "Ryan's waiting in the office."

"Certainly. I'll only take a few minutes of your time."

He led the way into the little house he'd once called home. Construction had begun this week to convert it into Off-the-Grid Adventures' headquarters. The living room would become the lobby and waiting area, and the three small bedrooms would be offices for him, Ryan, and Mark. Since their new furniture hadn't arrived yet, today they'd have to make do hosting Lorraine on the battered leather couch and arm chair in the living room.

"I'm going to fix myself a cup of tea," his grandmother said and headed in the direction of the kitchen.

Ryan walked out of the back bedroom, his future office, and introduced himself. "How can we help you, Ms. Hanaford?"

She perched on one end of the couch and folded her hands over her knees. "Well, as I'm sure you're aware, Haven is known as one of North Carolina's premier relaxation destinations. Our natural hot springs and the spa draw a lot of tourists."

"We know," Ethan confirmed.

Ryan sat in the chair by the window. "I'm a big fan of the hot springs."

"To be frank, we already had some concerns about the type of clientele your new business might attract." Lorraine looked between them, her hands still clasped over her knees. "But after hearing what happened on your property the other night, we're quite worried."

"I understand," Ryan said. "We're concerned as well. Ethan and I have already spoken about putting stricter safety precautions in place to secure the property at night."

"I should hope so," Lorraine said.

"It won't happen again," Ryan assured her.

She tilted her head. "Even so, Haven is known as a place where people come to relax, unwind, and leave their troubles behind. Your new business doesn't exactly fit that mold."

Ryan leaned forward. "On the contrary, I think a lot of folks might say that they find zip-lining and other outdoor adventures relaxing as well."

Lorraine made a face like she'd just stepped in dog shit. "Well, I think most people find those activities to be frightening, dangerous even. And if the teenagers the other night are any indication, the type of people interested in your new venture are not the type of visitors we're trying to bring to Haven. In fact, we were hoping you might reconsider the nature or the location of your business in the best interest of the town."

"In the interest of the town?" Ethan fumed. "I think anything that brings money and business into the town would be in its best interest, don't you?"

Lorraine looked down her nose at him. "Not at the expense of the town's image and other businesses, no."

"I fail to see how Off-the-Grid is going to have a negative effect on other businesses in town—"

Ryan put out a hand, silencing him. "Ms. Hanaford, how can we put your fears at ease?"

She sat up straighter. "Well, I suppose we'd like you to attend the next Town Council meeting and hear from the other concerned members of the council. We're going to need some reassurances before we can approve your rezoning application."

Ethan opened his mouth to let her know exactly where she and the rest of the Town Council members could shove it, but Ryan silenced him with a stony look.

"We'd be happy to attend the meeting. When is it?" Ryan asked.

Lorraine turned to Ryan with a pinched smile. "Next Friday the nineteenth at ten o'clock."

Ryan tapped the information into his phone and smiled. "We'll be there, and by next Friday, our third partner, Mark Dalton, should have arrived in town as well. I'm certain we'll be able to set your minds at ease."

Lorraine made a rude sound under her breath at the mention of Mark's name, and Ethan's fingers curled. Yeah, once upon a time they'd all been a bunch of teenaged hooligans, but they'd grown out of it—mostly, and Mark most of all. He was a decorated war veteran now, and he deserved better than to be judged by Lorraine Hanaford because he stole a pack of cigarettes from the convenience store when he was fifteen.

This was bullshit. They had to get Off-the-Grid up and running while Gram was here to see it. To hell with the Town Council and their stupid concerns.

"We look forward to seeing you there." Lorraine's smile more closely resembled a snarl. She stood, and Ryan showed her to the front door.

Thank God Ryan had agreed to come on board as Off-the-Grid's business manager because he was clearly better at this crap than Ethan was. All he wanted to do right now was punch a fist through the wall. A better idea would be to go out back to the pool, put on his trunks, and swim laps until the fire in his veins had been doused.

"You need to learn a thing or two about public relations." Ryan gave him a pointed look as he came back into the room. Ironic that Ryan, the hulking man with the motorcycle parked out front and tats up and down his arms, was the cool-headed peacekeeper of their group.

Ethan was known for his charm with the ladies, but his temper had always been on a short fuse. He blamed it on bad genes. "That's what I have you for. And Lorraine has always had a stick up her ass. Gram said so."

On cue, Dixie strolled in from the kitchen, a cup of tea in her right hand. "It's true. We were all so relieved when she quit coming to book club."

Ryan glanced between them. "Stick up her ass or not, she can make our lives a lot more difficult if she refuses to give us the zoning we need, so everyone needs to play nice."

Gram smiled sweetly. "I'm always nice."

Ryan patted her shoulder. "The best."

Ethan grunted. "I'll try."

"If you ask me, Lorraine is just jealous of Ethan's success," Gram said. "He was the one always playing pranks on the teachers in high school, and her Devon was supposed to go places. Now, Ethan's an Olympic champion with an exciting new business, and Devon is just a boring old accountant."

Ethan rubbed his neck. "I don't know about that."

"Well, it wouldn't hurt to butter her up in the meantime anyway," Gram said.

"No, it wouldn't," he agreed.

"On that note, I'm out." Ryan leaned in to plant a kiss on Dixie's cheek. "Always lovely to see you, Gram."

"You, too, sweetie." At one time or another, his grandmother had looked out for all three of them.

Ryan waved over his shoulder as he left.

"I'm just going to freshen up before you take me home." Dixie headed down the hall in the direction of the half-bath.

Ethan watched her go. Dr. Haskell had said she shouldn't drive herself any longer, in case the aneurysm burst while she was behind the wheel. He didn't like the idea of her living alone either, but hadn't broached the topic yet. For now, losing the ability to drive was a big enough setback. But she shouldn't be alone. She shouldn't die alone.

He raked a hand through his hair. *Shit*.

A knock at the door interrupted his thoughts. Gabby Winters stood on the other side.

* * *

Gabby was still fighting the urge to bolt even after she'd knocked. But she needed to return Ethan's T-shirt, and his Jeep was parked out front so she'd decided there was no time like the present. She would drop off the shirt, then be on her way to the animal shelter to pick up Sir Lancelot.

Ethan pulled open the door, and her breath caught in her throat.

"Hi." His hair once again had a finger-combed look, and there was something raw and painful in his eyes, something that made her want to reach out and comfort him, even though that was completely ridiculous. She barely knew him, he was perfectly capable of taking care of himself, and she was absolutely *not* here in Haven looking for a man.

"Hi." She felt her cheeks flush, which was equally silly. What was it about Ethan Hunter that always left her feeling like a shy teenager with a crush on the high school quarterback?

"My shitty day is suddenly looking up." He motioned her in with a smile that sent a happy shiver straight through her.

Goodness. She followed him into the living room, although they'd obviously begun construction to convert the house into a place of business. The room smelled like fresh paint, and the beginnings of what looked like it would become a reception counter bordered the foyer. "Looks like you have a lot going on here."

He nodded. "And lots more still to be done. I don't suppose you changed your mind about that zip-line tour?" His gaze dropped to her coral-striped skirt.

She twisted her fingers into its gauzy depths. "Not exactly."

"You always wear those." He gestured to her skirt. "Sexy."

It was true; she almost always wore long, bohemian skirts. She loved the way they felt against her skin, the way they moved when she walked. They were feminine but practical, especially paired with her favorite pair of Doc Martens, as she'd done today. "Thank you."

Her voice sounded annoyingly breathless. He'd just called her sexy, and she said *thank you*? She was terrible at this, which was for the better really. Because Ethan Hunter was clearly a player, and she did not want to be played, not by him or anyone else of his gender.

"My pleasure." His eyes locked on to hers.

"So . . . I just, um, came to give this back to you." She held the T-shirt out just as Dixie walked into the living room. *Ethan's grandmother was here.* Oh crap. The T-shirt slipped from her fingers and fluttered to the floor with a light plop.

"Gabby! What a surprise." Dixie looked between Gabby and Ethan with obvious delight.

Ethan stooped to pick up the T-shirt with an amused grin. Did nothing fluster him? Because his grandmother had just walked in on her returning his T-shirt to him, which looked like, *God*, it looked like they'd spent the night together.

"I was just—" She glanced helplessly at the shirt he now held, her cheeks burning.

Ethan winked. "Gabby, I hear you've already met my grandmother."

"Yes." Gabby forced a smile. "Dixie stopped by. It's great to see you again."

"It sure is. Well, don't let me interrupt. I'll be in the car. Take your time, you two." With a wave, Dixie gathered her purse and went out the front door.

Gabby blew out a breath with a nervous laugh. "That was embarrassing. It totally looked like... Well, you know." She gestured toward the shirt.

Ethan's smile said he knew exactly what it had looked like and didn't mind a bit. "Well, we can't have my gram getting the wrong idea about things. I mean, I would never want her to think I'd slept with a woman without at least taking her to dinner. So what do you say, can I take you to dinner?"

"Oh." She took a step backward. "Not that I wouldn't like to, but I just got out of a relationship so I'm kind of taking a break from dating right now."

Ethan pressed a hand to his chest in mock devastation. "That's a tragedy."

She twisted her hands together, wishing she wasn't silently agreeing with him right now, because dinner with Ethan? Yeah, it would be awesome. "Well, you shouldn't keep your grandmother waiting. Thanks again for your help last week, and for the flowers."

"Any time. And if you change your mind about that no-dating thing, you know where to find me." He winked, walking behind her as she headed for the front door.

"I won't, but I appreciate the sentiment." That sounded way too formal, but she couldn't help it. Ethan had strange effects on her ability to speak coherently.

His easy smile never faltered. "I totally respect that. But just so you're forewarned, I'm going to keep asking you to try the zip-line course."

Her palms got sweaty just thinking about it. "Not my style, Ethan."

"No?" His gaze drifted down over her skirt again. "I'd miss the skirt, it's true. But I bet you look great in jeans, too."

With a look that left her knees feeling ridiculously weak, he climbed into his Jeep and waved good-bye.

* * *

Ethan watched her drive away, feeling stupidly disappointed she'd turned him down, even though he had no right to. It wasn't like he had trouble getting a date in this town. Too bad the only woman who'd caught his eye recently had just driven away without him.

He glanced over at Gram. She'd nodded off in the passenger seat, hands clasped over the purse in her lap. In sleep, she looked...older maybe. More vulnerable.

That feeling was back in his stomach, a sick, clenching fear that slid upward, squeezing his chest until he could barely breathe. He cranked the engine, and the Jeep roared to life.

Dixie opened her eyes and looked over at him with a smile. "You and Gabby get things sorted out?"

"Yeah." He turned out of the driveway and headed toward Gram's house just a couple of miles down the road. Neither of them spoke during the short drive.

"Come in for a few minutes, will you?" she asked as he turned in at the brown-paneled house she'd bought over fifteen years ago when she'd pulled him out of foster care and settled here in Haven. Home, or the closest thing to it he'd ever known.

He followed her inside. She went into the kitchen and returned a few minutes later with two steaming cups of tea. He wasn't a huge fan, but he'd learned long ago that she wouldn't take no for an answer.

"We have a few things to talk about." She handed him a cup and sat on the couch.

Yeah, they did, and there was no sense putting it off. He sat opposite her in the overstuffed chair by the window. "Gram—"

She shook her head. "My time is coming, and there's nothing either one of us can do to change it. I just wanted you to know that I'm meeting with my lawyer tomorrow. I've put all of my final wishes in writing so that none of it falls on you. Everything will be taken care of."

He scrubbed a hand over his face. "Okay."

"There is one thing you can do for me."

He leaned forward. "Anything."

"I'd like to go to the beach one last time."

Whatever he'd been expecting her to say, it wasn't this. But this was a request he could definitely handle. "Consider it done."

She sipped from her tea and nodded, but he saw her chin quiver. "I always have loved the ocean."

That was the truth. Dixie had been born and raised by the beach in Wilmington, North Carolina, about five hours from Haven. She and his grandfather had planned to take a cruise around the world after they both retired, but his grandfather had died of cancer before they got the chance. Since she'd adopted Ethan, they'd gone to the beach every summer at least once. This year, between plans for Off-the-Grid Adventures and a visit from one of her longtime friends, they hadn't gone yet. "I'll see if I can rent our usual house in Emerald Isle. It's short notice, but they might have an opening."

"That would be perfect. Thank you, Ethan." She beckoned for him to come sit beside her.

He crossed the living room and sat next to her on the couch, his lungs getting smaller with each breath he took.

"I've been so worried about you...about leaving you." She took his hand and squeezed it tightly in hers. "When I told you I needed to see you settled before I go, I figured I'd have to make do with your new venture with Ryan and Mark. At least I'd know they were in town to watch out for you when I'm not here. And that's something I'm so grateful for."

He stared down at her small, wrinkled hand entwined with his.

"But I had no idea Gabby was about to come into your life. She's special, Ethan. I can see it, and I think you can, too. I know things are still very new between you two, but I've always had a sense for these things."

He drew back. "Gram—"

She shushed him. "I knew I was going to marry your grandfather within a few minutes of meeting him, and we had thirty glorious years together before he left this earth. I have the same feeling about you and Gabby. And now I can truly die in peace knowing that you've found the person who will love you as much as I do."

His stomach dropped like he'd just gone into freefall. *Fuck.*

* * *

Gabby let out a weary sigh. She was sitting on the worn linoleum in the kitchen, a dog biscuit clutched in her hand— by herself. As soon as she'd brought him home, Sir Lancelot ran inside the pantry to hide, and no amount of sweet talk could convince him to come back out.

"Come on, Lance." She'd decided on the nickname since he was obviously not up for knighthood just yet. "I've got cookies. And then I thought we could go for a walk in the woods."

His head appeared in the doorway of the pantry, cocked comically to the side.

"Did you hear a word you like? Cookie?" she asked.

His head cocked to the other side.

"Walk?"

He ran up to her, tail wagging shyly.

"You're a weirdo, Lance." She fed him the cookie, and he crunched contentedly at her feet. Quickly, she clipped the leash to his collar before he could run back inside the pantry. "Let's take that walk. I think a little fresh air might do us both some good."

Her new dog clearly needed to chill, and she was still flustered about her visit with Ethan earlier, so hopefully a walk would cool them both off. She led the way to the door, and they set out together along the path that led from her yard onto the town's hiking trails.

Today she'd be careful not to wander onto Ethan's property.

Lance trotted along at her side, head up and alert now that they'd left the house. He might not be much bigger than a cat, but the fact he could go hiking with her was a definite bonus.

She took them on a short walk, doubling back after only twenty minutes. It was his first day out of the shelter, after all. Even so, about halfway home, he curled up in the middle of the path and refused to go another step.

She propped her hands on her hips and looked down at him. "Seriously?"

He just stared up at her, panting.

With a sigh, she picked him up and tucked him under her arm for the rest of the walk home. She came out of the woods to the right of her house, startled to see Ethan's Jeep in the driveway. What in the world was he doing here?

He sat on her front steps, head in his hands, his back to her.

She walked up to him, but he didn't move, either so lost in his thoughts that he hadn't heard her approach or he'd fallen asleep. "Ethan?" she said softly.

He looked up, his eyes red and bloodshot, hair disheveled. She took a step back. Was he drunk? He pushed to his feet. "Can I come in?"

She narrowed her eyes, studying him. On second thought, he didn't seem so much drunk as...devastated. Had something happened? Her skin prickled with misgivings. "Sure." She walked past him and unlocked the front door.

"You lock up when you go for a walk? You've lived in the city too long," he said from behind her.

"Probably." Her stomach quivered. Yes, too long.

"Did you get a dog?"

"Yes." And Ethan still asked a lot of questions. She opened the door and motioned him inside. She put Lance down, and he darted toward the kitchen, no doubt to return to his favorite hiding spot in the pantry.

"He's...small," Ethan said. "What's his name?"

"Sir Lancelot."

"Hmm. That seems kind of ironic."

"It is. I call him Lance. Are you okay?" she asked, because he didn't look okay.

At her question, he turned away and walked into the living room.

Definitely not okay. "What happened?"

"It's Gram." His voice was flat, yet his words sent a chill down her spine. He stood there a long moment, a faraway look in his eyes. "She's dying."

"Oh, God." Her stomach somersaulted into her throat. "No."

He nodded, pain etched into the wrinkles that had appeared around his eyes. "She has a brain aneurysm. It's probably going to burst sometime in the next few weeks. And...she's going to die." His voice broke, ever so slightly, and the sound wrenched Gabby's heart right out of her chest.

"Oh, Ethan." She wrapped her arms around herself to keep from touching him. "I can't...I just can't believe it. She's so vibrant, so full of life. I'm so sorry."

"She thinks we're together." He walked to the window and looked out.

Gabby grimaced. "I was afraid she might. She saw the flowers you brought me, and today with the T-shirt..."

"She told me just now that she could die in peace knowing I'd finally found someone like you to love me as much as she does."

Gabby felt like her knees might give out beneath her. "Ethan—"

"I know." He looked as blindsided as she felt. "What can I do?"

"You have to tell her the truth." It was the only thing they *could* do.

He looked out the window again. "She lost her husband, my grandfather, to cancer twenty years ago. And my mother, her only child, was killed when I was ten. It was a year before she found out Mom had died, and another year before she got custody of me. Life's been nothing but unfair to her."

"And to you, it sounds like." She walked closer and rested a hand on his shoulder.

His muscles were so tight that her fingers practically bounced off him. "I did fine, thanks to Gram. Seems only fair to do what I can to return the favor."

It was all she could do not to pull him into her arms and hold him, kiss him, do everything in her power to ease his pain. "But we're not even dating. You have to tell her the truth. She deserves the truth."

"Here's the thing." He offered her a playful smile, but it fell flat. "I've never had a serious relationship. Never brought a girl to Gram's house. I didn't want to get her hopes up, because I don't ever want to get married. But this is really important to her, so I thought maybe you and I could just, I don't know, spend some time together these next few weeks..."

She drew back. "I'm not available for hire."

He raised his hands in the air. "Not even remotely what I was suggesting. You don't even have to kiss me. Just let me take you to dinner, come over and hang out with Gram and me, let her see us together. You might even have fun." He winked.

"You're attracted to me," she blurted out.

His blue eyes settled on hers, sending a high-voltage zing through her body. "I am."

She sucked in a breath, her body hot and tingly in all the right—or wrong—places.

He shook his head. "But I'm not a Neanderthal. You've told me you're not interested, and I respect that. Just let Gram see us hanging out together these next few weeks so that she can think there might be a future for us."

"That just feels...wrong." She rubbed her hands up and down her arms.

"We're not bad company."

"No, and I'd be happy to spend time with her. I really like your grandma. But I just don't feel right about lying to her."

"Please." The look on his face ripped at her heart.

"I can't. I'm sorry, Ethan."

He nodded, and without another word, he walked out the front door, leaving her feeling as if she'd just kicked a puppy.

CHAPTER FOUR

Gabby spent a restless night, tossing and turning in her bed. She couldn't forget the look on Ethan's face when he'd asked for her help. It haunted her every time she closed her eyes. Poor Dixie. How could she be dying?

It was unfair. The whole situation was unfair.

She rolled over in bed with a sigh and squinted at the clock. It was just past five, and she might as well accept the fact she wasn't getting back to sleep. Lance, disturbed by her movement, scurried across the bed and curled into a little ball on her spare pillow.

She left him there and climbed out of bed. A hot shower cleared some of the cobwebs from her head. By the time she'd dressed and had her morning cup of coffee, the sun was up, and she decided to take Lance for a quick walk and get an early start on work.

She needed to quit thinking about Ethan and his grandmother. She'd come to Haven to build something for herself without a man, or anyone else, interfering in her life. And as much as she hated what was happening to Dixie—and to Ethan—there wasn't anything she could do to help. Lying would only make everything worse in the end. It always did.

If she'd been honest with her friends and family about what was happening with Brad, maybe she wouldn't have stayed as long as she did. Maybe things would have ended differently.

Maybe she wouldn't be here in the mountains now hiding from the fallout.

She'd worked five hours by lunchtime while Lance napped on a pillow beside her desk. She'd need to stop by the local pet store later to get him some more supplies. He needed a dog bed, and maybe some toys.

One thing she'd realized in the last week was that it was time to show her face around town. She couldn't heal until she quit hiding. In fact, she was going to drive into town right now and have lunch. Maybe she'd stop by the deli for another Havenly Ham.

With that decided, she freshened up and put Lance in his crate to keep him out of trouble. She had driven halfway to town when she passed the little white house that was the future Off-the-Grid Adventures. There were several vehicles parked out front, including Ethan's red Jeep.

And she had absolutely no clue why she turned into the driveway. She just needed to see him, to be sure he was okay. To apologize for not being able to help. Hopefully then she could finally put this whole thing behind her and move on.

Shaking her head at herself, she parked and hopped out of her SUV before she could change her mind. He might have seen her already, and she'd look even sillier if she got back in her car and drove away now. Her cheeks burned as she walked toward the front door.

It opened, and a man stepped out, wearing worn jeans with a tool belt strapped low around his hips. He held the door for her with a polite nod. As she stepped inside, her eyes swept the room looking for Ethan. Instead they landed on another man hard at work behind the front counter—a man with dark hair and cold brown eyes and a smile that curdled the contents of her stomach.

"Gabby?" He wore an expression of surprise, but there could be nothing accidental about Brad Mobley turning up here in Haven.

"Do you two know each other?" The sound of Dixie's voice drew Gabby's attention to where she sat on the battered leather couch, a Kindle in one hand, a cup of tea in the other.

Oh God. *Oh shit.* She tried to run, but her legs had frozen in place.

Ethan strolled into the room from one of the back offices, his gaze locking on Gabby. He grinned, that dazzling, sexy grin that had the power to do all kinds of crazy things to her insides. Without another glance at her ex and without stopping to question what the hell she was doing, she went up on her tiptoes and pressed her lips to Ethan's. Just a quick "hello" kiss, just enough to let Brad know she had moved on. To leave her the fuck alone.

And all that went out the window the instant her lips touched Ethan's. His were warm, and soft, and sent a shot of sizzling heat right through her core. His eyes widened, and his hands settled on her hips. He didn't pull her closer, didn't trap her against him. In contrast, the contact felt warm and safe.

"Hey, baby," he murmured against her lips. Then he slid

an arm around her shoulders and started walking back toward the office he'd just come from. "If y'all will excuse us for a minute..." He was all relaxed charm as he towed her toward the privacy of his office, away from the prying eyes of everyone in the lobby who'd just seen her kiss him.

Gabby, on the other hand, was about to lose it. Her heart ping-ponged around in her chest, while the warm flutter of arousal battled the cold grip of fear in her belly.

Brad was here in Haven. She'd kissed Ethan, in front of Brad *and* Dixie. *Oh, God. She was so screwed.*

Ethan steered her into his office and closed the door softly behind them. His arm was still looped around her shoulder, and when she turned, she landed flush against his chest, his right knee pressed into the gap between her thighs. He made a low sound of approval, his hands sliding down to her butt.

And the last chill of her fear evaporated.

This was madness.

They stood like that for several long seconds, as her heart pounded and desire pooled low in her belly.

Ethan's lips curved in a slow smile, but his blue eyes were sharp as tacks. "Mind telling me what we're doing right now?"

"Um." She glanced down. Her hands were on his pecs, their hips flush together, his hands still gripping her butt. It was intense, and so sexy she could barely breathe. Ethan was looking at her like he wanted to devour her, but he was waiting for her to make the next move. He'd given her the reins, and somehow that made the whole thing even sexier.

"Not that I don't like kissing you..." He winked. "But you're sending out some seriously mixed signals here."

"I know." She pushed backward out of his arms.

He tucked his hands into his front pockets, holding her in the heavy weight of his gaze.

"I panicked," she said.

"Panicked?" He cocked his head to the side, so intense behind that casual demeanor. "Not what I like to hear right after a girl kisses me."

"I saw someone I knew, and I just...reacted."

His eyebrows drew together. "Someone you knew?"

She squeezed her eyes shut. *Brad was here in Haven.* This was a nightmare.

"Talk to me, Gabby."

"My ex, okay?" And he wasn't going to leave until he'd gotten what he wanted. Unless he thought she was off the market. Having a sexy alpha male like Ethan on her arm might be just the thing to get Brad to tuck his tail and slink home to Charlotte.

Ethan's blue eyes narrowed. "Your ex lives in Haven?"

She shook her head. "No. He must be here looking for me."

"He wants you back."

"Yeah." She bit her lip and looked away.

"And I hired him." His voice tightened.

She shrugged. "How would you have known? But that's not our biggest problem. Your grandmother just saw everything."

"Which means you and I need to have a serious chat. Not here." He motioned her toward the door.

Gabby dug her heels in. No way was she ready to go back out there and face the crowd that had seen her kiss Ethan. "Where are we going?"

"You stopped by to invite me to lunch, and I accepted. Let's go." His hand settled on the small of her back, propelling her toward the door.

With a fake smile plastered on her face, she turned the handle.

* * *

Ethan's gut churned with about twenty different emotions as he guided Gabby back through the reception area. He didn't like the idea of an ex following her to Haven. And he sure as hell didn't like her ex working here at Off-the-Grid. Ethan hadn't hired him directly—he'd hired Sinclair and Sons, now run by the oldest son, Martin, a longtime friend of his.

He'd be letting Martin know that Gabby's ex wasn't welcome on his property. But first things first. He and Gabby needed to have a little chat. No matter that he wanted in her pants in the worst way, she'd kissed him in front of Gram, and there was no undoing that.

"Gabby?" one of Martin's men—presumably her ex—said. *Schmuck.*

She tensed. "Brad, what in the world are you doing here?"

The schmuck glowered as Ethan slung an arm protectively around her shoulders. "Can I talk to you for a minute? Outside?" Brad asked.

"We were just on our way out," Ethan said, drawing her a little closer against him. *She's mine, buddy, so back the fuck off.*

"Please? Gabby?" The schmuck ignored Ethan entirely.

She ducked her head while Ethan guided her out the front door. They were down the front steps and headed for the Jeep when Brad came running after them. "Wait up."

"The lady said no," Ethan said coolly.

Brad scowled at him. "Actually, you did. I'm still waiting to hear from Gabby."

She lifted her chin. "I have nothing to say to you, Brad."

"Well, I do. Tell your boyfriend to wait in the car," Brad said.

"Watch yourself," Ethan warned him. "I don't like the way you're looking at my girl, especially not while you're on my dime."

The schmuck balked at that. "Hey, man, I don't want any trouble. Gabby and I go way back. I just wanted to catch up is all."

"Is that all?" Ethan stepped closer.

"This is ridiculous. Let's go, Ethan." Gabby marched toward his Jeep, showing a burst of temper he hadn't yet seen from her, but he liked it. Hell, he liked pretty much everything about her.

Except her ex.

"Want me to put the top on?" he asked as they reached the Jeep.

She shook her head as she climbed into the passenger's seat. He got in and cranked the engine, turning right onto Mountain Breeze Road, headed in the opposite direction of downtown Haven.

"Where are we going?" she asked.

"Silver Springs. Next town over. We need to talk, and there's no place to eat in Haven where I don't know half the staff."

She nodded, her jaw set. The wind whipped through her long hair, billowing it behind her and tossing strands in her face.

"Sure you don't want me to put the top on?" he asked.

She bent and rummaged in her purse. She came up with an elastic and tied her hair back with it. "What was with the caveman act back there?"

"Excuse me?"

"You," she said, "acting all caveman protective in front of Brad."

"You're the one who wanted him to think we were together." But the truth was, he'd have done it anyway. The schmuck really pissed him off, and he'd felt the need to mark his territory where Gabby was concerned. If that made him a caveman, then so be it.

She chewed her bottom lip. "I can take care of myself."

"I have no doubt." And that was the truth. "But Brad works for the contractor I hired, and that makes what he does on my property my business."

She didn't object to that, just sat there as the wind whipped her ponytail, looking so goddamn gorgeous it was all he could do not to pull over to the side of the road and kiss her the way he'd wanted to since he first laid eyes on her. Wild and untamed, not quick and chaste like the kiss they'd shared earlier.

"You like Mexican?" he asked as he guided the Jeep over the winding roads between Haven and Silver Springs.

She nodded. He drove to a little Mexican place off the beaten path where they could talk without worrying about any town gossips overhearing. They were seated at a table on the patio.

He ordered a Dos Equis. Gabby ordered a Diet Coke.

Today her skirt was white, long and flowing, and so damn sexy. Her shirt matched her eyes and hugged her curves perfectly. Her hair was windblown from the drive, giving her a bit of a sexy, rumpled look. He wanted to fist his hands in it and kiss her senseless.

"So let's talk," he said instead.

Gabby frowned, resting her elbows on the metal table between them. "I'll do it," she said.

"Do what?"

"Hang out with you so your grandma can think we're together." She was avoiding his gaze, and that pissed him off.

"And so that Brad can think we're together?"

"It might help him decide to leave town sooner."

"Getting his ass fired might help, too." Ethan's fingers tightened around his beer.

Gabby's eyes rounded. "You're going to fire him? Why?"

"I didn't hire him so I can't fire him, but I can make sure he doesn't set foot on my property again. What can I say? The guy really rubbed me the wrong way. So how is this thing between us going to work?"

Gabby straightened in her seat. "I meant what I said before about not dating—"

Their waitress interrupted then. Gabby ordered enchiladas suizas with extra sour cream. Ethan got the burrito special. He'd halfway expected her to order a salad and liked that she hadn't. He hated when women didn't order what they really wanted, thinking it would impress him if they were dainty or some such shit.

She looked at him across the table. "So it will just be for show."

He nodded. "Just for show."

"We'll hang out and spend time together with Dixie, but that's it. Behind closed doors, we keep our hands to ourselves."

He leaned back in his seat and took a long pull from his beer. "If that's what you want. But I don't think I'm the only one who enjoyed that kiss earlier."

"I think it would be best if there was no more kissing."

"Afraid you can't control yourself?"

She sucked in a breath. "Hardly."

He leaned forward, pinning her in his gaze. "Come on now, admit it. You want me just as bad as I want you."

Her eyes darted to the side. "Fine. You're not hard to look at. I'm sure you could have your pick of ladies in town."

"I'd pick you."

Her gaze flicked to his and held. "Well, that's good because I have another rule for us. No kissing or sleeping with anyone else while we're doing this. It might be just pretend, but I won't be made a fool of either."

"I would never make a fool of you, Gabby." He gazed into the honeyed depths of her eyes.

"Just so we're clear, you and I are not sleeping together either. So you're agreeing to no sex for as long as this lasts."

No sex. That well and truly sucked. "Okay."

"And this... attraction, it won't be a problem for you?" She closed her lips over the straw of her soda and sucked. He watched her swallow and felt himself go hard.

Oh, it was a problem all right. "I can control myself if you can."

Her cheeks flushed a warm pink. "It won't be a problem for me."

"Well then, I guess we have a deal."

* * *

Gabby forked another bite of enchilada into her mouth and tried not to stare at Ethan. Her pretend boyfriend. How in the world had she let that happen?

"So if we're going to pull this off, we need to get to know each other," she said.

"Okay." He met her gaze across the table. "So tell me about your family. Brothers? Sisters?"

"I have an older brother, John. He's an investment broker in Atlanta."

"And your parents?"

"They live in Charlotte. My mom's a doctor, and my dad is also an investment broker."

"Are you close?"

She lifted a shoulder halfheartedly. "We get along okay. We don't always see eye to eye, but they're good parents."

"And how long ago did you break up with Brad?"

"Last fall, so it's been almost a year now. I moved in with my parents for a while, but that just wasn't working out, so I packed up and came here." She sipped her Diet Coke. "And you? Siblings? Crazy ex-girlfriends?"

"None of the above. My relationships don't last long enough to get messy."

She wondered why. What made Ethan so sure he'd never want to settle down? He'd mentioned before that his mom died when he was ten. She didn't want to pry, and he didn't volunteer any more information, so she let the subject drop.

"Your grandmother says you're a local celebrity around here," she said.

"Does she now?" He shook his head, his expression softening with affection for Dixie.

"I guess I'd better do my homework and look for some YouTube clips of you in Beijing."

"Or you could come see me in action right here in Haven. I'm in the pool at Off-the-Grid every morning swimming laps." His smile had gotten flirtatious again.

And her cheeks were on fire. "Maybe."

He leaned forward. "So, Gabby, can I take you to dinner tomorrow night?"

A refusal rose on her tongue, but she bit it back. God, she wasn't ready for this. Not with any man, but definitely not with this man, who tempted her more than any man ever had before.

He grinned at her hesitation. "It's just a free meal and another chance for us to get to know each other better. I'm certainly not opposed to exploring the chemistry between us while we're at it, but you have my word that I won't put any moves on you. That ball is totally in your court."

She sucked in a breath and nodded.

His grin faded. "My grandmother knows everyone in town so we need to be seen out and about some."

Gabby sobered at the reminder of why they were doing this. Dixie was dying. She'd only met the woman a handful of times, but she liked her a lot. And Dixie had obviously done a fine job of raising her grandson. If not for the lying, Gabby certainly didn't mind doing whatever she could to help Dixie enjoy what time she had left.

"Dinner tomorrow then. But right now I need to get back to work," she said. She needed to get back to the quiet safety of her cabin so she could process everything that had happened in the past hour.

They finished up their lunch, and he drove her back to Off-the-Grid Adventures. She shivered at the sight of Brad's green Chevy Silverado parked around back. How had she not noticed it there before?

She hopped out of the Jeep and hurried back to her car. Ethan caught up to her before she could climb inside. He rested his hands against the car on either side of her, caging her in. Then he leaned in close, and *oh God*, he was going to kiss her! His word was no better than Brad's. Desire warred with disappointment inside her.

"In case anyone is watching," he whispered in her ear then pressed his lips to her cheek. At the angle they were standing, it would have looked like a real kiss to anyone inside the house.

With a wink, he stepped back. "Bye, Gabby. I'll call you about dinner, okay?"

She nodded, still feeling the warmth of his lips on her cheek, the tickle of his scruff on her skin. He'd kept his word.

And before she could question why she felt disappointed, she hopped into her SUV and headed home.

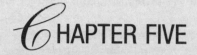

CHAPTER FIVE

*E*than unclipped from the zip-line and gave the all-clear for Ryan to come down the final line to join him. From there, they hiked toward the rock face where Ryan would teach rock climbing.

"Tell me again why you're having to bribe chicks to date you these days?" Ryan elbowed him in the ribs with a grin.

"Fuck you."

"But seriously, why this chick? Why not find a girl who actually wants to date you?"

"I told you. Because Gram thinks Gabby is the one for me."

Ryan sobered. "I just can't believe it, man. Gram's supposed to live forever."

"Tell me about it." They hiked for a few minutes in silence.

"Sure did look like you and Gabby were hitting it off, though," Ryan said.

"Chemistry's not the problem. She's messed up after her last relationship, I think."

"She doesn't seem like your type anyway. She's the type to put down roots, not jump into bed with a jerk like you."

Ethan had been very careful not to put down roots with a woman. He never let his relationships get that serious or that complicated. He'd seen the statistics. Children of domestic abusers were more likely to someday become one, and Ethan had been in enough fistfights to know he had at least some of his dad's temper in him. There was no way in hell he'd ever allow himself to become the monster his dad had been.

But Ryan was right. Everything about Gabby was serious. And complicated. Up until now, Ethan had been thinking about their relationship in terms of what it meant for him and Gram, but he hadn't really thought about what it might mean for Gabby, too. "No worries. It's hands off behind closed doors. Her rules."

"Fuck, man. You're dating the hottest girl in town, and you're still not getting laid."

A fact he was painfully aware of. "Oh yeah, when's the last time you got any?"

Ryan's face turned smug, and Ethan realized he was going to regret that question. "I've been out with Tina a few times since I got to town. We don't do much sleeping."

"You're an asshole."

"I'm an asshole who's getting lucky." The rock face came into view ahead of them, and Ryan picked up the pace. "Yo, that is sweet."

"I heard a rumor the property next door might be going up for sale at the end of the year," Ethan said as he tested out his footing at the base of the rock. "It would make a great addition. There are some wicked hills over there for a mountain biking course."

"Always been fond of mountain biking." Ryan hooked his

right hand in a crevice and began to climb. He was halfway to the top before Ethan had gotten both feet off the ground.

He enjoyed rock climbing, but he was an amateur. Ryan was a pro.

Ryan looked down at him. "This place is great, you know. I'm really glad you convinced Mark and me to come back home and make a go of it together."

Ethan drew a deep breath and lunged upward to grab a small ledge above his head. He knew what Ryan meant. It had been a long, hard road for all three of them, and it was pretty epically awesome that they were making this happen together. "Me, too, man. Me, too."

* * *

Gabby had no idea what to wear for a date that wasn't really a date. She finally settled on a long turquoise skirt paired with a slinky navy top. She ditched the Doc Martens in favor of matching strappy navy sandals.

She hadn't seen Brad since their run-in at Off-the-Grid yesterday, but she was under no illusions that he'd left town. He'd made it pretty clear that he wanted a second chance with her, and he'd never been very good at taking no for an answer.

She squeezed her eyes shut and pushed thoughts of him out of her mind. Better that she faced him now. Sooner or later he'd get the message and slink back to Charlotte. Then when she was ready to go home, she wouldn't have to dread running into him there.

Ethan knocked on her front door promptly at six thirty. Lance pinned his ears and ran for the pantry. Coward.

Gabby took a deep breath, unbolted the lock, and opened the door. Ethan stood on the other side, wearing khaki slacks, a blue button-down shirt that matched his eyes, and his usual panty-melting smile. He looked even more handsome all dressed up, and holy moly, she was in over her head even fake-dating him.

"Wow." His gaze slid from her face to her toes and back up. "You look gorgeous."

"Thank you." She felt herself blushing because the way he was looking at her made her *feel* gorgeous. And sexy. And she hadn't thought of herself that way in a long time. Under Ethan's heated gaze, she felt bold and daring.

Maybe a fake boyfriend had its benefits after all.

"So how do you feel about steak?" he asked as she motioned him inside.

"Love it." She walked toward the kitchen to extract Lance from the pantry. "Let me just take Lance out quickly and then I'm ready."

There were some other benefits of a fake boyfriend, too. Like, she hadn't had to worry about sexy underwear. And there were no pretenses. She could leave him standing in the kitchen while she took her dog out because he was definitely not expecting her to get cozy and make out with him before they left for dinner. And even better, there would be no awkward moment when he brought her home, deciding whether or not to invite him in.

"Does Brad have anything to do with the reason you always keep your deadbolt locked?" Ethan asked as she locked the door behind them.

She stiffened. "I'm from the city, remember?"

"You didn't answer my question." The steely look in his eyes told her he'd already drawn his own conclusion.

"I've always locked my doors. It's a responsible thing to do."

Ethan stepped closer. "He hurt you, Gabby?"

She flinched, and Ethan's scowl darkened.

"Godammit, if I ever lay eyes on him again—"

"No!" She whirled away from the door, away from Ethan. "It wasn't like that." Not until the end anyway. "He just liked to have things his way. That's all."

"If he so much as looks at you funny, I'm going to kick his ass." Ethan's eyes still snapped with anger.

Gabby managed a smile as she walked toward his Jeep. "You're awfully protective for a pretend boyfriend." Ethan had a rough side to him, a quick temper, and she had no doubt he could kick Brad's ass if he needed to. He'd probably handed out other ass-kickings in his lifetime. For some reason, that didn't bother her a bit.

"Any decent man would do the same," he said.

Was that true? She wasn't sure. "I appreciate the sentiment, but believe it or not, I'm perfectly capable of kicking Brad's ass myself should the need arise."

At that, Ethan grinned broadly. "I knew I liked you for a reason."

They kept the conversation casual on the drive to the restaurant. Ethan parked, and they strolled down Main Street hand in hand. Downtown Haven was so picturesque it belonged on a postcard. There were boutique stores for clothing, arts, crafts, jewelry, souvenirs, and even the most adorable bookstore. Ethan kept walking, leading her past the string of storefronts and around the corner onto Sullivan Street.

He held the door open for her at the Skyline Grille. "You been here before?"

She shook her head.

"Well, since you're stuck with me for the near future, the least I can do is show you around town. This place is great, and wait until you see the view."

She followed him inside, and the hostess led them upstairs to an outside deck overlooking the Smoky Mountains. It was even more spectacular than the view from her own back deck.

"Wow," she said as she took her seat. Their table was against the railing with uninterrupted views. In the distance, gauzy clouds wrapped around the mountaintops.

"Told ya." Ethan sat across from her, so handsome he was short-circuiting her brain just sitting there. He was awfully thoughtful and romantic even when he knew he didn't stand a chance of seducing her. She could only imagine what he was like when he was actually dating someone. No wonder he had such a reputation with the women in town.

"This is really nice, Ethan, but you don't have to wine and dine me. We should probably just hang out with your grandmother."

"We'll do that, too," he said.

"I'm going to her house tomorrow for book club."

"She'll love that." He smiled softly, looking out at the mountains beyond.

She and Ethan chatted easily while they stuffed themselves on steak and potatoes. She drank two glasses of wine, which was not the best idea in retrospect because she was feeling rather silly and a whole lot flushed by the time they'd finished eating.

The sun had dipped below the mountaintops, and their table was lit by a votive candle. She sighed as she stared into its flickering depths. "If this were a real date, you would *so* be getting lucky tonight."

* * *

Ethan choked on his wine. "That is a damn shame," he said when he'd finally regained the ability to speak.

Gabby giggled. She was tipsy, maybe a little past tipsy, and it only made her even sexier.

He leaned forward, resting his elbows on the table. "I wouldn't have pegged you as the type to put out on the first date."

Her eyes widened, and her pretty lips pursed. "Well, I'm not."

"I bet guys have gone to a lot of effort to woo you, Gabby Winters."

She gave him a puzzled look.

"Come on. What's the most extravagant thing a guy has ever done to get your attention?"

She frowned, then her eyes brightened. "There was one guy in college who sent a dozen roses and some chocolates after our first date."

That might be romantic by college standards. "How old are you?"

"Twenty-seven."

"Please tell me some guy since college has done something more romantic for you than have flowers and chocolates delivered."

"I guess my dating life is boring. Sorry."

"Well, shit, don't apologize. Absolutely nothing about you is boring, so the problem definitely lies with the men you've dated." And he really wanted to change that for her. He wanted to show her just how desirable and amazing she was, how a real man should treat her. But with the attraction simmering between them, he was already toeing a fine line he didn't dare cross.

She shook her head, and a lock of hair fell across her face. She swiped it back. "No, I think it might just be me."

"Not a chance. You're exceptional." He leaned closer. "You've probably got your dream date all planned out in your head. Tell me."

Gabby's breath caught, and she sucked her bottom lip between her teeth. "This is pretty nice. This restaurant."

"It's nice. But I want to know your most romantic fantasy date."

Her eyes fluttered shut. "The beach," she said softly. "Candlelit dinner on the beach, just the two of us. And afterward... you know."

"Sex on the beach," he said.

Her lips curved in a smile, and she nodded. "And maybe even skinny-dipping. I've always wanted to go skinny-dipping."

"Goddamn, Gabby. You are the opposite of boring." And holy hell, he was so turned on right now, his whole body ached with it.

Her eyes flew open, and she pressed a hand over her mouth. "I can't believe I just told you that."

He grinned. "That was hot. *You* are hot. And if a guy doesn't tell you so, then you need to show him the door."

She ducked her head with a shy smile. "Thanks."

Gabby's smiles were his weakness. They gave him a boost like a PowerBar after a long swim. When she smiled, she projected all the sweetness that made her so irresistible but with a hint of something wicked beneath, like she had a naughty side she rarely let anyone see.

"I have an important question." He said it with absolute seriousness, even though his intent was to lighten the mood. And shift the conversation so that he'd be able to stand up from the table without embarrassing himself.

"Okay."

"Pie or ice cream?"

She giggled again, and the sound of her laughter was definitely not helping the situation in his pants. "This place does a mean pecan pie, but the ice cream shop around the corner is pretty great, too."

"I've always been partial to ice cream," she said.

"All right then. Ice cream it is." While he paid the bill, she went to the ladies' room. He met her downstairs and took her hand to walk back outside.

The night was balmy, not too hot or too cold and not even all that humid. A perfect night for strolling down Main Street with a pretty girl on his arm.

"This is awfully romantic for pretend." She leaned against him, and at that moment, nothing about this felt like pretend. Sure as hell his attraction for her was the real deal.

"Anything worth doing is worth doing right," he said.

"That's a good motto." She still sounded a bit dreamy, reminding him that she was tipsy as hell.

They went into One More Scoop. He got a scoop of salted butter caramel, while she went for chocolate peanut butter crunch. Then they took their cones and walked across the street to the town commons, where they found an empty bench and sat together.

"Have you always lived in Haven?" she asked.

"Since Gram adopted me when I was twelve."

"And before that?"

"I bounced around a lot."

She licked her ice cream and watched him. "It must have been hard for you."

"Wasn't that bad." He crunched into his waffle cone.

"Tough guy." Her lips quirked.

He liked that. Not many women asked about his past, but when they did, they usually either responded with some sort of pity or got all awkward and couldn't change the subject fast enough.

Not Gabby. If he told her the darkest, ugliest truths about his childhood, the reason why he could never offer a woman his heart, would she take it in stride the same way? Probably.

They finished their ice cream, and he drove her home. He walked her to her front door and waited while she undid her deadbolt and opened the door. Then because he was the unlucky son of a bitch who had roped himself into a fake relationship, he drew her in and kissed her cheek.

He told her good night and went home. Alone.

* * *

Gabby walked to the kitchen for a glass of water, still feeling the heat of Ethan's lips on her cheek. Wishing they'd been on her mouth. He was probably a great kisser. Probably great in bed, too. It had been a long time since she'd yearned for the feel of a man's hands on her skin, to feel him inside her.

Sex with Brad had become an exercise in frustration. He'd been so focused on his own pleasure that he hadn't paid much attention to hers. Or that's what the therapist she'd seen a few times after she left him had said. Truly, she'd started to wonder if she just couldn't have an orgasm during sex. Or worse, maybe she was lousy in bed.

Because sometimes Brad would have trouble finishing, and he'd start swearing and ask her to try different positions until he found something that worked. It was a race to the finish line, to *his* finish line at least. It had been awkward and so *not* sexy. She'd gotten used to taking care of her own needs with the vibrator she kept tucked away in the back of her bedside table.

All the more reason she was taking a break from men

right now. All the more reason this pretend relationship with Ethan might turn out to be just what she needed. There could be no awkward sex, because there would be no sex. And just looking at him provided all the inspiration she needed for her late-night fantasies.

Pushing thoughts of Ethan out of her mind, she fetched Lance from his crate, took him outside, and headed for bed.

She didn't talk to Ethan the next day. Instead, she kept her nose buried deeply in her work, and when she'd finished, she took Lance for a short walk through the woods then baked a pan of strawberry lemon bars.

Actually, she was kind of excited about going to book club tonight at Dixie's house. She'd read and enjoyed the book, and she finally felt ready to meet some more people in town.

That confidence wavered slightly as she raised her hand to knock on Dixie's front door.

"Oh, you can just go right in," a voice said from behind her.

Gabby turned around and found a woman about her age standing behind her, her blond hair in a loose ponytail, a bottle of wine in each hand.

"I'm Emma," she said.

"Gabby. I'm new in town."

Emma nodded with a warm smile. "I know. And we can't wait to hear all about you and Ethan. Do you mind?" She nodded toward the door.

Gabby opened it for them, even as her heart lurched in her chest. "Me and Ethan?"

"Oh, come on. When you start dating one of the hottest, most eligible guys in town, everyone's going to talk about it. We're so glad you came tonight because we've all been wanting to meet you."

Gabby must have looked as horrified as she felt because Emma laughed.

"We want to meet you because you're new in town and we don't know you yet, not just because of Ethan. Come on." She nudged Gabby ahead of her into the house.

A handful of women were seated in the living room while the sounds of laughter and more conversation came from the direction of what Gabby assumed was the kitchen.

"Gabby!" Dixie waved from the far end of the living room. "I'm so glad you could make it. Come on in, and I'll introduce you around."

Emma lifted the bottles in her hands and whispered, "Red or white?"

Gabby smiled. She liked Emma already. "White. Thanks."

The women here ranged from Dixie's age to Gabby's. She smiled and made polite conversation as Dixie made introductions. Everyone seemed nice enough, and it was probably just paranoia that their friendliness might be motivated by nosiness about how the shy newcomer had landed charming, outgoing Ethan.

The table in the kitchen was overflowing with all kinds of finger foods and desserts. Gabby filled a plate and found a seat in the corner. Some of the women were already discussing the book, and she jumped into the conversation, grateful for a topic that didn't involve her dating life.

"Who made these?" a brunette about her mother's age asked, holding up one of the pink squares Gabby had brought.

"I did," she said, hoping she hadn't somehow screwed up the recipe. These were her specialty back home, one of her favorite things to bake.

"They're delicious," the other woman said with a smile. "What are they? I taste lemons, but I'm not sure what's making them pink."

"They're strawberry lemon bars," Gabby told her.

"They're fantastic," said the blonde sitting next to Emma.

"That's high praise considering she owns the bakery," Dixie whispered loudly.

The other woman smiled. "That's right. I'm Carly Taylor."

"You own A Piece of Cake?" Gabby had seen the bakery downtown but hadn't been inside yet.

"Yep." Carly took another big bite of her strawberry lemon bar with a smile.

Emma leaned toward Gabby. "*And* she's dating Sam Weiss."

"The rock star?" Gabby's eyebrows raised.

Carly nodded, her cheeks flushed. "Yes, that Sam Weiss."

"How are things going with you guys?" Emma asked her.

"Great. Really great." Carly was still blushing. "I flew out to visit him in L.A. again last week, and he'll be back in Haven later this month to stay for the rest of the summer."

"That's so awesome." Emma looked dreamy. Then she turned toward Gabby. "Speaking of hot guys, I want to hear all about you and Ethan…"

All eyes in the room turned to Gabby. Everyone wanted to know where she was from and what she did for a living. They oohed and aahed about her helping to develop video games.

Dixie sat there beaming with pride, which only made guilt twist in Gabby's stomach. It still didn't feel right lying to her, no matter the reasoning behind it. But that was Ethan's decision, and she'd agreed to go along with it.

"So tell us how you and Ethan met," Emma said.

Gabby grimaced. "I was out hiking, and I accidentally trampled a wasps' nest. He helped me out and took me to the clinic."

"Oh my God," Carly said. "That is like my worst nightmare."

"Were you stung badly?" someone else asked.

And before she knew it, the conversation had turned back to Ethan. It seemed everyone in town had either dated or wanted to date him at one time or another. Gabby got the impression he was quite the ladies' man. And they were all beyond proud of his Olympic success. She wanted to ask more about his past—surely these women knew the full story—but it seemed distasteful to ask in front of Dixie, knowing that her daughter, Ethan's mother, had died.

And besides, if she really wanted to know, she ought to just ask him herself.

The truth was, she did want to know. She wanted to know everything about him. Which probably meant she should try to learn as little about him as possible. Because already things felt a little too real between them, and she absolutely couldn't afford to make that mistake.

"I met someone new, too," a brunette about Gabby's age said. She thought the woman's name was Tabitha.

A collective murmur of excitement went around the room, and Gabby breathed a sigh of relief to have the attention turned to someone else.

"He's also new in town," Tabitha said. "He's a carpenter. His name is Brad. Brad Mobley."

HAPTER SIX

*E*than sank back in his seat with a mug of cold beer in his hand and a shit-eating grin on his face. "I told you not to friend a chick you're dating on Facebook."

"I am not even going there." Ryan shook his head with a scowl.

Mark eyed them from dark, unreadable eyes. "My first night back in town, and this is what you two losers decide to bicker about?"

"It's just like old times, man." Ryan clapped him on the back.

They were seated at their usual table at Rowdy's, a pitcher of beer between them, a platter of wings half demolished on the table beside it. Mark's right cheek was creased in a scar that had now faded into a shiny brown line a shade darker than his skin. There were other scars, Ethan knew. Scars that weren't visible, both physical and emotional.

He was so goddamn glad to have these guys back home. They'd met in foster care, lived together for a while in a group home here in Haven, and stayed tight even after Dixie had adopted him. In fact, the bond between them was a big part of the reason why his grandmother had settled here in Haven to raise him instead of bringing him to Wilmington, where she used to live.

Ryan and Mark had caused more than their fair share of trouble here in Haven, but Gram had done her best to keep Ethan on the right side of the law. She'd pushed him to pursue his talent at swimming, then kept him so busy with practice he'd had little time for anything else.

After graduation, life had sent Ethan, Ryan, and Mark in different directions. But now, ten years later, Off-the-Grid had brought them back together.

"Damn shame about Gram," Mark said.

Ethan sobered. "Yeah. It is."

"Anything you need, man, you just say the word."

"Thanks." Ethan swallowed past the tightness in this throat with another gulp of beer. Thank God he could walk home from Rowdy's. For one more night anyway. "She's hosting her book club tonight, so I stayed clear, but tomorrow I'm moving in with her."

"That's smart," Ryan said. "I'm taking her to lunch on Saturday. I know she can't drive anymore, so if you ever need backup to get her to an appointment or even just to pick up groceries, just say the word."

"Anything," Mark added, his expression deadly serious, which was usual for him, but Ethan knew he was true to his word. "Anything at all. You know how much we all love Gram."

Dammit, his throat was tight again. "I really appreciate that."

"Now fill me in on the girl." Mark cracked a rare grin.

"It's 'complicated.'" Ryan threw up air quotes and laughed until his eyes watered.

"Fucked up is what it is." Ethan drained his glass and reached for the pitcher to refill it.

Mark raised an eyebrow. "You—the stud of the Smoky Mountains—are dating a girl who won't sleep with you?"

"The stud of the Smoky Mountains?" Ryan laughed so hard he almost fell out of his chair. Ethan was tempted to lend an elbow to the process.

"We're not dating. We're just letting Gram think we're dating."

"But you took her to the Skyline Grille last night," Ryan said. "And I heard you guys shared ice cream in the park afterward."

"Aw," Mark said. "That's sweet. Are we back in high school?"

"Yo, I didn't take girls to the Skyline Grille back in high school," Ryan said

"You've never taken a girl to the Skyline Grille," Ethan pointed out.

"This is true." Ryan nodded. "I have much better luck getting laid by taking girls for a ride on my bike."

"The situation with Gabby is messed up. I'll give you that," Ethan said. "But you guys have got to keep it on the down-low. Not a word around Gram."

"You're walking a fine line trying to pull this off," Mark said. "Nothing gets past Gram."

Wasn't that the damn truth.

"The way you and Gabby look at each other, there's not a chance in hell it won't turn real before the gig is up," Ryan said.

Ethan lifted one shoulder noncommittally. "She's pretty

serious about not dating. Sure I'd love to get in her pants, but I respect her wishes."

"Of course you do," Mark said. "You're not a total asshole."

"But we will remind you of this conversation in a few weeks when you're still not getting any and you're frustrated as hell." Ryan tipped his mug in Ethan's direction.

Ethan was already frustrated as hell, but he'd deal. He might not be getting laid, but he enjoyed being with Gabby. There was something refreshingly different about her, and it wasn't just her funky style with the long skirts and boots. She really seemed to care about Gram and had gone out of her way to spend time with her. There was a wholesomeness to Gabby, but at the same time, she'd surprised him with her sexy fantasies.

And he couldn't fucking wait to see her again.

The next morning, he, Ryan, and Mark spent several hours at Off-the-Grid, walking the property and going over things that still needed to be completed before they opened for business. After what had happened last week, they had a whole checklist of new safety precautions to secure the place at night.

They'd already made it so far through the rezoning process. Notices had been mailed to adjacent property owners, giving them the chance to speak at a public hearing about the rezoning. When that hadn't yielded any complaints, Ethan thought they were home free. Now they had to persuade the Town Council they weren't out to corrupt the town.

A car pulled up out front just as they finished their meeting. Three elderly woman piled out and started walking around the house, peering off into the woods.

"Uh, what the hell?" Ryan asked.

Ethan recognized them from around town: Marlene Goodall, Helen Arkin, and Betsy Something-or-other. Marlene was Carly's grandmother and Gram's good friend. All three were active at the senior center. "I'll go see."

He walked outside.

"Oh, hi, Ethan," Marlene said. "We came by to see the place."

A lightbulb blazed in Ethan's head as he realized Marlene also sat on the Town Council. In fact, he had a sudden inkling that they all did. "That's great. Would you like a tour?"

Betsy nodded. "We would like that. We're concerned, you know, about safety."

Yeah, he'd figured that out. He almost went back inside to get Ryan since he was so much better at this shit, but surely even Ethan could handle showing these ladies around without blowing it. "It's all very safe, I promise. Follow me, and I'll show you the zip-line course."

The three women walked behind him, murmuring among themselves. An irritating prickle started between his shoulder blades. Who were they to tell him he couldn't open Off-the-Grid here? They didn't know the first thing about his new business—what it meant to him and what it might do for the town.

He reached the platform that marked the start of the zip-line course. "Well, here we are."

"Hmm, that doesn't look *so* bad," Marlene said.

"So you just zip right down that cable?" Helen asked.

"Not in a million years." Betsy shook her head.

"It's very safe," Ethan told them. "You're wearing a safety harness and helmet. You zip from one end of the line to the other. It feels kind of like flying. Anyone want to try it?"

"Heavens, no," Helen said.

"But I would like to see you demonstrate," Marlene said. "I think it would give me a better feel for how the whole thing works."

"My pleasure." Ethan left them and climbed the ladder to the platform. He showed them the new combination lock on the gear box and talked them through the process as he harnessed up, then kicked off from the platform, and soared. And...felt all of his frustration fade away.

Only thing that topped this was sex. And since he couldn't have any of that, he'd need the adrenaline rush of the zip-line to keep him sane this summer. By the time he'd unclipped at the other end and walked back to the group, he found Ryan and Mark outside talking to the ladies.

"Do you use a safety net for the rock climbing?" Marlene was asking Ryan.

"No, ma'am. Amateur climbers will wear a safety harness. More advanced clients can free climb."

Betsy covered her mouth in horror.

"So someone could theoretically fall to their death? Right here on your property?" Helen asked.

"In theory, yes," Ryan answered, looking pained. "There is risk involved in most any sport, but I can assure you that all necessary precautions will be taken to ensure the safety of our clientele. And we have all the necessary insurance to cover any injuries that may occur."

"Including the one last week?" Helen asked.

Ryan nodded. "Yes."

"I just can't imagine why anyone would want to climb up the side of a rock like that. Sounds like a death wish to me." Betsy shook her head, lips pursed.

"I enjoy pushing my body to its limits," Ryan said. "The adrenaline rush when you reach the top is worth every bit of pain and struggle to get there. There's really nothing else like it."

Helen shuddered, then turned to Ethan. "I do appreciate you demonstrating the zip-line."

"My pleasure." He was going to have to take another run to rid himself of the negativity rolling off these three women.

"We'll be going now. I hear we'll see you boys next Friday at the Town Council meeting," Marlene said.

"Yes, ma'am," Ryan said. "We're looking forward to it."

"See you there."

With a wave, they headed in the direction of their car.

"The fuck was that all about?" Mark asked.

"You heard the ladies," Ethan said. "We might start killing off locals left and right with our dangerous operations here."

"It's because of what happened out here last week with those teenagers. It gave them the excuse they needed to come after us," Ryan said. "They're worried we'll hurt Haven's reputation. But it'll all be fine once we get started and they see how we bring in new revenue for the town. You'll see."

Ethan scowled. "If they let us open our doors at all."

* * *

Gabby had spent the afternoon with Dixie. She'd taken her to nearby Silver Springs to do some shopping, then to Common Grounds for coffee, and now they were headed to Off-the-Grid to surprise Ethan. She really enjoyed spending time with Dixie, and they'd had a lot of fun today, but now Gabby was ready for a quiet evening home alone. These last few days, she'd been completely swept off her feet by Ethan and his family, and she was afraid she was starting to enjoy it a little too much.

They pulled into the driveway at Off-the-Grid, where a

black SUV was parked alongside Ethan's Jeep and Ryan's Harley.

Dixie clapped her hands with delight. "Oh, Mark must be here."

She hustled out of the car so fast Gabby had to rush to keep up with her. By the time she'd rounded the front of the car, Dixie was already walking around the side of the house, headed toward where Ethan, Ryan, and a third man stood in the side yard.

"Mark!" she exclaimed and threw her arms around him.

Mark was tall—very tall—with darkly tanned skin and a scar slashing his right cheek. His black hair was close-cropped, his demeanor rigid, until Dixie got to him. Then his face relaxed in a warm smile as he bent to kiss her cheek. It seemed like Dixie had been somewhat of a grandmother to all three of the guys. As Gabby watched them with her now, it felt a bit like seeing a family reunion.

Ethan's eyes found Gabby's, and he crossed the yard to pull her into his arms. "Hey," he whispered against her lips.

"Hey." Warmth flooded her at his touch and awakened a swarm of butterflies in her stomach. Impulsively, she pressed a quick kiss to his lips.

"I'm grilling burgers at Gram's house tonight. Join us?" His arms were still around her, his mouth tantalizingly close to hers.

She threaded her fingers into the front of his shirt, using their audience as an excuse to keep holding on to him. "I really shouldn't."

"You really shouldn't sit home alone on a Friday night when your friends are grilling burgers." His smile was infectious. "Come on."

"Okay, I guess. Just for a little while."

Ethan pulled her in for one more quick kiss, and then,

with a wink, he looped an arm around her shoulders and turned to his friends. "Mark, I don't think you've met Gabby yet."

Mark walked over to make introductions, then Ethan called out, "Burgers at Gram's. I'm cooking. Who's in?"

"Hell yeah," Ryan said.

Mark nodded with a smile.

"All right then. We'll see you over there." Ethan stepped back, although his hand lingered on hers and gave it a warm squeeze before he let go entirely.

And goodness, she wanted to drag him inside the house and kiss him until her knees melted and her toes curled and she'd completely forgotten all the reasons she'd insisted their relationship be only for show.

As much as she wished she wasn't so crazy-attracted to him, being around Ethan made her feel alive in a way she hadn't felt in a long time. Even if their relationship could never go beyond a few quick kisses in front of his grandmother, he reminded her what it was like to feel desirable.

And it felt good.

So good.

She turned to find Dixie watching, her face glowing like a kid on Christmas morning. That familiar guilt twisted Gabby's stomach. But was it so bad to let this sweet lady die thinking her grandson had a shot at true love?

Maybe if she had a grandma like Dixie, she'd have loved her enough to do the same. Gabby's grandparents were all gone now, but neither of her grandmothers had been as warm and fun and sweet as Dixie.

So she would swallow her guilt and do what she could to help this woman die in peace.

* * *

As it turned out, Mark took over the grill. With a cold beer in one hand and a spatula in the other, his friend looked more relaxed than Ethan could remember seeing him. Not for the first time, he said thanks for the fact that Mark was here, in Haven, scarred but in one piece.

Ethan took a swig from his own beer and walked to where Gabby stood at the edge of the deck, staring into the woods beyond.

"Hey." He walked up behind her, resting a hand on her shoulder, and she relaxed against him like it was the most natural thing in the world. He bent his head to inhale the honeysuckle scent of her hair, remembering that day not so long ago when he'd found her in the woods behind Off-the-Grid, looking so damn beautiful and so damn lonely.

She didn't look lonely now, surrounded by his family.

"It's nice here," she said, nestling her head against his shoulder, and hell if he didn't want this to be real. A kind of relationship he'd never had, where feelings ran deep and promises were made and kept.

He shook his head to clear it. "Do you do this with your family? Cookouts? Hanging out?"

She shrugged. "My parents aren't really cookout people. If they were going to eat out on the patio, my mom would probably have some kind of fancy takeout delivered."

"They're wealthy, then?"

"Upper middle class, I guess. We never wanted for anything, but I wouldn't call them rich. My mom just doesn't like to cook, and they're both more interested in what's going on with their jobs than hanging out and enjoying the view."

"I like to enjoy the view," he said. Both the mountains around them and the woman in his arms.

She turned her head, those warm caramel eyes locked on his. "That's one of the things I like about you."

It took every ounce of self-control not to kiss her. "Thank you for taking Gram around town today."

Gabby frowned. "I didn't do it as a favor to you. I enjoy spending time with Dixie."

"And that's one of the things I like about *you*." It meant a hell of a lot to him that she'd spent the afternoon with Gram. "Let's take a walk. There's something I want to show you."

She nodded, sliding her hand into his as they walked down the path leading from Gram's back patio into the woods. As the house faded from view, Gabby pulled her hand from his with a shy glance in his direction. The sound of water trickled through the trees, getting louder as they went. A few minutes later, they came out beside the waterfall that had been one of his favorite teenage hangouts. It trickled over rocks and splashed into a clear pool below.

"I used to sneak out of the house at night and meet up with Mark and Ryan here to drink beer or whatever else we'd been able to get our hands on," he said. "Couldn't do it too often because it messed with my training, but sometimes I just had to cut loose."

Gabby laughed. "I can picture that. You guys were close, huh?"

"Like brothers."

"It's great that they're back in town."

"Yeah. It is." He slid his arms around her, and even without an audience to fool, she melted against him.

She spun in his arms, chest to chest. "You ever bring girls here?"

"No." He'd never been the type to bring a girl home.

"I'm glad," she said, and then she kissed him.

And this time, it was no peck on the lips. Next thing he

knew, his tongue was sliding against hers, his hands were fisted in her hair, and he was gone. So fucking gone.

She let out a breathless moan, her body pressed tight against his.

He slid his hands down to her ass, gripping her through the thin fabric of her skirt. He kissed her until his head swam, until nothing existed but the taste, the feel of her mouth on his, and the soft sounds she made as she kissed the fucking daylights out of him.

"Gabby," he gasped when they finally came up for air.

Her eyes were dazed, her lips swollen from his kisses. "That was even better than I thought it would be."

"Oh yeah?" He bent his head and brushed his lips over her collarbone, rewarded by a shiver of need that rippled through her. "So you've thought about it?"

"Since I met you." She stepped back out of his arms, a guilty look on her face, and he knew they were about to go back to playing pretend.

"You are killing me here." He shoved his hands into his pockets.

"I wish I could do this for real. I do. But I came to Haven to stand on my own two feet, and I really need to do that. For myself." Her chin was up, and she looked so beautiful. So strong.

"You're doing it. And I'm not here to get in your way."

"But thank you for the kiss. I needed that." She touched her lips with a smile and he knew something else for sure. He could never make things between them real. Because she deserved a man who wanted to give her the world, and Ethan had nothing of the sort to give. All he could offer her was a good time in bed, but not his heart.

Never his heart.

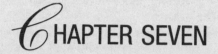

CHAPTER SEVEN

*G*abby's pulse had finally returned to normal by the time they made it back to the cookout. But holy crap, that had been the most amazing kiss. Now she finally remembered what she'd been missing. Actually, she wasn't sure she'd ever been kissed quite like that.

Ethan looked pretty pleased with himself, too. He caught her gaze and winked, then gave her hand a squeeze as they rejoined his friends and family.

Ryan gave them a knowing grin and passed Ethan a cold beer. "What are you drinking, Gabby?"

"I'll take a beer, too. Thanks."

Dixie sat in a white Adirondack chair facing the group, a peaceful smile on her face. "Have you guys started planning for the summer festival yet?" she asked.

Ryan, Ethan, and Mark gave her matching blank stares.

Dixie laughed. "I reserved a booth for Off-the-Grid when registration opened, remember? You just need someone to man it and some promotional things to go on it."

"Hmm," Ethan said.

"They're clueless, Gabby," Dixie said with a smile. "Maybe you can help them."

Gabby was feeling rather clueless herself. "What are we talking about, exactly?"

"The Haven Summer Festival," Dixie told her. "It's the weekend of July Fourth. There'll be all kinds of food and games, and local businesses will have booths to drum up new business. I knew these knuckleheads would forget so I booked them a booth."

"And we love you for it, Gram," Ryan said.

Ethan sat on the stone wall bordering the edge of the patio. "We do. We need this exposure. Can you help us?" He looked at Gabby.

She took a fortifying gulp from her beer. "I don't know anything about marketing or summer festivals so I don't know how much help I could be."

"You could at least give us feedback on shirts and stuff," he said.

"I've got a pretty good handle on promotional items," Ryan said, "Although, Gabby, I could definitely use your input on T-shirt styles."

She nodded. "I can do that, but you guys need to man the booth yourselves. You're the faces of Off-the-Grid, and you all have connections in town. People need to see you there and talk to you. Share your passion for Off-the-Grid and get them excited to come check it out."

"And make sure they know it's safe," Mark muttered.

Gabby looked between them. "Isn't it safe?"

"Oh, it's safe," Ethan said. "But the Town Council isn't so sure. They're holding up our rezoning request."

"Really?" Gabby sipped from her beer and sat beside him. "Why would they do that?"

"Because of what happened with those teenagers who snuck onto the property," Ethan told her.

Dixie made a sound of annoyance. "I can't see how that was your fault. Those kids were trespassing, and they're lucky you didn't press charges against them."

"And we're lucky that kid's family didn't sue us after he fell and broke his leg," Ryan said.

Dixie turned to Gabby. "The Town Council is worried because Haven was listed in *Carolina Magazine* as one of the top relaxation destinations in North Carolina, with the hot springs and the spa. They're afraid Off-the-Grid might knock us off that list next year."

"Well, that's just silly," Gabby said. "Zip-lining and rock climbing are things people do for fun while they're on vacation. I would assume that means they find them relaxing."

"That's what I told them," Ethan said.

Ryan smirked. "But not nearly as nicely."

"Have you planned a grand opening or anything?" Gabby asked.

Ethan glanced at Ryan and back at Gabby. "Uh, we thought we'd just start taking people out on the zip-line once our zoning comes through."

Dixie smiled broadly. "They need you, Gabby."

She opened her mouth to say that she probably wouldn't be in town long enough to see any of this through, but closed it again. Because she couldn't say that in front of Dixie. Couldn't even wrap her head around the fact that she was only here with Ethan because Dixie was dying. Even though she'd only known her a few weeks, her stomach tightened at the very thought.

"Who's ready for burgers?" Mark called from behind the grill.

And Gabby took the distraction and ran with it, grateful she hadn't had to make a promise she couldn't keep.

* * *

Ethan buried himself deeply inside Gabby's wet heat, thrusting harder and faster. The honeysuckle scent of her hair filled his lungs. Beneath him, she moaned, writhing with pleasure. His balls tightened as he grew closer to his release. So close...

He woke with a groan, his dick hard and aching. This was pathetic. He wanted her so bad she'd even infiltrated his dreams. He gripped himself, imagining it was Gabby's hands on his dick, stroking him.

He whispered her name into the darkness as his world started to go out of focus.

The soft sound of Gram's snores filtered through his lust-hazed brain. His eyes popped open, and he swore under his breath. *Fuck.* He was in Gram's guest room. In her guest bed. Lying under the floral-printed quilt that had been here ever since he'd moved out ten years ago.

He sucked in a ragged breath, then closed his eyes and counted backward from fifty, concentrating on Gram's even breathing on the other side of the thin wall until he was left with nothing but a dull ache in his balls and a raging bad mood.

His sexual frustration for the summer was now complete. The summer of blue balls. This had to be payback for all the women he'd dated and left before any emotional attachments could be made.

And as the saying goes, payback is a bitch from hell.

* * *

The next morning, Gabby grabbed on to every ounce of her self-respect and walked into Common Grounds, the local coffee shop. She inhaled the rich aroma, letting it settle some of her nerves as she approached the counter.

"Oh, hi. Gabby, right?" The barista gave her a friendly smile.

Gabby nodded. "Hi, Tabitha." They'd met at book club, and it had taken this long for Gabby to come in here and warn her about Brad.

"What'll you have?"

"I'll take a large caramel vanilla with cream and sugar." Gabby drummed her fingers against the counter, eyeing the gooey confections beneath its glass surface.

"The cinnamon buns are to die for. I get them from Carly's bakery across the street."

"They look amazing." Gabby had been meaning to stop by the bakery since meeting Carly the other night, and by the look of these cinnamon buns, she needed to go soon. "So at book club, you mentioned you were dating Brad Mobley."

"Yeah? So?"

"I know him." Gabby forced herself to look up and meet Tabitha's eyes.

Tabitha frowned. "Look, if this is some kind of jealousy thing, I don't—"

Gabby shook her head. "It's not that at all. I just thought you should know. He—" *He's controlling. He hit me.* "He's been abusive in the past."

Tabitha's eyes rounded. "Well, you'll need to tell that to some other girl because I dumped the jerk after he tried to order for me at dinner the other night."

"Oh." The uncomfortable knot that had been in Gabby's chest since she'd heard Tabitha's news the other night loosened. Thank goodness Tabitha had more sense where Brad was concerned than Gabby had. Her cheeks flushed.

The two women stared at each other for a few seconds of uncomfortable silence.

"So are you going to have that cinnamon bun with your coffee?" Tabitha asked.

"Um, sure." Why not bury her embarrassment under copious amounts of sugar?

Tabitha bagged the pastry and handed it to her with her coffee. Gabby paid, said good-bye, and hustled out of Common Grounds. God, that had been awkward.

And unnecessary in the long run, but that didn't make Gabby sorry she'd gone inside. She couldn't in good conscience have let Tabitha date her ex without a fair warning.

Clutching her sugary consolation prize, she hurried for her car and the safe sanctuary of her rental house.

* * *

Ethan sat in his Jeep, feeling irrationally disappointed that Gabby wasn't home. It was Saturday morning so he'd brought donuts and coffee and planned to surprise her with breakfast. That, and talk to her some more about the grand opening she'd mentioned. Because suddenly he felt like he had no idea what he was doing as far as launching a new business.

But she wasn't home.

Well, he could always go home to Gram's and surprise her with the goodies. The doctor had advised her to give up caffeine to keep her blood pressure down, but she might as well live it up with as many donuts as possible while she still could.

On that sobering thought, Ethan put the Jeep in reverse and almost backed into Gabby's blue SUV as she turned into her driveway. He couldn't help smiling. The sight of her had that effect on him.

Gabby parked beside him and stepped out of her car, a brown paper bag and coffee cup from Common Grounds in her hand.

Well, shit. He should have called ahead about the treats. In fact, she'd probably been in Common Grounds while he was across the street at A Piece of Cake.

"Looks like we had the same idea," he said as he got out of the Jeep with his box of donuts and two cups of coffee.

Gabby smiled, but it didn't quite reach her eyes. "Looks like we did. And you keep acting like we're really dating."

And it pissed him off that she kept pointing that out. "Just trying to do what feels natural. I wanted to see you this morning."

"Come on in." She motioned him after her as she went to her front door, where she paused to unlock the doorknob and the deadbolt.

He followed her inside. She set her things on the kitchen table and went to get the dog out of his crate. The thing was so small, he looked more like an overgrown rat to Ethan, with those giant ears and the long, skinny tail. He trotted into the room, took one look at Ethan, and darted into the pantry. "I think you could have gotten a better guard dog."

"I wasn't looking for a guard dog." She took two plates from the cabinet and set them on the table, then slid a cinnamon bun out of the paper bag she'd brought home, sliced it in half, and put one half on each plate.

"This one of Carly's?" he asked.

She nodded.

"These are like heaven. You had one before?"

"No."

He waited, watching as she took her first bite. Her eyes closed, and she let out a little moan, and oh, *hell yeah*.

She licked icing off her fingers. "Wow. That's like an orgasm on a plate."

Ethan's dick twitched. *Down, boy.* "It's good, but I could give you better."

Gabby's cheeks flushed red as she took another bite. "I can take care of myself."

Ah, hell, now he was hard as steel imagining her in bed pleasuring herself. "Do you think of me while you're at it?"

Her cheeks got even darker, and she choked on her second mouthful of cinnamon bun. She swallowed, coughed, and spluttered. "Oh my God. I didn't mean...that came out wrong...and *no*."

He grinned. "You're a terrible liar."

She covered her face with her hand. "I can't believe we're having this conversation. Change the topic, please."

"Talk to me about grand openings," he said.

Gabby peeked at him from between her fingers. "What?"

"Sweetheart, your mind is still in the gutter. Off-the-Grid. I don't have anything planned for a grand opening. What am I missing?"

Her hand dropped to her lap. "Oh. Well, I'm not sure I'm who you should be asking. I write computer code for a living, but you need something splashy, I would think. Get people's attention. Attract visitors from out of town. Show the Town Council that you guys are good for business, not a liability."

He nodded. "I like what you're saying. Like discount zip-line tours on opening day or something?"

"No, bigger." She stared thoughtfully at the remains of her half of the cinnamon bun. "What if you partner with the spa? Offer a weekend vacation package? Zip-lining, then relax at the spa afterward or something?"

"That's a great idea."

She shook her head. "I still think you need something bigger. Like... some of my friends back in Charlotte like to do those mud races. You know, with the obstacles in them? What if you did something like that for your grand opening? Donate the proceeds to a local charity."

Ethan nearly popped out of his chair. Yeah, he'd done several Spartan races in the past. They were hella awesome and what she was suggesting was so perfect it was all he could do not to jump up and kiss her. "You're a genius."

"Not really."

"This is exactly what we need, and it might even give us some ammunition when we meet with the Town Council next Friday." He picked up his half of the cinnamon bun and took a huge bite. Perfection. He devoured the rest of it, then opened the box of donuts.

Gabby sipped from her coffee with a smile. "You trying to put me in a sugar coma?"

"Nah. But if you want to work it off afterward, I know a few ways."

Her eyes widened. "We have an agreement."

He laughed as he plucked a powdered donut from the box. "And I was talking about Off-the-Grid. You still haven't let me show you around the place. Come over with me. Maybe you'll have some more ideas for the grand opening."

"Oh. Well, you can show it to me, but I'm not going on the zip-line." She reached for a chocolate frosted donut, then pointed a finger in his direction. "And don't you dare make a comment about how many sweets I'm eating."

He nudged the box in her direction. "Eat up, sweetheart. From where I'm sitting, every inch of you is perfect."

They finished their donuts, and Gabby took her little rat-dog outside, then she walked with him out to his Jeep. "All right," she said. "Show me what you've got."

* * *

Gabby watched from the ground as Ethan harnessed himself to the zip-line, but her mind was still on the enormous pool he'd just showed her. More specifically, she was fantasizing about Ethan shirtless and in swim trunks diving into that pool. Or Ethan stepping out of the pool. Soaking wet.

Her belly quivered.

"Sure you don't want to join me?" he asked from his perch high above her head.

"Positive."

"All right then. Let me know if you change your mind." He leaped off the platform, and Gabby's heart lurched into her throat. He bobbed on the line and began to zip to the other end, swaying from side to side as he went.

It looked crazy and terrifying and a little bit amazing.

He whooped as he whizzed by overhead. She smiled, walking after him. She still had no desire to defy gravity, but she could definitely understand why he loved it so much. And she thought a lot of other people would love it, too. This place should be really successful if they could just get the Town Council on board.

By the time he'd unharnessed himself and climbed down

the ladder from the second platform, she had almost reached him.

"Feel like taking a hike?" he asked.

She nodded. "I'd love to."

"Great, because I'd really like to show you the rest of the property. 'Course, it'd be a lot quicker if we were up there." He looked up at the zip-line platform above them.

"Never gonna happen."

"I warned you," he said as he started walking beside her. "I'm going to keep asking."

"Won't change my answer." Didn't piss her off either. Ethan wasn't pushy or judgmental, just persistent and passionate about his new business. And she respected that.

She enjoyed spending time with him. A lot. And pretending to date him didn't suck either. He pushed her outside her comfort zone in subtle—and not so subtle—ways, but it felt good to get out and have fun again.

She liked his friends and his grandma. And dammit, she *really* liked Ethan.

"Want to see the rock face where Ryan's going to take climbers?" he asked.

"Sure. You going to demonstrate that for me, too?"

He grinned. "Always happy to oblige."

They walked together through the trees along a path just barely worn into the ground, probably by Ethan himself. It was hot out today, but beneath the canopy of leaves, a cool breeze stirred, bringing with it the scent of pine and damp earth. "This must be a dream come true for you, owning this place," she said.

The gleam in his eyes said it all. "I'm a lucky SOB, that's for sure."

"I don't think luck had anything to do with it."

He turned to look at her with questioning eyes.

"You created this for yourself, and I'm guessing you worked pretty hard for it."

He shrugged. "Gram insisted I invest most of the money I got from endorsements after the Olympics, so I have her to thank for this really."

Hmm. Cocky, confident Ethan Hunter didn't know how to take a compliment. Not when it pertained to his self-worth. "Did you always dream about competing in the Olympics?"

He shook his head. "Gram signed me up for a whole bunch of sports after she adopted me, trying to keep me out of trouble. Turned out I was really good at swimming. At first, I was just doing it for her, but once I started competing, I was in it to win."

"You must have spent a lot of time training," she said.

"Hours a day in the pool and working out. I still can't go a day without swimming. It's in my blood." An intense look came onto his face when he spoke of his training.

She couldn't even imagine the kind of discipline involved in preparing for the Olympics. "Did you train here in Haven?"

"Gram found me a trainer in Boone, about a half hour from here. She drove me out there every morning before the sun came up so I could practice before school."

"Wow."

"She really turned my life around," he said, his voice gone husky. "I was headed for nothing but trouble before she adopted me."

"She's a special lady," Gabby agreed. Not just anyone would do what Dixie had, not only adopting her grandson but taking on the huge responsibility of helping him train for the Olympics as well. "Why'd you quit competing after Beijing?"

He shrugged. "I wanted to come home with a gold medal around my neck, and I did. Then it was time to try something else."

"It's pretty cool, you being a gold medalist." She elbowed him playfully. "I remember watching you on TV that summer."

"Yeah?"

She nodded. "I didn't place you until your grandmother told me, but I definitely remember you. You were hot."

He scowled. "Were?"

She rolled her eyes. "You know you still are. Cut it out."

"I don't know. You not wanting to kiss me has hurt my ego a little." He winked.

"It's not that I don't *want* to." She looked into his eyes, and suddenly she couldn't get enough air into her lungs. His blue eyes had heated, his playful demeanor edged with lust.

For her.

And then with another easy smile, he took her hand in his, leading her up an incline between two large rocks. "I get it, sweetheart. I really do."

And that was the thing. Even out here in the middle of the woods, with no one around for miles and knowing that Ethan wanted nothing more than to get in her pants, she felt totally safe. He would never pressure her to do something she wasn't comfortable with. And even though she wanted him just as badly as he wanted her—maybe more, since he'd probably had great sex a lot more recently than she had—she knew this was better than actually dating him.

He gave her confidence without stepping on her toes. If they made the relationship real, he'd have more power over her life than she felt comfortable giving anyone right now. Because Brad had been a nice guy, too, at least at first. It was only after things had gotten serious that he'd shown his true colors.

"I'm glad you brought me out here." She stepped over a tree root, lifting her skirt with her free hand so that she didn't trip.

Ethan squeezed her left hand. "Me, too. The rock face is right up this way."

They came around a corner and the path opened up to a big rock looming at least thirty feet into the air. There were some creases and cracks in it, but how anyone could scale it with only their bare hands—or why they would want to—was completely beyond her. "You can seriously climb that?"

"I can climb it. Ryan can kick its ass, though."

"Okay then. Show me."

With a cocky grin, he reached up and hooked his hand into a crack in the rock. He pulled himself up, his biceps flexing most impressively as he climbed. Holy shit, that was sexy. Soon she was left with nothing but a view of his very fine ass. And by the time he'd reached the top, she was so turned on, she could hardly stand it.

"So?" he called from the top. "You going to join me or what?"

"Not a chance. But I will enjoy watching you climb back down."

"Gotta give the lady what she wants." His fine ass reappeared over the edge as he started back down. He took his time on the descent, and if she wasn't mistaken, he might have reached for a few hand and footholds that made him flex his muscles a little more than was strictly necessary.

"You're a show-off," she said when his feet were back on solid ground.

He was a bit out of breath, his bronzed skin glistening

with sweat, trademark smile still in place. "No clue what you're talking about."

"No? You really needed to reach all the way to that notch?" She gestured above them. "Instead of the one closer to your shoulder that maybe wouldn't have shown off your lovely biceps quite as well?"

He flexed for her. "What, these old things? And for the record, I totally needed the leverage."

"Mm-hmm." For some reason, she put her hand on his biceps, and *oh crap*, that was a mistake. His skin was hot beneath her fingers, and his blue eyes blazed into hers.

"Killing me, Gabby," he murmured. "Killing me."

His words sent a bolt of red-hot desire right through her, and she must have made a sound because Ethan sucked in a breath, his gaze locked on her lips. His hands settled on her hips, burning into her skin through the thin fabric of her skirt.

Oh my God. Everything about the moment was intense. His chest heaved for breath, his eyes hooded and still focused on her lips. Desire pooled hot and aching inside her. He wouldn't kiss her, not without her permission.

And shit, she was being a tease. "Sorry," she mumbled, breaking free and turning away.

"You apologize too damn much." His voice was low, gruff. "Never be sorry for what you want or where you choose to draw the line."

"But I'm the one who said no kissing. So I shouldn't have done what I just did."

He laughed softly behind her. "It's okay, Gabby, really. I'll survive."

They hiked for a few minutes in silence, but it felt comfortable, not awkward. Ethan was relaxed at her side, again holding her hand as they walked along the trail.

"I'm thinking about that obstacle course," he said finally. "Like a team-building exercise. Everyone has to get their whole team through the course together. Winning team gets something really kick-ass, like a free lifetime pass to Off-the-Grid."

"I like it."

"You're a genius for coming up with the idea."

She laughed. "I have my moments."

"You know, smokin' chemistry aside, we make a good team," he said.

And the funny thing was, it was true.

CHAPTER EIGHT

Gabby stepped inside the deli and looked around for Emma. When she'd called yesterday to invite Gabby to lunch, she'd jumped at the chance. Now that she'd made friends in town, she realized how lonely she'd been these last few months. And she'd liked Emma a lot when they met at book club.

Emma waved from a table near the window, her blond hair again in a ponytail. "Hey!"

"Hi." Gabby sat across from her and settled her purse onto the empty chair.

Emma ordered a veggie wrap, and Gabby got the Havenly Ham special, remembering the day Dixie had shown up on her doorstep with lunch.

"Have you always lived in Haven?" Gabby asked.

Emma nodded. "I have. I'm thinking about leaving, though."

"Really? Change of scenery?"

"I don't have any family left here, and, I don't know, I want to try something new."

"I hear you. That's pretty much why I came here," Gabby said. "To try something new."

Emma gave her a conspiratorial smile. "I kind of have a reputation around here."

"You?" Gabby raised her eyebrows.

"Exactly," Emma said. "I'm the good girl. I never do anything unexpected or exciting."

"Well, I'm right there with you. Moving to Haven is the most outrageous thing I've ever done."

"So we need to mix things up," Emma said. "I'm thinking either a tattoo or shaving our heads."

Gabby took in her new friend's totally deadpan expression, then threw her head back and laughed. "I'll come with you for moral support."

Emma groaned. "God, you're as boring as I am. But seriously, the University of Georgia has an amazing landscape architecture program, and I've always wanted to apply for it."

"Really?"

Emma nodded. "I work at a landscape design company here in Haven—Artful Blooms—but I've always wanted to become a certified landscape architect. Someday I'd love to own my own business. Then I could do really amazing things. I could help design city parks and preserve the natural beauty around us."

Gabby sat back, taken with the sudden blaze of passion in Emma's eyes. "I think that sounds like a much better idea than shaving your head."

"I guess I'd better get started on my application then." Emma raised her Diet Coke. "To new beginnings."

"New beginnings." Gabby clinked her glass against Emma's with a smile. She liked Emma a lot—even with her good girl image still firmly intact. Gabby knew exactly where Emma was coming from. She'd always done what was expected of her, too, right up until she'd left Brad. Then, instead of happily moving on, she'd moved in with her parents, enduring their daily commentary on her life decisions until she'd decided to leave it all behind and come here to Haven.

They'd always thought she could do better than Brad. They wanted her to date someone more like the men in her family, with a well-paying office job and plenty of upward mobility. A carpenter hadn't fit that mold. And so when she'd come crawling home, there'd been a hearty "we told you so."

She hadn't even told them the whole truth. In fact, she'd never told anyone what happened during that last argument, when Brad had gotten so angry he'd slapped her, knocking her to the floor. Talk about a wake up call. She'd packed her bags that night.

Gabby drove home from the deli and retreated to her office to finish her workday. Once all her code had checked out, she took Lance for a long walk in the woods behind her house. He was really starting to come out of his shell these days. Today, he trotted at her side as they walked along the path.

"You like it here, right, Lance?"

He looked up at her, panting happily.

"Yeah, I like it, too. We're going back to Charlotte at the end of the summer, but I think you'll like that, too. You're small enough to share an apartment with me. And we'll still take lots of walks together."

When they got home, she sat in front of her computer, researching obstacle course races for Off-the-Grid's grand opening. The guys were going before the Town Council on Friday, and she wanted to help them get their zoning request approved, if there was anything she could do to tip the scales in their favor.

A knock at the door interrupted her thoughts.

She walked to it, fighting a smile at the thought of Ethan on the other side. What romantic thing would he do for her today? And why was she so giddy over the idea of seeing him again when they weren't even dating for real?

She pulled the door open without even bothering to check the peephole, then gasped at the man standing on the other side. "Brad."

"Hey, babe," he said. As if nothing had happened. As if they hadn't been broken up for almost a year.

As if he hadn't knocked her to the floor on that last night.

"What are you doing here?" She folded her arms over her chest. She wasn't afraid, not exactly. They'd lived together for over a year after all. But the more distance she got from their relationship, the more she realized how controlling he'd been. How unhappy she'd been.

"Well, I was driving by and saw your car so I took a chance this was your place."

Stalker much? "I meant, why are you in Haven?"

"I heard you were spending the summer here so I came looking for you, but when I got here, no one knew who you were. Couldn't believe it when you walked in the front door at Off-the-Grid last week. I miss you, Gab. If you give me another chance, I'll show you how great things could be for us." He gave her his best puppy-dog eyes, turning on the charm.

"Never going to happen." She'd never been more sure of anything in her life.

"You don't belong way out here in the sticks. Come home with me."

What had she ever seen in Brad? She stared at him now, with his sandy brown hair and dark eyes she'd once found so attractive. Not anymore. Everything from his neatly pressed pants to the dimple on his chin annoyed her now. "Actually, I'm glad you stopped by," she said.

His lips curved in victory. "I knew you'd come around." He stepped forward, inviting himself inside.

She blocked the doorway. "I'm glad you stopped by because now I can tell you in person that there is absolutely no chance of us ever getting back together. I want you to leave Haven, Brad. Please go home."

"Not without you."

She let out a frustrated sigh. "You don't want me. You've already put your moves on Tabitha and who knows how many other girls since I left you. You just don't like the idea that I'm happy with someone else."

"I only asked her out to make you jealous."

She shook her head. "I'm not jealous. I've moved on."

His gaze hardened. Gone was the slightly whiny man who'd been pissing her off ever since he stepped onto her front porch. In his place was the angry man who'd once made her cower in fear. And dammit, her stomach plunged straight to her toes.

"That idiot isn't good enough for you, Gabby."

"Ethan is twice the man you could ever be," she whispered, but her gaze had dropped to his boots.

"You can't do this." His voice shook with rage. "After everything I did for you? After all we went through together, you think you can just run off and shack up with some playboy in the mountains?"

"Please leave." She took a step backward, meaning to slam the door in his face, but he pushed his way forward, looming in the doorway. Had he always been so tall?

Gabby gulped for air, realizing with a sickening feeling that she'd left her cell phone in the office at the back of the house. She gripped the doorknob. If she slammed the door into him, would that get the message through his thick skull or would it just make him angrier?

"I think the lady asked you to leave."

She heard Ethan's voice from outside, and then Brad was shoved to the side, back onto the front porch, and Ethan stood next to her in the doorway.

Her knees wobbled, but no...dammit, no! This wasn't how it was supposed to go. How did Ethan always show up to fight her fights for her?

"I was just going," Brad said. "I have some business back in Charlotte, but I'll be back. We'll finish our conversation another time." He gave Gabby a long look.

"The hell you will," Ethan said. "Gabby asked you to leave. She doesn't want you to come back."

* * *

Ethan stood with his arm around Gabby's shoulders, watching as Brad stalked off to his pickup truck. She shrugged free and slammed the door behind them.

"What the hell was that?" she demanded, her cheeks flushed.

"Excuse me?" Because from where he was standing, it looked like she was mad...at him, instead of her asshole ex.

"I already told you how I feel about your caveman act," she said.

"No way in hell am I going to stand by and watch that guy walk all over you. You asked him to leave. I helped him leave."

Her bottom lip shook. "He wasn't walking all over me."

"Hey." He took her hand, drawing her closer. "I was just trying to help."

"And that's the problem with even pretend boyfriends." Her voice was soft, her eyes downcast. "I don't want help. I wanted to do that on my own."

Ah. Now he got it. He'd interrupted before she'd had a chance to send Brad packing on her own terms. "Look, I saw him being an asshole, and I reacted."

Gabby looked crestfallen. "It's okay. You were just trying to help."

He pulled her in for a hug. "Next time I'll try to remember that you don't need any."

She looked up at him. "Really?"

"Really." The earnestness in her voice struck him somewhere deep in his chest. She really needed to do this on her own.

"Okay." She backed out of his arms.

"I was on my way home from Off-the-Grid when I saw Brad's truck here. I'd love to hang around, but I assume you need to get back to work?"

She nodded.

He had something else he needed to run past her, too, but now wasn't the time. And he didn't like how quiet and unsettled she still seemed. "Let's get dinner together later."

She nibbled her lip, hesitation in her eyes.

"Just casual. What about burgers and beers at Rowdy's? Or whatever you're in the mood for."

"A burger does sound good," she said.

"Okay. I'll stop by around seven?"

She nodded, then followed him to the door. He was halfway to the Jeep when she said, "Ethan—thanks. For sticking up for me, even if I didn't want you to."

He smiled. "Any time."

With a wave, he climbed into his Jeep and drove to Gram's house. He found her on the couch with an ice pack on her forehead, her eyes closed. Cold, hard fear congealed in his gut. "Gram?"

"I'm okay," she said, waving her hand in his direction.

Not okay. None of this was okay. He sat beside her and took her hand in his. "Your head?"

"It's just a headache." She squeezed his fingers.

"What can I do?"

"I've already taken my medicine. Just sit with me. Talk to me."

Dammit, first Gabby didn't want his help, and now there was nothing he could do for Gram either. He fucking hated feeling helpless. But he sat with Gram, and they talked. For hours. Well, he talked mostly. He rehashed all of his most rebellious moments from his younger years. In fact, he was more honest with her about all the shit he and his buddies had pulled than he ever had been before.

What difference did it make? He was grown now. It was all water under the bridge. And there were so many great memories to share and laugh about before it was too late.

So many.

Finally, her headache eased. He fixed her a grilled cheese sandwich and heated up a can of tomato soup. The simplest foods had always been her favorites. They watched an episode of *Law & Order* together, and then she went to her room to rest her eyes while she listened to an audio book.

Ethan sat on the couch for a long time with his head in his hands. *Hell.* He wasn't ready to lose her. He'd never be ready to lose her.

Life was so fucking unfair sometimes.

A little before seven, he peeked through her open door and found her asleep in her bed, still wearing her head-phones. Morbidly, he stood in the doorway long enough to make sure her breathing was steady and even. Finally, assured she was okay—for tonight at least—he closed her door and headed for Gabby's.

He needed to feel something other than sadness tonight, and even if he wasn't allowed to kiss her, Gabby made him feel alive like no one else.

CHAPTER NINE

*G*abby pulled open her front door to find Ethan standing there, his eyes haunted the way they'd been the night he'd come asking her to pose as his girlfriend. Her breath caught in her throat. "Dixie?"

"She's okay," he said. "She had a rough afternoon, but she's asleep now."

Dixie might be okay, but Ethan wasn't. She tugged him inside and closed the door behind him. "I'm sorry."

He looked down at his hands. "I'm not ready to lose her."

"Oh, Ethan." The pain in his voice nearly brought her to tears. This badass, cocky man loved his grandma so much, *needed* her so much. She put her arms around him and pressed her cheek to his.

He sucked in a ragged breath, his arms closing around her waist. They stood like that for long seconds. So many emotions filled her, concern and compassion and sadness for what was happening to Dixie, but the longer she held on to Ethan, the more aware she became of his body against hers.

His chest heaving, his heart pounding, his stubble tickling her cheek.

"Gabby." His voice was raspy, thick with the same lust that pulsed through every inch of her body.

She turned her head, matching her lips to his. Sparks burst through her at the contact, shooting straight to her core, adding to the burning, aching need already building between her thighs.

His lips moved against hers, and she opened to him, devouring him. His tongue swept into her mouth, hot and demanding, dancing against hers until her toes curled inside her boots and she was up on her tiptoes, wanting more.

Needing more.

"You are the sexiest fucking thing," he rasped, his hands tightening around her, pulling her flush against him. He gripped her butt as he kissed the daylights out of her.

She rocked her pelvis against his, and he groaned, clutching her tighter. *Oh God.* She was so turned on, she might come right here in her entranceway, fully clothed, just from kissing him, from feeling his arousal pressed firm and hard against her belly.

How was that even possible? It had been years, *years*, since a man had given her an orgasm, in any way, shape, or form. And here she was, ready to combust in Ethan's arms before he'd even undressed her.

"Gabby." He clutched her against him, his chest heaving beneath her palms. "What are we doing here? Because this feels awfully damn real."

"I don't know," she whispered.

He groaned again, but this time the sound was heavy with regret. His hands, still clutching her hips, moved her back to a respectable distance. "When we do this, *if* we do this, I need you to be sure."

She blinked. Wow. It had always, *always*, been up to her to be the voice of reason in a relationship when things got hot and heavy. She might not have resisted if Ethan had swept her off to her bedroom, but she almost certainly would have regretted it in the morning. And somehow, his restraint made her want him even more.

"Christ." He looked away. "I want you so bad, Gabby. Let's go to dinner before I completely lose the ability to think straight."

She just nodded, then grabbed her purse and followed him outside to his Jeep. The ugly truth was that she liked him, and wanted him, even more because he hadn't taken her to bed. In her experience, the fantasy was always better than the real thing.

And fantasizing about Ethan was the hottest thing she'd ever experienced.

She'd never been to Rowdy's, but it seemed like the perfect place for them tonight: crowded enough to force them to keep their hands to themselves but not so loud that they couldn't talk.

"Hi, Ethan," a pretty blonde said as she strutted over with two menus. "Your usual?"

He nodded, then glanced over at her. "Gabby, what would you like to drink?"

"What do you recommend on tap?" she asked the waitress. "I like something light, not too hoppy."

"Try the Shepherd's Golden. It's a local brew. I can bring you a sample if you'd like."

"That would be great. Thank you."

"No problem. I'll be right back with that. I'm Tina, by the way. I'll be taking care of you guys tonight." Tina smiled, then headed back toward the bar.

"So you come here a lot," Gabby said.

"Yeah. Good food. Good beer. And they always have the game on." He glanced up at the TV over the bar. And while he obviously came here often enough to be on a first-name basis with his waitress, he hadn't looked at Tina with anything other than casual interest.

Nothing like the way he'd looked at Gabby earlier, like he wanted to taste every inch of her until she screamed with pleasure. Her cheeks heated. Her fantasies were *way* out of control.

Ethan scraped a hand over his face. "Don't look at me like that, Gabby."

She sat up straighter. "What?"

He gave her a look. "You know what. You're thinking dirty thoughts."

Her cheeks got even hotter. "How can you tell that?"

He winked. "Oh, I can tell."

A couple of brunettes in tank tops and short shorts sidled up to their table. "Hi, Ethan," one of them said.

He gave them a casual smile. "Hey, ladies. How's it going?"

"Just came by to say hi," said the second girl, giving Gabby an assessing stare.

Ethan introduced them to her as Lisa and Amanda. Old friends, he said.

They said polite hellos, then returned their attention to Ethan. "So how's the new zip-line course coming? When can you take me out?" Amanda asked.

"Hoping to be open by the end of the month," he said.

"It's sure to be a hit once people find out you're running the place," Lisa said. "You should keep your medals in a case in the lobby. Imagine all the tourists that would come by just for a look?"

Ethan's smile faded. "My medals have nothing to do

with Off-the-Grid. It's as much Mark's and Ryan's as it is mine."

"Oh," Amanda said. "Well, I've already seen them anyway." With a wink and a good-bye, she and Lisa headed off toward the bar.

"Sorry about that," Ethan said.

"No problem." Gabby guessed this was what Dixie meant when she said a lot of the women in town still considered Ethan a local celebrity. And she was trying really hard not to wonder when Amanda had seen his medals, because Gabby had never seen them.

In fact, maybe she should ask to, as a perk of being his pretend girlfriend.

Tina returned with a sample of the Shepherd's Golden for Gabby to try. It was light, crisp, a little bit fruity. "This is good. I'll take one. Thank you."

"Welcome. You guys ready to order?" Tina asked.

Gabby glanced down at her menu. She hadn't even looked at it, but Ethan had mentioned burgers earlier, and that sounded great.

"I'll have a Rowdy burger," he said, "with fries."

She glanced at the description of the Rowdy burger. Cheddar cheese. Bacon. Special sauce. "I'll have the same."

"You got it. I'll be right back with your beer." Tina collected their menus and walked off.

"So." Ethan's blue eyes raked over her, leaving heat everywhere they touched. "Where were we?"

* * *

Ethan took a long drink from his beer, but hard as he tried, he couldn't take his eyes off the woman on the other side of the table. Things had gotten way too fucking complicated in the past month. He needed Gram to be okay. Needed Gabby to be dating him because she wanted to, not some bullshit pretend relationship.

To hell with it. He polished off his first beer and signaled to Tina for another.

"I'm taking Gram to the beach this weekend," he said finally, when he had a fresh, cold beer in his hands.

"Oh." Gabby sat up straighter. "That's nice."

"It's something we do every summer. She asked...it's on her bucket list." He shook his head. He was rambling like a damn fool. "We'll leave after the Town Council meeting on Friday and come home Monday afternoon."

"It sounds wonderful."

"We'd love it if you could come with us." He looked up and met her eyes.

She twirled a lock of hair around her fingers. "I really shouldn't. This should be a special time for you and your grandmother."

"It will be, whether or not you're there, but we'd both like you to come."

"Um, I guess I could book a separate hotel room or something." Gabby fiddled with her beer, avoiding his gaze.

"I rented the beach house she and I usually stay in. There are two bedrooms and a loft. She sleeps downstairs, and I sleep up. I could use the pull-out couch in the loft after she's asleep, and she'd never know the difference." Or maybe they could just share the upstairs bedroom, and he could stop waking up every morning so hard he could barely see straight with no relief in sight.

But that had to be her decision. And she had to be sure about it.

"I do love the beach." Her voice had gotten softer, and a shy smile played at her lips.

He reached out and took her hand across the table. "You go a lot?"

She shook her head. "I haven't been in a few years actually. I used to go with my friends during college."

"So you'll come?" he asked.

She finally looked up and met his eyes. "If you're sure it's what you want. I know you're trying to keep up appearances for your grandmother, but maybe this should be a time just for the two of you."

"I'm sure. I'd really like you to come with us."

She smiled. "Okay, then. I'll come."

Relief loosened in his chest. It would mean a lot to Gram to have her there, and he would enjoy the extra time with Gabby. But seeing her in a swimsuit and sleeping under the same roof without sharing a bed might just drive him mad. "Thanks," he said. "It should be a fun weekend."

Their burgers arrived then, and the conversation slowed as they ate. Later, they strolled out to his Jeep hand in hand. Gabby gazed over at the town square with a dreamy expression on her face. "I really do like it here."

"Sure you can't stay?"

She shook her head. "All my friends and family are in Charlotte. I've never lived anywhere else."

"You're living here now," he pointed out.

"I'm just visiting. I'm here to prove a point to myself, but to stay feels like a cop-out. I need to get back to the life I left behind."

He shouldn't care that she was leaving at the end of the summer. He'd never dated a woman that long, not that he and Gabby were even truly dating. Maybe that was the difference. Maybe if she wasn't off limits, if he'd already slept with her, he'd be starting to put distance between them, the way he always did with women.

He drove her home and walked her to her front door, as much out of deeply ingrained manners as a need to make sure Brad wasn't lurking somewhere nearby, ready to hassle her again.

"Thanks for dinner. And for inviting me to the beach." A twig snapped behind her, and Gabby lurched into his arms with a startled squeak as some kind of creature scuttled off into the woods. "What the hell was that?"

He chuckled. "Probably a deer."

She shivered in his arms. "What if it was a bear? I'm not used to living where there are wild animals that like to munch on humans."

"Bears hardly ever bother us, as long as we don't bother them." His arms tightened around her, but it had nothing at all to do with her fear of bears.

"Let's go inside." She tugged him after her as she un-bolted the door and pushed them through it.

Somehow his arms were still around her as she slammed the door behind them, and he was powerless to let her go. Gabby stared at him for a long moment in silence, her eyes glazed with lust. She shifted her hips so that his dick pressed against the warmth of her body, and it took every ounce of self-control to hold himself still.

"I keep expecting you to...you know." Her voice was low and husky, her eyes locked on his lips.

"To what, Gabby? You made the rules."

"I really want to break them." She wiggled against him, her mouth moving closer to his.

He sucked in a breath and held it. His heart pounded, every cell of his body focused on hers, on the way she pressed against him and the whisper of her breath on his lips.

And then she kissed him. Softly, tentatively, her eyes still locked on his. He slid his hands down to cup her ass, yanking her more firmly against him, and kissed her back. Slow and thorough, until she moaned deep in her throat, her body plastered against his.

His tongue thrust against hers while his hands roamed her body, touching, teasing. He slid a hand between her legs, touching her through her skirt. She whimpered.

"Be sure, Gabby," he whispered against her lips.

He felt it, the slightest hesitation that tensed through her body at his words.

"Dammit." He dragged his mouth from hers, resting his forehead against hers as he gasped for breath.

"I didn't mean—"

"It's okay. I understand."

She bit her lip and looked away. "No, you don't."

"Then tell me."

"I just—what if the fantasy is better than the reality?"

He laughed softly. "Sweetheart, I promise you that won't be the case."

Her gaze flicked to the side, and she looked...hurt. *Fuck.*

His muscles tightened. "Did he hurt you, Gabby? Did he force you?"

Her eyes widened. "No! No, nothing like that. He just... it's nothing."

"It's something. Tell me."

She heaved a deep sigh. "It was just...this is so embarrassing. I didn't...it was all about him, okay?"

Ah, he thought he got it now, and his desire to deck the schmuck grew even stronger. "He didn't take care of you."

She blushed, still not meeting his eyes. "It's not like I need...God, I can't talk about this with you."

"Gabby, any guy that doesn't take time for his woman is a total dick. You have nothing to be embarrassed about."

She squeezed her eyes shut, her cheeks blazing even darker.

"But just so you know..." He bent his head to nibble her jaw. "My policy is ladies first."

She sucked in a breath, and he found himself wondering how long it had been since a man had gotten her off. Far too long, if his guess was right.

"It's not all Brad's fault," she whispered. "I think I might just not be very good at it."

Okay, he was *definitely* decking the schmuck if he ever laid eyes on him again. "Gabby, I promise you are not the problem."

She looked up at him, her eyes wide and swimming with self-doubt.

He took her hand and pressed it against the front of his shorts, just enough for her to feel him. "See the effect you have on me? Just kissing you is enough to make me crazy. You are so damn sexy, and I want you so bad it hurts. But what I want even more is to watch you come. Will you do that for me?"

He stroked her through the front of her skirt, and her head fell back, her eyes closed. He moved his hand to the waistband of her skirt, silently seeking her permission. She whimpered.

He slid his hand inside her skirt and panties, skimming over her bare flesh.

Gabby cried out, her hips thrusting against his.

"You are so hot," he whispered. "So sexy." He slid two fingers inside her, thrusting in and out while his thumb circled her clit.

Her hips bucked against him, her head back as she panted for breath. He captured her mouth with his, kissing the daylights out of her while he pleasured her with his fingers.

"Ethan," she gasped, her hips pumping against his to the rhythm of his fingers.

"Take your time, sweetheart." He increased his tempo, his free hand holding her close so that each movement of her hips brought her firmly against his aching cock. For tonight, that would be enough.

Tonight was all about Gabby.

She moaned as she came, her body tensing against his, then she relaxed in his arms, her face against his chest. "Holy shit," she whispered.

His thoughts exactly.

She peeked up at him through a wayward strand of hair that had fallen across her face. He brushed it back, then bent his head and kissed her. Holding her close, he savored the feel of her in his arms while they kissed.

After a few minutes, she lifted her head to give him a shy smile. "Would you like to stay for a bit?"

Hell yes, he would. "Yeah. Actually, there's something I was hoping you could do for me."

"Okay." Her pretty eyes clouded with worry.

"Can you show me how to play *King of the Desert*?"

Her mouth popped open. "Really?"

"Yeah. I want to see you in your element."

She backed out of his arms, still looking all flushed and sexy, the doubt that had clouded her features a moment ago replaced now with excitement. "Even if I kick your butt?"

"You'll definitely kick my butt. I can take it."

She grinned. "Okay then."

Ten minutes later, they were seated side by side on her couch, game controllers in their hands, while Gabby indeed kicked his ass in *King of the Desert*. His character—some dude named Sven with long, flowing blond hair—fell from halfway up a rock face and lost half his game health.

"We need to find you some food," Gabby said with a giggle as her character, a curvaceous brunette in a blue bustier, shimmied to the top of the cliff with no problem. "Press A to climb back up. X gives you a boost."

"A, then X. Got it." But he fell again, and this time his guy died. "Shit."

They played for over an hour, and he was finally getting the hang of it when a three-headed monster came out of nowhere and killed him again. Gabby slayed it effortlessly.

"I like watching you play," he said.

"Really?" She turned to look at him.

"Yeah. You smile a lot."

Her lips curved, and the next thing he knew, he was flat on his back on the couch with Gabby sprawled on top of him, kissing him senseless. Her warmth enveloped him as he lost himself in her kisses, his tongue thrusting against hers while his hands roamed her body, memorizing the feel of her curves.

Her knees slid down on either side of his hips so that she straddled him. He unbuttoned her top and pushed it aside so that he could kiss and caress her breasts, bringing her nipples into hard peaks. Gabby whimpered as he sucked on first one, then the other. Her hands fisted in his hair, holding him close while her hips rocked restlessly against his, driving him out of his fucking mind with need.

He rolled to the side, tucking her in next to him. She whimpered, wiggling to bring her hips against his again. Yeah, he knew the feeling. But he shifted back, keeping a few inches between them. "Not happening, sweetheart. I don't even have a condom on me tonight."

That was a flat-out lie. He never left the house without a condom, but he needed her to understand that tonight was all about her.

Her brow wrinkled. "But—"

"We're not having sex tonight."

"Oh." Her eyes widened. "Really?"

And dammit, he saw relief mixed with the disappointment in her eyes. She wasn't ready; maybe she never would be. And that was fine because already he could tell sex with Gabby would be so much more than just sex. He had sex for pleasure, not for the messy emotional entanglements that sometimes came with it.

With Gabby, there would definitely be emotional entanglements. His emotions were already a tangled mess, and he hadn't even gotten naked with her—yet.

"Really," he answered her, and he felt her relax beside him.

She pulled him in for another kiss, and he was lost in the feel of her, the taste of her. He brought his hand between them, teasing her through her skirt. She gasped, and her eyes fluttered shut as her hips thrust against his hand.

"Gabby, open your eyes."

She did, her caramel eyes soft and glazed with lust.

"The problem was definitely not on your end, okay?" He kept stroking her. "I want to fuck you so bad right now, but even though I can't, I want you to know that you have absolutely brought me to my knees here tonight."

She stared at him, her eyes wide.

"If I could"—he thrust his hips against hers, just once, hard enough to make them both gasp—"I have no doubt you would absolutely blow my mind."

A single tear trailed down her cheek. "Really?"

"Oh, hell yes. Really." He slid his hand inside her skirt and under her panties, trailing it over her skin until he reached her core, so hot and wet for him. "I want to bury myself in you until you're screaming my name." He thrust his fingers inside her, and she cried out.

"But just feeling you like this is so fucking good." He

pumped his fingers harder and faster. Gabby met him thrust for thrust with her hips, whimpering and panting as she grew closer to her release. He slowed his tempo, taking time to kiss her, to nip at her exposed nipples while his thumb traced lazy circles around her clit. "You are so fucking amazing."

"Please," she whispered, her body tensing, eyes closed.

"So sexy," he murmured as he gave her what she needed. He brought her to the edge, paused, then pushed her right over.

Her hips bucked against him as she came. "Ethan! Oh! Oh, Ethan."

She lay on the couch, limp and panting, looking like she'd just had a spiritual awakening.

And ten minutes later, as he headed for the door, his dick still straining the front of his pants, he'd never felt more satisfied.

CHAPTER TEN

*E*than, Mark, and Ryan worked long days the rest of the week. They spent their mornings in the office, working on details and plans for Off-the-Grid's grand opening. They'd decided to call the event the Adrenaline Rush. There would be a series of obstacles each team would need to work together to navigate, including a climbing wall and a ropes course. The final score would be determined based on overall time for the entire team to complete the course with deductions for any obstacles not completed along the way.

They hoped to not only bring the town together, but attract adventure-seeking tourists as well. Their event should be great publicity, both for the town and for Off-the-Grid. A win-win situation, or so they hoped. And while Ethan wasn't opposed to using his post-Olympic fame to their advantage, he wasn't trying to shine a spotlight on himself either.

In the afternoons, they worked on the property itself, putting finishing touches on the zip-line course and beginning installation of the ropes course that would be a part of the Adrenaline Rush as well as a new attraction at Off-the-Grid Adventures.

"This is sweet," Ryan said as he navigated along the rope bridge he, Ethan, and Mark had just finished constructing. It ran from one tree to another, with ladders at both ends, boards to step between, and a rope to hold on to for balance as you made your way across.

"Jesus. Be careful." Mark shook his head, reaching up to wipe the sweat from his brow.

They'd installed a line above that would connect to a safety harness, but the harness wasn't up yet. Ryan gleefully made his way across, unconcerned by the twenty-foot drop and his lack of safety equipment.

Ethan wasn't particularly worried either. They were all surefooted and athletic. But he sure as hell wouldn't be letting any paying customers up there without a harness.

"People are going to love this shit," Ryan said when he'd reached the other side. "Hell, *I* love this shit."

"Let's just hope the Town Council does, too," Ethan said. Because without the proper zoning, they were dead in the water. Starting over someplace new just wasn't feasible, financially or otherwise. They'd already built Off-the-Grid here, and this was where they were going to stay.

The incident a few weeks ago with the teenage joyriders was still hanging over their heads, but the blame for that was all Ethan's. He wouldn't make the same mistake twice. The ropes course would be fully enclosed behind a ten-foot chain-link fence, and the gate would be padlocked unless one of them was personally overseeing a group on the course.

"It'll be fine," Mark said.

"Fucking right." Ethan fist-bumped his friend then started up the ladder to try out the ropes course himself.

Living life without a safety net, the way he did best.

* * *

It was after seven by the time Ethan left Off-the-Grid. He'd asked Gabby to take Gram to game night at the senior center and decided to stop by on his way home to make sure she was holding up okay. He'd been a handful of times, and the seniors took their board games pretty seriously. He'd been locked into a game of chess with old Mr. Harmon for almost two hours.

He'd barely escaped with his sanity intact.

Fact: Ethan and board games did not mix well. Hoping Gabby had a higher tolerance, he pulled open the front door of the senior center. The noise greeted him first. Laughter, chatter, and the synthesized music of...video games?

He swept his eyes around the room, spotting all the usual suspects seated around tables containing their favorite board games. But across the room, Gram and Marlene stood in front of the TV, laughing and swaying from side to side. A video game was on the screen. In fact, it almost looked like Gram and Marlene were...

"Look, Ethan!" Gram called out to him. "I'm skiing!"

So she was. They were playing one of those games with a sensor where you controlled your player by moving your body. As he watched, Gram hopped in place, and her character went over a jump on the screen. She and Marlene bumped into each other, laughing themselves silly as the characters on the screen did the same.

He glanced around and spotted Gabby at a table in back,

playing chess with Mr. Harmon. Oh boy. Gabby's face was scrunched in concentration as she contemplated her next move. He decided to give her a few minutes, then see if she needed a break.

Mrs. Muth, who might have been the oldest resident in Haven at ninety-five, sat at a table by herself, staring at an iPad, brows furrowed. Concerned, Ethan walked over and sat next to her. "How's it going, Mrs. Muth?"

She looked up, her dark eyes now crinkled in a smile. "I'm still alive, so I can't complain. How are you, Ethan?"

"I'm good. You need help?" He gestured to the iPad.

She shook her head. "It's the most amazing thing. Look, I'm playing solitaire."

"Have you played it before?"

"Oh, yes. Solitaire has always been my favorite. I haven't been able to deal cards for years on account of my arthritis." She rubbed the swollen joints in her bony fingers. "So this is a real treat. I just have to touch the screen to move the cards. Gabby set it up for me."

"Did she now?" Ethan grinned, glancing at Gabby across the room. She caught his eye and smiled back.

"She's really livened things up for us here today," Mrs. Muth said. "I don't know when I've seen folks have so much fun. I even tried the skiing game earlier."

"That's great."

Mrs. Muth nodded. "You caught yourself a good one, Ethan. Make sure you hang on to her."

He laughed awkwardly. "I'll do my best, Mrs. Muth."

Gram walked over, cheeks rosy and eyes sparkling. "It's official. Gabby has to come to game night every month."

"And bring my video game equipment?" Gabby said with a smile, apparently having finished her game of chess, for she'd also joined them at Mrs. Muth's table.

Gram patted her shoulder. "It's you we love, although the video games sure have been fun, too."

Gabby beamed at the compliment, and Ethan felt an uncomfortable pressure in his chest, like he'd been underwater for too long. He was torn between the desire to bolt for the nearest door or to pull Gabby into his arms and kiss her senseless.

She took his hand, tugging him toward the TV in back with that sweet smile that was always his undoing. "So what do you say, want to see if you can beat me on the virtual slopes?"

Hell, yeah, he did. "Lead the way."

* * *

They walked into Town Hall on Friday morning feeling pretty damn good. Ryan had insisted they all wear button-down shirts and ties, and all three of them were freshly shaven. When Ethan had looked at himself in the mirror before leaving Gram's house, he thought he looked downright refined.

All hell-raising, bad boy attitude had been checked at the door.

After meeting and greeting their way across the room, he, Ryan, and Mark took their seats. Across from them were Lorraine Hanaford, Marlene Goodall, Helen Arkin, and the rest of the Haven Town Council. He was relieved to see that many of the council members were closer to his age than Gram's. Hopefully the younger members would be more enthusiastic about his new venture than Lorraine and her gang.

Ryan cleared his throat. "First of all, we'd like to thank you for the opportunity to be here this morning. We're

extremely excited about our new business venture and look
forward to showing you our vision for Off-the-Grid Adventures."

Ethan merely nodded in agreement. Despite the fact that
Off-the-Grid was his brainchild, they had agreed that Ryan
would do most of the talking this morning. He was their
PR guy, no question. Ethan would be the primary guide for
guests on the zip-line and ropes course. And Mark was their
behind-the-scenes guy. He got shit done, but he was a man
of few words.

"We're excited to hear from you guys this morning," said
one of the younger men on the council. "It's not every day
our own local Olympian opens a new business in town."

"Thank you," Ethan said as Lorraine shot him a withering
look.

Ryan took the Town Council members through an over-
view of Off-the-Grid and the activities they planned to offer.
He presented a shitload of information about outdoor adventure sports, the growing popularity of businesses like theirs
as part of a mountain vacation getaway, and the amount
of revenue similar businesses had brought into their home-
towns. He'd even put together a splashy slideshow to go
along with his presentation.

Last but not least, he explained in great detail all the
inspections and certifications that had been performed on
Off-the-Grid's equipment. He talked about their insurance
coverage and all the various new safety protocols that had
been put in place to protect guests—both invited and unin-
vited.

Ethan was impressed. He already knew Off-the-Grid
kicked ass, but if he hadn't, he'd surely buy in after Ryan's
presentation.

Even Mark was smiling with confidence.

"Well." Lorraine eyed her counterparts. "I certainly appreciate the time you've taken to come here today."

"We have one more idea we'd like to discuss with you, ma'am," Ryan said. They had agreed they'd save their ace in the hole for the end of the meeting, then go for broke.

"By all means," Lorraine said.

"We'd like to host a grand opening event of sorts, similar to a charity run or walk, but in this case, teams would work together to complete an obstacle course and other team-building challenges to be crowned the winner. We're calling it the Adrenaline Rush."

"Adrenaline Rush? Hmm." Lorraine glanced at Betsy to her left, and the two women raised their eyebrows.

"Yes, ma'am. We hope to build morale as local teams work together and hopefully also bring in some tourists interested in the challenge. Events like this have become very popular recently. People come from all over the place to participate. We would like to donate all the proceeds from the Adrenaline Rush to the Pearcy County Food Bank."

"Well, I think that sounds like a great idea and a lot of fun," Marlene said. "Sign me up."

"Ms. Hanaford?" Ryan asked. He sure looked the part today, with his brown hair neatly groomed, his tats hidden beneath a crisp blue button-down shirt. He might be hell on wheels when it came to his personal life, but he was also a hell of a businessman.

"You'd need a permit for the charity event, of course," she said. "Would you gentlemen mind waiting out front for a few minutes while we discuss this?"

"Not at all. Take your time." Ryan stood, and Ethan and Mark followed.

"Thank you so much for your time," Ethan said.

Mark just smiled, tipping his head politely.

They walked out to the lobby together. Mark ambled over to the water bubbler and filled a paper cup with cold water. Ryan walked to the front window and looked out at the cloudless blue sky.

"I think that went pretty well," Ethan said. "You kicked ass in there, bro."

"Thanks, man."

"You nailed it." Mark downed his cup of water, then crumpled it in his fist and sank it in the trashcan on the far side of the room with an easy toss.

"Hope so," Ryan said.

"We couldn't have done anything more. They'd be idiots not to give us our zoning," Ethan said. "We're going to bring a fresh crop of tourists into town. It's a win-win."

"In all fairness, if we weren't *us*, I think they'd have approved the application weeks ago," Mark said.

Ethan felt his temper rising. It was ridiculous that those tight-collared idiots might stomp on his and his friends' dreams because they'd once been hell-raisers. Shouldn't they get this chance to redeem themselves? Hadn't they already redeemed themselves by turning into at least semi-reformed adults?

Fifteen minutes later, Ethan's temper was sizzling good and hot when Lorraine finally called them back into the conference room.

Marlene flashed a quick thumbs-up, and his chest loosened as he slid back into his chair. He smiled at her, and she winked in return. He'd always liked Marlene. She reminded him a bit of Gram. In fact, she and his grandmother went way back.

"We have some good news for you," Lorraine said. "We all love the idea of your Adrenaline Rush competition. Charity events are always good for business, and as it happens, the Pearcy County Food Bank is a pet charity of mine."

Yeah, they'd known that. Mark had found it online, but as former foster kids, they'd all benefited from the food bank at one time or another in their childhoods so it was a natural fit for them as well.

"As a charitable event, it could be held on private property without commercial zoning in place," Lorraine continued, and Ethan felt disappointment sink in his gut. "We think this could be a great way to gauge public interest and get a better feel for your new venture before we approve your zoning request."

"We appreciate the opportunity," Ryan said, ever their peacekeeper.

Ethan swallowed his temper and kept his mouth firmly shut.

"So I wouldn't call it a grand opening event," Betsy said. "We still have some concerns about safety. But if all goes well, you could be in business soon after. We just need to see for ourselves what type of clientele Off-the-Grid will draw and whether or not things seem too dangerous for a town like Haven."

"Thank you very much," Ryan said. The men stood. "We look forward to the opportunity to prove ourselves to you."

Even if they shouldn't fucking have to. Ethan forced a smile as he followed his friends toward the door.

* * *

Gabby checked her duffel bag one last time. She'd dropped off Lance at Emma's house earlier that morning, and Ethan and Dixie should be here any minute to pick her up for their weekend at the beach.

She was excited. A little bit apprehensive, too, but mostly excited. It had been several years since she'd been to the beach, and a little fun in the sun might be exactly what they all needed right now.

A knock came at the front door, and she rushed to answer it with a smile on her face.

"Hi." Ethan stood there in khaki cargo shorts and a gray T-shirt, clean-shaven. And while she kind of missed the scruff, this looked good on him, too. She wanted to run her hands over his cheeks, but not with Dixie standing right behind him.

He pulled her in for a quick kiss anyway, which did all kinds of funny things to her stomach. It almost felt like what she imagined it would be like to ride his zip-line, a free-falling sensation that was equal parts terrifying and exhilarating.

They hadn't been alone together since Monday night—when he'd given her not one but two mind-blowing orgasms. But later tonight, after his grandmother was in bed? Well, she wasn't sure if she could, or even still wanted to, keep her hands to herself

But that was for later.

Dixie pulled her in for a hug. "I am so glad you're coming with us, Gabby. This weekend is going to be so much fun."

"I sure hope so," Gabby said. "Let me just grab my bag."

"I'll take it for you." Ethan stepped forward, ever ready to be of assistance.

Gabby slung it quickly over her shoulder, then picked up her purse. "I got it. Thanks."

His eyebrows rose. "No problem."

They walked outside together, where Dixie's SUV was parked in her driveway.

"I can't drive it, but it's roomier than his Jeep," she said.

"Would you mind if I sit in the front, at least to start? I tend to get carsick when I ride in the backseat."

"Not at all." Gabby grabbed the handle of the back door and pulled it open. "I don't get carsick so I'm happy to ride in the back."

"Thanks, hon." Dixie smiled as she climbed into the passenger seat.

Ethan slid into the driver's seat and cranked the engine. "Make yourselves comfortable, ladies. We've got a long drive ahead."

"How far of a drive is it from Haven?" Gabby asked as she fastened her seatbelt.

"Five and a half hours, give or take," he answered.

"Probably less the way he drives." Dixie looked over her shoulder at Gabby and winked.

They made it about an hour out of town before they stopped for lunch at a little diner in the middle of nowhere. The food was good, and the change of scenery was even better. As much as Gabby liked living in Haven, and she liked it a lot, she found that she was developing a taste for visiting new places and trying new things.

Which was weird since, other than college, she'd lived her whole life in Charlotte up until a few months ago. Or maybe not so weird at all. Maybe she was long overdue for some excitement in her life.

Dixie kept the conversation in the car lively for most of the ride. When she dozed off midafternoon, Gabby closed her eyes, too. But instead of sleeping, she found herself daydreaming about the things she and Ethan had done—or rather, the things she'd let him do—on Monday night.

It had really, truly shocked her that he hadn't even tried to have sex with her. She knew he was a gentleman, and he'd proven it time and again in abiding by her no kissing rule.

But he was a man with a reputation, a man who claimed his relationships were more about sex than emotions. So once she kissed him, she'd fully expected him to dive right into the main event.

Now she was left with the uncomfortable feeling that she'd misjudged him, underestimated him even. Ethan Hunter was not a player. He was kind, and thoughtful, and considerate.

He kept his relationships casual. No strings, no mess. Could she do the same if she slept with him? It could be a test for herself, enjoying the physical pleasure of sex with a man like Ethan without letting any of her emotional baggage weigh her down.

A test she would likely fail, but the ride might be worth the inevitable crash and burn.

They arrived in Emerald Isle just past seven o'clock. Ethan stopped at the rental office to get the key to their house, then drove down Ocean Drive past a variety of beach houses in every size, shape, and color of the rainbow. He parked behind a little turquoise house on the oceanfront side of the street.

A placard above the door read, SEASIDE DREAMING. Gabby adored the names people gave their beach houses, and this one seemed to suit their weekend perfectly.

Dixie was positively glowing. "I'm so glad you were able to get Seaside Dreaming. It makes this weekend even more perfect." She placed her hand over Ethan's and gave it a squeeze.

Gabby's heart clenched. "You've stayed here before?"

Dixie nodded. "Every summer since he was twelve. A lot of memories in this house."

Ethan had gone curiously quiet. He cleared his throat as he stepped out of the car, quick to busy himself with their luggage. Dixie looked after him, her eyes misty. And dammit, Gabby was battling tears of her own. This trip was so bittersweet for both of them.

She slipped out of the backseat and walked around to help Ethan get the bags out of the trunk. He handed her duffel bag to her with a dark look. She shrugged with what she hoped was a casual smile. So what if she liked to carry her own bag?

With his and Dixie's bags on his shoulders, Ethan led the way inside. The house was adorable, decorated in cool blues with splashes of vivid aqua and seashell accents everywhere.

"Our room is upstairs," Ethan said. He sounded harsh, but Gabby suspected he was still a bit choked up from that moment with his grandmother in the car.

God forbid a macho man should actually express what he was feeling.

He followed Dixie into the downstairs bedroom with her bag so Gabby headed up to find their room. The stairs led her to an open loft area with the pull-out couch Ethan had mentioned and a bedroom to the left that looked right out at the ocean with its own private balcony. "Wow," she whispered as she dropped her bag on the bed and walked to the window.

She'd never stayed at a beach house before. This was different from a hotel. Homier, and more comfortable, and way closer to the beach. She and her friends had usually rented a room at the cheapest motel they could find and hauled their beach bags several blocks to the sand every morning. It had been fun, but this...this was *nice*.

She pushed back the sliding door and stepped onto the balcony. The rhythmic hiss and slap of the ocean waves washed over her, and she smiled as she inhaled the salty sea breeze. The balcony had two white rocking chairs with a little table between them. It looked like the perfect place to sit and read.

She walked to the railing. From here, she could see the raised wooden walkway leading from their patio over the sand dunes to the beach. Beyond it, the ocean roared and crashed against the sand.

So amazing. Perfect.

She dragged herself away from the view and went back inside, finding that she had her own private bathroom, which she used to freshen up. She was about to go downstairs in search of Ethan and Dixie when he appeared in her doorway.

He crossed the room in several big strides, pulled her in close, and kissed her. When they finally came up for air, she was panting for breath, and Ethan's heart pounded beneath her palms.

"I'm glad you're here," he said.

"Me, too. Is this usually the room you stay in?"

He nodded, his blue eyes dark and glazed with lust. Then he winked. "I've spent many nights in that bed, and just so you know, I usually sleep in the buff. So tonight when you're lying there trying to fall asleep, think of me."

CHAPTER ELEVEN

*E*than did not sleep well. Being here at Seaside Dreaming brought back all kinds of memories, warm, happy, carefree memories that didn't mesh at all with their reasons for being here this weekend. Then there was the knowledge that Gabby lay on the other side of the door in the bed that was usually his.

And that knowledge had a predictable—as well as very uncomfortable—effect on his anatomy.

He rose with the sun and went for an early dip in the ocean before the women were up. Ever since his Olympic training days, he'd needed a good, long swim in the morning to get his brain going. The water was cold, crisp, and invigorating. By the time he got back to the house, he felt like a whole new man.

Dixie was in the kitchen making pancakes. The aroma made his mouth water and his stomach grumble. He bent to give her a kiss on the cheek as he walked by, headed for the refrigerator. He filled a glass of water and gulped it down.

"Feels good to be here," she said.

"Sure does. I'm going to go rinse off in the shower before we eat." He set his glass on the counter and jogged up the stairs to the loft. Luckily the door to the bedroom was open, which meant Gabby was up. Since Gram assumed they'd shared the bedroom last night, there was no good way to explain why he couldn't go in if the door was closed.

"Gabby?" He poked his head into the bedroom, at first not seeing her. She was on the balcony, dressed in a green tank top and a long, white skirt that billowed in the ocean breeze.

She looked up and smiled. "Hey."

"Gram's making pancakes. I'm going to take a quick shower."

"Oh." Gabby's gaze dropped to his bare chest, then lower. "I didn't realize she was up. I'll go down and help her."

Ethan grinned. She was totally checking him out. And now he didn't feel guilty that he was already fantasizing about her in a swimsuit. He ducked into the bathroom, stripped, and stepped into the shower.

Fifteen minutes later, they were sitting around the kitchen table with full plates in front of them, the ocean crashing in the distance. After devouring four of Gram's delicious pancakes, Ethan drained his coffee and leaned back with his hands clasped behind his head, stuffed and satisfied.

"Well, I don't know about you guys, but I'm ready to head to the beach," Dixie said when they'd all finished eating.

"You go on and get ready," Ethan said. "I'll clean up from breakfast."

"I'll help." Gabby stood and smoothed her hands over the front of her skirt.

He shook his head. "Nah, I got it. I can't cook for shit, but I sure can make myself useful after the meal's over."

Gram nodded, a proud smile on her face. "And he cooks just fine, too. I made sure he knows how to look after himself and his family."

He shooed the women out of the kitchen to get ready for the beach and spent the next ten minutes cleaning up their dishes. Gram was right. He could cook the basics. He just didn't enjoy it. Cleaning up, though, that he didn't mind too much. He could let his mind wander while he worked.

This morning it was churning over a thousand ideas for the upcoming summer festival, the Adrenaline Rush, and hopefully Off-the-Grid's opening thereafter. That, and the fact Gabby was upstairs putting on a swimsuit right now.

Would she wear a one-piece or a bikini? God, he hoped it was a bikini. While he loved her long, flowy skirts, he was painfully aware of the fact that he'd never seen her bare legs or the outline of her ass in a pair of tight jeans.

Hopefully today would be the answer to all of his fantasies.

With that thought in mind, he hung the dish towel on the bar in front of the stove and jogged upstairs. Again Gabby had left the door open for him. Thank goodness she was good at this role-playing thing because, thanks to her, Gram had no reason to suspect they weren't sharing the upstairs bedroom.

Gabby stepped out of the bathroom wearing a gauzy white cover-up that fell to her knees, leaving him with only a hint of the swimsuit beneath. But what he could see was purple and definitely a bikini, and he might just lose his mind when he got a good look at it.

She gave him a shy smile. "I'll be downstairs."

He nodded, his throat too dry to trust himself to speak. When she'd left, he pawed through his bag for a dry pair of trunks, then went into the bathroom to change. He slung a towel over his shoulder and headed downstairs.

Gabby and Dixie were in the living room, chatting as they shoved various items into their beach bags. Meanwhile he had his towel and was good to go.

Gram pointed to a cooler by the door. "I've got beer, water, and snacks all packed."

"I love you," he said.

He picked up the cooler, and Gram and Gabby took their bags. Outside, he grabbed Gram's beach chair and umbrella, then led the way down the raised wooden walkway over the dunes to the beach.

Gabby kicked off her flip-flops and sank her toes into the hot sand with a blissful smile. "This is so great."

"My very favorite place in the whole world," Gram said.

The beach was largely empty still. It never got crowded here, but this early in the summer season it was even emptier than usual. He picked a nice flat spot and set up the beach umbrella, then put Gram's chair and the cooler beneath it.

Gram wore a black sundress over her suit and settled into the chair happily with her Kindle. "You kids have fun."

Gabby chose a spot nearby and spread out her beach towel. Ethan laid his next to hers and sat on it, trying not to stare as she lifted the white cover-up over her head.

She was wearing a purple bikini with white trim and some kind of ruffly thing at the top that accentuated her cleavage, and *fuck*. She was breathtaking, all smooth curves and pale skin.

He leaned in close, his voice low. "You look hot."

She sucked in a breath, then her lips quirked. "So do you."

She reached into her bag and pulled out a bottle of sun block, which she started rubbing on her arms and chest. He tried not to watch. He really did. But then she rubbed cream across her stomach, and he was remembering the way he'd touched her the other night, and *hell*.

His attraction to Gabby was completely out of control.

She reached behind her head, awkwardly trying to spread it across her back.

"Let me." He slid the bottle from her fingers, squirted some cream onto his palm, and put his hands on her skin. Which was definitely a mistake.

Gabby let out a dreamy sigh as he rubbed sun block over her shoulders. He dipped his fingers beneath the strap of her bikini top, savoring the feel of her hot skin beneath his palms, then worked his way slowly down her back. Her head dropped forward as he skimmed his fingers down her sides.

He rubbed the cream into the delicate skin at her lower back, his fingers teasing the edges of her bikini bottom. Gabby sucked in a breath.

"That should do it," he said, his voice gruff.

She turned and smiled at him, looking adorably flushed. "Thanks."

"My pleasure."

She rolled up her cover-up and put it behind her head like a pillow, then lay back on her towel. Not really a sunbather, Ethan walked over to the cooler and pulled out a cold beer, then sat on his towel and tried not to stare at Gabby while he popped it open.

Hell, the beer was not a good enough distraction. He might be swimming the whole weekend because it was the only way to stop fantasizing about Gabby in her purple bikini. He took a long drink from his beer, then put it back in the cooler and jogged down the beach toward the surf.

* * *

Gabby watched him go, hoping no one could tell just how hard her heart was pounding. Wearing nothing but low-slung blue board shorts, Ethan was gorgeous. Sexy. Pretty much physical perfection.

She noticed a tattoo on his right shoulder, some kind of tribal symbol. It almost looked like the sun rising over ocean waves. And as he dove into the surf, she was reminded that he was a former Olympic champion. Gabby's best stroke was the doggy paddle. He surfaced and swam out until all she could see was a brown blob where his head broke the surface.

Yep, he was fast. He sliced through the water with powerful strokes, making it look effortless. And sheesh. Was it hot out, or was it just her dirty mind?

Either way, after she'd lain on the towel for a half hour or so, she was roasting. Dixie sat serenely in the shade of her umbrella, reading on her Kindle. Gabby smiled to herself, wondering what smutty book Ethan's grandma was reading this week. She'd gleefully confessed over lunch last week that although she faithfully read one serious book a month for book club, the rest of the time she consumed as many romance novels as she could.

She loved the sexy heroes and happily ever afters.

So did Gabby.

She set her sunglasses on her towel and walked down the beach, flinching as the sand scorched the soles of her feet. Ethan swam toward the shore to meet her.

"You comin' in?" he asked

"Thinking about it." She stuck her toes in the surf. It still felt awfully cold, and she was not at all a fan of cold water.

"Don't think, just jump." He splashed her, and she shrieked.

The water felt like ice on her overheated skin. "Not funny."

"No?" By the glint in his eyes, she knew she was in for it.

"Oh no, don't you even think about it."

She started to back up, but he was too quick. He swept her into his arms, her body flush against his cool, wet chest, and the next thing she knew, she was underwater.

She spluttered as water went up her nose, shoving at him while sand bit into her knees. She righted herself and surfaced, ready to let him have it, but he was already out of reach, treading water at a safe distance while he laughed himself silly.

"That was not funny." She tried to look indignant, but a wave slammed into her, nearly knocking her off her feet and totally ruining the moment. She waded out until the water reached her chest, then flopped backward and floated on the calm swells.

It wasn't so cold now that her body had adjusted. In fact, it felt good.

She hadn't been sure about coming to the beach with Ethan and his grandmother, but so far, it was turning out to be great. The house was lovely and so was the beach. And the company, including the man who—as she peeked in his direction—was currently staring at her like he wanted to eat her up.

She sank her feet back to the sandy bottom, hiding her body from his gaze. Not that she minded him looking, not really, but she'd always been self-conscious in a bikini. She'd gone shopping for this one yesterday after realizing in a panic that the only suit she'd brought to Haven was a black one-piece that had seen better days. This one was cute, and not too revealing, just enough to make her feel sexy.

Ethan stalked toward her, stopping close enough that each swell bumped her into him. She put her hands on his shoulders, meaning to push back to a safer distance, but somehow she wound up in his arms, her breasts pressed against his bare chest, her hips against his.

"Killing me," he said softly with a smile so hot her knees melted.

The waves kept rocking her against him, and his hands tightened on her hips, his blue eyes glazed with lust. He stepped them backward into deeper water, keeping her pressed close against him.

"What are you doing?" she whispered. She kicked off from the bottom to keep her head above water, and with a gentle tug, he settled her against him, her legs wrapped around his hips.

He was hard, and *oh God*, she was halfway to an orgasm just at the feel of him through the fabric of their swimsuits.

"I needed to show you just how fucking sexy you are in that bikini." His voice was low, rumbling through her, making her shiver in delight. And then his hand slid inside her bikini bottom. She let out an embarrassing squeak, even as pleasure rippled through her.

"Shh," he whispered, pressing his lips to hers. "We're just a happy couple out here kissing in the waves."

But his fingers were doing all kinds of naughty things, and she was too far gone to object. She wiggled against him, desperate for release, on fire beneath the cool caress of the water. Ethan swallowed her moans with his kisses as his fingers stroked her right over the edge.

She clenched her arms around him as she came. The orgasm took her hard, and she bit her tongue to keep herself quiet. Ethan groaned low and deep, seemingly aroused by her pleasure. His eyes were heavy with desire, his dick impossibly hard against her. "So fucking sexy," he whispered, then he kissed her again, crushing her mouth with his.

He tugged her bikini bottom back into place and lifted her free of his hips. The cold water where his hot body had been was a shock, knocking her back to her senses, and *whoa*. She couldn't believe she'd just done that!

She gave a panicked look around them, but there were no other swimmers in sight. No one nearby on the beach. Even Dixie was too far away to have seen anything, and still deeply engrossed in her Kindle.

"Oh my God," she whispered, looking back at Ethan.

With a wink, he dove into the surf.

She stood there, still humming with satisfaction and completely stupefied that Ethan had gotten her off right here on a public beach. That she'd let him. That it had been one of the hottest things she'd ever experienced.

That he'd now given her *three* amazing orgasms and never once expected her to reciprocate. Wow.

She lifted her feet and swam lazily toward shore, not in any hurry to get out of the water, not until she was sure she didn't look as post-orgasmic as she felt. And then she saw Dixie walking toward her, wearing a skirted black one-piece.

"How's the water?" she asked with a smile.

* * *

The summer of blue balls might just be the death of him. Ethan swam until the rest of his body had regained proper blood flow. It was worth it, though. Watching Gabby come was his new favorite pastime. He'd endure all the blue balls he had to if it meant getting to see her come apart in his arms like that again.

So fucking hot.

They spent the morning at the beach, then went back to the house for showers and a late lunch. After lunch, Gabby and Gram went into town to do some touristy shopping.

Ethan took his iPad and sat on the back deck to do some work. The kid they'd hired to design Off-the-Grid's website had created a graphic for them to use to promote the Adrenaline Rush. The Haven Summer Festival was two weeks away on the Fourth of July, and since they couldn't open for business until after the Adrenaline Rush, they'd decided to have their big event just two weeks later on July eighteenth.

It didn't give people much time to form teams and do any training so they were going to focus on the obstacle course aspect and less on any kind of distance running. People planned and trained for months for those things. This was going to have to be more of a spur-of-the-moment event because they just couldn't wait three or four months to open their doors.

Gram didn't have that much time, and frankly, neither did he, Ryan, and Mark. They needed to start bringing in some cash like yesterday. Ethan had saved up a cushion to last only through the summer, and his income from the swim lessons he taught wasn't enough to sustain him. Mark had been helping out part-time at the auto body shop, and Ryan had gone back to his bartending roots to cover the slack, but they needed to get Off-the-Grid up and running as soon as possible before they all went broke.

Today's task was to start getting the word out about their event. Ethan didn't use social media much, but he had a lot of "friends" on Facebook, most of them local, so that seemed like a good place to start. He posted the graphic on his wall with a link to the registration page and asked people to share it.

He glanced at his watch. As soon as Gram and Gabby got home, he needed to take the car and run a few errands of his own. He'd been thinking about it since they got here: the fantasy date Gabby had told him about that night at the Skyline Grille. Even if he couldn't get her naked, he could give her that romantic candlelit dinner on the beach. And he was going to pull out all the stops. She deserved to have a man work for her attention for a change.

After he'd worked on a few more things for the Adrenaline Rush, the warm sun proved too big of a distraction so he set his iPad aside and leaned back in the chair, closing his eyes. The next thing he knew his phone was ringing. He reached for it blindly, smiling when he saw Gabby's name on his screen, and wow, he'd been asleep almost two hours.

"Hello, gorgeous," he said.

"Ethan." Gabby sounded breathless, and not in a good way. "We're at the ER. They think it's just her blood pressure, but—"

He bolted upright, his heart slamming painfully into his rib cage. "What happened?"

"She got really dizzy and was having another headache. I got her here as fast as I could."

"Where are you?" He was already inside and walking

toward the front door of the house when he realized they'd taken the car. *Fuck.*

"Carteret General Hospital. We'd been shopping in Beaufort, and it was just down the road so I drove her straight here."

"The aneurysm?" A hot, prickly sensation crawled across his skin. If she died before he could get there...

"They don't think it burst, but they took her back for an MRI. She's in there now."

"I'm going to hang up and call a cab. Call me back when you know anything."

It took almost an hour to get a cab out to the house and to drive to Carteret General Hospital, one of the longest fucking hours of his life. When he barged through the Emergency Room doors, Gabby was waiting for him, her face pale.

"She's okay," she said.

"Where?" was all he could manage.

Gabby motioned him to follow, and they walked through a set of double doors, down a hall, and into a room divided by curtained partitions. Gram lay on a cot, chatting with a nurse.

The vise that had been squeezing his chest ever since Gabby's first call loosened at the sight of her. Gram was okay. She wasn't dying. Or at least, not right now.

She looked up at him and smiled. "I'm so sorry for all the fuss. Did you have to take a cab to get here?"

"What happened?" he looked from Gram to Gabby.

"Well, it's the silliest thing," Gram said. "They've got me on medicine to keep my blood pressure down because of the aneurysm, you know? I guess I got a little dehydrated today in the sun, and it made my blood pressure *too* low." She gestured to the IV taped to her arm.

"Too low?" He shook his head.

"She got really dizzy and almost passed out." Gabby looked stricken.

"I'll be careful to drink more water tomorrow," Dixie said.

"And limit your time in the sun," the nurse added.

"Yeah, yeah." Gram waved her hand. She didn't like being told what to do. Never had.

But he'd be damn sure she drank plenty of water from now on. Two hours later, they were back at Seaside Dreaming. Gram rested on the couch, watching a TV show about people redecorating their home, while Gabby worked in the kitchen, fixing them some kind of pasta dish for supper.

Not knowing what else to do, Ethan went out on the back deck, staring at the ocean, all those churning gray waves. He itched to jump back in for another swim, but there wasn't time before supper. Maybe later. Swimming had always helped him sort through all the shit in his head.

When Gabby called him in to eat, they sat together at the kitchen table, the mood notably subdued.

"Will y'all cut it out?" Gram said finally. "You're not at my funeral. Now who else saw that man in the banana hammock at the beach this morning?"

Ethan choked on the tortellini in his mouth. Gabby laughed until tears leaked from the corners of her eyes. Gram leaned over to whisper something in her ear, and the two women laughed even harder. Gabby looked at him and blushed.

He shook his head, a smile tugging at his lips. He wasn't even going to try to guess what his grandmother had just said.

They finished their meal, and Gram went to read in bed until she fell asleep. Ethan took over the job of cleaning up the kitchen. He was knee deep in dirty dishes when Gabby walked by, headed for the deck.

She had on a knee-length pink skirt and a white tank top, and his mind nose-dived straight into the gutter. There hadn't been time to shop for her dream date after what happened with Gram, but a new idea came into his head.

He might be able to salvage the evening after all.

CHAPTER TWELVE

Gabby walked along the beach, letting the surf slap her toes as she hunted for shells. Behind her, the sun settled on the horizon behind the row of beach houses, casting everything in a golden light. Her nerves were finally starting to settle for the first time since Dixie had collapsed that afternoon.

She'd gone down on her knees on the pavement, clutching her head, and Gabby's heart had stopped. Just stopped. The thought of losing Dixie...of Ethan not being there...

Gabby pressed a hand to her chest and swallowed hard.

The sun was fading fast now so she turned around and walked back toward their beach house. Her hand clenched around the collection of shells she'd gathered. Maybe she'd try to find something crafty to do with them when she got back home. Not that she was all that crafty, but she did try. Dixie might have an idea for her.

As she got closer to Seaside Dreaming, she saw that there was someone sitting on the beach towel she'd left spread out on the sand in front of their house. A man. And not just any man. The man who'd given her so many moments of pleasure, the man who'd put so much color back into her dreary life.

The man who felt like so much more than a pretend boyfriend.

Her heart thumped faster when he looked up at her, and a funny little tingle spread through her belly. She stopped a few feet away, just staring at him. He'd spread a second towel next to hers, and on it, he'd set a plate of fruit and cheese. A bottle of wine rested in a bowl of ice beside it. Several candles flickered from inside decorative green bowls nestled into the sand.

He looked up at her with candlelight dancing in his eyes. "I wanted to do this right, but with everything that happened this afternoon, I didn't get a chance to go shopping. So it's not quite a candlelit dinner on the beach, but I thought this might be a close second."

He'd remembered her dream date. And he'd tried to create it for her. Her heart flopped in her chest. "It might be even better."

"I hope so." He smiled as he poured two glasses of wine.

She sat beside him, tucking her skirt beneath her thighs. He handed her a glass, and she clinked it against his. "To your grandmother," she said.

"To Gram."

They drank. The wine was good, crisp, and sweet. It added to the warmth already flushing her skin just from sitting so close to Ethan. It was getting darker now, and while she could see a few other couples out strolling the beach, it was largely deserted.

The rhythmic slap of the waves against the sand felt like the pounding of her heart. Overhead, a gull screeched. She sucked in a deep breath of the moist, briny air.

"Lots of memories on this beach," Ethan said quietly.

"You guys always stay in this same house, right?"

He nodded. "Every summer for seventeen years."

And this summer would probably be the last. Gabby turned her head to look at him, saw the hard look in his eyes, the rigid set of his jaw. "That's a lot of summers."

"Never brought a girl here before." He winked, returning a playfulness to the mood the way he was so good at.

"And you wouldn't have brought me if we were dating for real." She plucked a piece of cheese from the plate and bit into it. Delicious.

"No." He stared at the waves, fading to a dark gray as the last sunlight left the sky. "We would have broken up by now. No offense."

"None taken." On the contrary, she appreciated his honesty. "So what, you date a girl for a few weeks, then dump her?"

He shrugged as he reached for a grape. "I try to keep it casual enough that it's a mutual thing. After a few weeks, the spark usually burns itself out."

Would it be that way if she and Ethan had sex? "I've never done that. Casual sex."

"I don't take you for a casual girl, Gabby." Something about the way he said it sent a thrill down her spine. Right now, she really wanted to be the kind of girl who had hot, wild sex with Ethan for a few weeks before moving on with her life.

She'd come to Haven to stand on her own two feet, but being with Ethan didn't feel like leaning on him. If anything, he made her feel stronger and more capable of tackling the world all on her own.

He lifted a strawberry from the plate and brought it to her lips. She bit into it, groaning as the tart flavor hit her tongue. "Mm, delicious."

"I think watching you eat it is even better." Though it was nearly dark now, she could see the glint of arousal in his eyes.

She felt an answering tug low in her belly. A few weeks ago, she'd been too unsure of herself to let go with a man. Ethan had given her back her confidence, at least somewhat. She no longer felt broken…that the only way she could have an orgasm was by herself.

Having sex with him would either give her back all her confidence and then some or, if it failed to live up to the hype like so many other things in her life, it might just crush her. But maybe it was time to take a risk and find out.

Candlelight flickered around them, dancing over his features. He'd asked her once what was the most romantic thing a man had done for her. *This.* It was definitely this. This was more romantic than anything she'd envisioned.

"You're thinking dirty thoughts." His voice had gone low and gruff.

"So are you." And hers was breathless.

"Sweetheart, I've been thinking dirty thoughts since I met you."

She grabbed another grape from the plate, desperate to maintain some sort of composure, but her throat had gone dry so she gulped the rest of her glass of wine, and *fuck it.* She leaned in and kissed him.

He let out a very masculine-sounding groan, his free hand coming to rest in her hair as he kissed her back. He tasted like wine and strawberries and everything sinful and delicious. His tongue thrust against hers, each stroke adding to the ache building inside her.

They kissed like that for a long time, until her body begged for more. A gust of wind ruffled her skirt and blew out most of the candles. As night fell heavy and dark around them, he lay back on the beach towel and tugged her on top of him. His hands roamed down her back to cup her butt. She nipped his lip, and his grip tightened.

"You are the sexiest fucking thing," he whispered, his breath tickling her neck.

"Nope. Pretty sure that's you." She sucked in a breath when his tongue brushed against the hollow of her throat. She slid forward so that she could feel his hard length between her legs, and then it was her turn to groan. She wanted this... more... everything.

His hand slid inside her panties, and she started to protest because it really wasn't fair that he kept doing this without letting her return the favor, but then he was stroking her, and she was already so close, and... *oh God*.

"Ethan," she gasped, squeezing her eyes shut as the orgasm built inside her. Everything faded away but the pleasure growing inside her, rising like a tidal wave higher... and higher. Ethan paused, and she tried not to scream because any second she was going to explode with one of the best orgasms she'd ever had. He thrust his fingers against her again, hard.

The wave crested, and she screamed, bucking wildly against him as pleasure pulsed through her. Then she collapsed on his chest. *Whoa*.

"Holy shit." Ethan sounded strangled. "That was hot."

He kissed her again, crushing her against him as aftershocks of pleasure pinged through her body.

"Ethan," she whispered. She was ready. She trusted him. She *needed* him.

"Remember what you said would come next on your dream date?"

Oh, she remembered, but now he was pushing her outside her comfort zone again. "Skinny-dipping?"

"I'm game if you are." As if to prove it, he sat up with her still in his lap and tugged his T-shirt over his head.

"This is a public beach!"

"And it's too dark to see a damn thing." He leaned forward and blew out the last candle, plunging them into total darkness. "Which is a shame, because I still won't have seen you naked."

"Ethan..."

"Come on." He stood, tugging her to her feet. Then he let her go, and she heard his shorts hit the ground.

"Oh my God."

He was naked. On the beach. Standing right in front of her. And she couldn't even see. He was right. It was too dark to see a thing.

"Last one in is a rotten egg." His lips brushed hers, and then he was off, running toward the surf.

This was total insanity. She glanced back at their beach house. Across the dunes, she could see that the light in the kitchen was still on, but Dixie's room was dark. Not that she'd be able to see them even if she were still up.

Shaking her head at herself, she slid her skirt down her legs, then shucked the rest of her clothes and felt around to place them at the end of the beach towel. She'd obviously lost her mind because now she was standing buck naked on the beach. Anyone could walk by and see her. Or not see her. But anyone could walk by!

She half walked, half ran down the beach to the water's edge, and there she stopped. The water lapped against her feet, cooler now that darkness had fallen. Dark. Dangerous. Who knew what lurked out there?

When she'd imagined skinny-dipping on her fantasy date, she had definitely *not* imagined swimming in the ocean at night.

"Ethan?" she whispered.

"Right here." His voice was close. Really close. His hands skimmed down her sides, sending a shiver of pleasure across her skin. "Nice," he whispered. "Come on."

He took her hand and tugged her forward.

"I can't believe I'm doing this."

"I can. This was your idea, remember?" His hand was warm in hers.

The water was up to her knees now, cool and soothing on her overheated skin. "It sounded a lot more fun when it was hypothetical."

"It's going to be just as much fun in real life." With a splash, he dove into the surf, leaving her standing there.

It was dark, and terrifying, and thrilling all at the same time. Cautiously, she took another step, then she squeezed her eyes shut and flopped backward into the water. It closed around her, as dark as the night around them, but still gentle and refreshing and salty, just like it had been when the sun was high.

Ethan's hand touched her shoulder, and she squeaked at the contact, her heart thumping harder. If anything *but* Ethan touched her out here in this dark ocean, she might completely lose her shit.

She turned toward him, and her body bumped his. He was so warm, so solid. She slid her arms around him, exploring the hard-muscled planes of his back. She couldn't help herself. Her hands slid down to his ass. It was firm and tight. And as she gave it a squeeze, his cock brushed against her belly. He hissed out a breath.

The water came to their waists now, each wave rocking them into each other until Gabby was so turned on, she could barely see straight. Not that she could see anyway. She reached down and gripped him in her hand, stroking up and down his shaft.

Ethan groaned, thrusting into her hand. He was so big. So hard. So hot, even beneath the cool caress of the ocean.

And she wanted him. Right here. Right now.

* * *

Ethan fought for control as Gabby's fingers slid up and down his cock. It felt so good. Too good. Then as he was about to let her go and swim until he'd regained his composure, she lifted her feet, wrapping her legs around his waist.

His cock pressed against the heat between her legs, and *fuck*. He was so gone. He thrust against her once, twice. She whimpered.

"Ethan." Her voice was soft, filled with want.

His cock strained against her. "Gabby."

He had to find the strength to let her go. His arms tightened around her, holding her firmly against him. He wanted her so fucking bad. Wanted to hear her scream his name while he was buried inside her. Wanted to lose himself in her. Wanted to wake up beside her.

Wanted things he had no business wanting, from Gabby or any other woman.

Never, ever, had he been this close to losing control with a woman. Unless she asked him to, he absolutely could not find the strength to pull away.

"Now, Ethan," she was saying.

"What?" He shook his head to clear it. Even if she was saying what he thought she was saying...they had a problem.

"Take me," she whispered, rocking against him. "Right here."

"Can't," he answered, even as his dick begged for the

chance. "Even if it wasn't a bad idea, I'm naked here. No condom."

"It's okay. I'm on the pill."

He went still. She was serious. "Not okay, Gabby. I always practice safe sex." Always. He'd never, ever gone without a condom. To go without was riskier, and also more intimate.

"But you've been tested?" she asked hopefully.

"Yeah. I'm clean."

"Me, too. I got tested after I ended things with Brad."

He couldn't believe they were having this conversation. Skinny-dipping in the ocean under nothing but a sliver of moon, his dick nestled against her heat. One thrust, and he'd slide home. He shuddered with the effort to hold back.

"So it's safe," she said. "Please?"

She lifted her hips so that she slid up and down his shaft, and like a rubber band that had been stretched to its breaking point, he snapped. He crushed her mouth against his, grinding her against him until she whimpered with need.

He positioned her against him, and she sank down onto him, hot and tight. His eyes rolled back in his head, and he had to lock his knees to keep from taking them under. She wiggled her hips, and he clutched her ass, holding her against him for a long moment. The darkness around them had heightened all his other senses. The chill of the water on the rest of his body contrasted with her heat, gripping him, driving him toward release.

"Gabby." He thrust inside her. Nothing had ever felt this good, this right.

She met him thrust for thrust, her soft cries fueling his need. They were one, moving together, lost in each other. The ocean rocked around them as wave after wave pounded the shore, and he thrust inside her, harder and faster.

"Oh," she gasped, her body clenching around him. "Oh!"

Her voice was soft, raspy, awestruck. He pumped faster, feeling his own release starting to gather at the base of his spine, tightening in his balls, pulsing in his dick. She gripped him again and again as she came, and as she screamed his name into the night, he groaned his own release.

"Oh God," Gabby panted, rocking against him.

He thrust one last time, his orgasm taking him so hard that his knees buckled, and he barely caught them before they went under.

"Holy shit." Gabby's arms and legs were wrapped around him, clinging to him.

Holy fucking shit indeed. He'd just had sex—unprotected sex—with Gabby. In the ocean. And it had been the hottest, most intense... most intimate thing he'd ever experienced.

* * *

Gabby awoke in her bed in the beach house, but she wasn't alone. Ethan lay beside her, naked. Gloriously naked. Once they'd gathered their things and come inside, they'd had sex again in the shower—with a condom this time.

He'd insisted.

And then they'd fallen asleep together.

Now, as she watched him sleep in the soft morning light, she knew she'd crossed a line last night. What they'd done had been so much more than just sex. She'd opened herself to him in every way, and he'd fulfilled every fantasy she'd ever had.

There'd been nothing awkward, nothing forced. No lack of chemistry, that was for sure.

Nothing like it had been with Brad.

With Ethan, she felt sexy and confident and in control.

And he'd given her, without a doubt, the best sex of her life. It certainly seemed like it had been pretty good for him, too. Men, in her experience, didn't tend to fake things the way women sometimes did.

"Mornin'," he whispered against her neck.

"Good morning." She smiled, still not quite over the fact that he was in her bed, the things they'd done, and how perfect it had all been.

Ethan's lips were nibbling under her jaw now, his fingers inching the sheet down her body.

She gripped it, bringing it back to her chin.

"I still haven't gotten a good look at you naked," he said, and with a yank, the sheet hit the floor.

She felt totally exposed and vulnerable for about one second, but Ethan was looking at her like she was a goddess, and beneath his gaze, she felt beautiful. Also...he was naked, too. And *wow*. She ogled him as blatantly as he was ogling her, from his tanned, washboard abs, to the trail of chest hair that led straight down to his penis, which was already hard. Every inch of him was hard, lean, and muscular. So sexy.

She glimpsed the tattoo on his right shoulder and leaned in for a closer look. It was done all in black ink, the sun climbing over churning waves. "What does it mean?" she asked.

"Dawn," he answered.

Ah, the sunrise. Dawn. But why?

"It was my mom's name," he answered her silent question.

She traced her fingers over the tattoo, absorbing the ache of his loss. "That's beautiful."

"It's just a tattoo. *You* are beautiful." He turned to face her, and then they were tangled up in each other, kissing and touching until she was on fire for him, desperate to have him inside her. He reached for the bedside table and sheathed himself in a condom.

Later, as they lay panting and breathless in each other's arms, she knew this was no longer pretend. For her at least. This was as real as it got.

Ethan trailed his fingers down her back. "I don't think I can ever get enough of you."

Did he mean that? He met her eyes, his gaze so full of warmth and affection. Her vision blurred as tears welled, slipping down her cheeks before she could stop them.

"What's wrong? Did I hurt you?" He reached out to wipe the tears from her face.

She shook her head. "No. The opposite of that."

"What?" He frowned. "Talk to me, Gabby."

"I just... I've had some bad experiences in the past. But this... with you... was different."

Ethan stared at her for a long beat of silence. Something stirred in his eyes, something that looked an awful lot like fear. "You know this is just temporary, right?"

A painful lump rose in her throat. "I know," she whispered.

"Okay." He slipped out of bed and pulled on a pair of swim trunks. "I need to go for my morning swim. You go back to sleep."

And with a quick kiss, he was gone.

CHAPTER THIRTEEN

Ethan swam until he couldn't swim anymore. Then he hauled his sorry ass out of the surf and walked back to the house. Gram sat on the deck, Kindle in hand.

"Have a seat," she said, pointing at the chair next to her.

He grabbed a dry towel off the railing and sat.

"You and Gabby have a fight?" she asked.

"What? No." He scrubbed the towel over his hair.

"Something's different. You look like a deer in the headlights."

"We're fine." But he couldn't shake the look in Gabby's eyes earlier. She'd looked at him like no woman ever had: like he meant more to her than just sex.

A whole fucking lot more.

"You're not fine." Gram gave him a long look. "I've known you long enough to know when you're panicking. Things are starting to get serious, and you're ready to bolt."

Ah, shit. "I'm not." He couldn't bolt out of a relationship that wasn't real. Except it *was* getting real, and he was not the man Gabby thought he was.

Dixie sighed. "You're not your father, Ethan."

He leaned forward, elbows on his knees, and stared at the boards on the deck. His head echoed with his mother's screams. His father's whiskey-fueled fury. The dull thump of his fist into her cheek. The sickening crunch of her skull slamming into the corner of the countertop.

The memories were as vivid today as they'd been nineteen years ago. Even now, he had to swallow past the bile that had risen in his throat.

"I have his temper," he said.

"You do not." Gram's voice hardened. "Your father was a mean son of a bitch. He alienated your mother from me and the rest of her family. He beat her. He hit *you* when you were just a boy. He took my daughter from me, your mother from you."

"I was there." He stared into his hands. "You don't have to remind me."

"I don't imagine you'll ever forget it. I know I won't."

He forced himself to look into her eyes, to see her pain, the pain they had both carried all these years. *I'm terrified of becoming him.* "I've hit people, Gram."

She scoffed. "A bar fight is *not* the same thing as domestic violence, and don't insult my intelligence—or yours—by pretending you don't know the difference."

"You're my grandmother. You see me through rose-colored glasses."

She leaned forward, her blue eyes blazing into his. "You're no saint. I know you raised whatever kind of hell you could when you were growing up. But your heart's always been in the right place. And I see the man you've become. Gabby is lucky to have you. Now go kiss and make up with her, you hear me?"

* * *

By the time the car pulled into her driveway on Monday afternoon, Gabby was ready to be home. The weekend had been a rollercoaster of emotions. Crazy highs and terrifying lows. Overall, though, it had been amazing. She wouldn't change a single moment of her time with Ethan, but it was time to get back to their regular lives now and see what happened.

Would they keep sleeping together? Would things go back to the way they'd been before the trip? She'd be smart to put a little distance back between them or at least have a conversation with him about redefining the rules. But she didn't. She just gave him a quick kiss good-bye and walked inside her house.

The rest of the day was a blur. She went to pick up Lance, washed a mountain of laundry, and spent several hours in her office catching up on work. It felt good to be home, to get back to her routine. This little house felt like home in a way no place ever had before. It was the first place she'd lived on her own. No parents, no boyfriend, no roommate.

Just Gabby.

She liked that. At dinnertime, she debated calling Ethan to see what he was up to, but decided she'd let him take the lead on whatever direction their relationship took now that they were back in Haven. So she threw together a salad and ate on the back deck with Lance.

Maybe she missed the ocean view and Ethan's sexy smile and the magic of the beach. And maybe she was a little bit disappointed he didn't call that night. But maybe he needed to get his head back on straight the same way she did.

On Tuesday, she barely came up for air. She started working at eight that morning and was still going as the sun sank below the mountains outside her window. She had one last string of code to test before she could call it a day.

A knock sounded at her front door. Lance hopped out of her lap and ran for the safety of the pantry. She shook her head. *That dog.*

Her heart thumped faster as she walked toward the door, imagining Ethan on the other side. Suddenly it felt like forever since she'd seen him, even though it had only been a day. She smoothed her hands over the front of her skirt, then pulled the door open to find Ethan standing there, wearing a green T-shirt and his trademark khaki cargo shorts.

And her body went all warm and tingly at the sight.

"Hi," he said, leaning against her doorjamb all nonchalant-like. But his eyes were intense. So intense they sent a sizzle of awareness down her spine.

Without thinking, she slid her arms around him and pulled him in for a kiss. "Hi, yourself."

Ethan's hands fisted in her hair as he kissed her back, slow and thorough until hunger burned inside her and her heart thumped against his. "You weren't answering your phone," he said finally when they'd come up for air.

"Sorry, I've been working. I must have left it in the bedroom."

His hands slid to her waist, anchoring her against him. "Want to get dinner?"

Her stomach growled in answer. "I'd love to. I just need to finish up one last thing I was working on."

He kissed her again. "Take your time. I can wait."

"Um. Okay." She backed out of his arms reluctantly, her body already missing the contact with his. "Make yourself at home," she said as she walked back to the office.

"Will do." He turned toward the kitchen.

She rushed back to her desk, completely distracted as she

tested her coding. What was Ethan doing? She imagined him lounging on her couch or searching for something manly to eat in her kitchen. He'd likely be disappointed there.

She stifled a giggle.

Thankfully her code checked out on the first try so she sent it through to be approved by the software architect, then hurried into the bedroom to freshen up her makeup. It had been half an hour since Ethan arrived by the time she made it back into the living room.

He wasn't there. Disappointment flopped in her belly that he might have changed his mind and left after all. But a sound drew her toward the kitchen, where she found Ethan sitting on the floor, a package of pepperoni in his left hand, his right extended toward the pantry.

"So tell me," he said in a conversational voice, and *goodness*, he must have been talking to Lance. She stayed back for a moment to watch, mesmerized. "What do you and Gabby do all day? Do you get to sit in her lap? I might be a little jealous about that, bro."

And to her complete surprise, Lance trotted out of the pantry, snatched the pepperoni slice from Ethan's hand, then trotted back inside. Ethan took out another slice and popped it in his mouth, then held his hand out toward her dog again.

Gabby stepped into the kitchen, doing her best to swallow the silly grin that had taken hold of her lips.

Ethan looked up at her with an answering grin. "Your dog is weird."

"I know."

He stood and tugged her up against him. "You finished with work?"

She nodded.

"What are you thinking tonight? Burgers? Pizza? Something fancier?"

"I ate healthy yesterday. A burger sounds perfect."

Ten minutes later, they walked into Rowdy's. They both ordered Rowdy burgers, just like they had last time, and Gabby felt herself blushing.

"What?" he asked.

"I was just thinking about the last time we came here."

His lips curved in a wicked smile. "I seem to remember we were having a hard time keeping our hands to ourselves that night."

"Yeah." She picked up her beer and took a sip, but it didn't cool the heat of his gaze.

He leaned forward until his mouth was just inches from hers. "Gotta say, I'm feeling the same way tonight."

So he did want to keep sleeping with her. *Good.* "Me, too."

He gave her a look that melted her from the inside out, then his gaze turned serious. "You okay with this? Breaking the rules here in Haven?"

Damn him for always being so thoughtful and considerate. "For now."

He slid around to her side of the table so that his thigh bumped hers as he leaned in close. "Because you know I can't keep this up long term."

He kept reminding her of that fact, as though she could forget. And maybe that was the problem, because she *wanted* to forget. "I know."

"Okay. I just wanted to make sure we were still on the same page."

She remembered what he'd said in Emerald Isle, about how if they'd been dating for real the whole time, his interest probably would have already fizzled. "Is it starting to fade for you now that we've slept together?"

* * *

"No. Fuck, no." Maybe he should have tried to play it cool, but the truth was, he wanted her even more now than he had before. He hadn't been able to stop thinking about her since they'd gotten home from the beach.

He'd stayed away for a day, hoping it would help set him straight, but it had only made him miserable. For right now, today, he needed to be with her. To hell with anything else.

Gabby sipped from her beer. "So we'll just keep doing what we started in Emerald Isle, until..."

Until Gram died.

She didn't say it. Didn't have to.

"Yeah." He took a long drink from his beer.

Their burgers arrived then. They didn't talk much while they ate, but the mood had shifted, and that pissed him off. So he leaned in to whisper in her ear. "I'm imagining my hands inside your panties right now."

She blushed. "You wish."

Oh, he did. He really did. And by the time he drove her home after supper, it was all he could think about. He pressed her up against the wall in the entranceway and kissed her until all the chaos in his brain had stopped.

This. This was what he needed.

He needed Gabby.

CHAPTER FOURTEEN

Gabby walked up the front steps of the Haven Spa, enchanted by the waterfalls trickling through rocks on either side of the entrance. In her hand, she held a flyer advertising the upcoming Adrenaline Rush.

She pushed open the door and stepped inside. "Wow."

The lobby was, for lack of a better word, a haven. With muted lighting, gentle flute music playing, and trickling waterfalls everywhere, Gabby already felt more relaxed. She smelled lavender and incense, and *oh*, why hadn't she been to the spa yet?

A pretty woman with shoulder-length brown hair looked up from behind the desk with a friendly smile. "Welcome to the Haven Spa. How can I help you?"

"I don't know yet, but you can definitely sign me up for something." Gabby took another look around the room and sighed.

The other woman laughed. "I'm Jessica Flynn. I own this place. Are you new in town or just visiting?"

"Gabby Winters. I'm here for the summer and wondering why it took me so long to stop by."

Jessica pointed a pen in her direction. "I like you already, Gabby. Do you prefer your spa treatments more traditional or a little bit on the earthy-crunchy side?"

"Earthy-crunchy," she answered without hesitation.

"I like you even more." Jessica's smile widened as she pulled out a brochure and placed it on the counter in front of her. "We have lots of options, but my personal favorite is the mineral mud bath to detox followed by a soak in one of our hot tubs fed by the natural hot springs. It's good for the soul, or so they say."

"Sign me up. Seriously, that sounds like perfection."

Jessica's eyebrows raised. "Really?"

"Yes. Definitely."

Jessica turned to her computer. "What's your schedule like? We could fit you in as early as Monday at four o'clock. You'll want to plan to be here for about two and a half hours."

"Monday at four would be perfect."

"You are easy to please." Jessica spent a few minutes running through the particulars of Gabby's upcoming spa treatment and handed her a full catalog with her receipt. "So what brings you to Haven?"

"Just looking for a change of pace for a little while." But she didn't feel nearly as cautious about that as she had even a few weeks ago when she'd met Ethan. Haven seemed to have been just what she needed.

Jessica's dark eyes were knowing. "It's a great place for a change of pace. I grew up here, but I left for a while after high school. Came back when I was ready for this." She gestured to the spa around her.

"It's a great town," Gabby agreed.

"Maybe you'll stay." Jessica winked. "So what's this?" She pointed to the flyer Gabby had set on the counter while she was signing her spa receipt.

Ah, that. The real reason for her visit, although she was not at all sorry she'd signed up for a spa treatment while she was here and, in thumbing through the brochure, had a feeling she'd be back for more. "I don't know if you've heard about the new outdoor sporting facility being built up the street from here, Off-the-Grid Adventures?"

"I've heard." Jessica's eyes shuttered.

Gabby nodded. "I figured. Small town, right?"

"Right." But Jessica's friendly exuberance had gone flat.

What was that about? "Well, as part of their grand opening, they're hosting a charity obstacle course challenge called the Adrenaline Rush. And we were wondering if you'd like to do some kind of a partnership. You know, like a spa discount to race participants or something."

"We?" The curiosity in Jessica's eyes was much more than casual. "Are you working with them?"

Gabby knew that look. Jealousy. Jessica must be a jilted ex. Her stomach soured at the thought of Jessica and Ethan having slept together. It was petty of her, because obviously it was in the past, but still. She felt weird having a spa treatment from one of Ethan's exes. "Sort of," she answered Jessica's question. "I was curious to check out your place so I offered to come over and tell you about the Adrenaline Rush."

Jessica took the flyer and studied it. "You're dating one of them, then."

"Yes." And Gabby had definitely been right in her jilted ex assumption.

Jessica tapped a finger against the flyer. "Yeah, I'll do a discount for race participants. I'll figure out the details and get in touch, okay?"

"Oh, thank you so much. It should be perfect, right? A relaxing soak in the hot springs after people get all banged up out on the course?"

"Should be good business for both of us."

Gabby walked out to her car. She had plans with Ethan for lunch so she drove straight from the spa to Off-the-Grid Adventures. She found him out back, talking to a couple of guys she didn't recognize. He waved when he saw her, a warm smile creasing his face.

Her heart turned a happy somersault in response. Goodness, she was so smitten with this man. Oh, how she hoped it would fizzle by the end of the summer like he had predicted, but she was awfully afraid her feelings were becoming too deep for that.

"Good news," she said when he walked over.

"Oh yeah?" He bent to give her a kiss, sending warmth through her body.

"I just came from the spa, and Jessica agreed to do some kind of discount for people running in the Adrenaline Rush."

He grinned. "That's great."

"I don't think she likes you all that much, though." She eyed him, nosing shamelessly into his business.

He chuckled as he shook his head. "She doesn't give a shit about me. It's Mark she's pissed at. They were high school sweethearts, and he was an idiot and dumped her after graduation when he enlisted."

"Oh." Relief swamped her, stupid, silly relief because she'd been jealous over nothing.

"She really ought to lighten up on the dude. He could have handled it better, but he was dealing with a shitty hand." Ethan's tone shifted, fiercely defensive of his friend.

Gabby shrugged. "I still think my high school sweetheart is a jerk for dumping me, so I might have to side with Jessica on this one."

Ethan stepped closer, the same jealousy she'd felt earlier now stamped on his face. "I'd have to agree. Any man who would dump you is a jerk."

"Including you?" she whispered.

His blue eyes clouded. "Including me."

* * *

Ethan felt like an asshole the way Gabby was looking at him right now. But then she smiled, and her expression softened. "You won't have to dump me. We have an agreement, remember?"

Yeah, he remembered, but he still had the uneasy feeling she was going to get hurt. "Want to see our new ropes course?"

"Is that different from the zip-line?"

"It is. We built this for the Adrenaline Rush. I think Mark and Ryan are over there now."

"Okay." She fell into step beside him.

He led her down a path from the main house to the clearing they'd converted into the ropes course. Mark sat straddling the top of the climbing wall, tinkering with one of the boards.

Gabby sucked in a breath. "I could not hang out with you guys long term. You'd give me a frigging heart attack."

"Oh, come on now. An adrenaline rush is good for you every now and then."

"No thanks."

He nudged her. "You've been all over town this week helping us spread the word about the challenge. You mean to tell me you're not going to participate?"

Her eyes widened. "Not a chance."

"Well, you know I can't participate." He, Ryan, and Mark would be overseeing the event. "So who's going to represent Off-the-Grid?"

"The whole event represents Off-the-Grid. Have you had a lot of signups this week?" She crossed her arms over her chest, glancing up at Mark again with wary eyes.

"No." And he was pissed about it, too. "Only two teams so far."

She touched his arm. "Well, it's only been a few days. I'm sure people are still figuring out their teams and things."

"Hope so." Because if this event was a failure, their entire plan for Off-the-Grid might fold.

"I know you don't like to bring a lot of attention to your Olympic fame, but maybe you should for this," she said. "You know, call the local news and ask them to cover the event?"

Dammit, she was right. "I should. I will."

"Any extra press in this case is a good thing, right?"

"Definitely."

"What's that?" Gabby asked, pointing to the hand trolley they'd installed over the pond.

"That," he said with a grin, "is the final event in the challenge. After the whole team has crossed the pond, it's a race to the finish line."

She pressed a hand to her mouth. "So you just hold on to that handlebar and try to make it over the pond?"

"Yeah. Momentum is key. Smaller people will need a bigger push. Want to try?"

She gaped at him. "Have you paid attention to me at all? No, I don't want to try!"

He grunted. "Well, you told me you're afraid of heights. This really isn't high. You're only a few feet over the water. Sure you don't want to?"

"Positive, but I'd love to watch *you* try." She grinned naughtily.

"Sure thing, sweetheart."

"What happens if you fall in?" she asked.

"Not going to happen, but if I fell, I'd just swim out. I don't know if you noticed, but I'm a pretty decent swimmer." With a wink, he left her standing there.

* ⁎ ⁎

Gabby watched mesmerized as Ethan stepped up to the short platform they'd installed and grabbed on to the handlebar. He blew her a kiss, leaned back as far as he could, then leaped forward into the air.

His legs swung out in front of him, the muscles in his forearms bunching impressively as he gripped the handle above his head and zipped across the pond. He dropped to his feet on the other side, gave her a silly bow, and jogged back to where she was standing. "See? Easy. You should try it."

No way. This didn't actually look that scary, but knowing her, she'd fall off halfway across and belly flop into the pond. And she had no desire to humiliate herself or get covered in icky pond muck.

"Don't let him pressure you." Ryan walked up beside her, an easy smile on his face.

"She never does," Ethan said.

"That's true." In fact, she never felt pressured with Ethan. It was one of the things she liked best about being with him.

Ryan glanced between them and shook his head. "Y'all still pretending this is fake?"

"What?" She took a step backward. Ryan knew about their arrangement?

"Your secret is safe with me." He chuckled as he walked off in the direction of a tall tree with a wooden ladder leading up its trunk.

"Ready for lunch?" Ethan asked.

"Yeah." She walked beside him back to the house. Their sign was up now, announcing Off-the-Grid Adventures in big, bold letters for the world to see. Surely the zoning problem was just a formality. She couldn't imagine that the Town Council would be so shortsighted as to keep them from going into business, but the guys seemed pretty worried about it, and they knew this town better than she did.

"You told your friends about our agreement?" she said as she climbed into the passenger seat of his Jeep.

He shrugged. "They know me too well to buy what we were selling otherwise."

"Hmm." For some reason, that pissed her off. Was the idea of Ethan dating plain, boring Gabby so outrageous that his friends would never believe it? Or was it the notion of him staying with her the whole summer because his usual relationships barely lasted a week?

Neither option sat well. And that was petty of her because she'd agreed to this. She'd agreed to all of it. And she'd gotten *so much* in return. Ethan had done wonders for her self-esteem in general, if not right at this exact moment.

He glanced at her as he pulled out onto Mountain Breeze Road. "Shit. You're looking at me like I fucked up."

"You didn't." She scrunched her nose. "I don't know what my problem is right now."

He nudged her with his elbow. "Are we about to have our first fight?"

"No." She let out a long sigh. "I've never done *this* before, and it all feels a little confusing right now."

His smile faded. "Define *this*."

"Fake relationships. Casual relationships. Whatever this is." She looked over at him. "What are we now, Ethan? Is this still all pretend?"

"I'm sure as hell not faking anything." His cocky grin left little doubt what he was referring to.

No, the chemistry was very real, and maybe that was part of the problem. "I'm not talking about sex."

He pulled into the parking lot behind the deli and looked at her. "Then what?"

"I don't know. *This* . . . you and me going to lunch, hanging out like we're dating. It all feels so . . . cozy. But then I wonder if you're just spending time with me because of Dixie. And wow, I sound super needy. I'm sorry." She pressed her hands over her eyes.

Ethan lifted them away, turning her to face him. "I'm not that complicated, Gabby, I promise. I'm always being straight with you, okay? I'm having lunch with you right now because I like you. I like being with you. And the sex is off the charts, right?"

"And after your grandmother's gone?" She hated to even say it, but there it was.

Ethan drew back, staring out the front window of the Jeep. "Then I guess that's that."

And that hurt, even though it shouldn't. He was only sticking to what they'd originally agreed to. She was the one feeling all kinds of stupid, mushy things she had no business feeling. She turned away, hiding the tears welling in her eyes.

"Dammit, I'm sorry. I didn't mean to say it like that." His voice sounded gruff.

"Then how did you mean to say it?" She paused, but he was silent. The air in the Jeep grew thick with the tension between them. "When we're together, it feels like more than just sex."

He exhaled harshly. "Gabby—"

She spun in her seat. "What? Does it make you uncomfortable that I have actual feelings?"

He just stared at her, a tortured look in his eyes.

"You treat me like I'm special." Her voice wobbled, and her face got all hot and prickly.

"You *are* special." The earnestness in his voice made her stomach quiver with longing. That this could be real. That Ethan could still want her, even after Dixie was gone.

She shook her head. "But you'll still walk away."

"I have to." He paused. "It's what we agreed on. It's what you wanted, too."

They stared at each other for a beat of heavy silence.

He rubbed a hand over his jaw. "Isn't it?"

"Right. Hey, look at that? I guess we had our first fight after all." And she climbed out of the Jeep, slamming the door behind her.

* * *

Ethan stayed late with the guys working on the obstacle course for the Adrenaline Rush. They'd spent the last three hours stringing tires from an overhead beam they'd installed between two trees. People would have to get from one end to the other using only the tires—no feet on the ground or they'd have to start over at the beginning.

By the time they'd finished, it was almost eight, and the last light was fading quickly in the Western sky. Ryan swung in one of the tires like a child, kicking his feet toward the treetops. Mark sat on the landing platform, tinkering with something. And Ethan...he felt the need to go punch something. Or swim some laps. Maybe both.

He'd been restless ever since his fight with Gabby at lunchtime. No doubt he'd handled it wrong, said all the wrong things. He was a guy after all. A guy who didn't do relationships. He should go to her tonight and try to smooth it over, but hell if he knew what to say. Everything about her twisted him up in knots, from the way his need for her grew each time they were together to the way she could turn his entire day around with just a smile.

"Yo, who wants beer?" Ryan asked.

"Yep," Ethan said.

Mark nodded, and they started walking back to the house.

"I left a package of bratwurst in the freezer earlier this week," Ryan said. "No grill at the condo, you know? You losers got plans tonight?"

"Nah, man, sounds good," Mark said.

"No hot date with the lovely Gabby tonight?" Ryan elbowed Ethan in the gut.

"Not tonight." Godammit, he was such an asshole.

"That settles it." Ryan led the way into the house. "Bro night. No girls allowed."

"What are we, fifteen?" Ethan shook his head as he walked over to the fridge. He pulled out three beers, popped the caps, and handed them out.

"We never would have done anything this lame when we were fifteen." Mark cracked a smile, then tipped his beer up for a drink.

"True story," Ryan said. "We'd have been out busting mailboxes or some such shit."

Ethan took the package of sausages out of the freezer

and led the way out back. It was true. He and Mark had been ten, Ryan eleven, when they were placed in the same group home in foster care. They'd quickly become thick as thieves, sneaking out together to wreak havoc or plot world domination from the roof of the neighbor's tree house.

Even though they'd lived together only a short time before Gram adopted Ethan, they'd attended the same middle and high schools, and the friendship had continued into adulthood.

"So what's the deal with your fake girlfriend?" Ryan said. "Because you've gone from frustrated and irritable to looking like a man who's getting laid."

Ethan fired up the grill, then took a long pull from his beer.

"He's definitely getting laid," Mark commented.

"Yeah, yeah." Ethan took another drink.

"And suspiciously tight-lipped about it," Ryan said to Mark. "Do you think that means the sex is awesome or terrible?"

"Have I ever discussed my sex life with you?" Ethan tossed three bratwurst onto the grill, then added a few more for good measure.

"And please don't start now," Mark said.

"But seriously." Ryan sobered. "I hope you know what you're doing. She's way too sweet for the likes of you."

"Tell me about it," Ethan muttered, then drained his beer. "She got upset with me earlier when we went to lunch. Something about how I wouldn't even be taking her to lunch if Gram had already passed."

"She has feelings for you. Real feelings," Ryan said. "And I don't think she's the only one."

"What?" He didn't do feelings, not with women. Sure as

hell not with Gabby, who'd just come out of a bad relationship. She deserved better. So much better.

But Mark was nodding, too. "You should see yourself when she walks into a room, man. You are totally whipped."

"Like hell." Ethan flipped the sausages with a little more force than was strictly necessary. "Speaking of women, apparently Jessica is still pissed at you." He pointed the spatula toward Mark.

Mark's expression hardened, and his jaw clenched.

"Jessica Flynn?" Ryan asked. "As in, the Jessica you dumped back in high school?"

"Yeah," Mark muttered. "That Jessica."

"That's a long time to hold a grudge," Ryan said.

Mark shrugged. "I had to end things between us when I enlisted. It was for the best."

"Doesn't sound like she agrees," Ryan said.

"When the hell has any of the three of us ever made a smart decision when it came to a woman?" Ethan threw his hands up in the air. "Smartest thing I ever did was decide not to ever let things get serious."

"And yet it sounds like you may have even screwed *that* up." Ryan clapped him on the back.

They drank a lot of beer, consumed their body weight in grilled sausage, and then, as the moon hung bright above them and the trees buzzed with the summer song of the cicadas, they trekked down to the ropes course for some old-fashioned fun.

Ryan went first, zipping across the pond with a loud whoop. Mark followed. But Ethan had a different idea. He stripped to his boxer briefs before he grabbed onto the hand trolley. "I'm goin' in."

"What?" Ryan called from the other side of the pond.

Ethan whizzed halfway across, then let go and landed

in the pond with a splash. The cool water closed over his head, and he kicked, his head breaking the surface as the moon grinned down at him from up high. "Fuck, yeah!" he yelled.

"Fall in, hot shot?" Ryan asked. Mark's laughter echoed in the darkness.

"Don't be a pussy. Come on. Try it," he said.

"I'm game," Mark said.

Ethan swam lazily toward the shore. He could just see his friend's outline as he kicked off and soared toward him, landing with a splash not far from where Ethan had gone in.

Mark surfaced silently and swam to the shore, all but invisible under the cover of night. Mr. Fancy Pants Special Ops. Someday Ethan needed to have Mark teach him a few tricks.

"Y'all are crazy," Ryan called from the shore.

"You chicken? The water feels great." Ethan's toes sank into the red clay at the bottom of the pond as he climbed ashore.

Ryan let out a good-natured groan, then with a splash, he followed them into the pond. And so went the rest of their evening, interrupted only to go get more beer from the house. It felt good having Ryan and Mark back home, the closest thing to brothers he'd ever had. And there was no way he was going to let those idiots on the Town Council shut down their dreams. He needed to keep his family together, now more than ever.

* * *

Ethan woke to a dull pounding in his skull and the sound of someone snoring. He opened his eyes to see Ryan sprawled across the other end of the couch, his face alarmingly close to Ethan's. After last night's debauchery, they'd all crashed here at Off-the-Grid, but the only face Ethan wanted to see at such close range first thing in the morning was Gabby's.

With a scowl, he rolled off the couch. He went into the bathroom to change into a pair of trunks then walked out back for his morning swim. The cool water closed over his head, welcoming him into his private realm, the place he still ruled and conquered every single day. An hour in the pool always set him straight.

Except this morning it didn't. The look on Gabby's face when she'd climbed out of the Jeep yesterday still gnawed at him. He'd been an ass not to go to her last night and smooth things over.

Damn it all.

Forty-five minutes later, he pulled into her driveway with a bag from the bakery and two coffees in his hands. His heart hammered against his ribs as he walked up the steps to her front door.

He knocked, then waited what felt like an eternity for her to come to the door. Finally, she opened it, looking all rumpled and sexy in a short pink robe, her hair a wild waterfall over her shoulders. She looked up at him with wide, questioning eyes.

"I'm sorry for being a jerk yesterday," he said. "I can't make promises for the future, but I hope you know that you're special to me, and not just because of Gram."

Her eyes got misty, and the air left his lungs in a whoosh. Hell, the last thing he wanted was to hurt Gabby. And yet he had the nasty suspicion that was exactly what was going to happen when it was time for him to walk away, no matter how much time he spent preparing them both for the inevitable.

She went up on her tiptoes and pressed her lips to his. "Thank you. But really, I was the one who got out of line yesterday, not you." She pulled back, a naughty look in her eyes. "Although technically, we *did* have our first fight, and I'm pretty sure that calls for makeup sex."

And then she yanked him inside and slammed the door behind them.

CHAPTER FIFTEEN

Gabby surveyed the table in front of her one last time. It was the Fourth of July, and the Haven Summer Festival was starting in less than an hour. She'd insisted that Ethan, Mark, and Ryan man the Off-the-Grid Adventures table themselves, but she'd let them talk her into setting it up for them.

And unless she was mistaken, she'd done a pretty good job. They had a full-color poster display on the left, advertising their new business with eye-catching photos of zip-lining and rock climbing. She'd arranged a stack of brochures, another stack of flyers about the Adrenaline Rush challenge, and a pile of Off-the-Grid T-shirts to be given away throughout the day to people who won one of the mini-challenges they'd be having every half hour during the festival.

She had placed a sign-up sheet for their e-newsletter next to the pile of registration forms for the Adrenaline Rush. They hoped to recruit lots of new participants today. And then, of course, there was the bucket of Off-the-Grid logoed Frisbees. Ethan had given her a budget for the promotional stuff, and she'd spent every penny.

"Wow," he said from behind her.

"What do you think?" She pressed her hands against the front of her shorts and watched for his reaction.

"It looks awesome. You've shown me this stuff before, but seeing it all together on the table, it looks really great. Thank you." He leaned in to press a quick kiss on her lips.

"You're welcome. I'm glad I got to be a part of this with you guys."

"Yo, this looks sweet," Ryan said as he sauntered up. He wore an Off-the-Grid T-shirt, tattoos peeking from beneath each sleeve. He was sexy, in a badass kind of way. All three of them were gorgeous, strong, and handsome in their own way. She was banking on them bringing in a lot of business today. The girls would flock to them because of their looks, muscles, and tattoos. The guys would come because they wanted to be a part of their dare-deviling new adventure.

"You're staying for the fireworks, right?" Ethan tugged her in close, his arms warm and strong around her.

"Sure." She couldn't remember the last time she'd gone to a fireworks show on the Fourth, but it sounded like fun, especially the part about lying on a blanket with Ethan. Things had been hot and heavy between them since they'd gotten home from the beach, but she couldn't shake the feeling that he'd started distancing himself somehow. Maybe she was being overly sensitive. Or maybe he was preparing her for what was to come after Dixie passed.

He was looking at her now, all casual and charming, but underneath it, something else lurked in his eyes: fear. If he was afraid she was falling for him, he had good reason. It was going to hurt like hell when she had to let him go, but she wouldn't be sorry about a single moment they'd spent together.

The commons were bursting with people, and even though the festival didn't officially start for another ten minutes, Ryan was already talking to a couple of women who'd approached their table.

"I'm going to walk around for a bit," she said.

"You'll love it," he said. "Tons of homemade, artsy-crafty stuff if you're into that. And so much good food."

"Sounds fun." Growing up in the suburbs of Charlotte, she'd never been to a small-town festival like this, and she was curious to poke around. "I'll take some Off-the-Grid flyers with me to pass out."

There were indeed a lot of local goods, and by eleven o'clock, she'd bought two pairs of earrings, a new skirt, and a pound of fudge that was probably going to melt under the hot sun before she ever got home tonight.

"Gabby!"

She turned and found Emma waving from behind a table. With a smile, she walked over. "Hey, Emma."

"Are you here by yourself?" Emma asked.

"Well, I helped the guys set up their booth for Off-the-Grid, but essentially yeah."

"A couple of the girls I work with are coming at noon to help out. Want to get lunch together?"

"I'd love to." Gabby looked around Emma's booth. It was full of bright, colorful flowers with a big banner advertising ARTFUL BLOOMS LANDSCAPE DESIGN. "How's it going so far?"

Emma's smile widened. "Great. I love events like this. I'm kind of a social butterfly, right? And the Summer Festival always brings new business for Artful Blooms."

"That's awesome," Gabby said.

"A couple of my friends and I are going to sign up for that obstacle course race together—Team Flower Power. Want to join us?"

Gabby threw her hands up in front of herself. "Nope. Thanks, but no. I don't really do adventure stuff."

Emma laughed. "No? But you're dating Ethan."

"And not even he can get me up on that ropes course, or the zip-line. Or any of it." She grimaced with a laugh.

"Hmm. Fear of heights?"

"Among other things."

"Well, let me know if you change your mind. I heard we need at least four people to make a team. I might ask Carly, but we could always use an extra person. I don't know how many all-girl teams there will be, but we're hoping to kick some butt."

"And I'm sure you will." Gabby stepped to the side as a couple of older ladies approached Emma's table. "I'll come back at noon, okay?"

Emma nodded.

Gabby moved on, browsing through a display of home-made wooden clocks and some kind of animal sculptures made out of metal scraps.

"Boo," Ethan whispered in her ear.

She spun, her bag of goodies smacking him right in the chest. "Sorry."

"No worries. Having fun?" He disentangled himself from her shopping bag to pull her into his arms.

"Yeah. And spending a lot of money. How are things going at the Off-the-Grid table?"

"Signed up a few people for the race. And the mini-challenges have been fun. People love competing for T-shirts. Want to get lunch?"

"Oh." She frowned. "I just made plans with Emma."

"It's okay. I'll grab a sandwich and walk around some before I head back to our table."

"Okay." But the longer she stood in his arms, the more she wanted to stay there.

"I'll see you later." He gave her another quick kiss, and then he let her go.

"So you and Ethan, huh?" Gabby turned to find Jessica Flynn watching from the Haven Spa's table.

"Yeah."

Jessica flashed her a friendly smile. "Well, good for you. If he's half as good in bed as he is to look at, you're a lucky girl."

Gabby felt herself blush. "Definitely lucky."

Jessica gave her a high five. "How was your treatment on Monday? I meant to stop in and check on you, but I got held up with another client."

"Oh, it was great. Really great." The best spa experience she'd ever had. "Those hot springs really are magical. I need to come again."

Jessica handed her a card from her table. "Well, here's a coupon for ten dollars off your next visit. I know the legend of the hot springs sounds hokey, but I'm a believer. There's something in that water that calms the soul."

Gabby remembered the way she'd felt as she soaked in a bubbling tub full of the natural spring water. "Count me in as a believer, too." Although truly, everything about this town seemed to be good for her soul. So good that it was hard to imagine leaving at the end of the summer.

* * *

Ethan had never spent the whole day at the Haven Summer Festival. He'd always stopped by, usually with whatever girl he was seeing at the time. They'd get something to eat, he'd

hang out while she shopped through all the crafts, and sometimes they'd stay for the fireworks.

But today had been nonstop. Every half hour, they'd
done some kind of game or challenge, from arm wrestling
to handing out clues and compasses to find prizes hidden
around the commons. They'd given away a lot of flyers and
Frisbees and signed up a modest number of people for the
Adrenaline Rush.

He and the guys had taken turns schmoozing at the table
and wandering around the festival, mingling and passing out
information and goodies. People seemed excited about Off-
the-Grid. Hopefully that would mean something when the
Town Council made their decision.

All day, he'd been scanning the crowd for Gabby. She'd
been here and there, chatting, making friends, buying crafty
shit, and seemingly having an awesome time. She'd really
come out of her shell here in Haven, and it stirred all kinds
of weird, warm things in his chest.

Pride. Protectiveness. Desire.

"Hey there, hotties." Emma Rush stood in front of their
table, her blond hair tied back in a ponytail, a wide smile on
her face.

"What's up, Em?" Ryan said. He and Emma had known
each other since they were kids. He'd been tight with her
older brother, Derek. Although right now, he was staring at
her like he'd never seen her before, and Ethan couldn't quite
figure what that was about.

"Can I take a registration form?" she asked. "I'm still
looking for a fourth person for our team, but my girls and I
are ready to rock it on Team Flower Power."

Ethan shook his head. "Flower Power?"

"Don't knock it." She pointed her finger at him. "We girls
are going to kick your butt."

"Not that he doesn't need a good ass-kicking, but we can't participate," Ryan told her. "We're running the thing."

"Oh," Emma said. "Well, we're going to kick butt anyway. I tried to convince your girlfriend to join our team." She looked at Ethan again.

"Bet that didn't go over well."

"Nope. Well, I'll see you guys later." With a wave, she walked off.

And Ryan was totally checking out her ass.

"I thought Emma was like the little sister you never had," Ethan commented drily.

"What?" Ryan turned his attention to straightening what remained of the stack of flyers on their table.

"You just checked out her ass."

Ryan didn't bother to deny it. "Yo, when did she get so... *hot*?"

Mark coughed into his hand.

"She's always been hot," Ethan said, "to those of us not related to her."

"I'm not related to her either, asshole." Ryan tossed a Frisbee at him.

Ethan caught it. "You guys staying for the fireworks?"

"Nah. Mark and I are going to watch the game at his place," Ryan said.

Mark was silent, his face a blank mask behind his mirrored lenses. But shit. The sound of fireworks was hard for him after Iraq, and Ethan had totally forgotten. He felt like a jackass.

A group of local teenagers descended on their table, curious about the zip-line course, and they got back to business. The rest of the afternoon passed quickly. They ran more mini-challenges, gave out more T-shirts, and schmoozed a few more people into signing up for the Adrenaline Rush.

Gram stopped by around three with her friend—and Town Council member—Marlene, both of them wearing oversized straw hats and eating funnel cake.

"Where's Gabby?" she asked.

"Around." He managed to keep himself from asking why she wasn't carrying water with her in this heat, knowing it would only earn him a lecture.

"Well, tell her I'm looking for her if you see her." Gram moved off into the crowd.

Ethan didn't see Gabby until she stopped by around five with a bag from Big Joe's BBQ on her arm, filling their booth with the tangy, smoky scent of barbeque. His stomach grumbled loudly.

"I brought brisket sandwiches," Gabby said. "They smelled really good, and I figured you guys might be getting hungry."

"I love you," Ryan told her as she handed him the bag of sandwiches.

She laughed, her eyes darting to Ethan. He felt the stupid urge to punch Ryan right in his cocky mouth.

"What?" Ryan's eyes widened in mock surprise. "Did I say it before you? Oh shoot, I hope I didn't just make things awkward."

"You're an asshole." Ethan's hands balled into fists.

Ryan threw his head back and laughed. Gabby's face flushed an adorable shade of red.

"I'm going to go grab us some beer," Mark said. He pointed at Ryan. "You're coming with me." The two of them walked off toward Untapped Brewery's stand at the other end of the street. Ryan was still laughing, the jackass.

Ethan stared at Gabby for a moment in awkward silence.

Then she smiled. "He was just joking around, Ethan. You should see your face."

He blew out a breath and motioned her to come behind the table with him. "I know. But he's still an asshole."

She went up on her tiptoes to press a kiss on his lips. "I laid our blanket out on the field for the fireworks."

"Great." He wrapped his arms around her, and everything else just disappeared. There was nothing but Gabby. The sweet honeysuckle scent of her hair, the warmth of her body against his, the way his heart seemed to slow down and beat in rhythm with hers.

Then she tipped her face up and kissed him, and he was a goner.

"You taste like powdered sugar," he whispered against her mouth.

"I ate funnel cake. And a lot of other really fattening stuff we won't talk about."

"That's exactly what you're supposed to do at the summer festival. That, and make out with me later on our blanket while we wait for the fireworks." He slid his hands down her back, lingering at her waist. He really, *really* wanted to feel her ass in those short pink shorts, but he'd have to wait until he got her somewhere more private.

"Get a room, you two." That was Ryan, but thanks to Gabby, Ethan no longer felt like punching his lights out.

Ryan and Mark both carried a beer in each hand.

"That was quick," Ethan commented. Usually the line for the beer was at least ten deep.

"I know the guy who runs the brewery," Mark said.

"So we got to cut the line," Ryan handed a beer to Ethan, while Mark handed one to Gabby. Then they all sat down to eat the brisket sandwiches she'd brought. Conversation was sparse while they stuffed their faces with beefy perfection.

One of the best things about living in a small town was the local grub. Good food. Great beer. Things like the summer festival to bring people together. He was a lucky SOB to live here. So damn lucky Gram had found him and taken him in when she did.

"You look like you're having deep thoughts," Gabby whispered in his ear.

He looked at her, her hair pulled back in a messy ponytail with damp curls framing her face and a smear of barbeque sauce on her cheek, and his brain short-circuited. "They're about to become dirty thoughts if you keep looking at me like that."

She winked.

Goddamn, he had it bad for this girl.

After they ate came the not-so-fun task of packing up everything they'd brought and hauling it out to his Jeep. Once everything was stowed, Mark and Ryan headed out, which meant—finally—he had Gabby all to himself.

Sort of. He still couldn't touch her without half the town seeing, but at least he could walk hand-in-hand with her through the rows of vendors toward the field where the fire-works would take place.

The air was thick with the scent of fried food, sweet with cotton candy and funnel cakes and caramel apples. Children shrieked as they darted between food stands, playing tag.

"I like it here." Gabby leaned in close.

He took the excuse to slide his arm around her waist. "Yeah?"

"It really is a haven."

"Sometimes." This place had definitely saved him once or twice.

Gabby dropped the bag she'd been carrying, and as she bent to grab it, he found himself staring at her ass. *Those shorts*. "Killing me."

She stood. "What?"

"Your shorts."

She touched them self-consciously. "Did I sit in something?"

"No, but they are turning me on. Big time."

"Oh." She blushed.

He took her hand and led her down the row of food stands and around the corner behind a supply truck. Then he pulled her in and kissed her, hard, while his hands slid to her ass. He cupped her through the thin cotton of her shorts, yanking her up against him. She let out a hungry whimper, her hips pressing into his, and his cock went from halfway aroused to hard as granite just like that.

He kissed her until they were both gasping for breath. Gabby looked up at him, her pink lips swollen from his kisses, her eyes all dazzled and drunk with lust.

"You are so fucking sexy." And he was so turned on, he could hardly see straight. Reluctantly, he disentangled himself from her. "I can't wait to take you out of these shorts later tonight."

"I'm looking forward to that part." She took his hand and led him back toward the bustle of the festival.

"You want ice cream?" he asked as they passed by a booth.

She shook her head, holding up the bag she'd dropped earlier. "I've got fudge."

He bought them cold bottles of water, and they wandered down to the field on the town commons, now covered with blankets and chairs. She led him to a green blanket off to the left side. The sun was setting through the trees, and more and more people were streaming into the commons in anticipation of the fireworks.

"Did Gram find you?" he asked, remembering she'd been looking for Gabby earlier.

She nodded. "She got me this. Isn't it beautiful?" She lifted her wrist to show him a turquoise bracelet.

"That's pretty." There'd been a lot of pretty things here today, and he hadn't bought anything for Gabby. *Stupid.*

She spun the bracelet so that he could see the symbol on the clasp. "It means hope."

Hope. From a dying woman. And how was that for ironic?

CHAPTER SIXTEEN

Sunset lit the field around them in varying shades of gold. Here and there, children ran with sparklers, laughing and shrieking. Cicadas hummed happily from the trees. Gabby scooted closer to Ethan on the blanket. Her knee bumped his.

His thumb brushed over the engraved clasp of her bracelet. *Hope.*

She understood the irony. She knew he was hurting. She wanted to help, but short of performing a miracle, what could she do? Was it foolish that she did hope? She hoped for happiness for herself, and for Ethan. If not together, then in whatever directions life took them.

"She's all I've got," he said finally, his voice gruff.

She took his hands in hers. "What happened to your mom?" It was way past time for her to know, because she was way past pretending he didn't matter to her.

He sat silent for so long, she didn't think he was going to answer. "My dad killed her."

She gasped, and a sick feeling churned in the pit of her stomach. "Oh, Ethan. How?"

He looked down at his hands. "Domestic abuse."

Nausea rose in her throat. "Oh...dammit. I'm sorry." She flung her arms around him, heard the catch in his breathing as he battled his emotions.

He sat like a statue, not hugging her back. "You've been here for months, and no one's told you about me yet?"

"No." But now that he was talking, she had a vague feeling she might have heard this story during news coverage of the Olympics. She held on to him, her hand on his chest, feeling his heart pounding against his ribs. "What should they have told me?"

"My dad...he was controlling. He convinced my mom to run away with him after she got pregnant with me when she was eighteen. They moved to Atlanta. He cut her off from her family. He was abusive. To her and, when she wasn't around, sometimes with me, too." He spoke without emotion, yet each word struck her to her core.

Oh, Ethan. Her heart wept for him.

"When I was ten, she left him. She remembered that her father, my grandfather, had grown up here in Haven, and she thought the town sounded perfect. She rented an apartment and tried to start a new life for us, but my dad did what abusive, controlling men do, and he followed her here. And when he found her, he tried to teach her a lesson. She fell and smashed her skull against the countertop. She died the next day."

"Was he arrested?"

Ethan nodded. "Died in a prison fight a few years later."

Gabby couldn't stop the spinning sensation inside her head. She clung to Ethan and whispered. "And you? Were you there when he attacked her?"

"I dialed 911." His voice was flat, but she felt his pain bunched in his muscles, saw it reflected in the stormy depths of his blue eyes.

Tears streaked her cheeks. "I'm so sorry."

"I didn't save her." His voice cracked, and she cried harder. For Ethan. For his mom. For Dixie, who'd lost her daughter and only child.

"You were just a boy."

"I was old enough to know what would happen when he found us. Old enough to have tried to help her."

But he'd been just a boy, a terrified boy who'd hidden while his father beat his mother, and now he was a big, strong man who carried a mountain of misplaced guilt on his shoulders. "He'd have hurt you, too, Ethan."

"Maybe I could have fought back. He fucking deserved for someone to hit him back." Rage finally boiled over in him, searing through his words, trembling in his muscles.

Gabby remembered how overprotective he'd gotten around Brad. How she'd fussed and called him a caveman. She'd had no idea he'd also been a victim of domestic violence. That he'd lost his mother to it. And now her whole world was out of balance with this new knowledge.

And now it was her turn to come clean. Her arms tightened around him. "There's something I need to tell you."

"Yeah?"

"You know things were . . . bad between me and Brad."

He nodded, his expression grim.

"He was controlling, and selfish, and so angry." She drew in a halting breath. "And he hit me. That's why I left."

"Ah, hell." Ethan inhaled harshly, his nostrils flaring. "I'm so fucking sorry, Gabby."

"Don't be. I guess we have something in common after all."

"Fuck," he muttered, pressing his forehead against hers, anchored to her in the fading light.

This man. He was so wrong for her yet so completely right. And right now, she never, ever wanted to let him go. They clung to each other, arms and legs entwined. Finally he sat back, nothing but a silhouette in the growing darkness. Hurt and sorrow radiated off him like a shimmering aura.

She touched the bracelet Dixie had given her. "I wish I could make it right for you. No one should have to go through what you and your grandmother have."

"There's no changing what's done."

"I wouldn't change anything that led me here to Haven. To you."

It was almost full dark around them now so, when his lips slammed into hers, it caught her by surprise. She gasped, her hands automatically reaching for him as she kissed him back. His tongue thrust against hers as all the heavy emotion hanging over them ignited into passion, a fiery need inside her that burned and throbbed with each stroke of his tongue.

She slid closer, and his hands gripped her ass, pressing her against his erection. And *oh*, he was so hard. Judging by the low growl in his throat and the way he ground his hips against hers, he was every bit as out of control as she was right now.

If half the town hadn't been sitting in the darkened field around them, she'd have freed him from his pants right then and there. But as he laid her back on the blanket, the sky exploded above them with a boom and a burst of golden sparks.

"Whoa," she whispered.

Ethan blew out a long breath as he flopped onto the blanket beside her. He was quiet as fireworks lit the night sky above them, his hand in hers, squeezing tightly. It was as if their emotions had been projected into the world around them: loud, fiery, and explosive.

And so very hot.

She lay mesmerized, watching the sky spark and sizzle with reds, blues, greens, purples, and dazzling whites. And when the finale began, as fireworks shot rapid fire into the sky, exploding in a kaleidoscope of color, Ethan took her hand and placed it on the front of his shorts.

He was still rock hard, and an answering tug of need grew within her.

"I need to be inside you," he whispered. "Right now."

His voice was taut, strained. And God, she needed him, too. But there was no way this could work. It would take forever for everyone to empty out of the field, and then the inevitable traffic jam in the parking lot. It could be hours before they made it home.

She gripped him through his khakis. "We have a slight privacy problem."

Even as she spoke, a couple of children ran by with sparklers, giggling as they went. Ethan swore under his breath. He clutched her hand in his, moving it to a more respectable spot on his chest. "Give me a minute, and then we'll go," he said.

They lay there like that for several long minutes as the crowd around them thinned out. Ethan's chest heaved, his muscles taut beneath her palm. Unable to help herself, she slid her hand down his stomach to the front of his shorts, and yep, he was still hard.

He hissed out a breath. "Not helping the situation."

"How about now?" She gripped him, feeling empowered by his arousal, by the way he thrust against her when she moved her fingers up and down his length.

"Definitely not." His voice was nothing but a whisper.

She scooted them to the side and wrapped the blanket around them, hiding her naughty hands from passersby. Behind them, people packed up their stuff and left, illuminated here and there by glow sticks, sparklers, and cell phones.

"Now?" She kept stroking him, thrilled by his needy gasps and the way he surged against her palm. She traced the outline of his head with her fingers, then gripped him and squeezed.

He shoved her hand away, lying still as a statue for a long minute. Finally he rolled toward her with a harsh laugh. "I damn near just came in my pants."

Her body clenched in response, desire pooling hot and wet between her legs. She was about a millimeter away from her own orgasm, and he hadn't even touched her.

He stood and tugged her to her feet, and then they were grabbing frantically for all their stuff. He grabbed the blanket, and she grabbed her shopping bags—hopefully all of them, but who knew, and who really cared?

Ethan zigzagged through the crowd and out into the parking lot, her hand gripped firmly in his. They didn't speak as they walked, both of them overcome with the urgency of the moment. He bypassed the crowded parking lot filled with people packing up their picnics.

"I'm in the exhibitor lot," he told her as they walked into another, farther lot. This one was much less crowded. She spotted his red Jeep near the end of a row, right underneath a streetlight. "We'll get your car tomorrow."

She sat in the passenger seat, watching wordlessly as Ethan put the top on the Jeep. He climbed into the driver's seat, cranked the engine, and drove them to the end of the row. It was dark here. Deserted, with woods on two sides, the mostly empty lot behind them.

He turned the engine back off and looked at her. In his

eyes, she saw everything he didn't and couldn't say. His need, his desire for her, the grief, pain, and guilt he'd carried these years for his mom and now for Dixie.

They couldn't change the past, but maybe, just maybe, they could find freedom from it here tonight, if only temporarily. She slid across the console into his lap, letting his erection settle between her legs, and *oh*, she was so close. Based on the shaky breath that escaped his lips, so was he.

He reached down, and the seat slid back, giving them more room.

He rocked her against him with a strangled groan. "I need you so bad."

"Hurry." She fumbled with the button on her shorts. Of all days, the one time she hadn't worn a skirt!

"Sweetheart, I don't think I could slow down if I tried." He unzipped his shorts, then reached for hers. She shimmied, semi-embarrassed about the fact she was now bare-assed to anyone who happened to walk by the car.

She reached over his shoulder to grab the picnic blanket off the backseat, which she draped over herself for privacy. Ethan freed himself from his shorts, rolled on a condom, and lifted her hips to position her over him.

She looked into his eyes as she sank onto him, seeing so much raw emotion reflected back at her. He moved inside her, lifting her hips up and down, and then there was nothing but their frantic movements as they fumbled toward ecstasy. She leaned forward, shifting the angle of their bodies, and *bam*, fireworks exploded inside her, hot and bright as the ones they'd seen earlier.

Ethan groaned. "How is it possible that it just gets better each time?" He looked into her eyes as he came, showing her the depths of his passion, his pleasure, his affection for her.

And *bam*, there went her heart, exploding with all the feelings she wasn't supposed to have for this man. Too late. She'd fallen for him, all right, and she wasn't even sorry.

* * *

Sometime in the dark hours of the night, Ethan slid out of Gabby's bed. She lay sleeping, a dreamy smile on her face. He felt a primeval urge to pound his chest and proclaim to the world that he was the one who'd put it there.

Instead he slipped out of her house and drove home. He needed to check on Gram. But also, he needed space. Things with Gabby had gone from hot and heavy to hot, heavy, and *intimate*. He felt exposed to the bone when he was with her, and the funny thing was...it felt so right. Like she fit into an empty place inside him and made him whole.

He drove slowly down Mountain Breeze Road, watchful for deer or other nighttime creatures in the road. His mind was replaying the way Gabby had driven him wild after the fireworks. The look on her face when she'd come apart in his arms right here in the front seat of the Jeep.

The understanding and compassion in her eyes when he'd told her about his past.

It was bullshit, total crazy bullshit, that he felt like turning the Jeep around and driving back to her. Instead, he parked in front of Gram's house and let himself quietly inside. He stood in the guest bedroom until he heard the soft sound of her snores through the paper-thin wall, then he collapsed into bed and slept.

He woke to sunlight streaming through the window and the smell of bacon. His stomach grumbled. And *dammit*. Even though he'd screwed Gabby's brains out last night, he still woke up hard, thinking of her. Morning wood would be so much more fun if he'd spent the night at her place instead of sneaking out in the middle of the night like a coward.

He closed his eyes and concentrated on the sounds of Gram puttering around in the kitchen until the tent in his shorts had eased. Then he rolled to his feet, grabbed clean clothes out of the duffel bag in the corner, and padded down the hall to the bathroom.

He showered and made it to the kitchen table just as Gram was setting out plates of bacon, eggs, and pancakes.

"You got home late last night," she said with a wink.

Shit. Why did he feel like a teenager caught sneaking in after curfew? "No offense, but I think you just go to bed early."

"Oh, I definitely do." She took a big bite of bacon. "But I got up to use the bathroom around one, and you weren't here yet."

He choked on a mouthful of pancake. "Gabby and I were out late after the fireworks."

"I'm just teasing, sweetie. You're a grown man. You don't have to come home at all. I'm just so happy for you and Gabby."

Nothing he could say to that. Instead, he shoveled food into his mouth until his plate was clean. "Thanks for breakfast, Gram. I'll cook tomorrow, okay? Whatever you like."

She shook her head. "Nonsense. I love cooking for you. I think we should have bacon every morning until…well, as long as I'm here to cook it."

"Bacon every morning? I can't argue with that." Couldn't breathe either. His stomach heaved at the thought of her not being here. He swallowed past it with a big gulp of coffee, then stood, pressed a quick kiss to her forehead, and headed for the Jeep.

Gabby's honeysuckle scent lingered inside it, or he just

couldn't get her out of his head. Or maybe both. He took the top down, then drove to Off-the-Grid and changed into his swim trunks. He needed to sort some things out, and the only way he could do that was by swimming.

After he dove in, everything came into focus as his body sliced through the water. At the end of each lap, he tucked, rolled, and kicked off toward the other end.

Steady. Even. Predictable.

Funny how he needed that here, when his life had never been any of those things. Except one thing in his life had always been just that.

Gram.

* * *

Gabby woke alone, which she'd expected, but still...maybe a small part of her had hoped he would stay this time. What they'd shared last night had been so intense, so emotional, so passionate. Her mind was still reeling from it all.

Reluctantly, she rolled out of bed and stepped into the shower. Then she took her morning coffee out on the back deck to enjoy with Lance. Rather than explore the woods below, he simply lay at her side, chin on his front paws, watching the birds swoop overhead.

"I don't think I've ever heard you bark," she said.

Lance looked at her, his right ear twitching as a fly buzzed around his head.

"You do know how to, right?" She took another long sip from her coffee. "I think I like that about you, though. Sometimes quiet is nice."

She finished her coffee and took him for a walk in the woods. Since it was almost noon already, she bypassed breakfast and fixed herself a peanut butter and jelly sandwich because she desperately needed to go grocery shopping but knew better than to go on an empty stomach.

She'd just finished making her sandwich when someone knocked on the front door. On cue, Lance scurried from where he'd been lying under the table and ran into the pantry.

"Seriously? It's probably Ethan. You like him, remember?" Her heart danced a happy jig in her chest as she rushed to open the door.

Her parents stood on the other side.

Gabby's smile withered and died. "Mom? Dad? What are you doing here?"

Her mom stepped forward to pull her into a tight hug. "Well, we hadn't heard from you in a while so we figured we'd stop by and surprise you."

"See what you've been up to out here in the mountains," her dad added. Even though it was Sunday, Harold Winters wore pressed gray slacks and a button-down shirt. Gabby had never seen her father in a pair of jeans, wasn't sure he even owned one.

"What a nice surprise. Come in." She tried to sound enthusiastic, but even to her ears it sounded forced.

Much like the smile on her mother's face. "What a lovely cabin."

"It's great, isn't it?" Gabby led her parents into the living room, where they ooh'ed and aah'ed over the view from her back deck. "Can I get you guys anything? Coffee? Water?"

"Water would be great. Thank you, sweetie," her mom said.

Her dad nodded. "I'll have the same."

Gabby walked into the kitchen, cursing under her breath. The last thing she was in the mood for today was a visit from her parents. There was no bad blood between them, but her parents had always been more focused on their careers than on Gabby. Growing up, her nanny had been the one to kiss her boo-boos, the one who taught her how to ride her bike without training wheels, and made sure her homework was finished before she went outside to play.

Debra and Harold had always been at work.

She filled two glasses with ice water and walked back to the living room. Her mom sat perched on the edge of the couch while her dad stood in front of the window, hands in his pockets.

"So, wow. You guys drove a long way to surprise me." She handed them each a glass.

"Thank you." Her mom took a long drink. "It had just been so long since we'd seen you. How are you doing?"

Gabby sat across from her on the love seat. "Really great actually. Haven's been good for me. I've made some new friends."

"Well, that's good." Debra looked relieved. "We were so worried when you just up and left home like that."

"I needed a change of scenery." And a chance to live her life without their constant judgment and criticism.

"At least you finally came to your senses where Brad was concerned."

Gabby bristled. Sure, Brad was a total loser, but her parents had no idea what he'd done. They just disliked him because he was a blue collar worker. But there was something else that had been bothering her. "Brad came here to Haven. Did you tell him where to find me?"

"Of course not," her mother said. "He came to see us, too, and I told him to leave us all alone. Good riddance, I say."

"But I didn't tell anyone else from home where I was staying," Gabby said quietly.

"For goodness' sake, Gabby." Her dad's voice was stern.

"You sound like you're accusing your mother of something here."

Debra blanched. "Well, I think I did tell him he could forget about seeing you again because you'd moved all the way out here in the mountains. I didn't think he'd *come*. I was telling him to move on."

Gabby shook her head. "It's okay, Mom. I told him to get lost, and he seems to have finally taken the hint."

"Well, that's good. So you like it here?" Her mother looked around the room as if searching for the answer to her own question.

"I do. I really do."

Another knock came at her front door. *Crap.* She didn't want to have to introduce her parents to anyone here. Haven's citizens weren't exactly their type, at least not any of the ones who might be standing on the other side of her front door right now.

"Excuse me." She smiled at her parents and hurried to the front door.

Ethan stood on the other side, wearing a wide grin and the same blue T-shirt he'd loaned her the day they met. The one that said, I'D RATHER BE GETTING HIGH.

Gabby held in a groan.

"Hey." He leaned in to give her a quick kiss. "I came to see if you wanted to get lunch, but it looks like you have company?"

"Oh—" She glanced behind her, then sighed. "It's my parents. They just...dropped by."

Ethan's eyebrows went up.

No doubt her parents had already seen him kiss her so there was nothing left to do but introduce them. "Sorry," she mouthed to him as she motioned him inside.

Debra stood from the couch, smoothing her hands over

the front of her black slacks. Harold moved to stand at her side. They both wore polite smiles as they stared at Ethan.

He turned on his trademark charm, extending a hand with a warm, genuine smile. "Hi, I'm Ethan Hunter."

"Debra Winters, Gabby's mother." She took his hand and shook.

"Well, I can certainly see where Gabby gets her looks. It's great to meet you."

Her mother patted her hair and blushed. "Nice to meet you, too."

As her dad shook hands with Ethan, he blatantly stared at Ethan's shirt. "That's a little inappropriate, isn't it?"

Ethan looked down at his shirt and laughed. "Sorry, sir. It's a hang-gliding joke. I haven't smoked weed in years."

Her dad's steely look made it clear he didn't find that at all reassuring.

But Ethan merely shrugged. "So what brings you guys to Haven? Has Gabby shown you around town yet?"

For a guy who always kept things casual and therefore probably didn't make it to the "meet the parents" stage often—if at all—he sure was handling this well.

"We just got here," her mother told him. "We decided to drive out this morning on a whim."

"Well then, I have perfect timing," Ethan said. "I've lived here most of my life so I'd love to help show you around. Have you had lunch yet?"

* * *

Ethan met Gabby's eyes across the table and winked. Her lips turned up in a hint of a smile. She'd been edgy ever since he barged in on her with her parents, but he couldn't say he blamed her. Mr. and Mrs. Winters both seemed like they could use a ride on his zip-line course—or two—to loosen them up some.

"So, Ethan, what do you do for a living?" Mr. Winters asked.

"I'm opening my own business this summer, Off-the-Grid Adventures. It's an extreme outdoor sporting facility. We'll have zip-lining, rock climbing, survival skills, that kind of thing. I'm really excited about it."

"Oh." Gabby's father looked less than impressed.

"That sounds... dangerous," her mother said.

He ought to introduce them to the folks on the Town Council; they'd probably get along great. "It's all very safe, I promise," he told her. "I'm also the swim coach at Pearcy County High during the school year and teach swim lessons year round."

"That's lovely," Mrs. Winters said, giving him her first real smile. "I swam on the Highland Country Club swim team all through high school."

"You did?" Gabby was looking at her mother like she'd never seen her before.

"Well, yes, honey. I'm sure I've mentioned it."

"I'm sure you haven't."

And here he'd thought he came from the only dysfunctional family at the table. "That's wonderful, Mrs. Winters. Swimming is the best sport as far as I'm concerned. Sure straightened me out when I needed straightening."

"Ethan won two gold medals at the Olympics in Beijing," Gabby told her mother, her voice laced with pride.

Apart from Gram, he wasn't sure anyone had ever looked at him the way she was right now. A funny, tingly feeling grew in his chest. He took her hand beneath the table and gave it a squeeze.

"Oh, I knew your name sounded familiar!" Mrs. Winters

was looking at him with respect now, and while he preferred that to the disapproval he'd gotten from her earlier, it pissed him off that his gold medals somehow made him more worthy in her eyes.

He kept them in a box in his closet. They didn't define who he was or even the greatest thing he'd accomplished. "Yes, that's me."

"I remember watching you compete that summer. In fact, if I'm not mistaken, Gabby and her friends all had a bit of a crush on you." Her mom elbowed her playfully, showing the first real affection toward her daughter that he'd seen.

Gabby blushed adorably. "*Mom*."

And it was all he could do not to reach across the table and kiss her, take her hand, and proclaim to the world that she was *his*. Because he couldn't imagine anything or anyone more perfect than Gabby.

Mr. Winters cleared his throat. "So how did you go from Olympic champion to riding zip-lines?"

His happy mood soured in an instant. "I'm pursuing a dream, sir. Opening my own business with two of my childhood friends. We hope Off-the-Grid will be very profitable."

"And if it's not?"

Ethan's hands balled into fists beneath the table. He'd brought in almost a million dollars in Olympic endorsements back in the day, and thanks to Gram's guidance, he'd invested it well. He could afford to pursue whatever dream he chose. "Then I'll try something else."

"And how do you plan to support yourself in the meantime?" Mr. Winters asked.

"Dad!" Gabby looked horrified.

"As I mentioned, I coach the high school swim team, teach swim lessons, and I also take odd jobs around town."

"Sorry." Mrs. Winters placed her hand over her husband's. "He's an investment broker. He's got money on the brain."

"I understand," Ethan said. Didn't change the fact that Gabby's father was also an ass.

He'd brought them to the Skyline Grille for lunch and requested a table on the upstairs open air patio, figuring they'd appreciate the upscale menu and the pricey view. And while they seemed impressed with the restaurant, the same couldn't be said about him.

He had a feeling her parents would be all too relieved when he and Gabby went their separate ways. And that shouldn't bother him. He usually didn't even meet the parents of a woman he was seeing and couldn't care less what they thought of him.

But for some reason this *did* bother him. He was royally pissed off that Gabby's parents didn't think he was good enough for her, and for some stupid reason, he found himself desperately wanting to prove them wrong.

CHAPTER SEVENTEEN

A dog?" Gabby's mother wrinkled her nose. "I didn't even know you liked dogs."

Gabby stroked Lance's fur as she once again sat on the love seat opposite her parents. Ethan had taken off after lunch, citing work, and she couldn't blame him. *God.* Her parents, especially her dad, had been so rude. Now she needed to find a tactful way to send them home. "I've always liked animals. Lance is a good companion."

"Never saw the point of a dog that small," her dad commented. "Can't guard. Probably can't even fetch."

She bit her tongue and looked away.

"So have you ridden this zip-line your boyfriend made?" her mom asked.

"No." And she'd been fine with that decision until about two seconds ago. Now she felt like a coward for not having at least tried.

"Good," her father said. "You're smarter than that."

"But I'm going to." If for no other reason than to tell her parents she had. But she was finished letting fear boss her around. To hell with that.

Her dad grunted his disapproval.

"Your father and I were talking in the car on the way home from lunch," her mother said.

Gabby looked between them, one hand clenched into Lance's soft fur.

"Ethan's gold medals are impressive," she continued, "and he's obviously a very ambitious and charismatic young man."

Gabby sensed a big *but* coming . . .

"He needs a job that reflects his potential," her father said. "Lockhart Investments is always looking for dynamic new people to join the team. Ethan might do well in communications or public affairs, or even sales. I'd be happy to put in a good word for him."

And there it was. Gabby shook her head. "Why would he want to come work with you, Dad? He's just opened a new business here in Haven, in case you weren't paying attention to anything he told you at lunch."

Her father's eyes narrowed. "He's taking people for zip-line rides. I could assure him a job with financial stability and growth. After all, you'll be coming home to Charlotte soon, and if Ethan's serious about you, he should consider his future, and yours."

"He *is* thinking about his future," Gabby said quietly. "He's fulfilling a dream with Off-the-Grid. And I don't need a man to provide for me, Dad."

"Well, of course not, Gabby," her mother said. "We raised you better than that. But listen to what your father's saying. He's offering Ethan an opportunity to do something more with his life. We just don't want to see you end up with another guy like Brad...you know, more interested in having a good time than settling down."

"All right, that's enough." Gabby stood from the couch. Lance, alarmed, scurried off toward the safety of the pantry. "For your information, Ethan is nothing, *nothing*, like Brad. If you'd taken the time to get to know either one of them, you'd be able to see that. I appreciate your concern, but if you just came here to meddle in my life, then you can leave. Because I'm happy here, and nothing you can say is going to change that."

* * *

Ethan taught two swim lessons, then spent the rest of the afternoon schmoozing local business owners to support the Adrenaline Rush or, better yet, form a team and join in the fun. He enjoyed networking, but lunch with Gabby's parents had left his patience running short, and after several hours of going door to door on Main Street, he'd had enough.

He was in serious need of stress relief, in the form of swimming laps or his zip-line course. But for some reason, as he headed toward Off-the-Grid, he found himself continuing down the road to drive by Gabby's place.

The silver BMW that had been parked in her driveway earlier was gone.

And he needed to see her. He turned into the driveway and parked. She opened the front door before he'd reached it, looking so goddamn gorgeous that he stumbled over his own feet in his hurry to pull her into his arms and kiss the daylights out of her.

"I'm so sorry." She pressed her face against his neck.

He buried his face in her hair, breathing in her honeysuckle scent. And all the tension in his body just faded away. "No need to apologize. Your parents had some valid concerns."

"Bullshit." She drew back and stared at him. "They were rude, and I told them so."

He grinned. "Wish I'd been here to see that."

She laughed softly, reaching up to brush a lock of hair from her face.

"So you had a crush on me during the Olympics, huh?"

Her cheeks flushed. "You were hot in a Speedo."

"I was a cocky kid high on the scent of gold."

She looked right into his eyes. "I like this version of you even better."

Yeah, he did, too.

Especially when he was with Gabby. She wrapped her arms around him and kissed him, hard. They kissed until her legs were wrapped around his hips, her back against the wall in her entrance hall, and his heart was about to burst right out of his chest.

"You are absolutely fucking amazing. You know that, right?" He nibbled down her neck, rewarded by a breathless gasp from Gabby.

"I'm working on it."

"Atta girl." And then he carried her down the hall to her bedroom, where he showed her exactly how amazing she was. Twice.

The sun was setting outside the window beside them as they lay in her bed, naked and entwined. She snuggled closer with a happy sigh. "I like this."

"Me, too." He tightened his arms around her, securing her against him. He liked it an awful fucking lot. More than he'd ever liked anything with a girl. And not just the sex. Everything with Gabby was great.

"I'm starving," she whispered.

"Me, too, but I don't want to move."

"Take-out?"

He liked the way she was thinking. "How does pizza sound?"

She smiled. "Perfect. And I have beer in the fridge."

He slid out of bed, pulled on his shorts, and walked to the living room, where he ordered a large pizza loaded with the works. Hell, they'd definitely burned enough calories earlier to justify it. And he'd noticed that Gabby didn't eat much of her grilled chicken salad at lunch today.

She walked into the living room wearing a gauzy pink gown that came to mid-thigh and was possibly the sexiest thing he'd ever seen. It gave him just a tease of the outline of her breasts, and as she passed him headed for the kitchen, he found himself staring at her ass, hoping for a glimpse to confirm whether or not she was wearing panties.

The gown was about an inch too long.

She came back with two beers, handed him one, and sank onto the couch. "What do you like to watch on TV?"

"Sports." He sat beside her.

Gabby wrinkled her nose. "What kind of sports?"

"Any kind."

"Hmm." She snuggled in close beside him, and her gown rode up her thigh, confirming that she was wearing panties— skimpy purple panties.

And he guessed she was not into sports. "We could watch a movie."

"That's so very…domestic." She gave him a funny smile.

Yeah, it was. He couldn't remember the last time he'd spent an evening hanging out with a woman, ordering take-out and watching a movie together. "I can be domestic." His gaze dropped to the video game equipment on the shelf beneath her TV. "Want to play something?"

Her eyes brightened. "Yes. That sounds more fun than a movie."

"Sweet. Got any more games like that skiing one you brought to the senior center?"

"Yeah, sure." She tapped a finger against her lips with a smile. "Guessing you wouldn't be interested in *Dance Central*."

He made a face at her, and she giggled.

"I've got a sports collection, a *Star Wars* adventure, and...oh! *Wipeout*."

"Like that TV show where you get whacked in the nuts and fall off stuff?"

She laughed. "Exactly like that, except the hits are virtual. You game?"

"Game on, baby." He got to his feet.

Five minutes later, he was jumping around and lurching from side to side, guiding his character through a virtual obstacle course while Gabby—predictably—whooped his ass. Although, to his credit, he couldn't be expected to pay full attention to the game when she was bouncing around next to him wearing next to nothing.

Their food arrived soon after, and they took a break to stuff themselves on pizza, then settled in with fresh beers to play *Super Mario Brothers*. Talk about a blast from the past.

"This was one of my favorite games when I was a kid," he said.

"Mine, too."

"My mom played with me sometimes." He had no idea why he was telling her this.

"Oh yeah?" Gabby scooter closer, her thigh against his. "What was she like?"

Tired, mostly. Beaten down by life. But…"She was really good at making me laugh."

She squeezed his knee. "She got that from her mom, I bet."

He exhaled slowly, surprised to find that he was smiling. "Yeah, bet she did. I didn't know Gram back then, but my mom had a lot of her mannerisms."

"You must miss her so much."

He didn't let himself think about his mom often, and when he did, it was usually to relive the horrific way she had died. He almost never remembered the happy moments, like playing video games with her or the way she'd hummed lullabies until he fell asleep when he was younger. "Thanks for asking about her."

Gabby leaned forward and pressed a gentle kiss to his lips. "Thank you for sharing her with me."

That night, when he fell asleep beside her, he didn't stir until morning light was streaming through the windows. Something cold and wet brushed his cheek, and he turned his head to find Gabby's dog sitting on the pillow staring at him.

"Hi," he said.

Lance cocked his head and stared at him some more.

"Look, if this is about that time in the kitchen…" Ethan shook his head at himself for talking to the dog. "I don't always carry pepperoni."

Gabby laughed softly beside him while Lance leaned in and licked his cheek.

"But I draw the line at kissing dogs. Sorry, buddy." He scooted the dog away, but he came right back, undeterred, still staring unwaveringly at Ethan.

"He hardly ever even comes out of the pantry when anyone else is in the house," Gabby said. "Maybe it's partly because he thinks you're hoarding pepperoni, but I think he really likes you."

"That's cool, man," Ethan told the dog. "You can come hang at Off-the-Grid anytime you like."

Gabby giggled. Her leg bumped his cock, reminding him that, for the first time in over a month, he didn't have to endure morning wood without her.

Fucking *finally*.

* * *

Gabby slid closer because, *wow*, Ethan was fully aroused, and they hadn't even started fooling around yet. In response, a warm ache grew between her thighs. She reached down to stroke him. "Well, good morning."

Ethan groaned. He nudged Lance off the bed, then pulled her up against him so that his cock pressed against her belly. "I've woken like this every day since I met you. You have no idea how many painful mornings I've suffered because you weren't in my bed."

"Really?" Wow. Knowing Ethan had woken every morning like this, thinking of her? That was sexy. And it turned her on, big time. She wiggled her hips, sliding up and down his hard length.

He sucked in a breath. "Baby, you have caused me more blue balls than you will ever know."

She gave him her best naughty smile. "Not this morning."

He reached for the box of condoms on her nightstand, and she made good on her word as they made love in the soft morning light. It was sexy, and passionate, and perfect. And when they'd finished and lay panting together, she rested her cheek on his chest, feeling his heart pounding beneath all that hard-muscled flesh.

"I'll think of you tomorrow morning," she whispered with a giggle.

He wrapped an arm around her waist, anchoring her to him. "You are evil."

"Well, you can think of me, too, while you take care of things." She reached down and touched him. His cock jumped beneath her palm.

"Yeah, see, that's the problem. Really can't take care of it with Gram on the other side of the wall. Her walls are paper thin, and anyway that's just weird."

"Oh." Yeah, that would definitely be weird. "Well, if the problem gets too bad, you know where to find me."

"Fuck, Gabby. I've mentioned that you're the most amazing woman ever, right?"

Yeah, he had, and it made her chest feel all warm and tingly. He said it with such conviction, such earnestness, and maybe she was naive, but she didn't imagine him saying it to every girl he slept with.

He kissed her again, then pulled back. "But speaking of Gram, I need to get home and check on her. I'll be working at Off-the-Grid all day today. Stop by?"

She nodded. "I'll bring lunch."

"Great." He slid out of bed, dressed, and after another kiss, he left.

She sighed, then looked down at Lance, sitting beside the bed, eyes wide, watching her with rapt attention. "Were you there that whole time?"

He cocked his head to the side.

"That's kind of perverted, dude. Next time I'm putting you in your crate."

She got up and got ready for her day, her mind wandering to Ethan the whole time, replaying their night together and counting down the minutes until she saw him again at lunch.

This had gone from a pretend relationship to explosive chemistry to real, *really real*, feelings almost before she'd realized what was happening.

And yet, it was all supposed to end after Dixie was gone. That thought brought on a whole host of feelings she didn't want to think about, so she pushed it out of her mind for now.

She munched a granola bar in the kitchen then retreated to her office to work. Luckily she was between major deadlines, since she'd been pretty distracted with Ethan and Dixie the last few weeks. The game she was coding right now, a kids' fantasy game called *Scion's Quest*, wasn't due until the end of the summer so it was no big deal if she took a few hours off here and there as long as she made up her time and had everything ready to go on schedule.

She spent the morning writing and checking code. It was almost noon before she reached a good stopping point, but before she left her computer, she checked her e-mail. Her mom had written, saying how nice it had been to see Gabby yesterday and how she hoped she would come home soon. And a friend of hers, Chloe, had also written.

Gabby and Chloe had been college roommates and good friends in the years since. She hadn't seen Chloe as much while she was dating Brad, and then she had avoided most everyone after she left him. She'd been a lousy friend. Case in point—Chloe was e-mailing to catch up and see if Gabby would like to go out sometime.

She didn't even know Gabby had moved to Haven.

That's how out of touch with her friends she was.

With a heavy feeling in her chest, she replied to Chloe's e-mail, giving her a quick update on her life and promising to get together as soon as she was back in Charlotte. She even invited Chloe for a visit here in Haven if she was interested.

She hadn't been herself when she was with Brad, or after she'd left him. But she was back now, and maybe even better than ever. And now it was time to go see her man.

With a smile, she walked Lance and put him in his crate, then drove to the deli and ordered sandwiches—four of them. Because she was betting all the guys would be hungry. She grabbed chips and sodas to go with the meals and headed for Off-the-Grid.

She pulled into the lot and parked next to Ethan's red Jeep, but when she went inside the house, no one was there. She left the food on the table in the kitchen and walked out back, following the sound of hammering from somewhere in the woods behind the house.

"Ethan?" she called, but there was no answer. He and the guys were probably so caught up in work, they had no idea it was lunchtime yet.

She walked down the path toward the zip-line course, and when the first platform came into view, she stopped, staring up at it.

"Have you ridden the zip-line your boyfriend made?"

Her mother's words echoed in her head. It was ridiculous that she hadn't. How could she stand on her own two feet when she was still letting fear rule her life? Standing here looking up, it didn't look *that* high.

Cautiously, she placed her hand on the wooden railing and started up the stairs. Her heart thudded hard and heavy against her ribs. With each step, her legs felt more and more like limp spaghetti. When she reached the top, she stood with her back against the tree trunk, her knees shaking, cursing a blue streak.

She closed her eyes and counted to twenty, slowly. At the very least, she would walk to the edge of the platform and have a look.

"Ready to fly?" Ethan whispered into her ear, and she shrieked.

She grabbed on to his arm as the platform tilted dangerously beneath her. Or more likely, her head was starting to spin. "As it turns out, no."

"Here, take my hand." He squeezed her hand firmly in his.

"I don't know what I'm doing up here," she said.

"Trying to take a leap of faith, it looks like."

Yeah, something like that. She really *wanted* to take a leap of faith.

"Want to see the harness?" he asked.

She nodded. He led her over to a bin against the back railing where the gear was apparently stored. He released her hand to punch a code into the lock on the bin, then opened it and pulled out a black harness with straps and buckles hanging everywhere.

"It clips on like this." He demonstrated on himself, fastening it around his legs and waist. "See?" He gave it a tug. "Couldn't fall out of this if I tried."

"What if it breaks?"

"Won't happen. These harnesses are top quality, and they're practically brand new. We inspect each one every morning before we use them, and they'll be replaced often once we're in operation to prevent wear and tear."

"Hmm." She watched him, standing there in that harness, looking so at ease, so strong and confident.

"Want to try one on?"

"Okay." There was no harm in trying it on. So what if her knees shook while he fastened it around her? It felt heavy and solid, but did nothing to ease the fear clogging her throat.

Ethan watched her for a minute in silence. "Unfortunately this rig's not built for tandem rides, or I'd take you with me."

"I want to go alone anyway." That was the whole point. She could lean on Ethan for small things, but not this.

"Atta girl." He nudged his fist against her biceps. "So why don't you sit right here in the middle of the platform and watch me take a ride, then see what you think?"

She managed a small smile. "I'd like that."

"Okay." He gave her a quick kiss, then clipped himself onto the line. She did as he'd suggested and sat cross-legged in the middle of the platform. It wasn't as scary from this position, probably because she couldn't see the ground. Just the line and the trees beyond.

With a whoop, he was gone, soaring off over the forest. She heard the whine of the zip-line mechanism over the cable mixed with Ethan's happy yell. He spread his arms wide, twisting back to grin at her before he'd bounced and swooped too far away for her to see his expression.

She watched until he'd landed on the next platform. It did look kind of fun. But the whole dangling way up in the air thing…

Nope. Just wasn't going to happen.

She sat rooted to the spot until Ethan had returned. He stood before her on the platform, still wearing his harness, looking exhilarated. "Ready to try?"

She shook her head. "Sorry."

He shrugged. "Doesn't matter to me whether or not you ride it, but it looks like it matters to you, so I'm guessing you'll do it when you're ready."

Tears burned the backs of her eyes. How did he read her so well? "If I'm ever ready."

He reached down and tugged her to her feet. "You will be."

* * *

Ethan left Off-the-Grid just past four and drove to Gram's house. Earlier he'd felt light as air up on that platform with Gabby. Now his body ached, weighed down with memories. For the past month, he'd been helping Gram check off the items on her bucket list, and tonight they would go together to visit his mom's grave.

It'd been far too long since he'd been there.

Gram was waiting in the entrance hall, wearing a blue-printed sundress that he often saw her wear to church on Sundays. They walked out to his Jeep together.

Memories of the day he'd buried his mother swamped him, dark and bitter. He remembered the temporary foster mother who'd been assigned to him straightening the tie on his child-sized suit and how that tie had felt like it was cutting off his air supply, squeezing the life right out of him.

He remembered the way it had felt looking at her grave after it was all over, like his whole life had gotten buried down in that hole with her. He hadn't even met Gram yet, didn't know she existed. On the day of the funeral, he had been completely alone in the world.

And it had been fucking terrifying.

He and Gram walked through the cemetery together, stopping in front of his mother's grave. Ethan looked over to see tears running silently down Gram's cheeks. *Shit.*

He put an arm around her, pulling her close.

"I miss her," Gram said. She dropped to her knees in front

of the headstone, tracing her fingers over his mother's name, etched in stone.

Dawn Marie Hunter

"Me, too," Ethan said. It had moved to the background now as the grief and the horror of losing her faded. In fact, some days he didn't think of his mom at all. But she was always there in the back of his mind, inked on his skin and forever in his heart.

But what he sometimes forgot was how her death had affected Gram. Not only had she lost her daughter, but she'd lost years of being a part of Dawn's life before she died. Gram hadn't been at her funeral, hadn't been able to mourn until a year after the fact.

It slammed into him like a battering ram that soon he'd be visiting the cemetery again, mourning Gram. And fuck. He wasn't ready. He'd never be ready.

His whole life was about to get sucked down in a big hole in the ground all over again.

CHAPTER EIGHTEEN

Ethan tossed and turned in bed that night, haunted by the nightmares of his past. After several restless hours, he finally turned his thoughts to Gabby. Gabby up on that platform looking so beautifully brave. Gabby beneath him in bed, screaming in pleasure.

Yep, that did the trick. He closed his eyes and fell into a fitful sleep.

When he awoke, sunlight was streaming through his window, and based on the tent in his sheets, Gabby was still on his mind. He closed his eyes and started counting backward from fifty, his morning tradition to relieve the pressure so that he could leave the bedroom without being indecent.

His dick was just starting to relax when his phone pinged with an incoming text. Welcoming the distraction, he reached over and grabbed it off the nightstand.

The text was from Gabby.

Thinking about you this morning and hoping that problem we talked about hasn't gotten too hard to handle.

She'd inserted a little winking emoticon at the end, followed by a sunrise and a tree. Morning wood. And yep, that problem had just gotten *really* hard again.

Killing me, he texted back.

That bad, huh?

Oh yeah, it was bad. Getting worse by the second.

I'd be happy to help you with it if you want to stop by... This was followed by several colorful hearts.

His poor cock ached at the thought. But... No can do. Gotta take Gram to an appointment.

Oh. Bummer.

No kidding. Gotta go. Chatting with you is not helping the issue.

He thrust his phone back onto the bedside table and lay there, concentrating on the sounds of Gram moving around in the kitchen until his dick finally accepted defeat. Then he went down the hall and took a long, cold shower.

That Gabby had a bit of an evil streak in her. He laughed into the shower's chilly spray, imagining what it might be like to wake up next to her more often. Hot, sweaty sex instead of painfully cold showers.

Something that would never happen because, when Gram passed, he and Gabby would part ways. Thoroughly chilled, he shut off the shower, dressed, and headed for the kitchen.

"Good morning," Gram said from the kitchen table, where she sipped a cup of hot tea and tabbed through who-knew-what on her iPhone.

"Morning." He headed straight for the coffeemaker, smiling when he saw she'd already brewed a pot for him. "Thanks, Gram. You rock."

"And you're very predictable." She looked up with a smile. "I'd like to check off another thing on my list this weekend."

"Oh yeah, what's that?"

"Visit the Biltmore." She held up her phone to show him that she'd been browsing the historic estate's website.

"You've never been?" That actually surprised him. The Biltmore Estate was one of North Carolina's most famous tourist destinations, a huge private estate with gardens, a winery, and all kinds of touristy things to do. It even had its own hotel.

"I never have, but I've always wanted to."

"Let's go then." It wasn't high on his to-do list, but it was definitely right up Gram's alley, and he'd love to be the one to take her.

"Bring Gabby. I'll get us a couple of rooms at the Biltmore Inn, and we'll make a weekend of it."

"Sounds great." They were making a lot of memories together this summer. As much as the reason for it sucked, Gram was making the most of it by doing and trying things she might not otherwise.

Wasn't there a song called "Live Like You Were Dying"? Maybe everyone should spend a summer like this, just not putting anything off and living each day like it was your last.

On that thought, he picked up his phone and texted Gabby, inviting her to Asheville with them for the weekend.

* * *

"I feel kind of bad tagging along with you guys on all these family trips," Gabby said as she hoisted her duffel bag onto her shoulder.

"Don't," Ethan said.

But she had to wonder, did he really, truly want her along for all this bucket list stuff with his grandmother? Or would he someday regret that he'd spent so much time canoodling with her during his grandmother's last weeks on this planet?

That thought curdled the contents of her stomach, but the last thing she would ever do was intentionally sour any part of this weekend for Ethan or Dixie. This was about them, after all. She was just along for the ride.

"You ever been to the Biltmore?" he asked.

She nodded. "I went with my parents when I was in high school. They go fairly often." Which was why she'd never had the desire to go back as an adult. But truly it was a lovely place. The gardens were stunning, and walking into that house felt like being on the set of a period movie—like stepping back in time, and up in class.

She'd never stayed there overnight, but the inn was supposed to be great, and it meant she got to spend the night with Ethan, which was worth the trip all on its own.

She gave one last glance around her house, then followed Ethan to the door. Dixie was outside, leaning against the back of her SUV and talking into her cell phone. She gave Gabby a friendly wave as she ended the call.

"I don't know about you guys, but I'm excited," she said.

"Me, too." Gabby opened the rear door and tossed her duffel bag onto the seat.

"And I am excited that you ladies are excited," Ethan said with a smile.

"Good man." Dixie patted his arm as she walked around to the front of the car.

They had a two-hour drive ahead of them, but it flew by with Dixie telling tales of Ethan's adolescent misadventures, and when she'd tired of that, she told stories about all the places she'd seen and visited on the many cruises she'd taken with her late husband.

Gabby heard a wistful note in her voice today that hadn't been there previously, and it made her chest hurt to think of what it must be like for Dixie, knowing each day could be her last.

After a stop at the gatehouse to buy tickets, Ethan guided them down a long driveway through the entrance gates of the estate. They wound through several miles of lush greenery to a parking lot, where they left the car and boarded a shuttle bus that brought them—finally—to the front steps of the Biltmore Estate. The big house loomed in front of them, looking like something right out of the history books with its steeped roof and turrets reaching toward the sky.

"Wow," Dixie said with awe in her voice. "It's even more impressive in person."

"It really is." Gabby hadn't appreciated a thing about it when she'd been here as a teen. She'd been too young to taste the wine when her parents dragged her along on a tour of the vineyard and too busy being pissed off that she'd had to miss a sleepover party with a group of her friends to do anything but sulk.

But now...now it took her breath away. The house alone was an impressive sight, but the flower gardens stretching out beside it really captured her attention. She'd always loved flowers. All kinds, all colors. They were so bright and vibrant and smelled so lovely.

Gabby and Dixie dragged Ethan along with them for a tour of the gardens before they went inside. He had to be bored out of his mind, but he wore an easy smile the whole time and willingly followed them wherever they wanted to go.

Dixie wore a wide straw hat on her head and looked so adorable, Gabby just wanted to squeeze her.

"Oh, these begonias are just beautiful," Dixie said. "I've never seen any quite so vividly pink before."

"They're gorgeous," Gabby agreed.

"I have one issue with the flower gardens here," Ethan said after his grandmother had wandered far enough up the path to be out of earshot.

"What's that?" she asked.

"No honeysuckle."

She smiled. "Well, honeysuckle isn't exactly pretty to look at."

"But it smells great, and you always smell like it." He gave her a look that made her chest swell with warmth.

"It's my body spray. The smell of honeysuckle reminds me of childhood afternoons playing outside. It's one of my favorite scents."

"Me, too, on all counts." He leaned in and nuzzled her neck.

She swatted him away as they came up behind Dixie on the path.

"I am in heaven," Dixie said with a radiant smile on her face. "Why on earth have I not come here before? I could spend all day right here in the garden."

"And you can if you want," Ethan told her. "But you might have to let me go get you some ice water."

"Iced tea would be even better," Dixie said.

"I'll see what I can do. Gabby?"

"Tea sounds great," she agreed.

"Be right back." Ethan placed a quick kiss on Gabby's

cheek and walked off in the direction of the house and its surrounding buildings.

"That man is a keeper," Dixie said with a wink as she watched him walk away.

"Yeah, he is." And Gabby really wished he was hers to keep.

"You might not believe in these things, but I knew the first time I saw you two together that it was meant to be. There's this energy between you. I can't describe it, but I know it when I see it." Dixie nodded her head, then bent to smell one of the many flowering roses around them.

"What?" Gabby straightened uncomfortably. Ethan had mentioned Dixie saying something like this to him, but she hadn't really thought about it since. She absolutely did not believe in love at first sight. Lust at first sight maybe, but love was a different thing entirely. It needed time to grow and took a lot of time to maintain, much like these flowers.

"I knew I was going to marry Ethan's grandfather the day we met. And we were blissfully happy for thirty years until cancer took him from me. I've seen it in other couples, too, and I'm always right. You might think I'm a crazy old lady, but I know what I'm talking about."

"Well, things are going really well for Ethan and me, but it's a bit early to be thinking about love and marriage and happily ever afters." Gabby busied herself reading the placard about the coral beauty roses in front of her.

"You might need to be patient with him," Dixie said. "He's probably going to be a complete idiot and do something stupid when things start getting more serious between you. He has a lot of baggage from his childhood that he doesn't like to talk about."

"I know." Gabby said the words quietly, tracing her finger over the delicate edge of a rose petal.

"Then you already know him better than any other woman he's dated."

"I don't know about that." Because she also knew that a whole lot of pain lurked behind his charming smile, pain that he wasn't eager to share with her or anyone else. Sure, they'd had a few moments when he'd let her in, but more often she could tell he was holding her at arm's length, trying to keep a distance between them.

"Well, I do." Dixie put a hand on her arm. "I'm just sorry I won't be around to see it when you guys finally figure it out."

Gabby swallowed over the sudden tightening in her throat. "I hope . . . I hope we don't let you down."

"You couldn't possibly. I only want him to be happy, and I know you'll both do your very best to that end."

Gabby nodded, her head swimming with guilt and regret. *But what if Dixie's right?* a tiny voice in her head wondered. What if she ought to fight for a chance with Ethan for real?

He came walking toward them then with three bottles of iced tea in his hands. "It's not fresh, but it'll have to do until you're ready to go up to the house." He handed them each a bottle and guided them toward a bench at the end of the path.

"It'll do just fine. Thank you, Ethan." Dixie unscrewed the cap from hers and took a long drink. She and Gabby sat on the bench while Ethan perched on the armrest, his hip against Gabby's side.

They sat for a few minutes, enjoying their tea and the view. But she knew they'd need to move inside soon. The sun had shifted from hot to scorching, and even with iced tea, they'd need to make sure Dixie didn't overdo it out here.

Already Gabby felt sweat trickling down her back, dampening the back of her skirt.

"Gabby?"

She looked up at the sound of an unfamiliar voice calling her name.

"Gabby Winters?" The middle-aged woman and man standing in front of their bench looked familiar, but it was taking her a moment to place them.

"Yes," she answered with a smile, trying not to feel like an idiot for not recognizing this woman who obviously knew her.

"Lois Barnes, I work with your mother," she said.

Ah, now Gabby remembered. Lois and her mom were both doctors at Carolinas Medical Center in Charlotte. Her parents had had Lois and her husband over for dinner many times, although it had been years now since Gabby had seen them. "Of course. It's so nice to see you." She stood to give Lois an awkward half hug.

"You remember my husband, George?" Lois gestured to the man standing beside her.

"Yes. Hi, George."

"Hello." George sounded bored.

Gabby turned toward the bench behind her. "This is my boyfriend, Ethan Hunter, and his grandmother, Dixie." At least in Dixie's presence she didn't have to fumble over what to call Ethan because, with Dixie, he was definitely her boyfriend.

Dixie and Lois complimented each other's hats, then Lois turned to Gabby. "How have you been? Your mother sure has been missing you at home." There was a hint of admonishment in the older woman's tone.

"I'm great. Mom and Dad came to visit just last weekend."

"That's right." Lois looked at Ethan with a new gleam in

her eye. "And she did mention that you were dating someone, an Olympic champion if memory serves."

"Two gold medals and one silver in Beijing," Dixie said
with pride.

Ethan flashed a megawatt smile but said nothing, always
reluctant to brag on his Olympic success. Gabby squeezed
his hand.

"Very impressive," Lois said. "I hear you may soon be
joining Harold at Lockhart Financial?"

Ethan straightened. "What's that now?"

Gabby's stomach turned to lead. She hadn't told Ethan
about her father's ridiculous offer. "Actually, Ethan's just
opened his own business in Haven."

"Oh." Lois frowned. "My mistake."

They made polite conversation for a few more minutes before Lois and George moved off down the path, but Gabby
couldn't shake the heavy feeling in her gut. It bothered her
more than it probably should have that her parents were going
around telling people Ethan was going to join her father at his
company. Why couldn't they accept him for who he was? And
for that matter, why couldn't they do the same for Gabby?

She glanced over at Ethan. He was smiling and laughing
as usual, but she knew better than anyone how skilled he was
at hiding his true feelings. Was he hurt? Angry?

He didn't say a word until later in the afternoon, when
Dixie had gone to the restroom. "You want to tell me what
that was about earlier?"

She sighed. "My dad offered to get you a job at the
company where he works. It was...insulting so I didn't
mention it."

He was quiet, but the rigid set of his jaw spoke volumes.

"I'm sorry," she said. "My parents are ridiculous. I already told them where to shove it."

"Appreciate that, but no worries. I'm sure they only meant to help." But as he walked off in the direction of the restrooms, Gabby felt an invisible wall rise up between them.

* * *

Ethan woke to the feel of Gabby's hands on him, stroking leisurely up and down on his shaft. He opened his eyes to see her facing him on the pillow, looking all sexy and sleep-rumpled.

"Good morning," she whispered.

"Sure as hell is," he croaked, his dick throbbing beneath her touch.

"I thought I'd get a head start since I'm here to help with your little problem this morning." She smiled sweetly, her innocent expression belying the way her hands worked him into a frenzy beneath the sheets.

"You just about gave me a wet dream." He pulled away before he came in her hands like a half-cocked teenager. "But I'd like to take my time and enjoy you this morning."

"Sounds good to me." She scooted closer, bringing her body against his.

He wrapped her leg around his hip and kissed her, slow and steady, until all the air between them had evaporated, their bodies pressed together, igniting a fiery friction everywhere they touched. They kissed while their hands roamed, exploring, touching, teasing. His cock was between her legs, and she rocked against him with a needy whimper.

He gripped her ass, grinding harder until they were both panting. She shifted her hips so that the head of his dick dipped inside her, and his eyes rolled back in his head.

"Condom," he gasped, clenching his muscles against the need to slide all the way home.

"Leave it off this time." Her breath tickled his neck. "I'm on the pill, and we're both clean. I want to feel you, just you, inside me."

"We shouldn't." He knew better. And yet, as she rocked her hips, taking him deeper, he was helpless to pull away. And as they made love in the soft morning light, he felt closer to Gabby than he'd ever felt to another human being, his skin on hers, inside her, taking them both out of their minds with pleasure.

Somehow it still got better every single fucking time.

"You have totally rocked my world," he whispered into her hair, their limbs still entwined, still panting for breath.

"Ditto." She pressed her forehead against his. "You have no idea how much."

But he did. Because he felt the same way.

"You helped me get my confidence back," she whispered against his lips.

He was starting to have trouble breathing. "You didn't need my help for that."

"I didn't think so either," she paused. "That's why I was so adamant about not making this real. I needed to do things on my own and on my own terms. But you make me feel sexy and...and *bold* in a way I never have before. You've shown me what a happy, healthy relationship should be like."

Fucking hell. He was the king of fucked-up relationships. He'd been born into one and never managed a real relationship with a woman since. He was the guy her parents only deemed worthy of dating her if he took a "real" job at her father's company.

And no matter how badly he wanted to be the man that Gabby thought he was, in the end he'd only wind up hurting her, too.

CHAPTER NINETEEN

Monday morning signaled the final countdown to the Adrenaline Rush on Saturday. So far, fifteen teams had signed up, a mixture of locals and race enthusiasts from out of town. Ethan had hoped for a bigger turnout, but this wasn't half bad, and hopefully there would still be a few last-minute signups.

Ryan had been busy planning all the logistics, hiring food vendors and all the other crap Ethan would have definitely forgotten about. When he wasn't putting the finishing touches on the course, Ethan was out and about in town trying to drum up more interest for the race and Off-the-Grid in general. Mark had spent much of the last week trekking through the woods, mapping out a course for each team to navigate by compass to find the clue that would lead them to the next part of the challenge.

It gave the race a unique spin from other Spartan-type races, and Ethan hoped it would be popular. He also hoped enough people would have trouble navigating with their compasses that it would drum up some interest for the survival skills classes Mark planned to teach once they'd officially opened for business.

Ethan had brought Gram along to the office today as she claimed to be withering from boredom at home all day by herself, which was probably true.

"Show me how the ropes course works," she said. "I want to be able to describe it to all my friends at book club on Thursday."

"You trying to help me out?" he asked.

"Well, of course. Is there an age limit?"

"No, but the course is fairly strenuous. There are definitely a few ladies in your book club I wouldn't recommend it for, but I'll let you be the judge of that."

"All the same, it might be fun to watch them try." Gram wore a positively evil grin on her face.

Ethan laughed as he shook his head. "So the ropes course starts here with the tires." He spent the next fifteen minutes demonstrating the course for her while she asked a million questions, most of which he had no idea why she needed to know, but hey, if she was able to drum up a few new participants from her book club, he wasn't going to second-guess her.

Just as he kicked off from the platform and soared over the pond on the hand trolley, he heard other voices coming from the bank. Women's voices.

Once he'd landed on the opposite bank, he turned and found himself facing Marlene, Helen, and Betsy from the Town Council.

"Hi, Ethan," Marlene said. "We just came to check in with you on your progress for the race this weekend. How are things going?"

"They're going really well," he said. "The course is

complete. We're just putting a few finishing touches on everything before the weekend."

"So this is part of the course for the race?" Betsy asked, gesturing around them.

"Yes. The race starts by the main house, where each team will receive a compass and directions to navigate to their next clue. They'll use that clue to get to the stream, where each team will receive a set of materials that they have to use to get everyone on their team safely across. From there, they'll follow a trail around the perimeter of the property with several obstacles along the way, ending here on the ropes course. Each team will need to successfully navigate the course together to finish."

"That sounds fun," Marlene said with a smile. "What's the prize if you win?"

"We've put together a prize package with donated goods and services from other local businesses in town, as well as local discounts for everyone who participates. And of course, a medal for everyone who completes the race."

"I like that you've involved other local businesses," Helen said.

"I heard the Haven Spa donated a full treatment package to the winning team to relax and unwind after the race," Dixie said.

"That's true," he confirmed.

"And have you had many people sign up?" Betsy asked. Of the three, she'd consistently been the most cynical. Even now, while the other two women were smiling and chatting with Dixie, Betsy maintained a sour expression.

"We have fifteen teams registered with a total of eighty-three race participants so far. We hope to exceed one hundred by race day."

Dixie's eyes gleamed with pride. "That is fantastic."

"It sounds like a good start," Helen said with a nod. "And you'll have all the facilities you need here on Saturday to host that many participants and whoever comes out to cheer them on?"

"Ryan has all of that under control," Ethan said.

"What about safety?" Betsy asked. "Will there be harnesses or nets to protect people?"

"Participants will wear harnesses on the rope bridge, but nothing else on the course requires safety gear. The zip-line course isn't part of the Adrenaline Rush, and the line over the pond here is low and slow enough so that anyone who falls will land safely in the water."

"Hmph," Betsy said, sounding unimpressed with that answer. "And what about first aid if someone does, God forbid, get injured?"

"Injuries are almost guaranteed," Ethan told her. "They happen at any race, and especially any race with obstacles. We'll have an ambulance here on standby in case of anything serious and first aid stations throughout the course to assist as needed."

"My granddaughter, Carly, signed up," Marlene said, her hands pressed together. "I'll be here cheering her on."

"That's great," Ethan said.

"What about Gabby?" Helen asked. "Will she be racing?"

"Unfortunately not," he said. "She's offered to volunteer here behind the scenes instead."

"Oh, that's a shame," Marlene said. "I was hoping to cheer for her. You know, the folks at the senior center are still talking about her. We're so excited she's coming to game night again this week."

"Oh, yeah?" He glanced over at Gram, who was grinning like a fool.

"Everyone loves Gabby," she confirmed.

"She's something, all right." Even Betsy was smiling.

Betsy? Smiling? Ethan just stared.

"I'll be here for the Adrenaline Rush, too, of course," Dixie said. "And as soon as this place opens for business, I'm planning to be the first customer on the zip-line course."

"Really?" He'd almost forgotten she'd said she wanted to ride the zip-line. Unlike the challenges in the Adrenaline Rush, just about anyone could ride the zip-line. It probably wasn't recommended for people with aneurysms just waiting to burst, but knowing Gram, he'd never talk her out of it. And having her as his first customer felt really right.

Having Gabby ride behind her felt even better.

"Oh yes," Gram was saying. "I've saved the best item on my bucket list for last. I can't wait. I want to ride the whole course, all five lines."

"*If* you receive the proper permits to open this place for business," Betsy said. "And just so you know, there are still several members of the council, myself included, who have some grave concerns about allowing a place like this here in Haven."

"Well"—Dixie raised her chin and shot Betsy a look—"I could ride the zip-line right now if I chose. Ethan can give rides to whoever he wants to on his private property without violating any zoning restrictions. But I hope I'll be riding as an official customer."

And dammit, Ethan really hoped so, too.

* * *

By Thursday, Gabby was getting the feeling that Ethan had added some space between them. She'd seen him only briefly since they got back from their weekend at the Biltmore Estate, once for lunch and once when she'd brought Dixie home after game night at the senior center.

Sure, she knew he was busy preparing for the Adrenaline Rush. But it felt like more than that. He was pulling away. No doubt he'd have dumped her long ago if not for their agreement. The thought of him being forced to stay with her for Dixie's sake really sucked, especially when Gabby was nowhere near ready to let him go.

And... *whoa*. These were not the thoughts of a woman committed to standing on her own two feet. On that thought, she took Lance for a walk then spent a very nice evening by herself drinking beer and playing video games online with a few of her coworkers.

On Friday, she brought sandwiches to the guys at Off-the-Grid as she often did. They wowed her with a demonstration of the ropes course. Her breath caught in her throat watching them boost each other over the climbing wall. It looked terrifying, but there was a whole lot of sexiness involved, too. Lots of tanned skin, toned muscles, and firm butts on display as they navigated the course together. All three of them were handsome, but her eyes never strayed far from Ethan.

"Want to join us?" he called from the rope bridge.

"Not even a little bit." She waved her hands in front of herself. "I'm enjoying watching you guys up there, though."

He flexed for her.

She grinned. "Yep. Great view from where I'm standing."

"That's because she's checking out your ass," Ryan said, giving his buddy a playful shove that set the rope bridge swinging.

Ethan grabbed on to an overhead rope to keep his balance, then shoved Ryan back, laughing the whole time.

Gabby sucked in a breath, her heart pounding. Her knees were shaking by the time Ethan made it safely to the far side of the bridge. She managed a smile as they took turns zipping across the pond. That part did look a little bit fun.

One benefit of their impending breakup was that she'd never have to find the courage to get up there herself. If they were dating for real, her own pride would force her up there sooner or later, with or without a little prodding from Ethan.

"So what do you think?" he asked as he came loping toward her, his skin gleaming with a sheen of sweat, his cheeks coated in enough scruff to be bordering beard territory.

Gorgeous, she almost said. "It looks great. A little terrifying, but I'm sure all the daredevils who've signed up for the race will love it."

"Sure hope so."

She thought she heard the tiniest amount of doubt in his tone. He had an awful lot riding on tomorrow's event. The whole future of their business might depend on it. She'd do whatever she could—from the ground—to help make the Adrenaline Rush a success.

After they ate, she went home to finish out her workweek. Everything for *Scion's Quest*, the game she was currently coding, was going according to schedule, but she'd been struggling with one code string since that morning. Once she'd gotten it straightened out, she planned to call it an early night.

She needed a good night's sleep because she'd be at Off-the-Grid all day tomorrow, helping out with the Adrenaline Rush. She was scheduled to work the registration desk in the morning and then float around wherever they needed her. Being a first-time event, there were bound to be kinks, and she was sure she'd be plenty busy.

Her phone pinged with a text message, and her heart

surged that it might be Ethan. But it was from Emma. Gabby's brow furrowed. She and Emma had hung out a few times but didn't generally text each other.

You around? was all Emma said.

Yep. What's up?

Mind if I stop by?

Well, she'd have to trade her pajamas for clothes, but otherwise... Sure, no problem.

She walked down the hall to put her bra back on and trade her lounge pants for a peasant skirt. Ten minutes later, Emma knocked at the front door.

Predictably, Lance dashed for the pantry.

"It's Emma," Gabby called after him. "She's the one who watched you last weekend when I was away. You like her."

No response.

With a shrug, Gabby pulled open the door. Emma stood there in black yoga pants and a purple tank top. "Sorry to bother you tonight, but I figured I might be more persuasive in person."

Gabby motioned her inside. "Persuasive?"

Emma clasped her hands in front of herself and drew a deep breath. "So you know I'm racing in the Adrenaline Rush tomorrow, and I've been looking forward to this for weeks. It sounds so fun, and it's an awesome chance to get to try some things I've never done, and our team—Team Flower Power—is the only all-girl team, so we really need to kick ass."

"Okay." Gabby nodded, cringing inwardly at the request she feared was coming.

"But Lisa, one of the girls I work with, came down with a stomach virus this morning, and it's a bad one. She can't keep anything down, and there's no way she's going to be able to run in the morning."

"Oh, I'm sorry. That sucks for her," Gabby said.

"It really does. That leaves me, Mandy, and Carly." She paused, giving Gabby a pleading look. "And you know, we have to have at least four team members to participate."

Gabby's stomach plunged right through her toes. "Oh, I...I can't. I'm really sorry, but I'm scheduled to volunteer all day."

"I'm sure Ethan would be happy to find someone to cover for you. Please?"

"Even if I could get out of volunteering, I've seen the ropes course, and there's just no way I could do it. I'm sorry." Gabby gulped air, feeling like a wimp.

"Oh yeah. You're afraid of heights, right?"

She nodded. "Terrified. So even if I agreed to join you, I'd only end up letting you down."

"Adrenaline is a great fear-buster. It's like being high, but better, because you're sober. Who knows what you might accomplish once you're out there?"

"Emma..."

Emma sighed. "You won't let us down. Maybe we won't finish, but without you, we can't even leave the starting line. I've asked everyone else I can think of, and you're my last hope."

Lance came trotting into the room, tail wagging at the sight of his new friend. Emma reached down to pet him, and he licked her hand.

"Okay," Gabby said quietly.

"Really?" Emma clapped her hands in excitement, and Lance darted several steps back toward the kitchen before deciding it was safe to stay.

"Assuming it's okay with Ethan." She twisted her fingers into the folds of her skirt. "But, Emma, I really don't think I'll make it through the ropes course."

"I think you will, but either way, we'll have given it our best, and that's all we can do, right?"

Maybe Gabby ought to adopt that as her new motto. But damn...just the thought of tackling that ropes course made her knees shake and her heart beat too fast. "I guess so."

"Okay. Unless I hear otherwise, I'll see you at Off-the-Grid tomorrow at seven. Oh, and wear this." She handed Gabby a purple T-shirt that read, TEAM FLOWER POWER.

"Cute shirt."

Emma smiled, then jutted a finger in Gabby's direction. "Seriously, be there. We're counting on you."

"I'll be there." She saw Emma out, then lifted Lance into her arms and carried him with her into the living room, where she settled him next to her on the couch. A sick feeling grew in the pit of her stomach. She was going to let Team Flower Power down tomorrow, and despite what Emma had said, that felt worse than accepting her limitations and staying on the sidelines.

Ugh. Why was she so eager to please that she'd let Emma talk her into saying yes? She stroked Lance absently with her left hand while, with her right, she dialed Ethan.

"Hey," he answered. "As it happens, I was just thinking about you, too."

"You were?" She pressed her knuckles to her lips with a smile.

"Yeah." He didn't elaborate, and an air of awkwardness fell over the line. No doubt about it, something between them had shifted, *changed*. He'd changed. He was pulling away.

"So I have a question," she said. "Could you manage tomorrow without me as a volunteer?"

"I'm sure I could swing it. Why?" A note of caution had entered his voice.

She sighed. "Somehow Emma just convinced me to join her team."

"No shit?" Now he sounded like Ethan again. She could hear the smile in his voice. "You're going to race?"

"In theory." She combed her fingers through Lance's soft fur.

"You totally got this. Need me to come over for a pep talk?"

As tempting as that sounded…"No. I'll be fine, and we both need our beauty sleep."

He laughed, and it tickled all the spots that had been missing him this week. "Seriously, though. You sure you're okay with this?"

Her heart melted at the concern in his voice. "I may not get far, but I'll give it my best."

"That's my girl," he said with pride. "And I think you'll go a lot farther than you think you will. In fact, I'm pretty damn sure I'll be giving you a victory kiss after you've crossed the finish line."

"I'm not going to make it through the ropes course."

"I wish I could have helped you practice on it, but it's already dark, and tomorrow morning's race time. But, and this might sound clichéd, seriously just don't look down. Have one of the other girls go ahead of you, and just keep your eyes on her the whole time."

"Okay." That might help. A little.

"I'll see you tomorrow bright and early," he said. "Sleep well."

"You, too." She hung up the phone and sat for a long time just staring at it. Then she walked down the hall toward her bedroom.

Eight hours later, she staggered out of bed, bleary-eyed. She hadn't slept a wink.

* * *

Ethan couldn't sleep. Two Olympic gold medals, and he'd never gotten nervous. But right now . . . he wasn't nervous exactly, but edgy. Restless.

Wishing he were in Gabby's bed.

Wishing he were giving her a pep talk as she got ready. She had to be scared to death. And he was so friggin' proud of her for tackling her fears like this. She was so strong, so much stronger than she gave herself credit for.

Finally, he gave up on sleep. It was just past five, and the sun hadn't even thought about peeping over the mountains yet. But there was lots to be done to get ready for the Adrenaline Rush, and he and the guys had to be there early.

He showered, doing his best not to wake Gram, but by the time he'd gotten dressed, she was in the kitchen fixing him breakfast. She wore a blue robe over her nightgown, her silver hair jutting from her head in all directions, and he had such a vivid memory of them in this house, her in the kitchen, looking so much the same as she'd fixed him a bacon and cheddar omelet before he boarded the flight to Beijing.

"My good luck special," she said as she placed the same omelet on the table. "You are going to kick butt out there today, sweetie."

"Thanks, Gram." He poured himself a cup of coffee and sat.

She slid another omelet onto her plate and sat opposite him with a cup of hot tea. "Marlene is bringing me by around eight so I can see the official kickoff."

"You're the best. You know that, right?"

"Well, of course," she answered playfully, but when she looked at him, her eyes were so tender, so filled with emotion, that his throat closed painfully.

He choked down the rest of his omelet, kissed her on the cheek, and headed for Off-the-Grid to start setting up. Mark and Ryan were already there—show-offs—running final safety checks on all the equipment.

Yesterday the porta-potties had been delivered, and they'd set up all the tables they would need for registration and refreshments. The race started at eight, with waves at eight fifteen and eight thirty to eliminate congestion on the course. After all the teams had crossed the finish line, their times and scores would be tallied and the winning teams would be announced.

He'd run the whole course with Ryan and Mark several times, and his only disappointment was that he wouldn't be competing today because it was a hell of a good time. His competitive nature fired up as the first racers began to arrive. It ought to be almost as exciting overseeing the event as participating, especially when he got to cheer for Gabby as she crossed the finish line.

They were short-staffed at the registration table without her so he stationed himself there, welcoming racers, handing out numbers and registration packets, and signing up those who'd decided to join at the last minute.

It was fun, and the turnout was great. Everyone looked pumped for the event. Some of the teams had even dressed in coordinating T-shirts and other outfits. And while he saw plenty of colorful accessories, he didn't see anyone who would be classified as "unsavory" by the Town Council.

TV crews from two local news stations were walking through the crowd, interviewing people. He recognized one of the anchors—Krissy Jenkins. They'd gone to high school together and dated briefly several years ago. He'd called her last week after Gabby suggested reaching out to the media.

Krissy stopped by the registration table, cameraman in tow, to ask him a few questions about the event for the evening broadcast.

"Good luck today," she said after they'd finished.

Ethan nodded. "Thanks for coming out to cover the event. I appreciate it."

With a wave, she headed off into the crowd, and he got back to handing out registration packets. The crowd just kept growing.

"Oh, shoot. You're stuck at the registration desk because of me."

He looked up to see Gabby standing on the other side of the table, wearing a purple TEAM FLOWER POWER T-shirt and black running capris, her hair pulled back in a ponytail fastened with a cluster of fresh-cut flowers, no doubt courtesy of Emma. "It's my event. The least I can do is show my mug here at registration."

"Do you need help?" She twisted her fingers. Judging by the dark circles under her eyes, she hadn't slept any better than he had.

"Sweetheart, I can handle the hell out of this. What about you? You ready?"

"As I'll ever be." She gave him a pinched smile.

He reached across the table and took her hand. "Remember, you're part of a team, and let the girls help you out. You'll help them, too, early in the course before things get elevated. Just focus on your teammates and never look down. You got this. No doubt in my mind."

"You're a lot more confident about that than I am." She tugged her hand from his and tucked a flyaway strand of hair behind her ear. "See you at the finish line."

"Atta girl."

She walked over to join her team, all dressed in matching

shirts with flowers in their hair. *Cute.* They were the only all-girl team, and he hoped they rocked that status.

Things got fast and furious for a while after that. He was so busy greeting and handing out registration packets that he barely had a chance to look up. When he did, the sight absolutely blew his mind. Off-the-Grid was packed, bursting with people, racers and spectators alike.

"Fucking awesome, man," Ryan said from behind him.

It was exactly as he'd envisioned it. Better. There was no way the Town Council could see this and not grant them their business permit.

"Hi. I'm here to register for the race."

Ethan turned toward the familiar voice and found himself staring into the smarmy eyes of Brad Mobley, Gabby's abusive ex.

CHAPTER TWENTY

Team Flower Power would be in the first wave of competitors starting at eight, and Gabby was both relieved and terrified about that. Relieved to get on with it because the anticipation was killing her, but terrified about what lay ahead.

She'd gone into the house to use the bathroom (as Ethan's girlfriend, she got to bypass the porta-potties, thank goodness) and was on her way to the registration area for a cup of water when she saw him.

Brad.

He stood at the registration table arguing with Ethan. *Oh God.* Brad was here and dressed like he intended to run the race. Ethan's expression was deadly. If she didn't get her butt over there and quick, they were going to fight, and she had no doubt Ethan would kick Brad's ass. As much as Brad deserved it, she didn't want that to happen. Not ever but especially not right now when she was already wound so tight with nerves, she was about to snap.

She jogged over to the table. "What are you doing here?" she demanded, relieved that her voice sounded strong. She sounded as pissed as she felt.

"News of your boyfriend's race traveled all the way to Charlotte. A couple of my buddies signed up, and I decided to join them." He was staring at her, and all she felt was furious.

"Over there. Right now." She pointed toward a big tree off to the side where they could talk without causing a scene.

"Bullshit," Ethan said, loud enough that he turned heads. "He was just leaving."

"The hell I was." Brad's ears were flushed, his body tensed for a fight.

Gabby cringed. Any minute now the fists were going to fly. But this was Ethan's big day, and no way was she going to let Brad ruin it. He wasn't worth it. She gave Brad a nudge, and with a final furious look at Ethan, he fell into step behind her and followed her to the tree.

She fisted her hands on her hips. "Go home, Brad."

"I have every right to be here. Your boyfriend can't keep me from registering." He stepped closer, too close, but she refused to give him the satisfaction of backing up.

She met his gaze evenly. "Actually, this is his private property, so I think he can."

"That's bullshit! Total bullshit."

The sound of his voice was like nails on a chalkboard. Gabby ground her teeth. "You've never run in a race before. We both know you're here because of me so let's just cut to the chase. What do you want? Why do you keep showing up here in Haven?"

Brad drew a deep breath. He paced a few steps away, dragging a hand through his hair. When he turned back to her, his expression had changed. "I want another chance with you, Gabby. We were good together."

"We were *terrible* together." She straightened her spine and stared him right in the eye. "You hit me."

He bowed his head. "That was a mistake, and I've apologized. It will never happen again."

"No, it won't, because I'll never give you the chance to do that to me again."

Something in her tone must have gotten through because he backed up, a startled look on his face. "But...I love you."

"No, you don't. You just want me back because I left before you were ready, and you like to be in charge of those decisions. But I made this one, Brad, and we are *finished*."

"No, we're not." Anger flared in his eyes again, the kind that used to make her shrivel in fear because she hated fighting.

But not today. "Yes, we are. There is not anything you could say or do that would ever convince me to give you another chance. I don't know how else to say it. I don't love you. I don't even like you. I don't ever want to see you again."

"You stupid, ungrateful bitch. After everything I did for you, you want to throw it all away for a fling with that loser?" He gestured to where Ethan stood behind the registration table, watching them, looking like a lion ready to pounce.

"Yeah, I do. Good-bye, Brad." She made it all the way to Ethan, fueled by anger and adrenaline, before her knees gave out. Her heart pounded, and her whole body shook.

Ethan was looking at her like he wanted to undress her right then and there, but instead he just held her in his arms until she'd stopped shaking. "I am so fucking proud of you."

And okay, maybe she was a little proud of herself, too. She'd finally told Brad off, hopefully for good. "Thanks."

"Now you're going to go out there and make me proud again, okay?" He kissed her, hard, so full of passion, but it was more than that. His kiss felt like all the words he'd never said: that this was real, that she was worth fighting for, that they had a chance together.

Tears stung her eyes. "Okay."

"You tell him to get packing?" he asked.

"Let him register. He's never run before. He'll probably fall on his face. It might be fun to watch." She managed a smile, but now that the adrenaline had faded, she sagged in Ethan's arms. Last night's sleeplessness, combined with her argument with Brad, had drained her.

"All right then." Ethan gave her an assessing look. "Here, eat this." He handed her a protein bar.

"Thanks." She opened it and took a bite, surprised to find her appetite had returned. When she'd gotten ready at home earlier, she hadn't been able to choke down a single bite of her breakfast. She ate the protein bar and chased it with a cup of water. "I better go find my team. It's almost eight."

He nodded, then pulled her in for another heady kiss. "Go get 'em, Tiger. I'll see you at the pond, okay?"

She nodded, then wove her way through the crowd of racers until she spotted Team Flower Power. Emma was busy fixing the flowers in Mandy's hair. Carly stood off to the side, kissing a guy that was—*holy shit*, it was Sam Weiss. Gabby tried not to stare, but she'd forgotten the girls had told her at book club that Carly was dating the famous rocker.

"There you are!" Emma said, sounding relieved. "We've been looking for you. I was afraid you'd gotten cold feet."

"Sorry," Gabby said. "I bumped into someone from back home."

Emma gave her a long look. "You okay? You look a little shaky."

"Just nerves. But don't worry, I'm ready to do this."

"Team Flower Power is going to kick some ass!" Mandy initiated a group fist bump. She did indeed look ready to kick ass. Beneath her purple team shirt and black knit capris, she was lean and muscular, built like an athlete.

Emma, though petite, also had an athletic build and looked ready to kick butt out on the course. Carly had a softer, curvier figure like Gabby's. She and Carly exchanged a nervous smile.

"Good luck, ladies," Sam said, waving as he turned to leave. "I'm going to go give Ethan a hand at registration, but I'll be waiting for you at the finish line."

A buzz rippled through the crowd as he walked toward the registration table. By the time he'd joined Ethan behind it, the table was mobbed with people—women in particular. Gabby saw a news crew headed that way, cameras blazing.

"There's a lot of star power at the registration table right now," Emma said with a giggle.

"Should be great publicity for the event," Carly said, and they all nodded.

Then Ryan was calling for the eight o'clock racers to gather at the starting line. Gabby gulped down her nerves and followed her teammates to the edge of the yard. Ryan read through the rules of the challenge for them one last time while Mark came around passing out a brown paper bag to each team.

"When I say go, you'll open your bag. Inside, you'll find a compass and directions to navigate to your next clue. Ready?"

Team Flower Power and the four other teams in the first wave all nodded and shouted in agreement. Adrenaline flooded Gabby's stomach.

"Go!"

A team in camouflaged clothes darted together across the field while everyone else remained where they stood to open their brown paper bag. Mandy, who'd been designated the team navigator, pulled out the compass, turning it over in her hand.

"Walk one hundred and fifty yards northwest," Emma read. "There you will find a trail with yellow markers. Follow it east until you reach the tree marked with an X. Your next clue is in that tree."

"Got it." Mandy stood, brow furrowed, tipping the compass as she turned slowly in a circle to orient herself. "Northwest is that way." She pointed toward the left side of the field.

"But that other team is going right," Carly said.

"I'm pretty sure we all have different directions," Emma said. "And some of them might not know how to read a compass anyway. Come on!" She took off at a jog across the field. Mandy overtook her to take the lead, while Gabby and Carly trailed behind.

The teams fanned out across the field, each headed into the woods at different points.

Team Flower Power entered the woods between two large oak trees, slowing to a walk as the vegetation became more dense. After a few minutes, they stumbled onto a thin trail marked with yellow ribbon tied around various tree branches.

"That was almost too easy," Carly said.

Emma smiled over her shoulder. "I told you we were going to rock this."

"East," Mandy said, pointing left.

They all fell into step behind her, jogging single file down the thinly cut path.

"X!" Carly said from behind Gabby, and they stopped to look where she was pointing. A tree to the right of the path had twine wound around it in a crisscross pattern, forming a thin X.

"That has to be it," Emma said. "Good eye, Carly."

No kidding. The rest of them had passed by the tree without noticing. Gabby's nerves had calmed some now, but while she hadn't held her team back—yet anyway—she hadn't contributed anything productive to their efforts either.

"Do you think we need to climb the tree?" Mandy asked.

"I'll climb it while you guys search around the trunk." Emma grabbed a branch, braced her feet against the tree's rough bark, and hauled herself up

Gabby walked around the tree, keeping her eyes on its gnarled roots, but nothing out of the ordinary caught her eye. If she were Ethan, where would she hide the clue? He was a straight shooter of a guy. He preferred a simple solution to something complicated.

Therefore, it made sense that the clue would be...

"Got it!" Mandy called, pointing to a brown paper bag wound into the twine at the back of the tree.

Yep. That sounded like Ethan.

"What does it say?" Emma called from overhead. She swung her feet down, dangling for a moment from a tree branch, then dropped to the ground.

Mandy removed a clue from the bag, leaving it for the next wave of racers. "Continue east on the yellow trail until you come to the blue trail. Take the blue trail northwest until you arrive at the stream. There you'll find a package of supplies marked with your team name. You'll use these supplies and whatever else you can gather from the surrounding woods to cross your team over the stream without falling in. If anyone falls in, that person must return to the starting side and try again. Once you've crossed the stream, you'll find directions to the next challenge."

Emma, Gabby, Carly, and Mandy set off at a jog down the path.

In the distance, she heard Ryan yell "Go!" as the next wave of competitors started out. She glanced down at her watch. Yep. It was eight fifteen. Soon they came to a larger trail, one Gabby recognized. In fact, it was the very trail she and Ethan had walked that awful day when they first met and she'd been attacked by yellow jackets.

Today, it had been marked with blue ribbon.

"Turn right," Mandy called, the compass still clutched in her hand. They all turned right, quiet as they jogged toward the stream.

The camouflaged team burst onto the trail in front of them, gave them a look, and took off running in the same direction. They jogged about ten minutes, during which time they were also joined by a team in red T-shirts, before they came to the stream.

The guys had selected an area where the stream ran wide and fast. Along its bank were approximately twenty rolled bundles, each labeled with a team name. Mark sat high on a rock, overseeing them.

Team Flower Power and the two other teams with them found and opened their bundles, hurrying to get across before the final two eight o'clock teams caught up. Inside their bundle were sticks and logs of varying lengths, rope, cloth, and a bottle of water for each team member.

Gabby drank while Emma and Mandy strategized. Carly was staring at the logs, a pensive look on her face. The camouflage team was already at work tying sticks together to make a makeshift bridge.

"These two are long enough to span the stream," Emma said, pointing at two logs. "We can slide them across and use the rope to tie the smaller sticks across them to make a bridge."

"Like what that team is doing?" Carly asked.

"Yeah, more or less."

"Or we could just try to balance beam on that biggest log to get across fast," Mandy suggested.

"I'd never make it," Carly said.

Gabby was remembering how she'd seen Ethan span the rope bridge back when it was under construction, the way he'd held on to an overhead rope for balance. "What if we run the log across, then Mandy can balance beam over to the other side holding one end of the rope. We tie the two ends to trees, and then the rest of us hold on to the rope as we go across for balance."

"That's brilliant." Emma clapped her hands in excitement.

Carly was nodding in agreement.

Mandy grabbed the end of the biggest log. "Okay, let's do it."

Together they helped her maneuver the log into place. It was no easy feat getting it across the stream with all of them on one side of the bank, but after a lot of work and even more swearing, they managed to swing one end of the log onto the opposite shore. They wiggled it until it settled into place securely enough not to roll beneath their feet.

The other two teams were still hard at work building bridges, but neither of them had laid anything across the water yet.

"Here I go." Mandy stepped onto the log. She bounced

lightly to test its strength, and then, with one end of the rope in her right hand and her arms out for balance, she started across.

Gabby watched, one hand pressed against her mouth, as Mandy inched her way across the log. Halfway there, it rolled a few inches beneath her, and Mandy landed in the stream with a splash. Laughing, she sloshed back to where she'd started. "Shit, this water is cold."

Gabby giggled as she remembered her dunk near this very spot when she'd been on fire with yellow jacket venom. "It's okay. No one else is even near starting across yet."

In fact, both other teams were watching with interest to see if the balance beam approach worked. Mandy started back out, and step by step, she crossed her way to the other side. They all yelled with excitement when she stepped onto dry land.

"Good so far," Mandy called. She tied her end of the rope around a sturdy tree, then Emma pulled it tight and tied it around a tree on the starting side.

"So who's next?" Emma asked.

"I'll go." Gabby took a deep breath, grabbed the guide rope, and stepped onto the log. The rope had a bit more give than she would have preferred, but it still did a good job of steadying her, and she made her way slowly and carefully to the other side without a single misstep.

Carly crossed next, and finally Emma, who took a tumble and had to start over. By the time Team Flower Power had crossed the stream, the camouflage team was laying their bridge over it, and a fourth team had arrived at the stream to begin building. A couple of volunteers rushed in behind them to begin disassembling Flower Power's balance beam to make room for new teams to build.

Gabby, Emma, Mandy, and Carly raced on. For the

moment, they were in first place, and that completely boggled Gabby's mind. But she also knew some of the hardest stuff still lay ahead. They jogged along a path through the woods headed for the ropes course, and her stomach grew heavier with each step.

They completed a few more obstacles along the way, and the camouflage team was back on their heels. It consisted of three athletic men and three equally fit women, and they were fast. Much faster than Team Flower Power.

But Flower Power was first on the ropes course, and therefore they got a head start on the first obstacle. The whole team had to complete each obstacle before they could move on. And up first were the tires, which, while tricky, weren't really all that terrifying.

Gabby was never more than a few feet off the ground, but she had to navigate from tire to tire all the way to the end without touching the ground. The tires swung and spun until she was dizzy. But by steadying each other, working slowly and carefully, the team made their way across.

Gabby had been doing as Ethan suggested, focusing on one obstacle at a time, and she'd been doing great. She was actually having fun, and they were *still* in first place!

They raced across the field, and *boom*, they were at the climbing wall, and just like that, her stomach dropped out through her feet. It was tall, so very tall. Ten feet, Ethan had told her. Straight up solid wood, and working together, they'd have to get everyone over it. On the backside, she knew, there was a ledge about two feet down so that the first person over the top could balance to reach back down and help their teammates.

On the other side of the field, she saw Ethan by the pond. He looked so official in his blue Off-the-Grid T-shirt and gray board shorts, ready to jump in and save anyone who might fall into the pond and need saving. It might even be Gabby herself, because she could totally see herself falling off the hand trolley halfway across.

But first, she had to get her butt over this wall. And then she had to conquer the rope bridge. *Oh God.* Her head spun.

"All right, girls. Are we ready?" Emma stood looking up at the wall.

"Ready," Mandy answered. "You're lightest, so maybe Gabby and I can boost you up, and then you can help from the top? Once I'm up, I can help pull up whoever's last."

Emma nodded. "Sounds like a plan."

The camouflage team arrived, and the men quickly started boosting the women up and over the wall. Not wanting to be left behind, Gabby and Mandy braced together and boosted Emma as high as they could go.

"I think I've got it." Emma grasped the top of the wall, reaching up with her right leg. Mandy braced beneath her, letting Emma put her left foot on Mandy's shoulder to get the leverage she needed to swing up and straddle the top of the wall. "Woohoo!"

Gabby smiled. Across the field, she saw Ethan flashing them a thumbs-up.

"Who's next?" Emma called down from the top.

"I'll go." Carly stepped up, and Gabby and Mandy repeated the process to boost her up, with the added help of Emma from above. Carly swung up and over and, with Emma's help, dropped safely to the ground on the other side.

The camouflage team cheered as their last team member dropped down on the other side. Emma shrugged from the top of the wall. "It's okay. We might catch back up, but honestly I never set out to win the race, and we're only the first five teams out of almost twenty anyway. But we're the only all-girl team so, just by crossing the finish line, we're winning."

"Damn straight." Mandy looked at Gabby. "I'm going to go up next, because Emma and I have the most upper body strength, so we can help to pull you up and over. Okay?"

Gabby nodded. The red-shirted team had arrived now, and another team she didn't recognize. A group from the eight fifteen wave. So much for any idea of coming in first. She didn't know if Emma was sincere about just wanting to complete the course, but for Gabby, it would truly be a win of epic proportions simply to cross the finish line.

Gabby braced her hands together and, as Mandy stepped into them, boosted upward with all her strength. Emma grabbed Mandy from above, and between the three of them, Mandy easily swung up onto the top of the wall.

"Ready?" she called down to Gabby.

"Yes." Gabby looked up at them, both reaching toward her. How in the world was this going to work? The wall loomed impossibly tall in front of her. Mandy and Emma's hands were just out of reach, much as her courage seemed always to be.

Her heart hammered, and her knees shook.

"Jump as high as you can. We'll grab your hands and pull, then kind of scramble with your feet until you can get one of your legs over. Okay?"

Gabby nodded. So *not* okay, but terrified or not, she was doing this. And by the time she zipped past Ethan on that hand trolley, she was going to be the strong, confident woman he already thought she was. She was going to scale this wall and leave her fears behind.

Determined, she took a deep breath and prepared to jump.

"Fancy seeing you here," Brad said from beside her, and

Gabby jumped, but not up toward her team. Away from him. Then she cursed herself for still being jumpy at just the sound of his voice.

She watched as his teammate boosted him up. He grabbed the top of the wall, flipped her the bird, and disappeared over the other side.

"Bastard," she muttered.

"Who was that jerk?" Emma asked from the top of the wall, eyes narrowed.

"An ex," Gabby said. "And I'm ready."

"Okay, we'll count you down, then jump as high as you can," Emma said. "Three, two, one...jump!"

Gabby jumped, hands outstretched. Her fingernails scraped over wood, and she scrambled but missed her teammates' hands, landing back on the ground.

"No worries. Again. Three, two, one."

She jumped. This time warm hands closed around her wrists, and she was hauled upward. Only after her fingers closed over the top of the wall did she realize her eyes were closed. She forced them open and dragged in a ragged breath. She was dangling from the top of the wall, Mandy's hand still gripping her right wrist.

"Now swing your legs," Mandy said.

Gabby tried to swing her legs, but they felt like lead weights, and her hands were starting to tire—she was never going to do this.

"You can do it," Emma said encouragingly. "Let go with your left hand and grab my hand, okay? I'll give you a boost."

But suddenly she didn't want Emma's help. Or Mandy's. Or anyone's. She'd been leaning on others, letting people help her out of a jam her whole life. Today she was going to do this, and she was going to do it on her own.

She kicked out with her right leg, reaching for the top of the wall.

"Grab my hand!" Emma called from above.

"Your fingers are starting to slip," Mandy said. "Grab Emma's hand. We'll get you up and over."

No. She was going to do this on her own, dammit. Her pride depended on it. She shook Mandy's hand loose from her right wrist. Her fingers burned, and as Mandy had pointed out, they were starting to slip. Desperate, she scrambled with her right leg again, but no dice.

"What are you doing, Gabby?" Mandy called. "Let us help get you over the wall."

"We're here for you," Emma said. "Grab my hand."

Gabby closed her eyes and put all her strength into one final swing. She kicked out with her left leg and swung high with her right. Her foot grazed the top of the wall, but her poor fingers chose that moment to give out. Her nails scored wood as she clawed wildly for a handhold, but she was free-falling.

Her stomach somersaulted as her worst fear came true. She plummeted to the ground. Her left ankle struck first, buckling beneath her. She crumpled into an awkward heap as her breath left her lungs in a whoosh.

"Gabby! Gabby, are you okay?" Emma's voice reached her from somewhere very far away.

White-hot pain radiated up through her left leg, and then everything faded to black.

* * *

Ethan stood by the pond, watching to see Gabby come over the top of the climbing wall. He'd been so fucking proud when he saw her team arrive first at the wall. They'd since been overtaken by several other teams, but they were still doing great, and he had full confidence she was going to conquer everything today.

This race was going to catapult her past all the fear and insecurity that had been holding her back. She'd finally realize how amazing she was, how strong and capable. And he was going to be here to see it.

Then someone screamed. Emma dropped from the climbing wall and started waving frantically in his direction. From the sidelines, two medics rushed toward the other side of the wall. The side where Gabby still was.

Ethan's chest constricted as he ran full-out across the field. He rounded the wall and found Gabby on the ground with the medics at her side, already surrounded by a crowd of onlookers. He crouched beside her. "What happened? Are you hurt?"

"My ankle." She gripped his hand, grimacing.

One of the medics felt along her spine, then asked her to move her head up and down and side to side. "Still no pain in your neck or back?"

Gabby shook her head. "Just my ankle. I landed full force on it, and it rolled under me."

"We'll get a brace on the ankle and get you over to the ambulance to finish checking you out," the medic said.

Ethan glanced down and saw that her left ankle was already swelling. "It's okay, sweetheart. Your ankle will heal."

Gabby nodded. Someone had pressed a wet cloth to her forehead, reminding him of the day they met, when he'd done the same for her after she was attacked by yellow jackets.

"You don't have good luck out here on my property, do you?" He laughed quietly as he gathered her in his arms and held her close.

"What I get for trying to climb over a wall," she muttered, pressing her face against his chest.

"Why didn't you grab my hand?" Emma said, crouching down beside them. "You scared the crap out of me!"

"I was trying to do it on my own." Gabby grimaced. "Now I've ruined it for all of you."

"Don't worry about it," Emma said. "We're just glad you're okay."

"Oh my goodness. What's happened?"

Ethan looked up to see Helen Arkin and Lorraine Hanaford rushing toward them. Fucking great. The Town Council showed up not to see all the amazing moments that had been made so far this morning, not the first team who ought to be crossing the finish line any moment now, but poor Gabby lying prone and injured on the ground.

"She fell and injured her ankle," he told them. "The medics are taking good care of her."

Helen looked up at the wall behind them, even now being climbed by three other teams. "Well, I can see how. My goodness!"

The medics finished bracing Gabby's ankle. "We're going to take you to the ambulance now, ma'am."

She looked up at Ethan, fear and humiliation in her eyes.

"I'll carry you." He stood with Gabby in his arms and carried her to the edge of the field, where the ambulance was parked. He set her gently on the cot inside. "I wish I could stay with you, but I've got to get back to my post."

"You get back to the pond, Ethan. I've got this." Gram pushed her way through the throng of people to take her place by Gabby's side. Gabby smiled weakly.

Relief loosened in his chest. "Okay. Thanks, Gram."

Ethan turned toward the pond. People were just starting to zip across it on the hand trolley. Cheers and whoops celebrated the first team crossing the finish line. Despite Gabby's injury, overall the day was going really well. The turnout was great, more than he'd expected. They'd surpassed the one hundred participants they'd hoped for, ending at one fifteen. They'd even had to add an eight forty-five wave of racers to accommodate the last-minute arrivals.

He was halfway across the field when he saw someone drop from the hand trolley into the pond, landing with a splash. He started to run, just in case. Seconds later, he heard screams.

"Oh my God, someone help!"

Ethan sprinted across the field and dove into the water.

CHAPTER TWENTY-ONE

*E*than surfaced with the disoriented swimmer in his arms. The man thrashed about like a feral animal, almost taking Ethan back under with him.

"Relax, man. I've got you. Just go limp and let me pull you to shore."

Thankfully, the man did as he said and went still, allowing Ethan to tow him to shore. A crowd had gathered, buzzing with concern. He helped the man onto the grass, where he sat gasping, but thankfully Ethan didn't hear any water rattling in his lungs.

"Thank you," the man said when he'd caught his breath.

"You okay? Did you swallow much water?"

The other man shook his head. "Think I just panicked when I hit the water. I'm not a very strong swimmer. Never figured I'd fall in."

His teammates surrounded him, patting his back and checking him over. Ethan stood and ran a hand through his hair, swiping excess water from it. The back-to-back crises left him jittery and unsettled.

"Yo, what the hell's going on?" Ryan pushed his way through the crowd, his brows knitted. "I just saw Gabby sitting in the back of an ambulance, and then I heard there was a near drowning here at the pond."

"It's okay. Everything's under control." Ethan looked back at the man he'd fished out of the pond. He was on his feet now, assuring the crowd of onlookers he was okay. "Gabby fell off the climbing wall and hurt her ankle, and this guy got disoriented in the water when he fell from the hand trolley. I pulled him out. He's fine."

Ryan leveled him with a hard look. "You need me to cover for you while Gabby goes to the hospital?"

He shook his head. "Gram's with her."

Ryan nodded. "All right then. I'm going back to the finish line to congratulate the teams and hand out medals as they finish."

Ethan watched as the man he'd pulled out of the pond walked off with his teammates. He saw the ladies from the Town Council watching, murmuring among themselves. Dammit to hell. And dammit, he did want to check on Gabby.

Soon. But racers were crossing the pond and heading to the finish line fast and furious now. He resumed his guard by the pond.

* * *

Gabby grimaced as she looked down at her ankle. The ER doctor had poked and prodded, then she'd been taken for X-rays, and now she sat waiting while her ankle throbbed, dulled only by the tremendous sting in her pride.

She'd been so intent on doing things her way, by herself, that she'd forgotten the whole point of the Adrenaline Rush, which was to work together as a team. And because she'd been such an idiot, she'd let her team down, and now they wouldn't get an official team placement in the race.

As if she'd read her mind, Dixie said, "Hurts not to finish, I know."

Gabby nodded. "I let my team down."

"Well, you did nothing of the sort. Anyone could have gotten hurt. It's the way these things go."

"Actually, this was pretty much my fault. I was trying to get over the wall by myself, to prove something to myself, and I didn't let them help me."

"Ah." Understanding shone in Dixie's blue eyes. "Well, just because that wall made of wood held you back doesn't mean you can't still scale the ones in your mind."

"I guess not." Gabby stared at her hands. "But it sure feels like it."

"We all have walls to climb, Gabby. You'll get over them when you're ready, just like Ethan's finally doing by opening himself up to you."

Tears stung Gabby's eyes. "He's not, not really." It just slipped out, as if she'd finally filled to bursting with guilt over the way they'd deceived Dixie. Or maybe the pain pills they'd given her had affected her tongue.

"Oh, I think he is." Dixie leaned forward and took her hand. "But my Ethan has a few walls of his own to get over. Has he told you about his parents? About how his mother died?"

Gabby nodded.

"He's a lot like Dawn, my daughter. They both would get these ridiculous notions in their head and never could let go of them, no matter how the situation changed. See, my husband and I had forbidden Dawn from dating Steve, Ethan's father. We saw what she was too young and naive to see: The guy was bad news." Dixie's eyes flashed with anger.

Gabby sat transfixed at this unexpected peek into Ethan's history.

"When Dawn got pregnant, she was afraid to tell us, afraid we'd disapprove, so she ran away with Steve. He was a terrible man, and he isolated her from us. We never heard from her again, never even knew we had a grandson."

"I can't imagine," Gabby whispered. The Hunters had endured so much pain, all of them.

"And when she finally found the courage to leave her husband, she clung to some silly, outdated fear of our disapproval, and instead of coming home to me in Wilmington, she ran here to the mountains and tried to make it on her own. If she'd only come back to me, she might still be alive." Dixie wiped a tear from her cheek.

Gabby pressed a hand to her chest. "Dixie, I don't know what to say."

"Secrets and lies can destroy a family." Dixie met her gaze, her eyes bright with anguish. "And Ethan is doing the same thing Dawn did, clinging to outdated beliefs. He's afraid he might turn out like his father if he ever settled down with a woman."

"No," Gabby whispered as tears flooded her eyes. "Oh, no."

"Nothing I can say or do will change his mind. That's up to you now." Dixie was looking at her like she held the keys to the universe.

Secrets and lies can destroy a family.

Gabby felt the air sucked from her lungs. Guilt rose up inside her until it threatened to swallow her whole.

"You don't understand. Our relationship wasn't real. Ethan wanted you to be able to die happy thinking that we were together."

As soon as the words left her mouth, she wanted to take them back. She'd wanted to clear her conscience, but instead of feeling relief, her stomach churned with nausea as she waited for Dixie's response.

Oh, Ethan. I'm so sorry...

She heard a rustle in the doorway and looked up and into Ethan's shocked—furious—eyes. She saw everything in that instant: hurt, betrayal, disappointment, and she knew she'd just made a horrible mistake. Her head swam with painkillers and heartbreak.

Before he could speak, before his grandmother even knew he'd overheard, a doctor stopped him in the hall, shook his hand, and walked off with him, talking a mile a minute.

Dixie had turned her head toward the window, her eyes misty. "Oh, honey, I'm no fool. I knew what Ethan did, and I knew why he did it."

"Wh—what?" Gabby sat forward, clutching her knees.

Dixie laughed softly. "When I told him I could die happy knowing he'd found you, I didn't expect him to start parading you around town as his new love. I know him better than that."

Gabby's heart took a nose dive. Dixie hadn't thought she and Ethan were meant for each other after all?

Dixie squeezed her hand. "Ethan is a stubborn, foolish man when it comes to his heart. When I said what I did, I only meant to give us both peace, because I knew what I knew, and I knew you guys would figure it out in due time."

"So you do think..." Gabby drew a shaky breath, still clutching Dixie's hand.

"Oh yes, I knew you two were meant for each other the first time I saw you together, and I have a spotless track record with these things. I didn't buy for a minute that Ethan had decided to get serious with you that quickly, but since he was putting on such a good show, I went along with it. I figured if you pretended long enough, eventually you'd figure out you weren't pretending at all. Am I right?"

Fresh tears leaked from Gabby's eyes. "I don't know."

Dixie dabbed at the corners of her eyes and smiled. "Don't try to fool me, my dear. Not this time."

Gabby's heart thumped painfully. No, she wasn't pretending. Not since their trip to the beach, maybe even before that. "I think...I think I'm falling in love with him."

"I know you are. It's written all over your face whenever you're around him."

She covered her face with her hands. "But I don't think it's the same for Ethan. He's pulling back." And he'd never forgive her for what he'd just overheard. She'd finally acknowledged her feelings for him out loud and simultaneously ruined everything.

"Oh, honey. If only you'd known him longer, you'd see how different your relationship with him is than with any other woman before you. He may think he's still pretending, too, but it's more real than anything he's ever done." Tears streamed down Dixie's cheeks. "I may not be here to see him figure it out, but please don't give up on him, because he needs you, Gabby, now more than ever."

* * *

Ethan stood outside the door of Gabby's exam room, his hands shaking with barely restrained fury. It had taken forever to disentangle himself from Dr. Nelson. The doctor had once patched Ethan up after he'd busted his collarbone falling out of a tree. Today he had talked Ethan's ear off about his son who would be a freshman at Pearcy County High in the fall and was interested in joining the swim team.

In the meantime, who knew what hell had broken loose in that exam room now that Gabby had spilled the beans about their fake relationship to Gram.

How could she? They'd had a deal. And...and he'd thought she really cared. For him and for Gram. Now he felt like he had ten years ago after he'd fallen out of that tree— like he could barely breathe past the painful crushing sensation in his chest.

He pushed the door open, not sure what to expect. How would Gram have reacted to the news? She might put on a brave front, but she had to be devastated. Inside the room, the two women were laughing. Both had slightly red-rimmed eyes, but if he hadn't overheard Gabby's earlier confession, he'd never have suspected a thing by looking at the two of them now.

Gram turned toward him with a wide smile. "Great news!"

Great news? This was great fucking news? He just stared. Gabby twisted her hands into the bedsheet beneath her, having the good grace to look ashamed.

"Her ankle is only sprained," Gram said.

"I just have to wear this boot for a little while." Gabby gestured to the orthopedic boot encasing her left ankle.

"That is good news." His voice sounded strange even to his own ears. After what Gabby had just done, neither of them had anything to say about it? *What the fuck?*

Gabby stared at him in awkward silence while Gram

chattered on about the race that morning. Before he could decide what to do, the door opened behind him and Marlene walked in.

"My ride's here," Gram announced, popping out of her seat. "Marlene and I are going to get something to eat, then she's taking me home. You take care of that ankle, Gabby. I'll check in with you tomorrow."

"Thanks so much for staying with me this afternoon." Gabby offered her a weak smile.

Gram gathered her purse while Marlene fussed over Gabby, and then they were gone. Gabby looked at him, her eyes shining with tears.

"What the fuck?" His voice shook.

"I'm so sorry," she whispered.

"How could you? Why?" He flung his hands in the air. He'd expected the rage, but not this feeling in the pit of his stomach like he'd just taken a hard punch. Whatever they were or weren't, he and Gabby had spent a hell of a lot of time together this summer and shared some crazy intense shit together. And whether he liked it or not, she meant a hell of a lot to him.

So this—this was betrayal. And it hurt like a son of a bitch.

"She was telling me about your mom. And she said secrets and lies can ruin a family. And"—she paused, and her bottom lip shook—"pain pills...I don't know. I'm so sorry."

"I had this one chance to fulfill her dying wish. One fucking chance." His voice rose, and he didn't care. "How could you do this to her?" *Or to me?*

Gabby looked down at her hands. "If I could take it back, I would. But—"

"I trusted you." His fists clenched, and his chest heaved.

No matter how hard he tried, he couldn't seem to catch his breath.

"Ethan—" She looked as destroyed as he felt.

"I just...I can't right now." He was already walking toward the door.

"No! Please. Let me explain—"

"Don't. I'll call Mark to give you a ride home."

"Ethan, wait!"

But he was already gone.

CHAPTER TWENTY-TWO

Gabby woke to a throbbing ankle and a sore heart. The cold fury in Ethan's eyes last night had cut right through her. And she deserved every bit of his anger. Sure, it had turned out okay because Dixie was a lot smarter than either of them had realized, but she had been totally wrong to confess.

She blamed it on the painkillers and an excess of adrenaline and emotion already pumping through her system. But if Dixie hadn't already known? If Gabby had crushed her dying wish just to ease her own conscience? Yeah, Ethan deserved to be pissed.

He hadn't called, hadn't spoken to her since he'd stormed out of her hospital room. She would give him today to cool off, but if he hadn't gotten in touch by tomorrow, she'd go to him to explain and grovel for his forgiveness.

Because what she'd told Dixie was true—she was falling for him. No, the truth was, she'd already fallen. Despite her best effort not to, she'd nosedived straight into love. She was standing on her own two feet all right, but with Ethan by her side, the path was a hell of a lot more fun than walking alone.

She wiped away tears as she dragged herself out of bed. Lance looked at her left foot as if it had morphed into a monster that might eat him, then he leaped off the bed. She hobbled to the door to let him out, then changed into a tank top and loose skirt to accommodate the boot. She'd taken it off briefly last night to shower off all the race dirt and sweat, and her ankle was a swollen, discolored mess.

But it wasn't broken. It would heal, just like her heart. She'd never seen Ethan as angry as he'd been yesterday. Oh, sure, he'd yelled. But it was his eyes that had really gotten her. They'd been dark with fury, but also hurt. He felt betrayed. By her.

And that was just the worst.

With a sigh, she hobbled into the kitchen and punched the button on her Keurig, then let Lance back inside.

A knock at the door sent her heart careening into her throat. *Ethan.* She rushed to answer it as quickly as she could manage in the stupid boot, her stomach flopping between excitement and dread because he was probably still furious.

Emma stood on the other side, holding up a bag from the bakery.

Gabby's whole body sagged in disappointment. She pasted on a smile as she opened the door. "Hi."

Emma handed her the bag and a cup of coffee with a laugh. "I don't think I've ever seen anyone look so disappointed to see me."

Gabby grimaced as she invited her in. "Sorry. I was hoping you were Ethan."

"Am I interrupting?" Emma paused in the doorway.

She shook her head. "No. I was hoping he'd come by, but we don't have plans." She led the way to the couch in the living room so she could put her foot back up. "Thanks so much for bringing coffee and whatever's in the bag."

"Cinnamon buns from Carly. We wanted to see how you were doing this morning."

"Oh, yum." Gabby opened the bag and breathed in the delicious scents of cinnamon and honey glaze.

"I'll go grab us some plates and napkins." Emma headed toward the kitchen with Lance at her heels.

"Thanks," Gabby called after her.

"So is it broken?" Emma asked after she'd taken a seat across from Gabby and they'd each helped themselves to a cinnamon bun.

She shook her head. "Just sprained. I rolled it when I landed. I'm so sorry I let you guys down yesterday."

"Oh please. Don't even worry about it." Emma bit into her cinnamon bun and moaned.

"I was so busy trying to prove something to myself I forgot to be a team player." Gabby bit into her own cinnamon bun and felt all her worries melt away, for a moment at least. "Man, these are good."

"It's no big deal, seriously. We wouldn't have gotten to race at all if you hadn't come out with us. As it was, we placed unofficially in twelfth place, according to Ryan. Although officially we didn't finish since the whole team didn't complete the course, but unofficial is good enough for me."

"That's great," Gabby said. "I'm so glad you kept going."

"It was awesome. That zip-line over the pond? So cool." Emma paused, and her eyes widened. "A man ahead of us almost drowned. Ethan had to rescue him."

Gabby gasped. "Really?"

Emma nodded. "I missed it, but I heard he was quite the hero."

Of course he was.

Emma's eyes narrowed. "You look all angsty. Did you guys have a fight?"

She put her cinnamon bun back on the plate, her appetite gone. "Worse. I told his grandmother something I shouldn't have, and he's super pissed at me about it. I'm not sure if we're still together, or... or what." She buried her face in her hands.

"Oh, my God. What did you tell Dixie?"

Gabby looked up at her friend. What difference did it make now? "That our relationship was pretend, for her sake. So that she could think Ethan had settled down before she dies."

"Holy crap! Really?"

She nodded miserably. "It was so stupid. I never should have agreed to it, but I did, and then things *did* turn real, for me at least. I felt so guilty about lying to Dixie... but it turns out she knew the whole time and was just playing along hoping we'd fall for each other while we were pretending, and oh my God, what a mess."

Emma laughed softly. "Take a breath. So Dixie already knew?"

Gabby inhaled shakily. "Yeah. She knew better than to think he'd fall for me so quickly."

Emma's lips quirked. "Well, she has a point. Ethan's got a reputation for a reason. He never gets serious, not even close. Nothing like what he has with you."

"But that was fake." Tears welled in Gabby's eyes. "He was just putting on a show for his grandmother's sake."

"Are you *sure*? Because you look pretty genuinely heart-broken right now."

"Because I was stupid and let it get real. But I don't think Ethan made the same mistake." She stared at the half-eaten cinnamon bun on her plate. It blurred as tears swam in her eyes.

"Oh, I don't know. You might be surprised. You've got to talk to him."

* * *

Ethan sat across from Gram at the Sunny Side Up Café. She'd insisted they go out to breakfast (right after she dragged him to church with her) to celebrate yesterday's Adrenaline Rush. In fact, she'd invited Ryan and Mark, too. He'd even had to fake a call to Gabby. Thankfully Emma's car was in her driveway as they drove past, giving her a legitimate reason not to join them.

"We had a few rough moments, but I'd call it a success overall," Ryan said.

"A total success." Gram raised her glass in his direction. "And boys, get that zip-line ready, because I'm going to ride it tomorrow morning."

"I thought you were waiting until we got our zoning?" Ethan said.

"Oh, I think I might be," she said with a wink.

"What do you know that we don't?" Ryan asked.

"Nothing for sure, but Marlene said you guys might be getting good news tomorrow."

"Excellent," Mark said.

"Yeah." Ethan felt the knot in his chest loosen. Last night, everything had been falling apart. Gabby had betrayed him, the Adrenaline Rush had been marred by safety mishaps, and then Gram had gone to bed early with a headache.

He'd barely slept, listening through the paper thin wall for the sound of her snoring. If she'd passed away last night, after the day they'd had...he wasn't sure he could have lived with that. But today was a new day, and whatever the reason, Gram seemed as happy and carefree as ever. It didn't lessen what Gabby had done, but it did make it a hell of a lot easier to breathe.

"It's the last thing on my bucket list," Gram said. "Riding that zip-line. One of you will be there to catch me on the other end, right?"

"Of course," Mark said with a warm smile.

"Well then, sign me up, boys. I can't wait." Dixie finished off her eggs Benedict and toasted them with what remained of her mimosa. "I'm so proud of you all, I just can't stand it."

"We couldn't have done it without you, Gram," Ryan said earnestly.

She turned to Ethan, her blue eyes warm and vibrant. "You've been quiet this morning, honey. I do wish Gabby could have joined us."

"Yeah."

Ryan's eyebrows went up. "Where is she?"

"She's with Emma," he said.

"We should have insisted they both come along," Dixie said, a hint of rebuke in her voice. "Poor Gabby, falling like that yesterday."

"I'll check on her later," he said. He should have gone last night, but he just couldn't bring himself to leave Gram. He was still too angry with Gabby to even form words. What was left for them to say?

Ryan was looking at him with a funny expression on his face. Ethan buried himself in the remainder of his omelet, trying his damndest to put Gabby out of his mind.

Instead, he spent the rest of the day with Gram. They hung out at her house, reminiscing over old photo albums. This was what was important right now: time with Gram. No matter that she hadn't mentioned it, she knew his relationship with Gabby was fake, so there was no need to rush over to her house to make amends for Gram's sake.

And the fact that nothing had felt right since he'd walked out on her yesterday made no difference. They'd had an agreement. She'd broken it. And he had no idea what to do now.

He made excuses for Gabby that afternoon after he'd put his phone on silent to avoid her calls. He and Gram watched some cheesy chick flick she'd been wanting to see, and she called it an early night.

He tossed and turned—again—his thoughts and dreams tangled up in Gabby, her scent, the feel of her in his arms, the stricken look on her face when she'd looked up and seen him in the doorway after she'd confessed all to Gram.

And dammit, despite the knife in his chest, he'd still woken hard and aching for her touch.

He rose with the sun and snuck out of the house without waking Gram. He drove to Off-the-Grid and let himself into the pool out back. He swam laps until all the kinks in his muscles were gone and his brain felt calm and focused.

Inside the house, he showered and changed, then sat and looked over some paperwork, enjoying the peace and quiet for once. He wound up on Off-the-Grid's Facebook page, reading comments that had been posted since the Adrenaline Rush. People were excited, asking when they'd be open for business and sharing photos from the event. He fist-pumped the air. Fuck yeah.

Somehow it had gotten to be nine o'clock, and he needed

to get back home to pick up Gram for her morning zip-line ride. His phone rang with an unknown number, and dread twisted in his gut. *Gram*...

"Ethan Hunter?" an unfamiliar female voice said.

"This is Ethan." He could barely breathe.

"This is Lorraine Hanaford with the Haven Town Council."

"Ms. Hanaford," he exhaled slowly, relief tingling in his veins. "How are you?"

"I'm doing well, thank you. I figured you'd want to know right away that we've just met, and the board has voted to allow commercial zoning for Off-the-Grid Adventures."

He popped out of his chair. "No sh—really? That's great."

She chuckled. "Thought you might think so. Well, the vote was not unanimous, just so you know. Please do be extra cautious about safety and keep the town's image in mind with your future events and marketing efforts."

"Yes, ma'am. I promise, you will not regret this."

"See that we don't."

He hung up with promises to do the town proud, then dialed Ryan and Mark with the news. His finger was on Gabby's number before he stopped himself. Later today. He'd go to her. It was past time for them to talk.

Meanwhile, he dashed out to the Jeep and drove home. Gram was going to get her final wish. She'd be their first official customer when she rode the zip-line this morning. So fucking perfect. He burst in the front door. "Gram!"

He'd expected to find her at the kitchen table, sipping tea while she checked the news on her iPhone, but the kitchen was empty.

"Gram?" he called again.

Her tea kettle wasn't on the stove, no cup in the sink. His chest turned to lead. *Gram.* Oh, no. Please, no. He walked toward the closed door to her bedroom, but he couldn't feel his fingers when he gripped the knob, couldn't hear anything but his pulse whooshing in his ears.

He lifted his fist and knocked. "Gram?"

Silence. The whole house seemed to have been sucked into a vacuum.

He knocked again, the sound echoing over the floorboards, rattling in his head.

Gram...

He pulled open the door as blackness tinged the edges of his vision. She lay in bed, on her side, eyes closed and peaceful, but he knew she wasn't asleep. *Oh, Gram. No.*

He forced his feet to walk, to cross the room. And he took her hand in his. It was cold. So cold. The world fell out from beneath him.

Gram was gone.

CHAPTER TWENTY-THREE

Gabby sat at the back of the church, knuckles pressed against her lips. The Haven Baptist Church was filled to bursting today. She'd come early and still taken one of the last seats. It seemed the whole town had come out to pay their respects to Dixie.

Through the sea of people, she saw three heads up front, apart from the crowd. Three big, strong men sitting together in the front row, Ethan's tousled blond hair in the middle. Mark and Ryan would become his family now, the only family he had left.

He'd been solemn, stoic, as he delivered the eulogy, but the heartfelt memories he'd shared hadn't left a dry eye in the house. Dixie had touched so many lives, been loved by so many people. Even Gabby.

The room spun out of focus as tears flooded her eyes. She wanted to be up front with Ethan. She wanted to hold his hand and kiss away his tears and help him through this.

Because she was absolutely heartbroken, and she'd known Dixie for only a month and a half.

"And now, I'd like us all to bow our heads and pray," the pastor said from the front of the church.

Gabby bowed her head and closed her eyes, feeling two tears trail down her cheeks.

I'm so sorry, Ethan.

The pastor spoke again, and then everyone was standing up, and the church filled with the murmur of voices. Gabby rose, grabbing on to the pew in front of her to steady herself, still off balance with the stupid boot on her left foot. Someone jostled her from behind, and she shuffled toward the aisle.

People crowded around Ethan, lining up for the chance to express their condolences. She needed to talk to him, needed desperately to apologize, to tell him how sorry she was for what he was going through. She wanted to throw her arms around him and tell him she loved him and beg him for a chance to see if this could work for real.

But she wouldn't line up with the rest of the town. She would wait until she could talk to him in private.

As she stood watching, he turned his head, and their eyes met. His were dark and empty. So empty. And yet the force of his gaze almost knocked her to her knees. Her whole body sizzled with it.

He'd avoided her calls all week, but he couldn't avoid her forever. They weren't finished. Not even close. Not if she had anything to say about it.

* * *

Ethan stood beside Gram's grave. While he'd been at home—at Gram's house—being plied with casseroles and

condolences by everyone in town, she'd been quietly low-
ered into the earth. Dead. Buried. Gone.

She lay beside her husband, Thomas Hunter, whom
Ethan had never met but who, by all accounts, had been
a great guy. A few feet to the left lay the empty plot
Gram had bought for her daughter, Dawn. Since no one
had known her relation to the Hunters at the time of her
death, Dawn had been buried in Silver Springs, where
she'd died.

Neither Gram or Ethan had been able to bring themselves
to sign the order to have her dug up and moved. So she remained in death how she'd lived her life...separated from
her family.

Ethan stared down at the freshly turned earth marking
Gram's final resting place. He imagined her up on the zip-
line at Off-the-Grid, grinning from ear to ear as she soared
over the forest. Why the fuck had she died before she got the
chance to do that? Why hadn't he insisted she ride it weeks
ago, when she'd still had time?

His throat swelled painfully.

"Ethan."

Gabby's voice filtered through the roaring in his ears, and
he didn't know whether to yell or kiss her. He turned slowly
and saw her standing at the edge of the little cemetery, still
wearing the black dress she'd worn to the funeral, her hair
pulled back from her face. And just the sight of her made
him lose his fucking mind.

"What are you doing here?" His voice was harsh, cold.

"Looking for you." She walked slowly toward him, her
gait hindered by the boot on her left foot.

"Well, you found me." He shoved his hands into the
front pockets of his black pants, wondering why he was
still wearing the suit he'd worn to the funeral. Why hadn't

he changed when he'd gone back to Gram's house after the service?

Why hadn't he taken Gram on the zip-line last week?

Why had Gabby betrayed him?

"I'm so sorry, Ethan. I can't even imagine what you're going through right now."

Yeah, he'd heard that before. So. Many. Fucking. Times.

"And I'm sorry for telling your grandmother the truth about our relationship." Gabby wrung her hands and blew a strand of hair out of her face. "I mean, I'm not sorry about how it turned out, but I'm so sorry for breaking your trust. I never should have done it."

"No, you shouldn't have, and I can't really imagine how you're not sorry about how this all turned out. What the fuck, Gabby?" His fists clenched inside the pockets of his pants.

She blanched. "Not *this*. I would have done anything to keep her from dying, but Ethan...she knew. Don't you see? She already knew."

"Knew what?"

"That we were fooling her. She said"—Gabby choked on a harsh laugh—"she said she knew you better than to believe you'd fall for me so quickly."

He tried to laugh, but it sounded more like a sob. *Shit.* Gram had known all along. Why had he ever thought he could fool her? "She always did know me better than anyone else. It still didn't give you the right to spill your guts like you did just to ease your own damn conscience. We had an agreement, Gabby, and you blew it."

She nodded, the movement jerky. "I did. I know. And I've been trying to apologize to you for a whole damn week."

"Well, forgive me. I've been busy burying my grand-mother."

She sucked in a breath. "And I wish I could have been there with you for that."

Her quiet words were knives to the gut because he wished that, too, somewhere deep inside. Something felt off…empty…without her. Which meant this whole thing was doubly disastrous because he'd stayed with Gabby for too long, let her become more than just a meaningless fling. "Deal's off. Gram's dead. You can go back to your own life now."

She took a hesitant step closer. "What if I don't want to?"

He inhaled sharply. "What are you saying?"

"I wasn't looking for a relationship, and I never would have jumped in so quickly with you if not for our deal." She paused, and when she looked up, the emotion in her eyes punched him hard, making his heart ache. "But your grandmother was right, at least for me. I did fall for you, Ethan, for real."

He saw the truth of her words reflected in her caramel eyes, and a warm feeling grew in his chest, seeping into the cold emptiness that had lived there since Gram died, since he'd walked out on Gabby after the Adrenaline Rush last weekend.

Then he glanced over his shoulder at his grandparents' graves, at the empty grave beside them where his mother ought to be. And he remembered the man who had put her there, the same man whose DNA flowed through Ethan's veins. "Don't do that. Don't make this more than it is. Sure, the chemistry between us was real. But that's all it was…chemistry. And chemistry has a habit of either fizzling or exploding. Guess what? *Boom.* We exploded."

She crossed her arms over her chest and glared at him. "Well, that's the stupidest thing I ever heard. If you're too scared to see if this could be a real relationship for us, then at least man up and say so."

He swung to face her, but no smart comeback rose on his tongue. He was just so fucking tired. "Just go home, Gabby."

She, too, looked defeated. "If you change your mind, you know where to find me."

"For a few more weeks anyway," he said. What was she spouting all this about feelings anyway? She was leaving town soon, and he'd never leave Haven.

She looked down at her feet. "Right."

"Good-bye, Gabby." And since she didn't make any immediate move to leave, he pushed past her and walked to the Jeep. Because every moment with her stirred all kinds of emotions inside him that he didn't want to feel. Ever again.

* * *

Gabby stood alone in the cemetery, staring at the freshly turned earth over Dixie's grave. *Please don't give up on him*, Dixie had said to her that afternoon in the hospital. "I haven't, Dixie. I'm trying."

She sat next to Dixie's grave and hung her head. "I do love him, but I have no idea what he's feeling or what to do. He's so hurt and angry right now." Her voice broke, and tears streaked her cheeks. "I miss you too, you know? You were a pretty awesome lady. Ethan was so lucky to have you in his life."

She sat for a few minutes, arms clasped around her knees, listening to the birds chirping and the wind rustling in the tree branches overhead. "I don't know if he'll want to try for a real relationship with me, but I promise you he'll be okay.

He's got Ryan and Mark to look out for him and Off-the-Grid to keep him busy. And I'll stick around long enough to give him a chance to change his mind about us, I promise you that, too."

She closed her eyes. It'd been a long time since she'd been to a cemetery or grieved a loss like this. She'd known Dixie only a short time, but she was one of those people that made a big impression. Gabby would always remember her warm smile and vibrant personality, the way she'd waltzed right in and taken Gabby under her wing when she'd been trying to hide away from the world in her cabin.

A loud buzzing sounded near her ear, and her eyes snapped open. A dark shape hovered beside her head, and *oh my God*, it was the biggest bug she'd ever seen. The horror of the yellow jacket attack reared in her memory, and this time Ethan wasn't there to save her.

She swatted at the thing with a shriek, but when it zipped off to the side, she saw that it wasn't a bug at all. It was a hummingbird, and *oh*, it was actually adorable! She'd never seen one in person before, had no idea that their wings moved so fast that they made the same buzzing sound as an insect.

The little bird hovered for a moment, looking at her, its wings a blur of movement, then it darted off in search of nectar in the nearby trees. She watched as it poked around in the honeysuckle blooms lining the perimeter of the cemetery, and with a smile, she remembered the honeysuckle body spray she used every morning.

The one Ethan liked so much.

Maybe the little bird had liked it, too.

She climbed to her feet, still awkward in the boot. Today marked a week since her accident, and her ankle no longer hurt unless she walked too much on it. She had an appointment on Monday to see about getting the boot off, and she couldn't wait.

Because she had some *very* important things to do once she could walk on her own again.

"I'll be back, Dixie, okay?" She wasn't sure why she was talking to the woman's grave, but she couldn't seem to help herself. "I'll be sure to let you know how things turn out, and if I leave town, I'll come and say good-bye before I go."

CHAPTER TWENTY-FOUR

*E*than gave the equipment a final check. He'd already checked and rechecked everything, but somehow, just minutes before Off-the-Grid officially opened for business, he found himself up on the platform going over it all one last time.

"All good?" Mark called from the ground.

"Ready to rock and roll," Ethan said.

"Now let's hope someone actually shows up for a ride today," Ryan said with a wry smile.

Because of the delay caused by the Town Council, they hadn't been able to hype any kind of grand opening event, but the Adrenaline Rush had helped to get their name out. A lot of people had signed up for their newsletter and followed them on social media.

So it was feasible a few people might show up. Ryan's rock-climbing lessons and Mark's survival skills classes had to be booked in advance, so they were banking solely on zip-line rides today. Until they'd built up more of a clientele, this would be their main event.

"Well," Ryan said. "It's almost ten so I'm going to mosey on over to the office and get ready just in case."

"I bet someone will show up." Ethan came down the steps from the platform, walking toward the house between Mark and Ryan. "And we'll make sure they have the time of their lives and invite all their friends to come back tomorrow."

"I think we'll see our first real business this weekend," Ryan said. "By then, word will be out that we're open. People will be looking for something fun to do on their day off, and some of the tourists in town might be curious, too."

"I think you losers are way overthinking this." Mark opened the back door and led the way inside.

The clock on the wall in the newly converted lobby read nine fifty-nine. They all stood staring at the front door as if it was going to burst open promptly at ten and fill the reception area with eager adventurers.

It didn't.

Nothing happened at ten o'clock. Or ten fifteen. They grew bored of watching the front door and turned to their own devices. Ethan played *Candy Crush* on his phone, trying like hell not to think about how bad he wished Gram were here taking that first ride on the zip-line. Ryan sat in his office inputting numbers into a spreadsheet. And Mark puttered around in the kitchen doing...well, Ethan had no idea what he was doing, but it involved peanut butter and the food processor.

"We're going to need a better way to manage our time than sitting around waiting for customers to show up," Ethan said at ten thirty after they'd spent a half hour doing just that.

Ryan poked his head out of his office. "Speak for yourself. I've been busy in here."

"I beat level three hundred in *Candy Crush*." Ethan waved his phone in the air.

"I can keep an eye on things here if you want to get some stuff done on the property," Ryan said. "There's a checklist of low-priority things I left on the table in the kitchen."

"On it." Mark snatched up the note and headed for the back door.

Outside, a car pulled into the lot. Ethan, Ryan, and Mark all stared at the front door.

"This could be our lucky day," Ryan said.

Ethan stepped behind the reception counter, ready to greet whoever came in the front door and hoping like hell it would be a paying customer and not someone from the Town Council checking to see if they'd maimed any tourists yet.

The door opened, and Shirley Meyers, the town nurse, walked in with Marlene Goodall at her side. Both women wore sweatpants and T-shirts, looking ready for their aerobics class...or maybe even a zip-line ride.

"Morning, ladies." Ethan greeted them with a big smile. "What can I do for you?"

Shirley put her hands on the counter. "Well, you see, I made a deal with your grandmother, and I'm here to uphold my end of the bargain even though she's not here to see it."

Ethan's smile faltered. "What?"

"Well, hon, she talked me into going on that zip-line with her. Me, Marlene, Victoria, Joan...and I'm not sure how many others. We were all supposed to ride together, but now we're here to ride in her honor." Shirley paused, and her expression softened. "She promised it would be fun and that we're not too old."

Ethan swallowed past the hard lump in his throat. "She

was right. It'll be one of the most exhilarating experiences you've ever had, and there is absolutely no age limit."

"That's good news because I just turned seventy-two," Marlene said. "I've been thinking it looked kind of exciting every time I've been out here."

"Truth be told, I'm terrified," Shirley said. "But a promise is a promise, and I would do anything for Dixie. I'm honored to ride that zip-line for her."

The front door opened, and two more women walked in, Gram's friends Victoria and Dorothy, followed by Joan. By the time Ethan had gotten their paperwork, the crowd in the lobby had grown to ten, all friends of Gram's and all over the age of sixty. Ryan joined Ethan to help get everyone paid and waivers signed.

"The full zip-line tour will take about an hour and a half," Ethan said. "I'll give everyone the safety spiel and demonstration here on the ground, and then I'll take you up on the platform."

The women nodded, their faces ranging in expression from genuine excitement to complete horror. Ethan walked them through all the safety information they would need while Ryan and Mark went around fitting them with harnesses.

Ethan led them up the steps to the platform, and ten minutes later, Shirley soared out over the treetops. She let out a screech that startled birds out of the trees.

"Oh, Lordy," Marlene said as Ethan clipped her harness onto the line.

"Don't you worry," Victoria told her. "I think she just had the time of her life."

Sure enough, by the time Ethan had gotten them all across the first zip-line and joined them on the next platform, the general consensus was that it had been fun. And two hours later, as he led them through the woods back to the house, they were chattering excitedly and showing off selfies they'd taken along the way.

If only Gram could have been here to ride with them.

An empty feeling settled in his chest, nagging at him through the rest of the day. Grief, maybe. But the woman whose face he saw when he closed his eyes smelled like honeysuckle and felt like home every time he held her in his arms. And it had been a long fucking time since he'd held her in his arms.

He pushed Gabby out of his mind as a young couple entered the lobby. They had a handful of afternoon zip-line customers, but nothing like the morning marathon of Gram's friends. By closing time, they were restless, a combination of excitement and boredom, and so they found themselves, by unspoken mutual agreement, sharing a pitcher of beer and a platter of wings at Rowdy's.

"To Gram," Ryan said as he lifted his frosted mug.

"To Gram." Ethan clunked his beer to Ryan's as Mark chimed in beside him.

The three of them drank in silence. Ethan's beer splashed into the gaping void inside him, cold and unsatisfying.

"Doesn't feel real that she's gone." Ryan set his mug on the table.

"But she sure as hell saved our asses today," Mark said quietly.

"It's true," Ryan said. "Thanks to her, our first day was a pretty decent success. And if any of those ladies are half as chatty as Gram was, they'll send more business our way."

"We can hope." Ethan stared into his beer.

"I *know* those ladies are chatty." Mark chuckled as he plucked a wing off the platter.

"It was a good start. I made notes on areas where we can

improve," Ryan said. Then as Ethan and Mark both gave him dirty looks, he added, "Yo, just doing my job. We'll figure out the rough spots as we go. Someone booked a survival skills class through the website today."

"Yeah?" Mark's dark eyes gleamed. "That's cool."

"Great," Ethan said.

"You were right," Ryan told him. "Thanks for dragging our sorry asses back to Haven to do this with you. Off-the-Grid is going to be epic."

"Yeah." But Ethan couldn't muster any excitement of his own. It was going to be great, no doubt. And he'd feel like celebrating soon. Just when he didn't feel like an empty shell about to be crushed under the weight of his own misery.

Ryan snagged a wing off the pile and pointed it in Ethan's direction. "You going to tell us why we haven't seen Gabby around lately?"

"Gram's gone."

"And? Please don't tell me you just ditched her when Gram died."

"Not just because Gram died, but that was our agreement, after all."

"Shit, man." Ryan shook his head. "That's harsh. You could have at least stayed with her through the funeral."

"And don't even pretend it was all fake." Mark gave him a look Ethan imagined might have made the men under him in the Army squirm in their uniforms. "Because you're not that good an actor."

Ethan rubbed the back of his neck. "The chemistry was real. But then she told Gram the truth about our relationship."

"Why the fuck would she do that?" Ryan asked.

Ethan shrugged because he still didn't know. "She claims it was a combination of her conscience and pain meds."

Mark shook his head. "She wouldn't last a minute in the military."

Ryan laughed. "No kidding. But seriously, that blows. Was Gram upset?"

"That's the kicker. Apparently Gram was on to us from the start. She was just playing along hoping we'd fall for real while we were pretending."

"And I'd say she was right," Ryan said.

Ethan's chest felt too tight. "That's what Gabby said, too. My fucking fault for even pretending to have a real relationship."

"So she fell for your sorry ass, huh?" Ryan shook his head as he bit into another wing.

"Apparently."

"And you dumped her rather than see if there might be anything real on your end, too?"

Ethan set his mug down so hard, beer sloshed on the table. "I dumped her because of what she did to Gram."

"Which was apparently only telling her something she already knew," Ryan said. "And that sucks, but in the end, no harm was done. Are you sure none of this has anything to do with baggage from your own fucked-up childhood?"

"What are you, a shrink?" Ethan glared at him. "Who fucking cares if my lousy childhood is why I don't want to settle down and get married?"

"Because if you're holding back because you're afraid you'll turn into your father, then that's a problem."

Ethan slammed his fist into the table. "Dammit, we all know I have his temper. Forgive me for being smart enough to realize it before I put myself in a situation where I might do something unforgivable."

Ryan and Mark both stared, their expressions almost comical.

"Fuck you both." Ethan shoved back from the table.

"Sit your ass back down," Ryan said, his voice harder than Ethan had ever heard. He sat. "I should have seen this and set you straight sooner. I'm sorry I didn't. But I'm telling you now...you do *not* have your father's temper."

"No?" His fists clenched. "You haven't been hassling me all summer to watch myself in front of the Town Council?"

"Oh yeah, you're hotheaded, and you run your tongue like an asshole sometimes, but would you ever hit a woman?" Ryan leaned forward, slamming his own fist onto the table. Heads swiveled in their direction.

Ethan stared into his beer. "I'd like to say no, but I'm not willing to take the chance."

"That's bullshit," Mark said. "Have you ever raised your fist at a woman? Ever felt even the tiniest urge to hit the woman you're with?"

"No. Shit, no." He glanced toward the bar, saw the bartender watching, making sure they weren't about to brawl.

"That's because you'd never do it," Ryan said. "I've known you since you were ten, man. Even when you were a punk-ass teenager picking fistfights left and right, you've never given me any reason to believe you'd ever be anything but a fucking knight in shining armor for your future wife."

"It's true," Mark said.

"Doesn't matter." Ethan shook his head. "I'm happy with my dating life the way it is. No reason to change things."

"Are you happy?" Ryan asked. "Because you look miserable."

"I buried my grandmother two days ago, asshole."

"I bet Gabby could put a smile on your face," Mark said. "If you let her."

"Gabby and I are done." He couldn't go there. Not now. Not ever.

"Now I realize I'm no expert on the subject"—Ryan held his hands up in front of himself—"but from where I was standing, you and Gabby looked pretty hung up on each other these last few weeks. *Both* of you. And now you look miserable without her. I think we've established that you'd never, ever hit her. So why the fuck aren't you driving to her house right now, begging for another chance?"

* * *

By the time he left Rowdy's that night, Ethan wanted nothing more than to drive to Gabby's house, yank her into his arms, and lose himself in her warm, welcoming body. But wanting her didn't mean it was a good idea, and anyway he was too toasted to do anything other than stagger home with Mark and Ryan. He climbed the stairs to his condo, slammed the door behind him, and collapsed onto the bed, asleep before his head hit the pillow.

He woke to a dull ache in his head and the all-familiar and overpowering ache for Gabby, one that he was beginning to think might be a permanent morning status. Would he ever stop needing her this way?

Because he'd certainly never spent two months wanting the same woman before. By now, the flame between them should have burned out. So why was she still the last thing on his mind when he went to bed and the first thing on his mind when he awoke?

Why couldn't he get her out of his head?

They'd been broken up for over a week, and yet the thought of going to Rowdy's to pick up some random chick held about as much appeal as getting a root canal. He wanted Gabby. Only Gabby. Forever Gabby.

And *fuck*. Ryan was right. He needed to get his ass over to her house and beg for her forgiveness. Why had he ever thought she was just another girl he could date and leave before things got complicated? Things with Gabby had been complicated from the moment they met. Gram had seen it. And Gram was never wrong.

He rolled out of bed and into a hot shower to make himself presentable, then popped two ibuprofen and chased them with a glass of water and a candy bar. Breakfast of champions.

And the whole time, he was thinking about Gabby. Her smile. The way her eyes gleamed like warm honey when she was excited. The honeysuckle scent of her hair. The way it felt when her arms were around him—like nothing else in the world mattered.

Because she was everything.

He grabbed his keys and raced out the front door. The wind whipped in his hair as he drove the deserted early morning streets of Haven. Maybe he shouldn't show up at her front door at seven o'clock in the morning, but dammit, he couldn't wait another minute to see her.

Except when he got to her cabin, she wasn't there. The lights were off, and her SUV wasn't parked in the driveway. And disappointment turned into flat-out panic that she'd already left town.

But he tamped it down. Chances were she'd gone out for breakfast with Emma, and if she had left town, well, he could look up her parents and track her down that way if he had to.

He turned the Jeep toward Off-the-Grid. Without Gabby, the only way to tame the emotions churning inside him right now was the pool. He pulled into the lot, went inside to change into a pair of trunks, and dove in.

The water hit him like a cold slap to the face. A much-needed cold slap. His legs started kicking, his body falling into familiar rhythms as he swam. His first few laps were fast and furious as he worked out all the extra adrenaline, then he slowed to a steady pace until his body had cooled.

But not even the chill of the pool could cool the fire raging in his heart.

* * *

Gabby couldn't explain why she was sitting in front of Dixie's grave at seven o'clock in the morning. She only knew she hadn't been able to sleep, and for whatever reason, in death, Ethan's grandmother seemed to have become her most trusted confidante.

She sat with her elbows hooked around her knees against the chill of the early morning mountain air. A whole summer in Haven, and she still hadn't gotten used to that. In Charlotte, the temperature never cooled once summer hit. Two o'clock in the morning and it could still be eighty-five and muggy.

Her boot had been downgraded to an Ace bandage yesterday, and Gabby had decided that was good enough. "I've got something important to do this morning," she told the grave in front of her. "I needed to do it a while ago, but I'm really good at putting stuff off. I've spent my whole life putting things off because it was just easier that way."

A hummingbird darted out from the nearby bushes, and this time Gabby smiled. "So cute. I wish you were here to see it. But I came here this morning to tell you something. You never got to do the last thing on your bucket list, right?

You wanted to ride Ethan's zip-line more than anything. And that thing scares me silly. But I'm ready to get over my fear of heights."

She paused and watched as the hummingbird was joined by a friend, zipping about together in search of fresh nectar. "Actually, I'm ready to get over fear in general, and I think the zip-line is a good place to start. So I'm going to ride it this morning. For you, Dixie, and for me. If you're up there somewhere, watch over me and make sure the rope doesn't snap, okay?"

Gabby blew out a breath and stood, shaking off the dirt that had gathered on the back of her yoga pants. Off-the-Grid didn't open until ten, but she was planning to have been and gone before the guys showed up for work. She was doing this for herself, not for Ethan. But he'd showed her how to work the harness that other day when she'd almost jumped, and she knew the combination to the lock on the gear box.

So she would harness up and zip across to the second platform. She didn't need to ride the other four sections of the zip-line. One would be enough to scare a few years off her life and hopefully fling her right past her fear of heights.

She waved good-bye to Dixie and climbed into her SUV. Off-the-Grid was only a five-minute drive from the cemetery, which was good because any longer and she might lose her nerve. No, that wasn't true. Nothing was going to deter her today. She was doing this.

Ethan's red Jeep was parked in the lot. Gabby felt the air whoosh from her lungs. She hadn't counted on him being here so early, hadn't wanted to see him, not with those cold, angry eyes replacing the vibrant blue ones she'd fallen in love with.

Oh yeah, she loved him.

And she'd stick around Haven until he'd healed from Dixie's death enough to know if he might love her back. But this morning, she just wanted to ride the zip-line and be on her way. With a sigh, she pulled in next to his Jeep and walked up to the house.

It was dark inside, the front door still locked. She walked around back and heard a faint splash from the direction of the pool. *Of course.* He'd come here early to swim, as he so often did. Perfect. He couldn't see the zip-line from the pool so he'd never know she was there, but he might actually hear her scream if the line snapped and she plummeted to her death, so that was good. At least she wouldn't lie out there on the forest floor for hours waiting to be found.

She laughed at herself. She was *not* going to die this morning. She wasn't even going to get hurt. Nope. Not happening.

She limped down the path toward the zip-line, her heart pounding. A cold sweat popped out on her forehead and slicked her palms. Her knees shook like Jell-O as she climbed the steps to the platform.

Don't look down.

Ethan's advice came back to her. She looked straight ahead, all the way to the platform at the other end of the line. It was far, but not so scary as long as she kept her focus on it and not the ground fifty feet below.

She went to the box where they stored their gear, punched in the combination she'd watched him use before, and opened it. Carefully, she fastened a harness behind her thighs and around her waist, snugging it as tight as she could get it. No wiggle room to fall out.

All right then.

She inched her way forward to the middle of the platform and reached up to clip the harness onto the line. And she looked down. *Oh God.* Her head swam as she took in the ground so far below. Had the platform started to sway, or was that just her legs?

Oh. She slumped to her knees with an embarrassing squeak. Her heart felt like it might burst out of her chest at any moment. Her head spun. A sour taste filled her mouth.

No. Nope. She was not giving up. Not this time.

She sucked in a deep breath and held it as she climbed to her feet. Dammit, she was doing this, and she was doing it now.

The clasp on her harness clamped on to the metal trolley with a solid clink. She squeezed her eyes shut and tensed her legs to kick off.

Here goes nothing...

"Gabby, wait!"

She opened her eyes to see Ethan sprinting down the path wearing nothing but wet blue swim trunks. And at the sight of him, her knees gave out again, dropping her in an ungraceful heap on the platform.

CHAPTER TWENTY-FIVE

*E*than could hardly believe his eyes when he got out of the pool and saw Gabby up on the zip-line platform, ready to jump all by herself. He raced toward her, hardly feeling the sticks and stones on the path beneath his bare feet.

Gabby was here. And holy shit, she was about to jump. And she was *here*.

He took the steps three at the time, bounding onto the platform. Gabby sat there, pale and shaky, staring up at him with wide eyes. He gripped her hands and tugged her to her feet, wanting desperately to crush her in his arms, but he was soaking wet and ice cold, and he owed her an apology first in any case.

"I wanted to do this before you saw me," she said, nodding toward the zip-line behind her. The zip-line she was attached to—backward.

"And I am so fucking proud of you, but unless you're certified, you should never jump alone." He held on to her fingers lest she get any ideas.

Her chin went up. "I paid attention when you showed me the gear last time."

"I see that, and you did a great job. But"—he ran his hand up the line attaching her harness to the trolley overhead, showing her the twist in the nylon—"you attached yourself backwards, and I don't recommend trying it that way. Not on your first run anyway."

"Um..." She looked up at the cable, and he could practically see the courage leaking out of her.

"You should always have one of us inspect your gear before you jump." He slid his hands over her harness, checking all the buckles and straps, trying not to feel her up while he was at it. Gabby sucked in a breath regardless. "But once I've inspected you, I assure you this ride is a hell of a lot safer than your drive over here. Nothing's going to happen to you up here. Got it?"

She nodded.

"Now I need you to stay right here on the platform while I go back down and run over to the next platform to catch you, okay?"

She frowned. "I don't need anyone to catch me. That's why I wanted to do this by myself."

"You're going to jump by yourself, and that's the important part. I'm just here to make sure you don't get hurt on the other end." He thought of the way she'd gone down on the climbing wall, trying so hard to make it over by herself instead of leaning on her team. "Gabby, some sports are team sports for a reason, right? The idea isn't to play every position on the team, just your own. And right now, your job is to jump off this platform, keeping your hands right here." He wrapped her fingers around the hand hold at the top of the harness. "Hold on tight, and have the ride of your life, and I'll catch you on the other end."

She looked into his eyes, her gaze hitting him like a jolt of adrenaline. Her caramel eyes gleamed with emotion, that warm, sweet spirit that made Gabby so special. His heart was pounding like a jackhammer, but the empty, aching void in his chest was gone. Just standing here with her filled him with this weird, warm feeling he had no name for.

Love. Holy shit. He was in love with Gabby. Of course. Of course he loved her. Gram had been right all along. Hell, the rest of the town had been telling him for weeks how much they all loved her. Why had he been the last one to figure it out? And was there still a chance for them? He'd been an ass, pushed her away when he'd needed her most.

"I'm sorry," he whispered.

Her eyes widened. "For what?"

"For everything. I was an idiot. I screwed things up, but I'm not going to ruin this moment for you. You jump, and then we'll talk." He gripped her fingers. "Wait for me. I'll give you the all clear, and then I want you to count to five and jump, the bigger the better. Wait for me," he repeated as he let her go.

She stood still as a statue, watching as he raced back down the steps and over the path to the next platform. He stubbed his toe on a rock and held in a swear because it would all be worth it when Gabby came soaring toward him over the line.

He raced up the steps and stood at the edge of the platform looking back at her. Gabby was just a tiny figure at the other end of the line now, too far away to see the expression on her face, but he had every confidence she was going to do this.

"Whenever you're ready," he called.

On the other platform, Gabby didn't move. Had she heard him?

"All clear!" he shouted.

She took a tiny step forward, and then, if he wasn't mistaken, she started shaking her head.

Hell, no. She'd come too far to back down now. "You got this, Gabby."

"No, I don't," she shouted back.

"There's something I really need to tell you when you get here," he shouted.

Gabby shook her head again. "What?"

"There's something I need to tell you!"

"I can't." She reached up as if she was going to unclip herself from the line.

"I love you." The words just slipped out, ricocheting through the trees from his platform to hers, but he didn't want to take them back. He loved her so much that he wondered how he'd ever not realized it, how he'd ever thought he could give her up and go back to living without her.

She froze. "Wh—what?"

He cupped his hands around his mouth and shouted, "I love you! Now please get over here so I can finish apologizing for being such an ass these last few weeks and beg for your forgiveness."

Gabby was silent for several long beats, long enough that he started to worry he'd waited too long to come to his senses. He'd been too big of an idiot. And then she jumped. She twirled out into the air, her feet kicking as she let out a wild cry—half scream, half whoop.

He stood rooted to the spot as she zipped over the woods toward him. As she came closer, he saw that tears streaked her cheeks. And she had a white-knuckled grip on the harness. But she was smiling! She soared onto the platform, but instead of putting her feet down for a landing, she lifted them. Her body slammed into his, nearly knocking him off his feet.

He wrapped his arms around her as her legs went around his waist, anchoring him to her. He reached up and un-clipped her from the line before it yanked them off balance. "I love you," he whispered against her lips.

Gabby pressed her forehead to his. "I love you, too. So much."

He wound his fingers into her hair and kissed her, slow and fierce. "I'm sorry it took me so long to figure it out and for all the many ways I was a total jerk these last few weeks."

She shook her head, fresh tears streaking her cheeks. "You had every right to be mad. If Dixie hadn't already fig-ured it out, I might have really upset her, and right before she died. I don't know how I would have lived with that."

"Luckily, she was smarter than the both of us." He tight-ened his arms around her. "I feel like I've spent my whole life running away from my past, but I never could get away from it."

She met his eyes. "I don't think anyone ever does."

"Probably not. But now that I let it catch up to me, it feels…okay."

"I'm glad." She pressed her lips to his. "I don't want to run away from things anymore either. From now on, we only run to each other. Deal?"

"Gabby, I would run to you any damn day. Every damn day for the rest of my life."

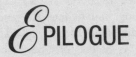

EPILOGUE

Gabby hung by her fingertips, the rough wood biting into her skin. Her feet kicked against the wall, seeking but not finding purchase.

"Gotcha, sweetheart." Ethan's shoulder landed beneath her right foot, and as he straightened, she boosted herself up to swing her leg over the top of the wall.

Straddling it, she looked down at him. He was staring up at her with that trademark charming smile on his face, but the love in his eyes made the smile that much more authentic. Her chest swelled with pride, for herself for making it to the top of this damn wall, and for him for overcoming the hang-ups from his past to trust her with his heart.

"Here I come." He jumped up and grabbed the top of the wall, swinging himself up to sit facing her with a ridiculous lack of effort.

She scowled at him. "Seriously, you could at least make it look like that was hard for you. It might boost my confidence or something."

"Making things look easy is my specialty." With a wink, he swung over the other side and landed on the ground with all the grace of a cheetah.

Gabby blanched as she looked at the ground ten feet below. The scene of her infamous, ridiculous fall during the Adrenaline Rush. But today she'd scaled the wall. With Ethan's help, she'd mostly overcome her fear of heights these last few months. Last week, she'd ridden the entire zip-line course, and it really had been awesome. Life in general had been pretty great since she'd decided to stay in Haven.

"Whenever you're ready," he called.

She drew a deep breath and swung her left leg over the wall. As she again dangled by her fingertips—this time on the far side of the wall—Ethan's hands came around her waist, ready to catch her.

But when she let go, she fell like a rock, knocking him off balance. They tumbled to the ground together, arms and legs tangled. Well, she'd made it over the wall in typical klutz style.

"I keep falling into you like this." She giggled.

"I don't mind."

She popped up to her feet, dusting herself off. Ethan put one knee up, then paused, reaching toward his right thigh.

"Oh, no. Are you hurt?"

Ethan was shaking his head, a wide smile on his face. He reached into his pocket and pulled out a little black box, and *oh my God*, he was on one knee. No way. She clapped a hand over her mouth.

He pulled the box open and held it up to her, revealing the ring inside, an intricately carved silver band with three delicate diamonds in the center. It was exquisite. Tears sprang into her eyes.

"It was Gram's," he said, his own eyes suspiciously glossy. "She'd want you to have it, don't you think? Will you marry me?"

"Oh my God." She laughed as tears streaked her cheeks. "Yes."

He took her left hand in his and gently slid the ring into place. It was a perfect fit. The diamonds winked up at her, and she knew Dixie was beaming down on them, wherever she was. They had just made her final wish come true.

"Wow." Ethan looked down at her hand, still clasped between his big, masculine fingers. "That looks even better on you than I could have imagined." He looked up, and their eyes met.

A hummingbird darted past, and Gabby smiled. "I think your grandmother approves."

"She is having a dance party up there right now." He turned his eyes toward the sky.

"I know it. I'm so happy, Ethan." So happy she felt like she might burst with it.

"Me, too." He leaned in and kissed her again. "Thank you for helping me get here."

"Likewise. Now if you don't mind, I've been waiting a long time to try out that hand trolley over the pond."

He grinned. "You got it."

He stayed right behind her as she traversed the ropes course and over the swinging bridge. Her head swam, and her knees shook, but she kept walking slow and steady until she'd made it to the other side. They high-fived when their feet once again touched the ground.

"It's go time," he said as they walked toward the pond.

Gabby reached up and grabbed on to the hand trolley, the diamonds on her new ring winking in the sunshine. She smiled. "Here I go."

"Enjoy the ride," Ethan called as she kicked off and soared.

"Oh, I will." The wind whipped through her hair, and she whooped for joy. It felt like flying. And what a ride it would be from here on out, with a wedding to plan and a happily ever after to live with Ethan.

Emma Rush is the good girl who has always done what's expected of her. But when tattooed Ryan Blake returns to town on his motorcycle, Emma is sure she's found the perfect man to help her walk on the wild side...

A preview of *Crazy for You* follows.

$\mathcal{B}$y eleven, only a handful of people remained at the bar. Ryan poured a scotch on the rocks for a man sitting alone near the door. Based on the way he fiddled with his bare ring finger, Ryan pegged him as either going through a divorce or a man looking to mess around on his wife. Neither option sat well when he caught the dude staring in Emma's direction.

He walked over to her. "Why are you sitting here alone at the bar on a Monday night, Em?"

She looked up at him, her blue eyes bright and twinkling with mischief despite—or maybe because of—the drunken giggle that revealed how much beer she'd consumed tonight. "Because I'm having fun."

He smiled in spite of himself. "Wouldn't have pegged you as the type."

She gave him a funny look. "Well, I'm trying to broaden my horizons."

"Hang tight," he told her, then went down the bar to settle up with the trio of tourists. They left him a sweet tip before heading out into the night. He wiped down the bar as he made his way back to Emma. "You ready for me to call you that cab?"

"What time are you off?" she asked.

"We close at midnight."

She leaned closer, and her floral scent teased his nostrils. "Any chance you could give me a ride?"

"It's the first week of March, and I only have my bike. You'd be more comfortable in a cab." And so would he, because the sight of her here at the bar, all that silky hair loose around her shoulders and the sexiest hint of cleavage showing at the neckline of her shirt...it was doing all kinds of weird things to his mind. Like making him fantasize about her on the back of his bike, her arms around his waist. Her lips on his. Emma in his bed, screaming his name.

"I've always wanted to ride on a motorcycle," she said softly.

"You've never..."

She shook her head. "So what do you say, will you be my first?"

Ah, hell. *Derek's little sister.* He repeated the words in his head until he'd dragged his mind out of the gutter. "It's cold out there. You're not dressed to go for a ride."

"I only live a few miles down the road. I'll survive."

This was a terrible idea. He should insist she take a cab, for his own sake if not for hers, but... "All right then, if you don't mind waiting around while I close up."

"Not at all. It's kind of fun hanging out at the bar by myself. A couple of guys have even flirted with me. Maybe I should let my hair down more often. What do you think?"

He thought those guys were too smooth for a woman like Emma, and if the cheater by the door tried to put a move on her, he might "accidentally" spill a drink in the douche's lap. "I think you're beautiful however you wear your hair, but it does look really nice tonight."

She sat up straighter. Yeah, he hadn't expected to hear himself say that either.

"Thanks."

He grabbed a cloth and wiped down the bar, more as a distraction than out of necessity.

She leaned closer, those blue eyes hitting him like a punch to the gut. "I'm trying to shake things up a little this year, not be so much of a goody two-shoes."

He blinked. "Say what?"

"I want to have some fun." She smiled, not the practiced take-me-home-tonight smile he received from so many women every time he tended bar, but a warm, honest smile that seemed somehow much sexier. "I'm thinking about getting a tattoo. And I want to sign up for rock-climbing lessons when you guys get started back up again."

His brain got fuzzy somewhere around the mention of a tattoo. "Oh, yeah?"

She nodded, tucking a lock of hair behind her ear. "It looks exciting."

"Almost as good as a ride on my bike." And dammit, he was flirting.

"You could bring all kinds of excitement into my life," she said with a giggle, reminding him that she was borderline drunk.

"Water for you until we close," he said, plunking an empty glass on the bar in front of her, which he filled from the tap.

She grumbled but took it without protest.

Ryan ventured down the bar to check on the cheater by the door and the other lone couple still remaining. The couple paid their tab and left, leaving only Emma and the cheater. And luck must be on Ryan's side because that guy paid up, too, and headed out into the night.

"I've never been the last one at the bar before," Emma said, watching as he cleaned up.

"The place is dead tonight. Monday night outside of tourist season."

"Can I help?" she asked as he placed dirty mugs into the dishwasher beneath the counter.

"Nope, but I do appreciate you keeping me company." He hadn't paid much attention to her when they were kids, but grown-up Emma was pretty cool, even if she was totally messing with his head tonight.

She chattered away while he cleaned up the bar. Jason,

the manager, swung through and flipped the sign on the door from OPEN to CLOSED. Emma went to the restroom while Ryan finished up in back.

"Since when did you start picking up chicks during your shift?" Jason asked.

"Since never," Ryan answered. Business was business and not to be mixed with dating, no matter how many women he casually flirted with while he tended bar. "She's an old friend who needs a ride home."

"On your bike?"

He shrugged. "Only ride I've got. I've known Emma since she was a kid. She's just a friend."

"Whatever you say, man." Jason slapped him on the shoulder and headed for the back door.

Ryan turned to find Emma in the doorway, a funny smile on her face. "It might sound better if you said you'd known me since *we* were kids, instead of since *I* was a kid."

"Same thing, isn't it?" He zipped his jacket and led the way toward the back door.

"As long as you're not still thinking about me like I'm twelve," she said with a wink as she pushed the door open ahead of him. She wore a blue jacket now, not nearly thick enough to keep her warm on his bike.

He glanced at her ass. Yep, she was definitely all grown up now. "You sure you want to do this? If Mark's still up, I could get his keys and drive you home in his SUV."

"I'm positive I won't freeze to death in the time it takes you to drive me home."

"All right then." It was cold tonight, but he'd always found it exhilarating to feel the icy rush against his body as he rode. Emma might regret her decision later, but she was right, she wouldn't freeze to death in the time it took to get her home. "You got gloves?"

She pulled a pair of black gloves out of her pockets and slipped them on.

He led the way around the corner and down two blocks to the renovated building he, Ethan, and Mark had bought condos in last year. Ethan's condo was noticeably empty these days as he spent more and more time at Gabby's place.

Emma walked up to the Harley and rested her hand on the handlebar. She turned to look at him with a gleam in her eyes. She really did want to ride on it. Well, he'd be damned. Maybe he'd underestimated her.

He unlocked the door to his first-floor unit and grabbed the spare helmet he kept for just this occasion. Except usually the woman riding on the back of his bike was someone he was either sleeping with or hoping to sleep with. *But this is Emma.*

"You ready?" Ryan asked as he held it out to her.

"You have no idea." She took it with a smile and slid it onto her head.

And…*fuck*. The combination of the skintight jeans, jacket, and his helmet on her head was too much. He'd never been able to resist a woman dressed to ride, let alone a woman on his bike. Which meant he was crazy to give her this ride.

He handed her a pair of glasses, then put on his own helmet.

"What are these?" she asked.

"Eye protection." His slid his pair into place. Too bad they did nothing to obscure his view of Emma, because damn, she was turning him on big time right now. Those jeans… "All right, wait for me to give you the all clear, then you're going to put your left foot on the peg, grab my shoulders, and climb on."

She nodded, excitement dancing in her eyes.

He mounted the bike, settled himself, and cranked the engine. It roared beneath him with barely leashed restraint. This bike was his pride and joy, the first thing of value he'd ever bought for himself. He'd worked his ass off for this beast and never regretted a single penny he'd spent.

Once the engine settled beneath him, he gave Emma a nod. As she swung into place, her hands settled on his waist, searing his skin even through all the layers of their clothing. No doubt about it, she was going to be his undoing tonight.

* * *

Whoa. Emma closed her eyes and let out a shriek as Ryan guided the bike onto Main Street and picked up speed. The cold wind whipped her face, taking her breath away. Beneath her, the engine rumbled and roared like a wild thing. *Holy shit.* She was on the back of Ryan Blake's bike, and it was amazing.

The wind bit through her thin knit gloves, hitting her fingers with an icy blast. Actually, every part of her was freezing, but she didn't care. She wrapped her arms more firmly around Ryan's waist, anchoring herself to him so she didn't tumble off the back of the bike, and somehow her hands slipped beneath his jacket. *Ahh.* That was better. Toasty warm, and also...her hands were on his T-shirt. Even through her gloves, she felt the hard contour of his abs, and nope, she wasn't cold now.

And this was absolutely freaking amazing.

She hung on tight as he guided them over Haven's twisting mountain roads, deserted at this hour. Overhead the moon shone like a beacon, illuminating the night in its soft, silvery glow. The roar of the engine and the slap of the wind against her face shocked her senses. It was thrilling, invigorating, so completely different from riding inside a car.

She'd never have done this if Mandy hadn't dared her, and now she felt like her eyes were open for the first time in years. *This* was what she needed. Somewhere along the way, as she sat at the bar talking to Ryan, she'd realized she was having fun, *really* having fun. And she wanted more. She wanted it all, every last wild and crazy fantasy.

All too soon, her building came into view. Ryan cut the engine and guided them quietly into the driveway, coming to a stop behind her Honda Civic.

"Don't worry," she told him. "I share this place with students. They're probably still up, but if not, I've suffered through enough of their late-night parties that they'd sure as hell better not complain about a little motorcycle noise." She rented the front half of this multi-unit cabin. The back half had two apartments, both occupied by college students.

He turned his head to look at her, so sexy in his helmet and riding glasses. "So how was it?"

"Even better than I thought it would be." She gulped for air. His lips were way too close to hers, and she was still a little bit drunk on beer and a whole lot drunk on her first motorcycle ride. Mandy's words echoed in her ears, *Bonus points if you kiss him. Just stand up a bit, lean over his shoulder, and kiss him...*

Emma leaned forward, her chest sliding up his back as she tipped her face to his. Holy hell, she had completely lost her mind, but she was going for it. Every nerve in her body went haywire.

Clunk. Her helmet smacked into his, drawing her up an inch short of his lips.

Ryan sucked in a breath, his dark eyes locked on hers.

She froze. Oh God, this was so embarrassing! She was pressed against him, her hands still on his waist, her face so close to his, so awkward, so obvious she'd been about to kiss him. Foiled by the stupid helmet.

"Emma." His voice was low, his face a blank mask behind his glasses.

"Um—" Well, now the moment was ruined, and she felt like a total idiot. She scrambled off the bike, pulled off her helmet and glasses, and turned her back to him.

He came up behind her, put a hand on her shoulder, and spun her to face him. "What just happened?"

She just shook her head, crossing her arms over her chest.

He stared at her for a long second, looking so disreputably rumpled, she almost went for it again—this time without helmets to get in the way.

"You had too much to drink tonight."

"I'm not drunk." Or wait—maybe she should have let him think she was. That might be less embarrassing, and it's not like she was totally sober, after all.

His gaze slipped to her lips. "It wouldn't be a good idea."

And there it was. She absorbed the sting of his words. "Oh. You don't—I mean, I get it. Those other women at the bar are a lot more—"

"Emma," he interrupted her, his dark eyes nearly knocking her off her feet with their intensity, "it's got nothing to do with them. You're…any guy would be lucky to kiss you, but I can't." Something flickered in his expression. It almost looked like desire…for her.

Whoa. "Why not?"

A muscle in his jaw flexed. "You know why."

She jabbed a finger at him. "Don't you dare bring up my brother right now."

"I promised him I'd look out for you. I specifically promised him that I would *not* take advantage of you."

"Well, that's insulting because I wouldn't call anything that happened tonight you taking advantage of me. And that was over ten years ago, Ryan." She paused as hot tears pressed against the backs of her eyes. "Derek's gone."

The words hung between them, crisp and cold. Ryan had been there beside her at Derek's funeral. He'd always been there for her. But he didn't want to be *with* her. And it hurt even more than she'd feared.

His eyes shone with regret. "And I can never get his okay on this."

"You don't need his permission. I'm twenty-seven years old, Ryan."

"Em—"

She waved him off. "Forget it. Thanks for the ride."

* * *

Emma woke up the next morning to the ding of an incoming text message, followed by another, and another. Her head ached, and *ugh*, her pride stung even worse. She pressed a hand over her eyes with a groan. A heavy weight plopped onto her chest, knocking the breath from her lungs.

"Meow."

Emma peeked through her fingers at the gray cat perched on top of her, regarding her from wide blue eyes. "Good morning to you, too, Smokey."

She shifted the cat to the side so that she could grab her cell phone off the nightstand. The screen showed five new text messages, all from her friends.

Rumor has it you did indeed catch a ride on Ryan's bike, Gabby said.

Details. We need details! From Mandy.

I've got fresh cinnamon buns. Come and get 'em, and let's gossip. From Carly, who owned A Piece of Cake bakery and made the best cinnamon buns Emma had ever tasted.

I'm in, Gabby texted.

Be there in thirty. Emma, wake up! From Mandy.

I'll be there, she texted. But the details are less exciting than you're imagining. I'm going to need extra frosting, Carly.

Then she rolled out of bed. Smokey meowed again as she hopped victoriously onto Emma's pillow and sat, lifting a paw to wash her face.

"You are such a diva," Emma said as she headed for the bathroom. She stepped into the shower, submersing herself in the hot spray. Forty-five minutes later, she walked through the doors of A Piece of Cake, finding her friends already gathered at the counter, drinking coffee and munching on cinnamon buns.

She scowled. "You could have at least waited for me."

"Long night?" Mandy gave her an assessing look, one eyebrow raised.

"More like too much beer." She rubbed her forehead as she sat on an empty stool. "What happened with you and Carl?"

"Eh, he turned out to be a dud." Mandy shrugged. "But we want to hear all about your night with Ryan."

"Extra frosting," Carly said, passing a plate across the counter with a cinnamon bun dripping with gooey white goodness. She set a steaming cup of coffee beside it.

"You're the best." Emma inhaled the rich aroma of cinnamon and French roast, feeling her system starting to perk up already.

"So?" Gabby asked. "What happened?"

Emma held up a finger. She took a big, fortifying sip of her coffee and popped a forkful of sinfully delicious cinnamon bun into her mouth. Once the sugar and caffeine had taken effect, she turned to her friends. "Ryan gave me a ride home on his bike."

"And?" Carly asked.

"Was it amazing? I've always wanted to ride on a motorcycle," Gabby said.

"It was great." So much more than great. A shiver of excitement snaked down her spine as she remembered the feel of the bike beneath her, the wind in her hair, the moon illuminating them like a scene out of a movie.

"Just great?" Mandy gave her a look that said *we want more*.

"It was fantastic. Is that better?" Emma shook her head. "You guys really pushed me last night, and you know what? I loved it. I had so much fun hanging out at the bar, and riding home on Ryan's bike was the most fun I've had in ages."

"So why the extra scoop of frosting?" Carly asked, leaning her elbows on the counter.

"Because between the dare, the beer, and the motorcycle ride, I completely lost my mind, and I kissed him. Or I *tried* to kiss him." She pressed a hand over her eyes as her friends squealed in surprise.

"Did you kiss him or not?" Mandy asked.

"I went for it, but, at the last moment, we bonked helmets instead." She cringed.

"That sounds kind of adorable," Carly said, a wistful note in her voice.

"It wasn't. It was awkward and embarrassing." For a moment right before their helmets bumped, she'd been so sure he wanted to kiss her, too. "And then he gave me some speech about how he'd promised Derek he'd never take advantage of me."

"Really? He promised Derek he wouldn't go after you?"

She nodded. "Which was reasonable at the time. I was fifteen and as innocent as they came, and he was an eighteen-year-old troublemaker who surely would have broken my heart."

"But Derek never came home from the war," Gabby said softly.

"That was twelve years ago," Emma said. "Things change. We're adults now."

"What are you going to do?" Mandy asked.

She took another bite of her cinnamon bun. "Easy. I'm going to pretend it never happened."

"But you do have feelings for him?" Carly asked.

Emma spluttered. "Feelings? No! Like, of course he's hot, and I'm sure the kiss would have been great, but feelings? No. No way."

They were all staring at her. Gabby's mouth dropped open.

"Whoa," Carly said. "You totally do."

Emma felt her cheeks start to burn. "What? Don't be ridiculous. I do not have feelings for Ryan Blake."

"Ever hear that saying about how 'the lady doth protest too much'?" Mandy said.

"Cut it out, seriously." Emma gulped from her coffee and scorched her throat, making her sputter again.

"Interesting. Very interesting." Mandy tapped her fingers against her lips. "Well, I'd say last night's dare was a success. Now we have to keep the momentum going. You need an excuse to see him again."

"I'm seeing him in a couple of hours," Emma mumbled, still coughing. "I'm going out to Off-the-Grid to talk about spring landscaping."

"Something more interesting than talking about work," Mandy said. "You need to get back on his bike or—"

"Remember last night how you said you wanted a tattoo?" Gabby asked. "Ryan used to manage a tattoo parlor. It would make perfect sense for him to take you."

"After last night? No way."

"I dare you." Mandy grinned. "C'mon. You said you wanted a fling with a bad boy. This is your chance, girl. Don't blow it."

Fall in Love with Forever Romance

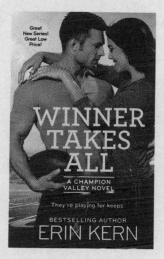

WINNER TAKES ALL
By Erin Kern

The first book in Erin Kern's brand-new Champion Valley series, perfect for fans of *Friday Night Lights*! Former football player Blake Carpenter is determined to rebuild his life as the new coach of his Colorado hometown's high school team. Annabelle Turner, the team's physical therapist, will be damned if the scandal that cost Blake his NFL career hurts *her* team. But what she doesn't count on is their intense attraction that turns every heated run-in into wildly erotic competition…

LAST KISS OF SUMMER
By Marina Adair

Kennedy Sinclair, pie shop and orchard owner extraordinaire, is all that stands between Luke Callahan and the success of his hard cider business. But when the negotiations start heating up, will they lose their hearts? Or seal the deal? Fans of Rachel Gibson, Kristan Higgins, and Jill Shalvis will gobble up the latest sexy contemporary from Marina Adair.

Fall in Love with Forever Romance

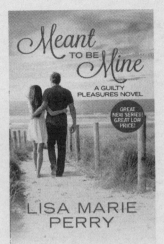

MEANT TO BE MINE
By Lisa Marie Perry

In the tradition of Jessica Lemmon and Marie Force, comes a contemporary romance about a former bad boy seeking redemption. After years apart, Sofia Mercer and Burke Wolf reunite in Cape Cod. Their wounds may be deep, but their sizzling attraction is as hot as ever.

RUN TO YOU
By Rachel Lacey

The first book in Rachel Lacey's new contemporary romance series will appeal to fans of Kristan Higgins, Rachel Gibson, and Jill Shalvis! Ethan Hunter's grandmother, Haven, North Carolina's resident matchmaker, is convinced Gabby Winter and her grandson are meant to be together. Rather than break her heart, Ethan and Gabby fake a relationship, but if they continue, they won't just fool the town—they might fool themselves, too...

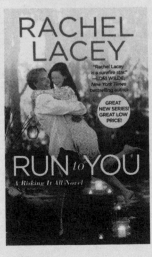

Fall in Love with Forever Romance

AN INDECENT PROPOSAL
By Katee Robert

New York Times and *USA Today* bestselling author Katee Robert continues her smoking-hot series about the O'Malleys—wealthy, powerful, and full of scandalous family secrets. Olivia Rashidi left behind her Russian mob family for the sake of her daughter. When she meets Cillian O'Malley, she recognizes his family name, but can't help falling for the smoldering, tortured man. Cillian knows that there is no escape from the life, but Olivia is worth trying—and dying—for...